'What exact[ly are you]
proposing with [...]
and by taking [...]
Croix? That's a[...] I'll agree to
go,' she added quickly.

Alix looked at Leila. She was pale, and even more beautiful than he remembered. Were her eyes always that big? The moment he'd seen her standing in the foyer his blood had leapt, as if injected by currents of pure electricity.

'You'll come because you're carrying my heir, and the whole world knows it now.'

Leila looked hunted. Her arms were crossed tightly over her chest again, pushing the swells of those luscious breasts up. The thought of Leila's body ripening with his seed, his child, gave him another shockingly sudden jolt of lust.

Leila was pacing now. 'What is the solution here? There *has* to be a solution…' She stopped and faced him again. 'I mean, it's not as if you're really intending to marry me. The engagement is just for show…until things die down again.'

She looked so hopeful Alix almost felt sorry for her. *Almost*. Her reluctance to marry him caught at him somewhere very primal and possessive.

'No, Leila. We will be getting married. In two weeks.'

One Night With Consequences

When one night...leads to pregnancy!

When succumbing to a night of unbridled desire
it's impossible to think past the morning after!

But, with the sheets barely settled, that little blue line
appears on the pregnancy test and it doesn't take long
to realise that one night of white-hot passion
has turned into a lifetime of consequences!

Only one question remains:

How do you tell a man you've just met
that you're about to share more than just his bed?

Find out in:

Nine Months to Redeem Him by Jennie Lucas
January 2015

Prince Nadir's Secret Heir by Michelle Conder
March 2015

Carrying the Greek's Heir by Sharon Kendrick
April 2015

Married for Amari's Heir by Maisey Yates
July 2015

From One Night to Wife by Rachael Thomas
September 2015

More stories in the *One Night With Consequences* series
can be found at millsandboon.co.uk

AN HEIR
FIT FOR A KING

BY
ABBY GREEN

MILLS
BOON

Published in Great Britain 2015
by Mills & Boon, an imprint of Harlequin (UK) Limited,
Eton House, 18-24 Paradise Road, Richmond, Surrey, TW9 1SR

ISBN: 978-0-263-25081-7

Printed and bound in Spain
by CPI, Barcelona

Irish author **Abby Green** threw in a very glamorous career in film & TV—which really consisted of a lot of standing in the rain outside actors' trailers—to pursue her love of romance. After she'd bombarded Mills & Boon with manuscripts they kindly accepted one, and an author was born. She lives in Dublin, Ireland, and loves any excuse for distraction. Visit abby-green.com or e-mail abbygreenauthor@gmail.com

Books by Abby Green

Mills & Boon Modern Romance

Forgiven but Not Forgotten?
Exquisite Revenge
One Night with the Enemy
The Legend of De Marco
The Call of the Desert
The Sultan's Choice
Secrets of the Oasis
In Christofides' Keeping
The Virgin's Secret

The Chatsfield

Delucca's Marriage Contract

Billionaire Brothers

The Bride Fonseca Needs
Fonseca's Fury

Blood Brothers

When Falcone's World Stops Turning
When Christakos Meets His Match
When Da Silva Breaks the Rules

**Visit the Author Profile page at
millsandboon.co.uk for more titles.**

This is for Sheila Hodgson…
thanks for your support and calming influence
while life got seriously in the way of this book!

I'd also like to thank the beautiful stranger working
in the perfume shop in the Westbury Mall in Dublin,
who sparked the original idea for this story, and a very
special thanks to Penny Ellis of Floris, London, who
gave me my first experience in how to build a perfume.
Any glaring errors are purely my own!

CHAPTER ONE

LEILA VERUGHESE WAS just wondering morosely to herself what would happen when her dwindling supplies of perfume ran out completely when out of the corner of her eye she spotted something and turned to look, glad of the distraction to her maudlin thoughts.

It was a sleek black car, pulled up outside her small House of Leila perfume shop. The shop she'd inherited from her mother, on the Place Vendôme in Paris. When she took a closer look she saw a veritable *fleet* of sleek black cars. The lead one had flags flying on the bonnet, but Leila couldn't make out what country they were from—even though she'd spent most of her life identifying the glamorous comings and goings from the exclusive Ritz Hotel across the square.

A man hopped out of the front of the car, clearly a bodyguard of some sort, with an earpiece in his ear. He looked around before opening the back door and Leila's eyes widened when she saw who emerged. As if they had to widen purely to be able to take him in better.

It was a man—unmistakably and unashamedly a man. Which was a ridiculous thing to think… One was either a man or a woman, after all. But it was as if his very masculinity reached out before him like a crackling energy. He uncoiled to a height well over six feet, towering over the smaller, blockier man beside him. Powerfully built, with broad shoulders in a long black overcoat.

He looked as if he was about to come towards Leila's shop when he stopped suddenly, and Leila saw a moment of irritation cross his face before he turned back to talk to someone who had to be in the back of the car. A wife? A girlfriend? He went and put a big hand on the roof of the car as he consulted the person inside.

Leila caught a glimpse of a long length of bare toned thigh and a flash of blonde hair and then the man straightened again and began striding towards the shop, flanked by his minders.

It was only now that Leila even registered his face. She'd never seen anything so boldly beautiful in all her life. Dark olive skin—dark enough to be Arabic? High cheekbones and a sensual mouth. It might have been pretty if it hadn't been for the deep-set eyes, strong brows and even stronger jaw, which had clenched now, along with that look of irritation.

He had short hair—dark, cut close to his skull. Which had that same beautiful masculine shape as his face.

Shock held Leila still for a long moment as he got closer and closer. For a second, just before the shop door opened, his eyes caught hers and she had the strangest notion of a huge sleek bird of prey, swooping down to pick her up in his talons and carry her away.

The dark-haired shop assistant behind the glass of the shop barely impinged on Alix Saint Croix's consciousness as he strode to the door. *Surprise me.* His mouth tightened. If he'd been able to say that the previous night had been… pleasurable, he might have been more inclined to 'surprise' his lover. He was a man who was not used to obeying the demands of anyone else, and the only reason he was indulging Carmen's sudden whim for perfume was because he was all too eager to get away from her.

She'd arrived in his suite the previous evening, and their subsequent lovemaking had been…*adequate.* Alix had found himself wondering when was the last time he'd been so consumed with lust or by a woman that he'd lost his mind in pleasure? *Never,* a little voice had whispered as his lover had sauntered from the bed to the bathroom, making sure all her assets were displayed to best advantage.

Alix had been bored. And, because women seemed to have a seventh sense designed purely to detect that, his lover had become very uncharacteristically compliant and sweet. So much so that it had set Alix's teeth on edge. And after a day of watching waif-thin models prancing up and down a catwalk he was even more on edge.

But, as his advisor had pointed out when he'd grumbled to him on the phone earlier, 'This is good, Alix. It's helping us lull them into a false sense of security: they believe you have nothing on your agenda but the usual round of socialising and modelising.'

Alix did not like being considered a *modeliser,* and he pushed open the door to the shop with more force than was necessary, finally registering the shop assistant who was looking at him with a mixture of shock and awe on her face.

He also registered within the same nanosecond that she was the most beautiful woman he'd ever seen in his life.

The door shut behind him, a small bell tinkling melodically, but he didn't notice. She had pale olive skin, a straight nose and full soft lips. *Sexy.* A firm, yet delicate jaw. High cheekbones. Her hair was a sleek fall of black satin behind her shoulders and Alix had the bizarre compulsion to reach out and see if it would slip through his fingers like silk.

But it was her eyes that floored him… They were huge light emerald gems with the longest black lashes, framed by gracefully arched black brows. She looked like a Far Eastern princess.

'Who are you?'

Was that his voice? It sounded like a croak. Stunned. There was an instant fire kindling in his belly and his blood. The fire he'd lamented the lack of last night. It was as if his body was ahead of his brain in terms of absorbing her beauty.

She blinked and those long lashes veiled her stunning eyes for a moment.

'I'm the owner of the shop, Leila Verughese.'

The name suited her. Exotic. Alix somehow found the necessary motor skills to put out his hand. 'Alix Saint Croix.'

Recognition flashed in her eyes, unmistakable. She flushed, her cheeks going a pretty shade of pink and Alix surmised cynically that of *course* she'd heard of him. Who hadn't?

Her hand slipped into his then, small and delicate, cool, and the effect was like a rocket launching deep inside Alix. His blood boiled and his hand tightened reflexively around hers.

He struggled to make sense of this immediate and extreme physical and mental reaction. He was used to seeing a woman and assessing her from a distance, his desires firmly under control. This woman…*Leila*…was undeniably beautiful, yes. But she was dressed like a pharmacist, with a white coat over a very plain blue shirt and black trousers. Even in flat shoes, though, she was relatively tall, reaching his shoulder. He found himself imagining her in spindly high heels, how close her mouth would be if he wanted to just bend down slightly…

She took her hand back and Alix blinked.

'You are looking for a perfume?'

Alix's brain felt sluggish. Perfume? Why was he looking for perfume? *Carmen*. Waiting for him in the car. Immediately he scowled again, and the woman in front of him took a step back.

He put out a hand. 'Sorry, no…' He cursed silently—what was wrong with him? 'That is, *yes*, I'm looking for a perfume. For someone.'

The woman looked at him. 'Do you have any particular scent in mind?'

Alix dragged his gaze from her with an effort and looked around the small shop for the first time. Each wall was mirrored glass, with glass shelves and counters. Glass and gold perfume bottles covered the surfaces, giving the space a golden hue.

The decor was opulent without being stifling. And there wasn't the stench of overpowering perfume that Alix would normally associate with a shop like this. The ambience was cool, calm. Serene. Like her. He realised that she exuded a sense of calm and that he was reacting to that as well.

Almost absently he said, 'I'm looking for a scent for my mistress.'

When there was no immediate reaction such as Alix was used to—he said what he wanted and people jumped—he looked at the woman. Her mouth was pursed and an unmistakable air of disapproval was being directed at him. Intriguing. No one ever showed Alix their true reactions.

He arched a brow. 'You have a problem with that?'

To his further fascination her cheeks coloured and she looked away. Then she said stiffly, 'It's not for me to say what's an appropriate term for your...partner.'

Leila cursed herself for showing her reaction and moved away to one of the walls of shelves, as if to seek out some perfume samples.

Her father had once offered the role of mistress to Leila's mother—*after* she'd given birth to their illegitimate daughter. He'd seduced Deepika Verughese when he'd been doing business in India with Leila's grandfather, but had then turned his back on her when she'd arrived in Paris, disgraced and pregnant, all the way from Jaipur.

Her mother had declined his offer to become his kept woman, too proud and bitter after his initial rejection, and had told Leila the story while pointing out all the kept women of the various famous people and dignitaries who'd come into the shop over the years, as a salutary lesson in what women were prepared to do to feather their nests.

Leila's mind cleared of the painful memory. She hated it that she'd reacted so unprofessionally just now, but before she could say anything else she heard the man move and looked up into the glass to see him coming closer. He looked even larger reflected in the mirror, with his dark image being sent back a hundred times.

She realised that his eyes were a very dark grey.

'You know who I am?'

She nodded. She'd known who he was as soon as he'd said his name. He was the infamous exiled King of a small island kingdom off the coast of North Africa, near Southern Spain. He was a renowned financial genius, with fingers in almost every business one could think of—including most recently an astronomical investment in the new oil fields of Burquat in the Middle East.

There were rumours that he was going to make a claim on his throne, but if this visit was anything to go by he was concerned with nothing more than buying trinkets for his lover. And she had no idea why that made her feel so irritable.

Alix Saint Croix continued. 'So you'll know that a man like me doesn't have girlfriends or partners. I take mistresses. Women who know what to expect and don't expect anything more.'

Something hardened inside her. She knew all about men like him. Unfortunately. And the evidence of this man's single-minded, cynical nature made her see red. It made her sick, because it reminded her of her own naivety in the face of overwhelming evidence that what she sought didn't exist.

Nevertheless she was determined not to let this man draw her down another painful memory lane. She crossed her arms over her chest. 'Not all women are as cynical as you make out.'

Something hard crossed his face. 'The women who move in my circles are.'

'Well, maybe your circles are too small?'

She couldn't believe the words tripping out of her mouth, but he'd pushed a button—a very sensitive button. She almost expected him to storm out of her shop, but to her surprise Alix Saint Croix's mouth quirked on one side, making him look even sexier. Dangerous.

'Perhaps they are, indeed.'

Leila suddenly felt hot and claustrophobic. He was looking at her too intensely, and then his gaze dropped to where the swells of her breasts were pushed up by her crossed arms. She took them down hurriedly and reached for the nearest bottle of perfume, only half registering the label.

She thrust it towards him. 'This is one of our most popular scents. It's floral-based with a hint of citrus. It's light and zesty—perfect for casual wear.'

Alix Saint Croix shook his head. 'No, I don't think that'll do. I want something much earthier. Sensuous.'

Leila put down the bottle with a clatter and reached for another bottle. 'This might be more appropriate, then. It's got fruity top notes, but a woody, musky base.'

He cocked his head and said consideringly, 'It's so hard to know unless you can smell it.'

Leila's shirt felt too tight. She wanted to undo a top button. What was wrong with her?

She turned back to the counter and took a smelling strip out of a jar, ready to spray it so that he could smell it. And go. She wanted him gone. He was too disturbing to her usually very placid equilibrium.

But before she could spray, a large hand wrapped around her arm, stopping her.

Heat zinged straight to her belly. She looked up at him.

'Not on a piece of paper. I think you'd agree that a scent has to be on the skin to be best presented?'

Feeling slightly drugged and stupid, Leila said, 'It's a woman's scent.'

He cocked a brow again. 'So spray some on your wrist and I'll smell it.'

The shock that reverberated through Leila was as if he'd just said *Take off all your clothes, please.*

She had to struggle to compose herself, get a grip. She'd often sprayed perfume on her own skin so that someone could get a fuller sense of it. But this man had made the request sound almost indecent.

Praying that her hand wouldn't shake, Leila took the top off the bottle and pulled up her sleeve to spray some of the scent. When the liquid hit the underside of her wrist she shivered slightly. It felt absurdly sensual all of a sudden.

Alix Saint Croix still had a hand wrapped around her arm and now he moved it down to take the back of her hand in his, wrapping long fingers around hers. He moved his head down to smell the perfume, his dark head coming close to her breast.

But he kept his eyes on her, and from this close she could see lighter flecks of grey, like silver mercury. Leila's breath stopped when she felt his breath feather along her skin. Those lips were far too close to the centre of her palm, which was clammy.

He seemed to consider the scent until Leila's nerves twanged painfully. Her belly was a contracted ball of nerves.

A movement over his head caught her eye and she saw a sleek, tall blonde emerge from the back of the car with a phone clamped to her ear. She was wearing an indecently tight, slinky dress and a ridiculously ineffectual jacket for the cool autumn weather.

He must have picked up on her distraction and straightened to look out of the window too. Leila noticed a tension come into his body as his girlfriend—*mistress*—saw him and gesticulated with clear irritation, all while still talking on the phone.

'Your…er…mistress is waiting for you.' Leila's voice felt scratchy.

He still had his hand wrapped around hers and now let her go. Leila tucked it well out of reach.

He morphed before her eyes into someone much cooler, indecipherable. Perversely, it didn't comfort her.

'I'll take it.'

Leila blinked at him.

'The perfume,' he expanded, and for a moment a glint of what they'd just shared made his eyes flash.

Leila jerked into action. 'Of course. It'll only take me a moment to package it up.'

She moved to get a bag and paper and quickly and inexpertly packaged up the perfume, losing all of her customary cool. When she had it ready she handed it over and avoided his eye. A wad of cash landed on the counter but Leila wasn't about to check it.

And then, without another word, he turned around and strode out again, catching his…whatever she was…by the arm and hustling her back into the car.

His scent lingered on the air behind him, and in a very delayed reaction Leila assimilated the various components with an expertise that was like a sixth sense—along with the realisation that his scent had impacted on her as soon as he'd walked in, on a level that wasn't rational. Someplace else. Somewhere she wasn't used to scents impacting.

It was a visceral reaction. Primal. His scent was clean, with a hint of something very *male* that most certainly hadn't come out of a bottle. The kind of evocative scent that would make someone a fortune if they could bottle it: the pure essence of a virile male in his prime. Earthy. Musky.

A pulse between Leila's legs throbbed and she pressed her thighs together, horrified.

What was wrong with her? The man was a *king*, for God's sake, and he had a mistress that he was unashamed about. She should be thinking *good riddance*, but what she was thinking was much more confused.

It made alarm bells ring. It reminded her of another man who had come into the shop and who had very skilfully set about wooing her—only to turn into a nasty stranger when he'd realised that Leila had no intention of giving him what he wanted…which had been very far removed from what *Leila* had wanted.

She looked stupidly at the money on the counter for a moment, before realising that he'd vastly overpaid her for the perfume, but all she could think about was that last enigmatic look he'd shot her, just before he'd ducked into the car—a look that had seemed to say he'd be back. And soon.

And in light of their conversation, and the way he'd made her feel, Leila knew she shouldn't be remotely intrigued. But she was. And not even the ghost of memories past could stop it.

A little later, after Leila had locked up and gone upstairs to the small flat she'd shared with her mother all her life, she found herself gravitating to the window, which looked out over the Place Vendôme. The opera glasses that her mother had used for years to check out the comings and goings at the Ritz were sitting nearby, and for a second Leila felt an intense pang of grief for her mother.

Leila pushed aside the past and picked up the glasses and looked through them, seeing the usual flurry of activity when someone arrived at the hotel in a flash car. She tilted the glasses upwards to where the rooms were—and her whole body froze when she caught a glimpse of a familiar masculine figure against a brightly lit opulent room.

She trained the glasses on the sight, hating herself for

it but unable to look away. It was him. Alix Saint Croix. The overcoat was gone. And the jacket. He had his back to her and was dressed in a waistcoat and shirt and trousers. Hands in his pockets were drawing the material of his trousers over his very taut and muscular backside.

Instantly Leila felt damp heat coil down below and squeezed her legs together.

He was looking at something in front of him, and Leila tensed even more when the woman he'd been with came into her line of vision. She'd taken off the jacket and the flimsy dress was now all she wore. Her body was as sleek and toned as a throughbred horse. Leila vaguely recognised her as a world-famous lingerie model.

She could see that she held something in her hand, and when it glinted she realised it was the bottle of perfume. The woman sprayed it on her wrist and lifted it to smell, a sexy smile curling her wide mouth upwards.

She sprayed more over herself and Leila winced slightly. The trick with perfume was always *less is more*. And then she threw the bottle aside, presumably to a nearby chair or couch, and proceeded to pull down the skinny straps of her dress. Then she peeled the top half of her dress down, exposing small but perfect breasts.

Leila gasped at the woman's confidence. She'd never have the nerve to strip in that way in front of a man.

And then Alix Saint Croix moved. He turned away from the woman and walked to the window. For a second he loomed large in Leila's glasses, filling them with that hard-boned face. He looked intent. And then he pulled a drape across, obscuring the view, almost as if he'd known Leila was watching from across the square like a Peeping Tom.

Disgusted with herself, Leila threw the glasses down and got up to pace in her small apartment. She berated herself. *How* could a man like that even capture her attention? He was exactly what her mother had warned her about:

rich and arrogant. Not even prepared to see women as anything other than mistresses, undoubtedly interchanged with alarming frequency once the novelty with each one had worn off.

Leila had already refused to take her mother's warnings to heart once, and had suffered a painful blow to her confidence and pride because of it.

Full of pent-up energy, she dragged on a jacket and went outside for a brisk walk around the nearby Tuileries gardens, telling herself over and over again first of all that nothing had happened with Alix Saint Croix in her shop that day, secondly that she'd never see him again, and thirdly that she didn't care.

The following evening dusk was falling as Leila went to lock the front door of her shop. It had been a long day, with only a trickle of customers and two measly sales. Thanks to the recession, niche businesses everywhere had taken a nosedive, and since the factory that manufactured the House of Leila scents had closed down she hadn't had the funds to seek out a new factory.

She'd been reduced to selling off the stock she had left in the hope that enough sales would give her the funds to start making perfumes again.

She was just about to turn the lock when she looked up through the glass to see a familiar tall dark figure, flanked by a couple of other men, approaching her door. The almost violent effect on her body of seeing him in the flesh again mocked her for fooling herself that she'd managed not to think about him all day.

The exiled King with the tragic past.

Leila had looked him up on the Internet last night in a moment of weakness and had read about how his parents and younger brother had been slaughtered during a military coup. The fact that he'd escaped to live in exile had become something of a legend.

Her immediate instinct was to lock the door and pull the blind down—fast. But he was right outside now and looking at her. The faintest glimmer of a smile touched his mouth. She could see a day's worth of stubble shadowing his jaw.

Obeying professional reflexes rather than her instincts, Leila opened the door and stepped back. He came in and once again it was as if her brain was slowing to a halt. It was consumed with taking note of his sheer masculine beauty.

Determined not to let him rattle her again, Leila assumed a polite, professional mask. 'How did your mistress like the perfume?'

A lurid image of the woman putting on that striptease threatened to undo Leila's composure but she pushed it out of her head with effort.

Alix Saint Croix made an almost dismissive gesture with his hand. 'She liked it fine. That's not why I'm here.'

Leila found it hard to draw in a breath. Suddenly terrified of why he *was* there, she gabbled, 'By the way, you left far too much money for the perfume.'

She turned and went to the counter and took out an envelope containing the excess he'd paid. She'd been intending to drop it to the hotel for him, but hadn't had the nerve all day. She held it out now.

Alix barely looked at it. He speared her with that grey gaze and said, 'I want to take you out to dinner.'

Panic fluttered in Leila's gut and her hand tightened on the envelope, crushing it. 'What did you say?'

He pushed open his light overcoat to put his hands in his pockets, drawing attention to another pristine three-piece suit, lovingly moulded to muscles that did not belong to an urban civilised man, more to a warrior.

'I said I would like you to join me for dinner.'

Leila frowned. 'But you have a mistress.'

Something stern crossed Alix Saint Croix's face and the grey in his eyes turned to steel. 'She is no longer my mistress.'

Leila recalled what she'd seen the previous night and blurted out, 'But I saw you—you were together—' She stopped and couldn't curb the heat rising. The last thing she wanted was for him to know she'd been spying, and she said quickly, 'She certainly seemed to be under the impression that you were together.'

She hoped he'd assume she was referring to when she'd seen the woman waiting for him outside the shop.

Alix's face was indecipherable. 'As I said, we are no longer together.'

Leila felt desperate. And disgusted. And disappointed, which was even worse. Of course a man like him would interchange his women without breaking a sweat.

'But I don't even know you—you're a total stranger.'

His mouth twitched slightly. 'Which could be helped by sharing conversation over dinner, *non*?'

Leila had a very strong urge to back away, but forced herself to stand her ground. She was in *her* shop. *Her* space. And everything in her screamed at her to resist this man. He was too gorgeous, too big, too smooth, too famous...too much.

Something reckless gripped her and she blurted out, 'I saw you. The two of you... I didn't intend to, but when I looked out of my window last night I saw you in your room. With her. She was taking off her clothes...'

Leila willed down the embarrassed heat and tilted up her chin defiantly. She didn't care if he thought she was some kind of stalker.

His gaze narrowed on her. 'I saw you too...across the square, silhouetted in your window.'

Now she blanched. 'You did?'

He nodded. 'It merely confirmed that I wanted you. And not her.'

Leila was caught, trapped in his gaze and in his own confession. 'You pulled the curtain across. For privacy.'

His mouth firmed. 'Yes. For privacy while I asked her to put her dress back on and get out, because the relationship was over.'

Leila shivered at his coolness. 'But that's so cruel. You'd just bought her a gift.'

Something infinitely cynical lit those grey eyes and Leila hated it.

'Believe me, a woman like Carmen is no soft-centred fool with notions of where the relationship was going. She knew it was finite. The relationship was ending whether I'd met you or not.'

Leila balked. She definitely veered more towards the *soft-centred fool* end of the scale.

She folded her arms and fought the pull from her gut to follow him blindly. She'd done that with a man once before, with her stupid, vulnerable heart on her sleeve. It made her hard now. 'Thank you for the invitation, but I'm afraid I must say no.'

His brows snapped together in a frown. 'Are you married?'

His gaze dropped to her left hand as if to look for a ring, and something flashed in his eyes when he took in her ringless fingers. Leila's hands curled tight. Too late.

The personal question told her she was doing the right thing and she said frostily, 'That is none of your business, sir. I'd like you to leave.'

For a tiny moment Alix Saint Croix's eyes widened on her, and then he said coolly, 'Very well, I'm sorry for disturbing you. Good evening, Miss Verughese.'

CHAPTER TWO

ALIX WAS HALFWAY across the quiet square, fuelled by a surge of angry disbelief, before the thought managed to break through: no woman, *ever*, had turned him down like that. So summarily. Coldly. As if he'd overstepped some invisible mark on the ground. As if he was...*beneath* her.

He dismissed his security detail with a flick of his hand as he walked into the hotel, with staff scurrying in his wake, the elevator attendant jumping to attention. Alix ignored them all, his mind filled with incredulity that she had said *no*.

He'd ended his liaison with Carmen specifically to pursue Leila Verughese.

When Carmen had undressed in front of him in his suite he'd felt nothing but impatience to see her gone. And then, when he'd gone to his window and seen the light shining from a small window above the perfume shop and that slim figure, all he'd seen was *her* alluring body in his mind's eye. The hint of generous curves told of a very classic feminine shape—not exactly fashion-forward, like Carmen, with tiny breasts and an almost androgynous figure, but all the more alluring for that.

He wanted her with a hunger he hadn't allowed himself to feel in a long time. And that impatience to see Carmen gone had become a compelling need.

When Alix got to his suite of rooms he threw off his coat and prowled like a restless animal. He felt animalistic.

How *dared* she turn him down? He wanted her. The exotic princess who sold perfume.

Why did he want her so badly?

The question pricked at him like a tiny barb and he couldn't ignore it. He'd only ever wanted one other woman in a similar way. A woman who had made him think she was different from all the others. When she'd been even worse.

Alix, young and far more naive than he'd ever wanted to admit at the age of eighteen, had been seduced by a beautiful body and an act of innocence honed to perfection.

Until he'd walked into her college rooms one day and seen one of his own bodyguards thrusting between her pale legs. The image was clear enough to mock him. Years later.

As if his own parents' toxic marriage hadn't already drummed it into him that men and women together brought pain and disharmony.

Ever since then Alix had excised all emotion where women were concerned. They were mistresses—who pleasured him and accompanied him to social events. Until the time came for him to choose a wife who would be his Queen. And then his marriage would be different. It wouldn't be toxic. It would be harmonious and respectful.

Alix thought about that now. Because that time would be coming soon. He was already being presented with prospective wives to choose from. Princesses from different principalities who all looked dismayingly like horses. But Alix didn't care. His wife would be his consort, adept at dealing with the social aspects of her role and providing him with heirs.

So why is this woman getting under your skin?

She's not, he affirmed to himself.

She was just a stunningly beautiful woman who'd connected with him on some very base level and he wasn't used to that.

Alix didn't like to recall that first meeting, when just seeing her had been like a defibrillator shocking him back to life.

His was a life that needed no major distractions right

now. He had enough going on with the very real prospect that in a couple of weeks he was going to regain control of his throne. Something he'd been working towards all his life.

And yet this woman was lingering in his mind, compelling him to make impetuous decisions. And despite that Alix found himself drawn once again to the massive window through which he'd seen Leila across the square last night. The shop was in darkness now, the blind pulled firmly down.

A sense of impotent frustration gripped him even more fiercely now. The upstairs was in darkness too. Was she out? With another man? Saying yes to him? Alix tensed all over at that thought and had to relax consciously. He did not *do* jealousy. Not since he'd kicked his naked bodyguard out of his traitorous lover's bed. And had that even been jealousy? Or just young injured male pride?

He emitted a sound of irritation and plucked a phone out of his pocket. He was connected in seconds and said curtly, 'I want you to find out everything you can about a woman called Leila Verughese. She owns a perfume shop on the Place Vendôme in Paris.'

Alix terminated the connection. He told himself that she was most likely playing a game. Hard to get. But he didn't really care—because he was no woman's fool any more and, game or no game, he *would* have her and sate this burning urge before his life changed irrevocably and became one of duty and responsibility.

She didn't have the power to derail him. No woman did.

For two days Leila stood in her shop, acutely aware of Alix Saint Croix's cavalcade sweeping in and out of the square. Every time his sleek car drove past she tensed inwardly— as if waiting for him to stop and get out and come in again. To ask her to dinner again.

She hated it that she knew when his cars were parked outside the hotel. It made her feel jittery, on edge.

Just then her phone rang, and she jumped and cursed softly before answering it. It was the hotel. They wanted Leila to bring over an assortment of perfumes for one of their guests.

She agreed and put the phone down, immediately feeling nervous. Which was ridiculous. This wasn't an unusual request—hotel guests often spotted the shop and asked for a personal service. At one time Leila had gone over with perfumes for a foreign president's wife.

Even though she would be venturing far too near to the lion in his lair, she welcomed the diversion and set about gathering as many diverse samples of perfumes as she could.

On arrival at the hotel, dressed smartly in a dark trouser suit and white shirt, hair up, and with her specially fortified and protective wheelie suitcase, Leila was shown to the top floor by a duty manager.

The same floor as Alix Saint Croix's suite.

She felt a flutter of panic, but pushed it down as the lift doors opened and she stepped into the opulent luxury of one of the hotel's most sumptuous floors.

To her vast relief they were heading in the opposite direction from the suite she'd watched so closely the other night.

The duty manager opened the door to the suite and ushered Leila in, saying, 'Your clients will be here shortly—they said to go ahead and set up while you're waiting.'

Leila smiled. 'Okay, thank you.'

When she was alone she set about opening her case and taking out some bottles, glad to have the distraction of what she did best. No time to think about—

She heard the door open behind her and stood up and turned around with a smile on her face, expecting to see a woman.

The smile promptly slid off her face when she saw Alix Saint Croix and the door closing softly behind him. *Client*, not clients. For a long moment Leila was only aware of her heartbeat, fast and hard. He was dressed in a white shirt and dark trousers. Sleeves rolled up, top button open. Hands in his pockets. He was looking at her with a gleam in his eyes that told her the predator had tracked down his prey.

So why was she suddenly feeling a thrum of excitement?

He took a step further into the room and inclined his head towards her suitcase, which was open on an ottoman. 'Do you supply men's scents also?'

Leila was determined not to appear as ruffled as she felt. She said coolly, 'First of all, I don't appreciate being ambushed, Mr Saint Croix. But, as I'm here now—yes, I do men's scents also.'

Alix Saint Croix looked at her with that enigmatic gaze, a small smile playing around his mouth. 'The hotel told me that you regularly come to do personal consultations. Do you regard *all* clients as ambushing you?'

Leila's face coloured. 'Of course not.' She felt flustered now. 'Look, why don't we get on with it? I'm sure you're a busy man.'

He came closer, rolling his sleeves up further as he said, with a definite glint in his grey eyes, 'On the contrary, I have all the time in the world.'

Leila's hands clenched into fists at her sides. She boiled inside at the way he'd so neatly caught her and longed to be able to storm out…but to where? Back to an empty shop? To polish the endless glass shelves? He'd just suggested a lucrative personal consultation—even if his actions were nefarious. Not to mention the wad of cash he'd left her the other day…

Swallowing her ire, and not liking the way he was getting under her skin so easily, she forced a smile and said, 'Of course. Then, please, sit down.'

Leila was careful to take a chair at a right angle to the couch. Briskly she took out some of her sample bottles containing pure oils and a separate mixer bottle.

As he passed her to sit down she unconsciously found herself searching for his scent again, and it hit her as powerfully as it had the first time. Leila had a sudden and fantastical image of herself having access to this man's naked body and being allowed to spend as much time as she liked discovering the secret scents of his very essence, so that she could try to analyse them and distil them into a perfume.

She cursed her wayward imagination and said, without looking at him, 'Had you any particular scent in mind? What do you usually like?'

She was aware of strong thighs in her peripheral vision, his trousers doing little to hide their length or muscularity.

'I have no idea,' he said dryly. 'I get sent new perfumes all the time and usually just pick whatever appeals to me in the moment. But generally I don't like anything too heavy.'

Leila glanced at him sharply. His face was expressionless, but there was an intensity in his eyes that made her nervous. For a moment she could almost believe he wasn't talking about scents at all, and felt like telling him to save his breath if he was warning her obliquely that he wasn't into commitment—because she had no intention of getting to know him any better.

She couldn't deny, though, how her very body seemed to hum in his presence.

Instinctively she reached for a bottle and pulled it out, undoing the stopper. She sniffed for a moment and then dipped a smelling strip into the bottle and extracted it and held it out towards him. 'What do you think of this, Monsieur Saint Croix?'

'Please…' he purred. 'Call me Alix.'

Leila tensed, her hand held out, refusing to give in to

his unashamed flirtation. Eventually, eyes sparkling as he registered her obvious struggle against him, he took the sliver of paper and Leila snatched her hand back.

He kept his eyes on her as he smelled it carefully, passing it over and back under his nose. She saw something flare in his eyes, briefly, and felt an answering rush of heat under her skin.

Consideringly, he said, 'I like it—what is it?'

'It's fougère—a blend of notes based on lavender, oakmoss and coumarin: a derivative of the tonka bean. It's a good base on which to build a scent if you like it.'

He handed her back the tester and lifted a brow. 'The tonka bean?'

Leila nodded as she pulled out another bottle. 'It's a soft, woody note. We extract ingredients for a scent from anything and everything.'

She was beginning to feel more relaxed, concentrating on her work as if there *wasn't* a whole subtext going on between her and this man. Maybe she could just ignore it.

'It was developed in the late eighteen-hundreds by Houbigant and I find it evocative of a woody, ferny environment.'

Leila handed him another smelling strip.

'Try this.'

He took it and looked at her again. She found it hard to take her eyes away as he breathed deep. Every move this man made was so boldly sensual. Sexy. It made Leila want to curl in on herself and try not to be noticed.

'This is more…exotic?'

Leila answered, 'It's oudh—quite rare. From agarwood. A very distinctive scent—people either love it or hate it.'

He looked at her, his mouth quirking slightly. 'I like it. What does that say about me?'

Leila shrugged minutely as she reached for another bottle, trying to affect nothing but professionalism. 'Just that you respond to the more complex make-up of the scent. It's perhaps no surprise that a king should favour such a rare specimen.'

Immediately tension sprang up between them, and Leila busied herself opening another bottle.

Alix Saint Croix's voice was sharper this time. 'A king in exile, to be more accurate. Does that make a difference?'

Leila looked at him as she handed him another sample and said, equally coolly, 'I'm sure it doesn't. You're still a king, after all, are you not?'

He made a dissenting sound as he took the new tester. Leila wondered how much more patience he would have for this game they were playing. As if someone like him *really* had time for a personal perfume consultation...

She looked to see him sniff the strip and saw how he immediately recoiled from the smell. He grimaced, and Leila had to bite back a smile.

'What is *that*?'

She reached across and took the paper back. 'It's extracted from the narcissus flower.'

His mouth curled up slightly. 'Should I take that as a compliment? That I don't immediately resonate with the narcissus?'

Leila avoided looking at him and started packing up her bottles, eager to get away from this man. 'If you like any of those scents we tested I can make something up for you.'

'I'd like that. But I want you to add something I haven't considered...something you think would uniquely suit me.'

Leila tightened inwardly at the prospect of choosing something unique to him. She closed the case and looked at him. 'I'm afraid I will be bound to disappoint you. Perfume is such a personal—'

'And I'd like you to deliver it personally this evening.' He cut her off as if she hadn't even been talking.

Leila stood up abruptly and looked down at him. 'Monsieur Saint Croix, while I appreciate the custom you've given me today, I'm afraid I…'

He stood up then too, and the words dried in her throat as his tall body towered over hers. They were too close.

His voice was low, with a thread of steel. 'Are you seriously telling me that you're turning down the opportunity to custom make a scent for the royal house of Isle Saint Croix?'

When he said it like that Leila could hear her mother's voice in her head, shrill and panicked, *Are you completely crazy?* What was she doing? In her bid to escape from this disturbing tension was she prepared to jeopardise the most potentially lucrative sale she'd had in years? The merest hint of a professional association with a *king*, no less, and her sales would go through the roof.

In a small voice she finally said, 'No, of course I wouldn't turn down such an opportunity. I can put a couple of sample fragrances together and deliver them to the hotel later. You can let me know which you prefer.'

His eyes were a mesmerising shade of pewter. 'One scent, Leila, and I want you to bring it to me personally. Say seven p.m.?'

Her name on his lips felt absurdly intimate, as if he'd just touched her. She glared at him but had no room to manoeuvre. And then she told herself to get a grip. Alix Saint Croix might be disturbing her on all sorts of levels but he was hardly going to kidnap her. *He wouldn't need to.* That was the problem. Leila was afraid that if she had much more contact with him, her defences would start to feel very flimsy.

Hiding her irritation at how easily he was sweeping aside her reservations, she bent down and closed her suitcase—but before she could lift it off the ottoman he brushed her hand aside and took it, wrapped a big hand firmly around the handle.

Leila straightened, face flushed. He extended a hand and lifted a brow. 'After you.'

Much to her embarrassment, he insisted on escorting her all the way down to the lobby and seemed to be oblivious to the way everyone jumped to attention—not least his security guards. He called one of them over and handed the thickset man the case, instructing him to carry it back to the shop for Leila. Her protests fell on deaf ears.

And then, before she could leave, he said, 'What time shall I send Ricardo to escort you to the hotel?'

Leila turned and looked up. She was about to assert that she'd had no problem crossing the square on her own for some two decades, but as soon as she saw the look in his eye she said with a resigned sigh, 'Five to seven.'

He dipped his head. 'Till then, Leila.'

Once back in his own suite, Alix stood looking across the square for a long time. Leila's reluctance to acquiesce to him intrigued him. Anticipation tightened his gut. Even though he knew this was likely just a game on her part, he was prepared to indulge it because he wanted her. And he had time on his hands.

He felt a mild pang of guilt now when he thought of what his security team had reported to him about her.

The Verughese family were wealthy and respectable in India. A long line of perfumers, supplying scents to maharajas and the richest in society. There were a scant few lines about Deepika Verughese, who had been Leila's mother. She'd come to France after breaking off relations with her family, where she'd proceeded to have one daughter: Leila. No mention of a father.

In all other respects she was squeaky clean. No headlines had ever appeared about her.

He felt something vibrate in his pocket and extracted a small, sleek mobile phone. Without checking to see who it was, and not taking his eyes off his quarry across the square, he answered, 'Yes?'

It was his chief advisor, and Alix welcomed the distraction, reminded of the bigger picture.

He turned his back to the view. 'How are the plans for the referendum coming along?'

Isle Saint Croix was due to vote within two weeks on whether or not they wanted Alix to return as King. It was still too volatile for Alix to be in the country himself, so he was depending on loyal politicians and his people, who had campaigned long and hard to restore the monarchy. Finally the end goal was in sight. But it was a very delicate balancing act that could all come tumbling down at any moment.

The ruling party in Isle Saint Croix were ruthless, and only the fact that they'd had to reluctantly agree to let international observers into the country had saved the process from falling apart already.

Andres was excited. 'The polls are showing in your favour, but not so much that it's unduly worrying the military government. They're still arrogant enough to believe they're in control.'

Alix listened to him reiterate what he already knew, but it was still reassuring. Something bittersweet pierced his heart. When he regained the throne he would finally have a chance to avenge his younger brother's brutal death.

Alix tuned back into the conversation when the other man cleared his voice awkwardly and said, 'Is it true that your affair with Carmen Desanto is over? It was in the papers today.'

Alix's mouth tightened. Only because of the fact that Andres was one of his oldest and most trusted friends did he even contemplate answering the question. 'What of it?'

'Well, it's unfortunate timing. The busier you can look with very *un*political concerns the better—to lull the regime on Isle Saint Croix into a false sense of security. Even if they hear rumours of you gaining support from abroad, when they see pictures in the papers…'

He didn't need to finish. Alix would appear to be the louche and unthreatening King in exile he'd always been. Still, he didn't like to be dictated to like this.

'Well,' he said with a steely undertone, 'I'm afraid that, as convenient a front as Carmen might have proved to be, I wasn't prepared to put up with her inane chatter for any longer.'

An image popped into Alix's head of another woman. Someone whose chatter he wouldn't mind listening to. And he very much doubted that *she* ever chattered inanely. Those beautiful eyes were far too intelligent.

On the other end of the phone Andres sighed theatrically. 'Look, all I'm saying is that now would be a really good time to be living up to your reputation as an eligible bachelor, cutting a swathe through the beauties of the world.'

Alix had only been interested in a very personal conquest before now, but suddenly the thought of pursuing Leila Verughese took on a whole new dimension. It was, in fact, completely justifiable.

A small smile curled his lips. 'Don't worry, Andres. I'm sure I can think of something to keep the media hounds happy.'

When the knock came on Alix's door at about one minute past seven that evening he didn't like to acknowledge the anticipation rushing through his blood. The reminder that Leila was getting to him on a level that was unprecedented was not welcome. He told himself it was just lust. Chemical. Controllable.

He strode forward and opened the door to see Leila with a vaguely mutinous look on her beautiful face and

Ricardo behind her. Alix nodded to his bodyguard and the man melted away.

Alix stood back and held the door open. 'Please, come in.'

He noted that Leila hadn't changed outfits since earlier. She was still wearing the smart dark trouser suit and her hair was pulled back into a low, sleek ponytail. She wore not a scrap of make-up, yet her features stood out as if someone had lovingly painted her.

The pale olive skin, straight nose, lush mouth and startling green eyes combined together to such an effect that Alix could only mentally shake his head as he followed her into his suite… How did such a woman as this work quietly in a perfume shop, going largely unnoticed?

She turned to face him in the palatial living room and held up a glossy House of Leila bag. 'Your fragrance, Monsieur Saint Croix.'

Alix bit back the urge to curse and said smoothly, 'Leila, I've asked you to call me Alix.'

Her eyes glittered. 'Well, I don't think it's appropriate. You're a client—'

'A client who,' he inserted smoothly, 'has just paid a significant sum of money for a customised fragrance.'

Her mouth shut and remorse lit her eyes. Alix was fascinated again by the play of unguarded emotions. God knew he certainly hadn't revealed emotion himself for years. And the women he dealt with probably wouldn't know a real emotion if it jumped up and bit them on the ass.

She looked at him and he felt short of breath, acutely aware of the thrust of her perfect breasts against the silk of her shirt.

'Very well. Alix.'

Her mouth and tongue wrapping around his name had an effect similar to that if she'd put her mouth on his body intimately. Blood rushed south and he hardened.

Gritting his jaw against the onset of a fierce arousal that

made a mockery of any illusion of control, Alix responded, 'That wasn't so hard, was it?' He groaned inwardly at his unfortunate choice of words and reached for the bag she still held out in a bid to distract her from seeing her seismic effect in his body.

With the bag in his hand he gestured for her to sit down. 'Please, make yourself comfortable. Would you like a drink?'

Leila's hands twisted in front of her. 'No, thank you. I really should be getting back—'

'Don't you want to know if I like the scent or not?'

Her mouth stayed open and eventually she said, 'Of course I do... But you could send word if you don't like it.'

Alix frowned minutely and moved closer to Leila, cocking his head to one side. 'Why are you so nervous with me?'

She swallowed. He could see the long slim column of her throat, the pulse beating near the base. Hectic.

'I'm not nervous.'

He came closer and a warm seeping of colour made her skin flush.

'Liar. You're ready to jump out of that window to get away from me right now.'

One graceful brow arched. 'Not a reaction you're used to?'

Alix's mouth quirked. The tension was diffused a little. 'No, not usually.'

He indicated again for Leila to sit down and after a moment, when he really wasn't sure if she'd just walk out, she moved over to the couch and sat down. Something relaxed inside him.

He put down the bag containing the scent while he poured himself a drink and glanced at her over his shoulder. 'Are you sure I can't get you anything?'

She'd been taking in the room, eyes wide, and suddenly all its opulence felt garish to Alix.

Those eyes clashed with his. 'Okay,' she said huskily. 'I'll have a little of whatever you're having.'

It was crazy. Alix wanted to howl in triumph at this concession. At the fact that she was still here, when usually he was batting women away.

'Bourbon?'

She half nodded and shrugged. 'I've never tried it before.'

There was something incredibly disarming about her easy admission. Like watching the play of emotion on her face and in her eyes. Alix brought the drinks over and was careful to take a seat at right angles to the couch, knowing for certain that she'd bolt if he sat near her.

He handed her the glass and she took it. He held his out. '*Santé*, Leila.'

She tipped her glass towards his and took a careful sip, as he took a sip of his own. He watched her reaction, saw her eyes watering slightly, her cheeks warming again. His own drink slipped down his throat, making his already warm body even hotter.

'What do you think?'

She considered for a moment and then gave a tiny smile. 'It's like fire… I like it.'

'Yes,' Alix said faintly, transfixed by Leila's mouth, 'It's like fire.'

A moment stretched between them, and then she dropped her gaze from his and put her glass down on the table to indicate the bag she'd brought. 'You should see if you like the scent.'

Alix put down his own glass and took the bag, extracting a gold box embossed with a black line around the edges. It had a panel on the front with a label that said simply *Alix Saint Croix*.

Alix opened the box and took out the heavy and beautifully cut glass bottle, with its black lid and distinctive gold piping. It was masculine—solid.

'It's quite strong,' Leila said, as he took off the lid and looked at her. 'You only need a small amount. Try it on the back of your hand.'

Alix sprayed and then bent his head. He wasn't ready for the immediate effect on his senses. It impacted deep down in his gut—so many layers of scent, filtering through his brain and throwing up images like a slideshow going too fast for him to analyse.

He was thrown back in time to his home on the island, with the sharp, tangy smell of the sea in the air, and yet he could smell the earth too, and the scent of the exotic flowers that bloomed on Isle Saint Croix. He could even smell something oriental, spicy, that made him think of his Moorish ancestors who had given the island its distinctive architecture.

He wasn't prepared for the sharp pang of emotion that gripped him as a memory surged: him and his younger brother, playing, carefree, near the sea.

'What's in it?' he managed to get out.

Leila was looking concerned. 'You don't like it?'

'Like' was too flimsy a word for what this scent was doing to him. Alix stood up abruptly, feeling acutely exposed. *Dieu*. Was she a witch? He strode over to the window and kept his back to her, brought his hand up to smell again.

The initial shock of the impact was lessening as the scent opened out and mellowed. It was *him*. The scent was everything that was deep inside him, where no one could see his true self. Yet this woman had got it—after only a couple of meetings and a few hours.

CHAPTER THREE

LEILA STOOD UP, not sure how to respond. She'd never seen someone react so forcefully to a scent before.

'I researched a little about the island, to find out what its native flowers were, and I approximated them as closely as I could with what I have available in the shop. And I added citrus and calone, which has always reminded me of a sea breeze.'

Alix Saint Croix looked huge, formidable, against the window and the autumnal darkness outside. Her first reaction when she'd met this man had been fascination, a feeling of being dazzled, and since then her instinct had been to run away—fast. But now her feet were glued to the floor.

'If you don't like it—'

'I like it.'

His response was short, sharp. He sounded almost... *angry*. Leila was completely confused.

Hesitantly she said, 'Are you sure? You don't sound very pleased.'

He turned around then and thrust both hands into his pockets. His chest was broad, the darkness of his skin visible under his shirt. He looked at her closely and shook his head, as if trying to clear it.

Finally he said, 'I'm just a little surprised. The fragrance is not what I was expecting.'

Leila shrugged. 'A customised scent has a bigger impact than a generic designer scent...'

His mouth quirked sexily and he came back over to the couch. Leila couldn't take her eyes off him.

'It certainly has an impact.'

'If it's too strong I can—'

'No.' Alix's voice cut her off. 'I don't want you to change it.'

A knock came on the door then, and Leila flinched a little. She was so caught up in this man's reaction and his charisma that she'd almost forgotten where she was. The seductive warmth of the bourbon in her belly didn't help.

Alix said, 'That's dinner. I took the liberty of ordering for two, if you'd care to join me?'

Leila just looked at him and felt again that urge to run—but also a stronger urge to stay. *Rebel.* Even though she wasn't exactly sure who she was rebelling against. Herself and every instinct screaming at her to run? Or the ghost of her mother's disappointment?

She justified her weakness to herself: this man had thrown more business her way than she'd see in the next month. She should be polite. *Ha!* said a snide inner voice. *There's nothing polite about the way you feel around him.*

She ignored that and said, as coolly as she could, 'Only if it's not too much of an imposition.'

He had a very definite mocking glint to his eye. 'It's no imposition…really.'

Alix went to the door and opened it to reveal obsequious staff who proceeded straight towards a room off the main reception area. Within minutes they were leaving again, and Alix was waiting for Leila to precede him into the dining room—which was as sumptuously decorated as the rest of the suite.

She caught a glimpse of a bedroom through an open door and almost tripped over her feet to avoid looking that way again. It brought to mind too easily the way that woman had stripped so nonchalantly for her lover. And how Alix had maintained that nothing had happened in spite of appearances.

Why should she even care, when he was probably lying?

Leila almost balked at that point, but as if sensing her trepidation, Alix pulled out a chair and looked at her pointedly. No escape. She moved forward and sat down, looking at the array of food laid out on the table. There was enough for a small army.

Alix must have seen something on her face, because he grimaced a little and said, 'I wasn't sure if you were vegetarian or not, so I ordered a selection.'

Leila couldn't help a wry smile. 'I *am* vegetarian, actually—mostly my mother's influence. Though I do sometimes eat fish.'

Alix started to put some food on a plate for her: a mixture of tapas-type starters, including what looked like balls of rice infused with herbs and spices. The smells had her mouth watering, and she realised that she hadn't eaten since earlier that day, her stomach having been too much in knots after seeing Alix Saint Croix again, and then thinking about him all afternoon as she'd worked on his fragrance.

She could smell it now, faintly—exotic and spicy, with that tantalising hint of citrus—and her insides quivered. It suited him: light, but with much darker undertones.

He handed her the plate and then plucked a chilled bottle of white wine out of an ice bucket. Leila wasn't used to drinking, and could still feel the effects of the bourbon, so she held up a hand when Alix went to pour her some wine.

'I'll stick to water, thanks.'

As he poured himself some wine he asked casually, 'Where are your parents from?'

Leila tensed inevitably as the tall, shadowy and indistinct shape of her father came into her mind's eye. She'd only ever seen him in photos in the newspaper. Tightly she answered, 'My mother was a single parent. She was from India.'

'Was?'

Leila nodded and concentrated on spearing some food with her fork. 'She died a few years ago.'

'I'm sorry. That must have been hard if it was just the two of you.'

Leila was a little taken aback at the sincerity she heard in his voice and said quietly, 'It was the hardest thing.'

She avoided his eyes and put a forkful of food in her mouth, not expecting the explosion of flavours from the spice-infused rice ball. She looked at him and he smiled at her reaction, chewing his own food.

When he could speak he said, 'My personal chef is here. He's from Isle Saint Croix, so he sticks to the local cuisine. It's a mixture of North African and Mediterranean.'

Relieved to be moving away from personal areas, Leila said, 'I've never tasted anything like it.' Then she admitted ruefully, 'I haven't travelled much, though.'

'You were born here?'

Leila reached for her water, as much to cool herself down as anything else. 'Yes, my mother travelled over when she was pregnant. My father was French.'

'Was?'

Leila immediately regretted letting that slip out. But her mother was no longer alive. Surely the secret didn't have to be such a secret any more? But then she thought of how easily her father had turned his back on them and repeated her mother's words, used whenever anyone had asked a similar question. 'He died a long time ago. I never knew him.'

To her relief, Alix didn't say anything to that, just looked at her consideringly. They ate in companionable silence for a few minutes, and Leila tried not to think too hard about where she was and who she was with.

When she'd cleared half her plate she sneaked a look at

Alix. He was sitting back, cradling his glass of wine, looking at her. And just like that her skin prickled with heat.

'I hope I didn't lose you too much custom by taking up your attention today?'

He looked entirely unrepentant, and in spite of herself Leila had to allow herself a small wry smile. 'No—the opposite. The business has been struggling to get back on track since the recession…niche industries like mine were the worst hit.'

Alix frowned. 'Yet you kept hold of your shop?'

Leila nodded, tensing a little at the thought of the uphill battle to restore sales. 'I've owned it outright since my mother died.'

'That's good—but you *could* sell. You don't need me to tell you what that shop and flat must be worth in this part of Paris.'

Leila's insides clenched hard. 'I won't *ever* sell,' she said in a low voice. The shop and the flat were her mother's legacy to her—a safe haven. Security. She barely knew this man…she wasn't about to confide in him.

Feeling self-conscious again, she took her napkin from her lap and put it on the table. That silver gaze narrowed on her.

'I should go. Thank you for dinner—you really didn't have to.'

She saw a muscle twitch in Alix's jaw and half-expected—*wanted?*—him to stop her from going.

But he just stood up smoothly and said, 'Thank you for joining me.'

Much to Leila's sense of disorientation, Alix made no effort to detain her with offers of tea or coffee. He picked up the bag that she'd had with her when she'd arrived and handed it to her in the main reception room.

Feeling at a loss, and not liking the sense of disappointment that he was letting her go so easily, Leila said again, 'Thank you.'

Alix bowed slightly towards her and once again she was struck by his sheer beauty and all that potent masculinity. He looked as if he was about to speak some platitude, then he stopped and said, 'Actually... I have tickets to the opera for tomorrow evening. I wonder if you'd like to join me?'

Leila didn't trust his all-too-innocent façade for a second—as if he'd just thought of it. But she couldn't think straight because giddy relief was mocking her for the disappointment she'd felt just seconds ago because he was letting her go so easily.

She was dealing with a master here.

This was not the first time a man had asked her out but it still hit her in the solar plexus like a blow. Her last disastrous dating experience rose like a dark spectre in her memory—except this man in front of her eclipsed Pierre Gascon a hundred times over. Enough to give her a little frisson of satisfaction.

As if *any* man could compete with this tall, dark specimen before her. *Sexy.* Leila had never been overtly aware of sexual longing before. But now she was—she could feel the awareness throbbing in her blood, between her legs.

And it was that awareness of how out of her depth Alix Saint Croix made her feel that had Leila blurting out, 'I really don't think it would be a good idea.' *Coward*, whispered a voice.

He lifted a brow in lazy enquiry. 'And why would that be? You're single...I'm single. We're two consenting adults. I'm offering a pleasant way to spend the evening. That's all.'

Now she felt gauche. She was thinking of sex when he certainly wasn't. 'I'm just...not exactly in your league, Monsieur Saint Croix—'

'It's Alix,' he growled, coming closer. 'Call me Alix.'

Leila swallowed, caught in the beam of those incredible eyes. 'Alix...'

'That's better. Now, tell me again exactly why this is not a good idea?'

Feeling cornered and angry now—with herself as much as him—Leila flung out a hand. 'I own a shop and you're a king. We're not exactly on a level footing.'

Alix cocked his head to one side. 'You're a perfumer, are you not? A very commendable career.'

Unable to keep the bitterness out of her voice, Leila said, 'To be a perfumer one needs to be making perfumes.'

'Something I've no doubt you'll do when your business recovers its equilibrium.'

His quiet and yet firm encouragement made something glow in Leila's chest. She ruthlessly pushed it down. This man could charm the devil over to the light side.

'Don't you have more important things to be doing?'

A curious expression she couldn't decipher crossed his hard-boned face before his mouth twitched and he said,'Not right now, no.'

Leila's stubborn refusal to accede to his wishes was having a bizarre effect on Alix. He could quite happily stay here for hours and spar with her, watching those expressions cross her face and her gorgeous eyes spark and glow.

'Don't you know,' he said carefully, watching her reaction with interest, 'that feigning uninterest is one sure way to get a man interested in you?'

Immediately her cheeks were suffused with colour and her back went poker straight with indignation. Eyes glittering, she said, 'I am *not* feigning uninterest, Mr Saint Croix, I am genuinely mystified as to why you are persisting like this—and to be perfectly frank I think I'd prefer it if you just left me alone.'

He took a step closer. 'Really, Leila? I could let you walk out of this suite right now and you'll never see me again.' He waited a beat and then said softly, 'If that's *really* what you want. But I don't think it is.'

Oh, God. He'd seen her disappointment. She'd never been any good at hiding her emotions. She'd also never felt so hot with the need to break out of some confinement holding her back.

She hadn't felt this hungry urgency with Pierre. He'd been far more subtle—and ultimately manipulative. Alix was direct. And there was something absurdly comforting about that. There were no games. He wasn't dressing his words up with illusions of more being involved. It made her breathless.

Her extended silence had made something go hard in Alix's eyes and Leila felt a dart of panic go through her. She sensed that he would stop pursuing her if she asked him to. If he did indeed believe she was stringing him along. Which she wasn't. Or was she? Unconsciously?

She hated to think that she might be capable of such a thing, but she couldn't deny the thrilling rush of something illicit every time she saw him. The rush of sparring with him. The rush each time he came back even though she'd said no.

Leila felt as if she was skirting around the edges of a very large and angry fire that mesmerised her as much as it made her fear its heat. She'd shut down after her experience with Pierre, dismayed at coming to terms with the fact that she'd made such a huge misjudgement. But now she could feel a part of her expanding inside again, demanding to be heard. To be set free. Another chance.

She'd never been to the opera. Pierre's most exciting invitation had been to a trip down the Seine, which Leila had done a million times with her mother. The sense of yearning got stronger.

She heard herself asking, 'It's *just* a trip to the opera?'

The hardness in Alix's eyes softened, but he was careful enough not to show that he'd gained a point.

'Yes, Leila, it's just a simple trip to the opera. If you can close a little early tomorrow I'll pick you up at five.'

Closing a little early would hardly damage her already dented business. She took a deep breath and tried not to let this moment feel bigger than it should. 'Very well. I'll accept your invitation.'

Alix took up her hand and raised it to his mouth before brushing a very light, almost imperceptible kiss across the back of it. Even so, his breath burned her skin.

'I look forward to it, Leila. *A bientôt.*'

At about three o'clock the next day Leila found herself dealing with an unusual flurry of customers, and it took her a couple of seconds to notice the thickset man waiting just inside the door. When she finally registered that it was Ricardo, Alix's bodyguard, she noticed that he had a big white box in his hands.

She went over and he handed it to her, saying gruffly, 'A gift from Mr Saint Croix.'

Leila took the box warily and glanced at her customers, who were all engrossed in trying out the samples she'd been showing them. She looked back to Ricardo and felt a trickle of foreboding. 'Can you wait for a second?'

He nodded, and if Leila had had the time to appreciate how out of place he looked against the backdrop of delicate perfume bottles she might have smiled.

She suspected that she knew what was in the box.

She ducked into a small anteroom behind the counter and opened it to reveal layers of expensive-looking silver tissue paper. Underneath the paper she saw a glimmer of silk, and gasped as she pulled out the most beautiful dress she'd ever seen.

It was a very light green, with one simple shoulder strap and a ruched bodice. The skirt fell to the floor from under the bust in layers of delicate chiffon. On further investigation Leila saw that there were matching shoes and even underwear. Her face burned at that. It burned even more when she realised that Alix had got her size spot-on.

She felt tempted to march right across the square and tell him to shove his date, but she held on to her temper. This was how he must operate with *all* his women. And he was arrogant enough to think that Leila was just like them?

'What do you mean, she wouldn't accept it?'

Ricardo looked exceedingly uncomfortable and shifted from foot to foot, before saying *sotto voce*, mindful of the other men in the room, 'She left a note inside the box.'

'Did she now?' Alix curbed his irritation and said curtly, 'Thank you, Ricardo, that will be all.'

Alix had been holding a meeting in his suite, and the other men around the table started to move a little, clearly anticipating a break from the customarily intense sessions Alix conducted. He dismissed them too, with a look that changed their expressions of relief to ones of meek servitude.

When they were all gone Alix flicked open the lid of the box and saw the plain piece of white paper lying on the silver paper with its succinct message:

Thank you, but I can dress myself.
Leila.

Alix couldn't help his mouth quirking in a smile. Had any woman ever handed him back a gift? Not in his memory.

He let the lid drop down and stood up to walk over to the window of his suite, which looked out over the square below.

For a large portion of his life, ever since his dramatic escape from Isle Saint Croix all those years ago, he'd felt like a caged animal—forced into this role of pretending that he *wasn't* engaged in an all-out battle to regain his throne. The prospect of being on his island again, with the salty tang of the sea in the hot air... Sometimes the yearning for home was almost unbearable.

Alix sighed and let his gaze narrow on the small shop that glinted across the square in the late-afternoon sunlight. He could see the familiar slim white-coated shape moving back and forth. The caged animal within him got even more restless. The yearning was replaced with sharp anticipation.

It would be no hardship to pursue Miss Verughese and let the world think nothing untoward was going on behind the scenes. No hardship at all.

Leila looked at herself in the mirror and had a sudden attack of nerves. Maybe she'd been really stupid to send Alix's gift back to him? She'd never been to the opera—she wasn't even sure what the dress code was, except posh.

The scent she'd put on so sparingly drifted up, and for a moment she wanted to run and wash it off. It wasn't her usual scent, which was light and floral. This was a scent that had always fascinated her: one of her mother's most sensual creations. It had called to Leila from the shelf just after she'd locked up before coming upstairs to get ready.

It was called *Dark Desiring*. Her mother had had a penchant for giving their perfumes enigmatic names. As soon as Leila had sprayed a little on her wrist she'd heard her mother's voice in her head: *'This scent is for a woman, Leila. The kind of woman who knows what she wants and gets it. You will be that woman someday, and you won't be foolish like your mother.'*

She felt the scent now, deep in the pit of her belly. Felt its dark sensuality, earthy musky notes and exotic floral arrangement. It was so unlike her...and yet it resonated with her. But she felt exposed wearing it—as if it would be obvious to everyone that she was trying to be something she wasn't.

The doorbell sounded... Too late to remove it now, even if she wanted to.

She made her way downstairs, her heart palpitating in her chest. She thrust aside memories of another man she'd let too close. It had been as if as soon as her mother's influence had been removed Leila had automatically sought out proof that not all men weren't to be trusted. But that had spectacularly backfired and proved her *very* wrong.

Walking through the darkened shop, Leila forced the clamouring memories down. She'd learnt her lesson. She was no fool any more. She still wanted something different from her mother's experience, but Alix Saint Croix was the last man to offer such a thing. So, if anything, she couldn't be safer than with this man.

She sucked in a big breath and opened the door. The sky was dusky outside and Alix blocked most of it with his broad shoulders. He was dressed in a classic black tuxedo and white bow tie under his overcoat. Leila's mouth went dry. That assurance of safety suddenly felt very flimsy.

She wasn't even aware that Alix's eyes had widened on her when she'd appeared.

'You look beautiful.'

She stopped gawking at him long enough to meet his eyes. And those nerves gripped her again as she gestured shyly to her outfit. 'I wasn't sure... I hope it's appropriate?'

Alix lifted his eyes to hers. 'It's stunning. You look like a princess.'

Leila blushed and busied herself pulling the door behind her and locking it to deflect his scrutiny.

The outfit was a traditional Indian *salwar kameez* with a bit of a modern twist. The tunic was made out of green and gold silk, with slim-fitting trousers in the same shade of green. She had on gold strappy sandals that she'd bought one day on a whim but never worn. A loose chiffon throw was draped over her shoulders and she'd put her hair up in a high bun. She wore ornate earrings that had belonged to her mother—like a talisman that might protect her from falling into the vortex that this man created whenever he was near.

The driver of the sleek car parked nearby was holding the door open, and Leila slid into the luxurious confines as Alix joined her from the other side. She plucked nervously at the material of her tunic as they pulled away.

Alix took her hand and she looked at him.

'You look amazing. No other woman will be dressed the same.'

Leila quirked a wry smile, liking the feel of Alix's hand around hers far too much. 'That's what I'm suddenly afraid of.'

He shook his head. 'You'll stand out like a bird of paradise—they'll be insanely jealous.'

Leila gave a small dissenting sound and went to pull her hand back, but Alix gripped it tighter and lifted it up, turning her wrist. He frowned slightly and bent to smell. Leila's heart thumped, hard.

He looked at her. 'This isn't your usual scent?'

Damn him for noticing. Leila cursed her impetuosity and felt as if that scarlet letter was on her forehead for all to see. She pulled her hand back. 'No, it's a different scent—one more suitable for evenings.'

'I like it.'

Leila could smell his scent too. The one she'd made him. She knew that it lingered on his skin from when he'd put it on much earlier that day—it didn't have the sharp tang of having been recently applied. She thought of their scents now, mingling and wrapping around one another. It made her feel unbearably aware of the fact that they were so close. Aware of the warm blood pumping just under their skin, making those scents mellow and change subtly.

It was an alchemy that happened to everyone in a totally different way, as the perfume responded uniquely to each individual.

She finally looked away from Alix to see that they were leaving the confines of the city and heading towards the grittier outskirts. Nowhere near the Paris opera house.

She frowned and looked back at him. 'I thought we were going to the opera?'

'We are.'

'But we're leaving Paris.'

Alix smiled. 'I said we were going to the opera. I didn't say where.'

Flutters of panic made her tense. 'I don't appreciate surprises. Tell me where we're going, please.'

His eyes narrowed on her and Leila bit back the urge to lambast him for assuming she was just some wittering dolly bird, only too happy to let him whisk her off to some unknown location.

Alix's voice had an edge of steel to it when he said, 'We're going to Venice.'

'*Venice?*' Leila squeaked. 'But I don't have my passport. I mean, how can we just—?'

Alix took her hand again and spoke as if he was soothing a nervous horse. 'You don't need your passport. I have diplomatic immunity and you're with me. The flight will take an hour and forty minutes. I'll have you back in Paris and home by midnight. I promise.'

Leila reeled. 'You said flight?'

Alix nodded warily, as if expecting another explosion.

'I've never been on a plane before,' she admitted somewhat warily. As if Alix might be so disgusted with her lack of sophistication that he'd turn around and deliver her home right now.

He just frowned slightly. 'But…how is that possible?'

Leila shrugged, finding to her consternation that once again she was loath to take her hand out of Alix's much bigger one. 'My mother and I…we didn't travel much. Apart from to other parts of France. We went to England once, to visit a factory outside London, but we took the train. My mother was terrified of flying.'

'Well, then,' said Alix throatily, 'do you want to go home? Or do you want to take your first flight? We can turn around right now if you want.'

That was like asking if she wanted to keep moving forward in life or backwards. Leila felt that fire reaching out to lick at her with a tantalising flash of heat. Alix's thumb was rubbing the underside of her wrist, making the flash of heat more intense. Leila thought of the car turning around, of returning to that square and her shop. She felt nauseous.

She shook her head. 'I'd like to fly with you.'

Alix brought her hand to his mouth and kissed it lightly before saying, 'Then let's fly.'

Leila might not be half as sophisticated as his usual women, but even she knew that they were talking about something else entirely—just as the flames of that fire reached out to consume her completely and Alix moved close enough to slant his hard sensual mouth over hers.

She'd been kissed before—by Pierre. But his kiss had been insistent and invasive. Too wet, with no finesse. This was…

Leila lost any sense of being able to string a rational thought together when her mouth opened of its own volition under Alix's and she felt the first electrifying contact of his tongue to hers. She was lost.

CHAPTER FOUR

THE ONLY THING stopping Alix exploding into orbit at the feel of Leila's lush soft mouth under his and the shy touch of her tongue was the hand he'd clamped around her waist. He was rock-hard almost instantaneously. He'd never tasted such sweetness. Her mouth trembled under his and he had to use extreme restraint to go slowly, coaxing her to open up to him.

He felt the hitch in her breathing as their kiss deepened and he gathered her closer to feel the swell of her breasts against his chest. Right at that moment Alix couldn't have remembered his own name. He was drowning in heat and lust and an urgent desire to haul Leila over his lap, so that he could seat her against where he ached most.

She pulled back suddenly and he cracked open his eyes to look down into wide green ones. Leila had her hands on his chest and was pushing at him.

'Please—don't do that again.'

Alix was on unsure ground. Another first. He wasn't used to women pushing him away. And he knew Leila had been enjoying it. She'd been melting into him like his hottest teenage fantasy, and he felt about as suave as a teenager right then. All raging hormones and no control.

Drawing on what little control he *did* still have, Alix moved back, putting space between them. He looked at her. Cheeks flushed, chest rising and falling rapidly, eyes avoiding his. Mouth pink and wet. It made him think of other parts of her that might be wet. He cursed himself silently. Where was his finesse?

He reached out and cupped her jaw, seeing how she tensed. He tipped her chin up so that she had no choice but to look at him. Her eyes were huge and wary. There was an edge of something in her eyes that he couldn't read. He felt a spike of recrimination. Had he been too forceful? But he knew he hadn't. It had nearly killed him to rein himself in.

'Did you have a bad experience with a previous lover?'

She pulled his hand down. 'That's none of your business.'

She avoided his eyes again and he wanted to growl his frustration. But they were pulling into the small private airport now, and staff were rushing to meet the car.

Alix got out and pulled his coat around his body, not liking that he had to conceal his arousal. He glared at the driver who was about to help Leila out of the car and the man ducked back to let Alix take her hand. When she stood up beside him, the breeze blowing a loose tendril of dark hair across one cheek, he had to forcibly stop himself from kissing her again.

Gripping her hand, when he usually avoided public displays of affection like the plague, he led her over to the waiting plane: a small sleek private jet that he used for short hops around Europe. He realised then how much he took things like this for granted. Leila had never even flown before.

He stopped and turned to her. 'You're not frightened, are you?'

She glanced from the plane to him and admitted warily, 'It looks a bit small.'

He grinned and felt the dense band of cynicism around his heart loosen a little. 'It's as safe as houses—I promise.'

He urged her forward and up the steps, past a steward in uniform. He chose two seats opposite each other so he could see Leila's expression. He buckled them both in, and then the plane was taxiing down the runway. With a roar of the throttle, it lifted up into the darkening Paris sky. Alix had had a discreet word with the pilot, and watched Leila's face for her reaction as they climbed into the air.

Her hands were gripping the seat's armrests, and when she cast him a quick glance he raised a brow while shrugging off his overcoat. 'Okay?'

She smiled and it was a bit wobbly. 'I think so.' She put a hand to her belly as if to calm it.

Alix was charmed by her reaction. Her expression was avid as the ground was left behind, and her hands gradually relaxed as the plane rose and gained altitude and then found its cruising level. And then her face became suffused with wonder as she took in the fact that they were flying directly over the city of Paris.

It was perfect timing, with all the lights coming on. Alix looked down through his own window and saw the Eiffel Tower flashing. He'd taken this for granted for so long it was a novelty to see it through someone else's eyes.

Leila felt as if she was in a dream. Her stomach had been churning slightly with the motion of the plane, but it was calming now. To be so high above the city and all its glittering lights…the sheer beauty of it almost moved her to tears. And it was distracting enough to help her block out how amazing that kiss had been. How hard it had been to pull away.

What had finally made her come to her senses had been the realisation that she was being kissed by an expert— who'd kissed scores of far more beautiful women than her.

'Why did your mother hate flying so much?'

Leila composed herself before she looked at Alix, where he was lounging in the chair opposite, long legs stretched out and crossed at the ankle, effectively caging her in. Despite her best efforts, one look at his hard, sensual mouth was bringing their kiss back in glorious Technicolor…the way it had burnt her up.

She forced her gaze up to his eyes and tried to remember his question. 'My mother flew only once in her life, when she came to France from India. It was a traumatic journey for her... She was in disgrace, pregnant and unwed, and was suffering badly from morning sickness.' Leila shrugged lightly, knowing she was leaving so much out of that explanation. 'She always associated flying with that trauma and never wanted to get on a plane again.'

'Aren't you curious about your Indian roots and family?'

An innocuous enough question, but one that had a familiar resentment rising up within Leila. Her mother's family had all but left her for dead—they'd never once contacted her or Leila. Not even when a newspaper had reported that some of them were in Paris for a massive perfume fair.

Leila hid her true emotions under a bland mask. She forced a smile. 'I'm afraid my mother's family cut all ties with us... But perhaps one day I'll go back and visit the country of my ancestors.'

She took refuge in looking at the view again, hoping that Alix wouldn't ask any more personal questions. The lights of the city were becoming sparser. They must be flying further away from Paris now.

But it was as if Alix could read her mind and was deliberately thwarting her. He asked softly, 'Why did you pull back when I kissed you, Leila? I know it wasn't because you really wanted me to stop.'

She froze. She hadn't expected Alix to notice that fleeting moment when she'd felt so insecure. She hadn't wanted it to stop at all...she'd never felt such exquisite pleasure. And the thought of him kissing her again—she knew she wouldn't be able to pull back the next time.

An urgent self-protective need rose up inside her. She had to try and repel Alix on some level—surely a man of a blue-blooded royal line wouldn't want anything to do with the illegitimate daughter of a disgraced Indian woman?

She looked at him, and he was regarding her from under hooded lids.

'You asked before if I'd had a bad experience with a lover...'

Alix sat up straighter. 'You told me it was none of my business.'

'And it's not,' Leila reiterated. 'But, yes, I had a negative encounter with someone, and I don't really wish to repeat the experience.'

Alix went very still, and Leila could see the innate male pride in his expression. He couldn't believe that she would compare him to another man.

'I'm sorry you had to experience that, but you can't damn all men because of one.'

Leila took a breath. Alix wasn't being dissuaded. In spite of the flutters in her belly she went on. 'In fact, if you must know, my mother was rather overprotective.' The flutters increased under Alix's steady regard. 'The truth is that I'm not as experienced as you might—'

'Are you ready for supper, Your Majesty?'

They both looked to see the steward holding out some menus. Relief flooded Leila that she'd been cut off from revealing the ignominious truth of just how inexperienced she was. She welcomed the diversion of taking the menu being proffered.

She imagined that Alix would believe she was still a virgin as much as he'd believe in unicorns. But thankfully, when they were alone again, he didn't seem inclined to continue the discussion.

When she glanced at him, he just sent her an enigmatic glance and said, 'I recommend the risotto—it's vegetarian.'

Leila smiled. 'That sounds good.'

When the young man came back, moments later, Alix

ordered. Then he poured them both some champagne. When the flutes were filled and a table had been set between them, Alix lifted his glass and said, with a very definite glint in his eye, 'To new experiences, Leila.'

She cringed inwardly. He didn't have to pursue the discussion. He'd guessed her secret. She lifted her glass too, but said nothing. She got the distinct impression that he still wasn't put off. And, as much as she'd like to tell Alix that flying in a plane was the *only* new experience she was interested in sharing with him, she couldn't formulate the words. Traitorously.

'Why is everyone looking at us?'

Alix looked at Leila incredulously. She had no idea what a sensation she was causing—*had* caused as soon as they'd stepped from his boat and into the ancient *palazzo* on the Grand Canal where the opera was being staged. Leila stood out effortlessly—like a jewel amongst much duller stones. Now it was the interval, and they were seated in a private area to the right of the stage. Private, yet visible.

His mouth quirked. 'They're not looking at us—they're looking at *you*.'

She looked at him and blushed. 'Oh…it's the clothes, isn't it? I should have—'

Alix shook his head, cutting her off. 'It's not the clothes…well, it *is*. But that's because you are more beautiful than any other woman here and you're putting them to shame with your sense of style. Every woman is looking at you and wondering why their finger is not on the pulse.'

Leila's blush deepened, and it had a direct effect on Alix's arousal levels.

'I'm sure that's not it at all. I've never seen so many beautiful people in one place in my entire life. I've never seen anywhere so breathtaking—the canal, this *palazzo*…'

She ducked her head for a moment before looking back at him. 'Thank you…this evening has been magical.'

Alix had to school his features. He couldn't remember the last time a woman had thanked him for taking her out.

'You're glad you overcame your reluctance to spend time with me?' he queried innocently.

Her green gaze held his and Alix felt breathless for a second. *Crazy.* Women didn't make him breathless.

Her mouth twitched minutely. 'Yes, I'm glad—but don't let it go to your head.'

An unfortunate choice of words when it made him aware of the part of his anatomy that refused to obey his efforts to control it.

Leila looked so incandescent in that moment—a small smile playing around her mouth, eyes sparkling—that Alix had to curl his hands into fists to stop himself from kissing her again.

The lights dimmed and the cast resumed their places. Alix tore his gaze from her, questioning his sanity and praying that he'd have enough control not to ravish her like a wild animal in the darkened surroundings.

After the opera had finished Alix took Leila out of the *palazzo* and along the Grand Canal in his boat, to a small rustic Italian restaurant where he was greeted like an old friend by the owner. They ate a selection of small starters and drank wine, and to Leila's surprise the conversation flowed as easily as if they'd known each other for months, not days.

Something had happened—either as soon as she'd agreed to this date or on the plane, when events had become a dizzying spectacle. Or maybe it had been when she'd chosen a different perfume for herself…

She'd stepped over a line—irrevocably. She felt as if she was a different person, inhabiting the same skin. As if she'd thrown off some kind of shackle holding her to the past. She was a little drunk. She knew that. But she'd never felt so light, so…effervescent. So open to new possibilities, experiences.

She wasn't naive enough to think that it would be anything more than transient. Especially with a man like Alix. And that was okay. If anything it was a form of protection. He was practically emblazoned with *Warning!* And *Hazardous!* signs.

She must have giggled a little, because Alix said dryly, 'Something I said was funny?'

Leila shook her head and looked at him, all of a sudden stone-cold sober again. He was beautiful. Their mingled scents wrapped around her. Leila imagined them curling around her brain's synapses, rendering them weak. Making her want what he was offering with those slate-grey eyes— hot with a decadent promise she could only imagine.

Leila realised with a sense of desperation that she *wanted* whatever he was offering. She wanted to lose herself and be broken apart. She wanted to know what it was like. She wanted to taste the forbidden.

She didn't want to go back to her small poky apartment above her failing shop and be the same person. Looking at life passing by across the square. She wanted life to be happening *to her*. She'd never felt it this strongly before. It was his persistent seduction, the perfume, the wine, the opera…leaving her country for the first time. It was his kiss. It was *him*.

Impetuously she leaned forward. 'Do we have to go back to Paris tonight?'

Immediately his gaze narrowed on her. She was acutely conscious of the fact that his jacket and bow tie were gone and his shirt was open at the throat, revealing the strong bronzed column of his neck.

'What are you suggesting?'

Feeling bold for the first time in her life, Leila said, 'I'm suggesting…not going back to Paris. Staying here… in Venice.'

'For the night?'

She nodded. The enormity of what she was doing was dizzying, but she couldn't turn back now. Her heart was thumping.

Alix cocked his head slightly. 'I think you might be a little drunk, Miss Verughese.'

'Perhaps,' she agreed huskily. 'But I know what I'm saying.'

'Do you now…?' Alix looked at her consideringly.

For a second something cold touched Leila's spine. Maybe she had this all wrong. Maybe Alix was just toying with this gauche girl from a shop until a more suitable woman came along? No doubt he was getting a kick out of her untutored reactions to flying and seeing the opera.

And now this… Maybe the thought of bedding a virgin wasn't palatable to a man of his undoubted experience and sophisticated tastes? She thought of how that woman had undressed in front of him and her insides contracted painfully. She could never do that.

She looked away, searching for her bag and wrap. 'Forget I said anything. I'm sure you have meetings—'

Suddenly her hand was clasped in his and reluctantly she looked at him. He was intense.

'Are you saying you want to stay in Venice for the night to share my bed, Leila?'

She hated it that he was making her spell it out, but she lifted her chin and said, 'If you're not interested—'

His hand tightened on hers. 'Oh, I'm interested. I just want to make sure you're not going to regret this in the morning and blame it on too much wine.'

Leila stared back, suppressing an urge to say *I'm blam-*

ing it on much more than that. He wouldn't understand. 'I want this—even if it's just one night.'

Alix interlaced his fingers with hers. It felt like a shockingly intimate caress.

'It won't be one night, Leila, I can guarantee that.'

She shivered lightly. The way he said that sounded like a vow. Or a promise.

'Signor Alix…?'

He didn't even look at his friend. He just said, 'We're finished, Giorgio, thank you.'

But it was a long moment before Alix broke his gaze from hers and let go of her hand to stand up.

Leila couldn't remember much of leaving the restaurant, or of the boat ride along the magical Grand Canal at night. She was only aware of Alix's strong thighs beside hers on the seat, his arm tight around her shoulders, his hand resting disturbingly close to the curve of her breast.

She was only aware that she was finally leaving a part of her life behind and stepping into the unknown.

She couldn't believe she'd been so forward, and yet she knew that even if given a choice she wouldn't turn back now. This man had unlocked some deep secret part of her and she wanted to explore it. She didn't care about the fact that Alix Saint Croix was famous or rich or royalty. She was interested in the man. He called to her on a very basic level that no one had ever touched before.

And as the boat scythed through the choppy waters she reassured herself that she was going into this with eyes wide open. No romantic illusions. She was *not* starry-eyed any more. Pierre had seen to that when she'd let him woo her. That had been just after the death of her mother, when she'd been at her most vulnerable. She wasn't vulnerable any more. And Leila had no intention of shutting herself away like a nun for the rest of her life.

They were approaching a building now—another grand

palazzo. A man stood on the small landing dock and threw a rope to the driver. They came alongside the wooden jetty and Alix jumped nimbly out of the boat before turning back to lift Leila out as easily as if she weighed nothing.

As he let her down on the jetty he kept her close to his body, and her eyes widened when she felt her belly brush against a very hard part of him. Her pulse quickened and between her legs she felt damp.

Then he turned, and held her hand as he strode through the open doors. Leila had to almost run to keep up and she tugged at his hand. He looked back, something stark etched onto his face. She refused to let it intimidate her.

'What is this place?'

'It belongs to a friend—he's away.'

'Oh...'

A petite older woman dressed in black approached them and Alix exchanged some words with her in fluent Italian. It was only then that Leila looked around and took in the grandeur of the reception hall. The floor was marble, and there were massive stone columns stretching all the way up to a ceiling that was covered in very old-looking frescoes.

Then Alix was tugging her hand again and they were following the woman up the main staircase. The eyes from numerous huge stern portraits followed their progress and Leila superstitiously avoided looking at them, sensing a judgment she wasn't really blasé enough to ignore in spite of her bravado.

The corridor they walked into had thick carpet, muffling their footsteps. Massive ornate wooden doors were closed on each side. At the end of the corridor the woman came to some double doors and opened them wide, standing aside so they could go in.

Leila's breath stopped. It was the most stunningly sumptuous suite of rooms she'd ever seen. She let go of Alix's hand and walked over to where the glass French doors were open, leading out to a stone balcony overlooking a smaller canal.

She heard the door close softly and looked behind her to see Alix standing in the centre of the room, hands in his pockets, legs wide. Chest broad.

He took a hand out of his pocket and held it out. Silently Leila went to him, kicking off her sandals as she did so.

When she got to Alix, he drew her chiffon wrap off her shoulders and it drifted to the floor beside them. Then he reached around to the back of her head and removed the pin holding her hair up. It fell around her shoulders in a heavy silken curtain and he ran his hand through the strands.

'I wanted to do this the moment I saw you,' he said.

Feeling suddenly vulnerable, she blurted out, 'Did you really not sleep with that woman after you pulled the curtains that night?'

His grey gaze bored into hers. 'No, I did not sleep with Carmen that night. I wouldn't lie to you about that, Leila.'

She found that she believed him, but she still had to battle the insidious suspicion that he would say whatever he wanted to get her into bed. Not that he'd had to say much—she'd all but begged him!

Furiously she blocked out the raising clamour of voices and reached up, touching her mouth to his. 'Take me to bed, Alix,' she whispered.

CHAPTER FIVE

AGAINST THE MUTED lighting of the opulent suite Alix looked every inch the powerful man he was. He took up so much space, and a sudden flutter of fear clutched at Leila's belly. Could she really handle a man like this?

But then he took her hand and led her into another room. The bedroom.

Its furnishings were ridiculously, gloriously lush. A four-poster, canopied bed stood in the centre of the room, surrounded by thick velvet drapes held back by decorative rings. Through the windows Leila could see the Grand Canal, and boats moving up and down. The curtains fluttered in the breeze and yet she was hot. Burning up.

Alix came and stood in front of her. Leila was at eye level with the middle of his chest. Never more than now had she been so aware of his sheer masculinity and strength. She wished she had the nerve to reach out and touch him, but she didn't. The boldness that had led her here seemed to be fleeing in the face of the stark reality facing her.

Alix tipped up her chin with a curled forefinger and Leila couldn't escape his gaze.

'We'll take this slow.'

Leila swallowed. So much for trying to repel him with her inexperience. His eyes burned. And something melted inside her at his consideration. He pulled her forward then, until her breasts were touching his body, her nipples tightening in reaction. Both his hands went to her jaw, caressing

the delicate bone structure before tilting her face upwards.
And then his head dipped and his mouth was over hers.

Leila made a soft sound in the back of her throat. His
tongue explored along the seam of her mouth until she
opened up to him, and then he was stroking her tongue
intimately, teeth nipping at her full lower lip. Her hands
curled into his shirt, clutching. He was all hard muscle and
heat and he tasted of wine.

When Alix drew back after long, drugging moments,
Leila followed him, opening her eyes slowly, all her senses
colliding and melting into one throbbing beat of desire.
She'd never imagined it could be like this. After just a kiss.

Alix brought his hands to the small buttons running
down the front of her tunic. His skin was dark against the
silk and Leila watched as slowly the front of her tunic fell
open to reveal her lacy bra underneath.

'So beautiful...' breathed Alix as he saw her breasts
revealed, more voluptuous than Leila had ever been comfortable with.

He slid a hand inside her tunic and cupped one, testing its shape, its firm weight. The effect on her body was
so intensely pleasurable that Leila was too embarrassed
to look at Alix. She ducked her head forward and her hair
slipped over her shoulders, the ends touching his hand.

She gave a little gasp when Alix's other hand caught
her hair at the back of her head and tugged gently. His fingers were squeezing her breast now, and her nipple was
pinched tight with need. Leila wanted something but she
wasn't sure what. *More.*

When he bent to take her mouth again she whimpered.
And then his hand was pulling down the silk cup of her
bra and he was palming her naked breast, fingers trapping
her nipple, squeezing gently.

Alix's kiss was rougher than before, but Leila met it
full-on, already feeling more confident, sucking his tongue

deep, nipping his mouth. He was pushing her bra up now, over her breasts, freeing them. Pulling the top part of her tunic wide open.

When he eventually broke the kiss he was breathing harshly, eyes glittering like molten mercury.

There was something raw in his expression that made excitement mixed with sheer terror spike inside Leila. Alix moved back, tugging her with him, until he sat down on the edge of the massive bed.

Leila's breasts were exposed—framed by her pushed-up bra and the tunic. She should have felt self-conscious, but she didn't. Alix's gaze rested there and then he cupped one breast and brought his mouth to it, teasing the hard tip with his tongue before pulling it into his mouth and suckling.

Leila thought she might die. Right there and then. She'd never experienced anything so decadent, so delicious, as this hot, sucking heat. When he administered the same attention to her other breast her legs buckled and she landed on Alix's lap, his mouth and tongue lapping at her engorged flesh, making her squirm and writhe as a coil of tension wound higher and higher between her legs.

He broke away suddenly, his voice gruff. 'I need to see you.'

He carefully stood Leila up again and she felt momentarily dizzy, holding on to his arm to steady herself. He stood in front of her and slowly started to peel her tunic up and over her head. After a moment's hesitation Leila lifted her arms and it came all the way off, landing on the floor at their feet.

Then Alix deftly removed her twisted bra, and that disappeared too. Now she was naked apart from her trousers and underwear.

He was looking at her, eyes dark and unreadable. His hands were tracing her contours as reverently as if she was a piece of sculpted marble.

'I want to see you too.' Leila heard the words coming from her mouth and wasn't even aware of thinking them. *Dangerous.*

He dropped his hands and stood before her, silently inviting her to undress him. Leila lifted her hands to his shirt and slowly undid his buttons, his shirt falling open as she moved down his massive chest.

When she got to where his shirt was tucked into his trousers she hesitated for a moment, before pulling it free and undoing the last buttons. Soon it was open completely, and she pushed it wide open and off his shoulders. Alix opened his cufflinks, and then the shirt slid off completely.

Leila was in awe. The sleek strength of his muscles under the dark olive skin was fascinating to her. There was a little hair around his pectorals and a dark line down through his muscle-packed abdomen, disappearing enticingly into his trousers.

She reached out and put her hands on him, spread her fingers wide. His scent was hypnotising her...earthy and musky and *male*. The scent she'd made for him mixed with his own unique essence. She bent forward to press her lips against his hot skin, her mouth exploring and finding the small hard point of his nipple. She licked it experimentally and Alix jerked.

She pulled back, looked up. 'Did I hurt you?'

He shook his head and smiled. 'No, you didn't hurt me...*sorcière*. Lie down on the bed,' he instructed.

Leila was only too happy to comply. She felt shaky. The taste of his skin was addictive. She collapsed onto the bed and Alix moved over her before pressing a kiss to her mouth and moving down, trailing his lips over her jaw and neck, down to her breasts, anointing one and then the other.

He pulled back slightly and looked at her before saying, 'I'm going to take your trousers off...'

Leila bit her lip and then nodded. Her belly contracted

when Alix's fingers came to her button and zip, undoing them both, and then he put his hands to the sides of her silk trousers to slide them down.

She lifted her hips to help. When they were off Alix's hands went to his own trousers, and with a swift economy of movement they were off too. Along with his underwear. He was now gloriously and unashamedly naked. Leila came up on her elbows, her eyes going wide at the sight of him.

His body was a honed mass of hard muscles and masculine contours. She'd never seen anything like it. All the way from his shoulders and chest, down to slim hips and strong muscled thighs. Between his thighs and lower belly was a thicket of dark hair, out of which rose the very core of his virility. Long and thick and hard. Proud.

As Leila watched he brought a hand to himself, stroking gently. It was so unbelievably sensual that her mouth dried even as other parts of her felt as if they were gushing with wet heat.

When he took his hand from himself Leila fell back against the soft covers of the bed. Alix reached forward and gently pulled her panties free of her hips and legs. Dropping them to the floor.

Now they were both naked, and Alix came alongside her on the bed. She could feel his bold erection against her thigh. A potent invitation. But she was too shy to explore him there.

Instead, he kissed her—long, drugging kisses that sent her out of her mind completely as his hands explored her body, squeezing her buttocks, her breasts, following the contours of her waist and hips. And then he was pushing her legs apart and long fingers were exploring her *there*, where no one had ever touched her. Not even herself.

In a moment of panic at this intimate exploration she

reached down and put a hand on his, stopping him. She looked at him, breath laboured, feeling hot.

One of Alix's thighs was between her legs and she could feel the heat of him there, very close to the apex of her legs, where his hand was. And as suddenly as she'd felt panic she felt an urgency she couldn't understand. She took her hand away again.

'I won't hurt you, Leila.' Alix promised. 'Any moment you want to stop, just say and I will.'

She nodded her head. 'Thank you...'

His hand started moving again, and when she felt him push one finger and then two inside her she let out a gasp, her head going back, eyes shut tight, as if that could control the almost violent reactions happening in her body.

He was moving his fingers in and out and she could feel how wet she was. His movements got faster and the heel of his hand pressed against a part of her that needed more friction. Without even realising she was doing it Leila lifted her hips, pushing into him, seeking more.

She was unaware of the smile of pure masculine satisfaction on Alix's face as he watched her.

There was something coiling so tight and deep within her that Leila begged incoherently for it to stop, or break, or do *something*. It was painful, but it was also the most exquisitely pleasurable thing she'd ever felt. And then suddenly her whole body was caught in the grip of a storm and she broke into a million pieces. She felt like the sun, the moon, stardust, pleasure and pain. All at once.

When her body was as lax as if someone had drained every bone out of it, she opened her eyes and blinked.

Alix looked vaguely incredulous. 'That was your first orgasm?'

Leila nodded faintly. She guessed it was. Living in such a small space with her mother hadn't exactly been conducive to normal female exploration. And then she'd been so grief-stricken and busy...

The expression on Alix's face changed from incredulous to intent. He moved so that his body lay between her legs, forcing them apart. Leila still felt sensitive down there, but as Alix moved against her subtly she found that excitement was growing again—a need for more even though *more* surely couldn't be possible...

Alix kissed her, surrounding her in his heat and strength. Leila moved her hands all over him—down his torso to his hips, his muscular buttocks. And all the while he was rocking against her gently, and that urgency was building in her again...for something...for *him*.

He pulled his mouth away from her breast and she could feel the tip of his erection nudging against her opening, sliding in tantalisingly.

'Are you okay?'

She nodded. She wasn't on earth any more. She was on some new and exotic planet where time and space had become immaterial. There was no real world any more.

'Yes,' she said out loud, so that there was no ambiguity.

Alix's jaw tightened. 'This might hurt at first... Stay with me—it'll get better, I promise.'

And with that he thrust in, deep into Leila's untried flesh, stretching her wide. She gasped and arched against him, part in rejection of his invasion and part in awe at how right it felt in spite of the pain—which was blinding and red-hot. But she took a breath and looked into Alix's eyes, trusting him.

He was so big and heavy inside her. And then he moved—slowly, deeper. Pushing against her resistance. And then he pulled out again. Leila could feel sweat break out on her brow, between her breasts. She'd never thought sex would be so gritty, *base*.

Alix was relentless, moving in a little deeper each time,

and as Leila's flesh got used to him, accommodated him better, the awful sting of pain faded, becoming something else. Something much more pleasurable. Even more pleasurable than before.

Something about Alix's urgency was transmitted to her and Leila instinctively wrapped her legs around him. She felt inordinately tender in that moment, cradling this huge man between her legs, feeling the force of him inside her body.

His movements got stronger, more powerful. And Leila's hips were moving, circling. He reached down between them and touched her *there*, close to where he was thrusting. Circling his thumb, making stars explode behind her eyes, making her body tight with need again.

She was gasping, her body arching against him, buttocks tightening as he pushed her to the very limit of her endurance and she fell again, down and down, from an even higher height than the first time.

She was coasting on such a wave of bliss that she was barely aware of Alix's own body, pumping hard into hers, before he too went taut and with a guttural groan exploded in a rush of heat inside her.

Leila came to when she felt herself being lifted out of the bed, pliant and weak. She managed to raise her head and open her eyes to see he was walking them into a dimly lit bathroom...acres of marble and golden fixtures.

Steam was rising from a sunken bath that looked big enough to swim in, and Alix knelt and gently deposited Leila into the pleasantly hot water.

She looked at him, properly awake now. 'What are you doing?'

He grimaced. 'You'll be sore...and you bled a little.'

Leila thought of the bed and the sumptuous sheets. Mortified, she said, 'Oh, no!'

Alix looked stern. 'It was my fault. I should have known to prepare…'

Another expression crossed his face then, something like dawning horror, but it was hard to see in the shadows of the room, and then it was gone, replaced by something indecipherable.

He stood up and Leila saw that he'd wrapped a towel around his waist. It still didn't disguise the healthy bulge underneath, though, and her face flamed as she sank down into the bubbles.

'I'll be back in a minute.'

Alix left the bathroom and Leila moved experimentally, wincing when she felt the sting of something between pleasure and pain between her legs. She ached too—all over. But pleasurably.

Letting her head fall back, she allowed the water to soothe her body. Her brain was foggy but one thing was crystal clear: she was no longer a virgin. She'd allowed Alix Saint Croix to be more intimate with her than anyone else. And it had felt…*amazing*. Stupendous. Transformative.

It was as if this body she'd had all her life was suddenly a new thing. Her hand moved of its own volition up over the flat plane of her belly and cupped her breast. Her nipple was roused to a hard peak under her hand, still slightly sensitive. When Leila brushed it a zing of pleasure went to her groin.

She felt emboldened—empowered. Like a woman for the first time in her life. That perfume she'd chosen earlier…she got it now. She could own a scent like that and wear it with sensual pride. Dreamily, she smiled, her hand over her breast, fingers trapping her nipple, squeezing gently as Alix had done…

Alix felt marginally more under control dressed in his trousers. Up until a couple of minutes ago he had felt as if someone had drugged him and he'd lost any sense of rationale or control. And he *had*. And about something so fundamentally important to him that he was still reeling.

But he was already becoming distracted again, losing focus. He stood in the doorway of the bathroom, watching Leila cup her breast in her hand, a small smile playing around her mouth, and just like that Alix was hard again, ready for her.

That first initial thrust into her body... It had been heaven and hell—because he'd known that while he was experiencing possibly the most exquisitely sensual moment of his life she'd been in pain. Even though he'd been as gentle as he could... And then, when that pain had faded from her eyes and her body had begun to move under his, Alix hadn't had a hope of retaining any sense at all. He'd become a slave to the dictates of his body and hers.

He'd had to push her over the edge—touching her intimately, taking advantage of her inexperience—because he'd known he couldn't wait for her completion.

And then he'd exploded. Inside her. Without any barrier of protection.

Alix curbed the panic. Stepped into the bathroom. 'How are you feeling now?'

Leila immediately dropped her hand from her breast and tensed, opening her eyes, her smile fading. But then it came back...shyly.

'I'm okay. I think.'

Alix reached for a towel and held it out. Leila stood up and Alix couldn't help watching as the water sluiced down her perfect body. Her skin was like silk. She was exquisite. Slim and yet all woman, with full hips and breasts. Alix gritted his jaw to stop thinking about how it had felt to be cradled by her hips and thighs. How right it had felt. Right enough to send him mad—to make him forget important things. Like protection.

Leila rubbed herself dry with the towel, avoiding his eye now, and then Alix offered her a robe. She turned her back to him to put her arms into it and when she turned around again, belting it, she looked worried.

'Is something wrong?'

Alix felt a weight on his chest. Her eyes were so huge, so green. So innocent.

'Come into the bedroom. I asked the housekeeper to send some food and drinks up.'

He took her hand and led her out. A table was set up near the window. A candle flickered in the dim light. The sounds of the canal lapping against the building came faintly from outside.

They sat down and Leila looked even more worried. 'What is it, Alix? You're scaring me… '

'We didn't use protection.' He grimaced. 'That is, *I* didn't think of it. I presume you're not on any form of contraception?'

Leila shook her head, damp tendrils of dark hair slipping over her shoulders. Her cheeks coloured. 'No…I didn't think of it either.'

Alix's voice was harsh. 'It was my responsibility.'

She avoided his eyes for a long moment, and then she looked back at him. 'I think I'm okay, though. It's not a fertile time in my cycle. I've just finished a period.'

Something eased in his chest even as something else pierced him. A sense of loss. *Strange.*

He took her hand. 'I wasn't thinking. Ordinarily I never forget. And I can't *afford* to forget…'

He saw when comprehension dawned in those huge eyes.

Leila pulled her hand back. Her voice was stilted. 'Of course. A man like you has to be more careful than most. I understand.'

Alix felt a bizarre urge to say something to reassure her,

to tell her that it was nothing personal. But he couldn't. Because it was true. He would have to father an heir with his Queen and no one else. His own father had created a storm of controversy by bedding numerous mistresses, who had all come forward at one time or another claiming to have had children by him.

It had been one of the many reasons the people of Isle Saint Croix had become so disillusioned with their King and overthrown him.

'It won't happen again, Leila. I'm sorry.'

Her eyes snapped back to his and Alix quirked a smile. 'I don't mean *that*. We *will* be doing that again, I just won't forget about protection again.'

Food lay on the table between them, unnoticed, and Alix forced himself to try and retain a modicum of civility. He held up a piece of cheese. 'Are you hungry?'

Leila shook her head and then looked away, embarrassed.

Alix reached across and took her chin, tipping it up. He smiled. 'But you *are* hungry for something…?'

It entranced Alix that she seemed to have no sense of guile, or of playing the coquette. And why would she? She'd been a virgin. Her gaze dropped to his mouth and he saw the same insatiable appetite that had been awoken inside himself. His body hummed and soared with it.

She nodded, telling him silently what she was hungry for. Alix wanted to groan. 'But you're going to be too sore…'

Leila shook her head, her eyes on his now. Feminine and full of that innate knowledge that a man couldn't possibly ever fathom. Amazing that she already had it. Alix had never really noticed it before now, because he'd never seen it as a spontaneous thing. The women he was usually with were all too cynical even to attempt it.

'I'm okay. Really.'

Her husky words took him out of his reverie. He needed no further encouragement, so he dropped the food, stood up and led Leila back over to the bed.

When Leila woke up again it was morning. She opened her eyes and saw that the room was bathed in sunlight. She was on her own. But just as she thought that, Alix strolled out of the bathroom, straightening his tie. He was impeccably dressed. Shaved. Cleaned up. When Leila felt utterly wanton.

She sat up and clutched the sheet to her body, thoroughly disorientated. Alix leaned against one of the four posters of the bed and crossed his arms. A sexy smile played around his mouth. 'You look adorable...all mussed up.'

Leila scowled, and then grew hot when she thought of how *mussed up* she'd become when Alix had taken her to bed for the second time. Somehow in the dimly lit bathroom and bedroom last night it had been easier to face this man. Now it was daylight, and a return to reality and sanity was here. And it was not welcome.

Twinges and aches made her wince as she leant out to the side of the bed to look for some clothes.

Alix was there in seconds. 'Are you okay?'

Leila looked at him and couldn't breathe. 'I'm fine... What time is it?'

She had no clue what the etiquette of this kind of morning-after scenario was. A morning-after in *Venice,* after a night of more debauchery than she'd ever known she was capable of. Mortification washed through her in a wave.

Alix glanced at his watch, oblivious to her inner turmoil. 'It's after ten. I'm sorry about this, but I do need to get back to Paris for a lunchtime meeting.'

Leila forced herself to meet his eyes, even though she

wanted to slither down under the covers and all the way to Middle Earth. 'Of course. I need to get back too.'

Alix put his hands either side of her hips, effectively trapping her. 'You're not regretting anything, are you?'

His face was so close she could see the lighter flecks of grey in his eyes. And she knew that no matter how embarrassed she was right now, how gauche she felt, she really didn't regret a thing.

She shook her head and he pressed a firm kiss to her mouth before pulling back.

'Good. The housekeeper has sent up some breakfast, and I had some clothes sent over for both of us.'

'You did?' Leila boggled.

Alix shrugged and stood up. 'Sure—I called my assistant in Paris and she got them sent from a boutique here in Venice.'

Of course, Leila thought wryly to herself. She'd almost forgotten for a moment who Alix was. The power he wielded. The ease with which he clicked his fingers and had his orders obeyed. The ease with which she'd fallen into bed with him...

She had to stop thinking about that.

Galvanising herself, Leila got out of bed and pulled the sheet off the bed, tucking it around her body, all the while acutely aware of Alix's amused gaze.

'I'll have a quick shower,' she said, and walked to the bathroom with as much dignity as she could while trailing a long length of undoubtedly expensive Egyptian cotton behind her.

Once in the bathroom, Leila could hear Alix's phone ring and his deep tones as he answered. It was a welcome reminder that he was itching to move on, to get back to Paris and his life. And she needed to get on too.

As she stepped under the hot spray of the shower she

told herself that if all she had was this night in Venice with a beautiful exiled king then she would be happy with that.

She valiantly ignored the physical pang in the region of her chest that told her otherwise. She was *not* her mother, and she was *not* going to fall for the first man she'd slept with.

An hour later they were back on Alix's private jet, taking off from Venice. Alix was talking in low tones in another guttural language on his phone. She guessed it must be a form of Spanish. It was a relief not to have his attention on her for a moment.

Leila looked out of the window and took a shaky breath. Hard to believe her world had changed so irrevocably within less than twenty-four hours.

She wore the new clothes Alix's staff had sent over. Beautifully cut slim-fitting trousers and a loose long-sleeved silk top, with a wrap-around cashmere cardigan in the most divine sapphire-blue colour.

They'd even sent over fresh underwear and flat shoes. She felt cossetted and looked after. *Dangerous*. Because he did this sort of thing with women all the time.

When they'd been eating breakfast, just a short while before, she'd caught him looking at her intently. 'What?' Leila had asked. 'Have I got something on my face?'

Without make-up she'd felt bare. Exposed.

Alix had shaken his head. 'No. You're beautiful.'

And then he'd reached for her hand and she hadn't been able to look away from him.

'I want to see you again. Today...tonight. Tomorrow.'

Her heart had stopped, and then started again at twice the pace. 'But this was just one night...'

Wasn't it?

That was how she'd justified her outrageous behaviour. It had been a moment out of time.

Alix had looked a little fierce. 'Is one night enough for you?'

Trapped in his steely gaze, she'd asked herself if she could do this. Agree to an affair with this man? Have more of him? *Yes*, a pleading voice had answered.

Would he even let her go after she'd acquiesced so spectacularly? She knew the answer. Slowly she'd shaken her head. It wasn't enough for her either. She wanted more—shamelessly.

Alix's fingers had tightened around hers. 'Well, then...'

And now here she was, hurtling back towards the real world and a liaison she wasn't sure she knew how to navigate. She heard Alix terminate his call and thought of the dress he'd bought for her to go to the opera, and these new clothes.

She turned away from the view and found him looking at her. Before she could lose her nerve she said quickly, 'I don't want to be your mistress. I appreciate the clothes this morning, but I don't want you to buy me anything else.'

He looked at her for a moment, as if he truly couldn't understand what she was saying, and then he shrugged nonchalantly. 'Fine.'

Leila thought of something else and felt the cold hand of panic clutch at her gut. The prospect of press intrusion. Being photographed with Alix. It would inevitably bring scrutiny, and she did not want that under any circumstances.

She said, 'We can't go out in public. I don't want to end up in the papers. I'm not prepared for that kind of intrusion.'

Alix straightened, and something flashed across his face—surprise?—before it was masked and Leila thought she might have imagined it.

'I have an entire team at my disposal. I will make sure you're protected.'

Leila looked at him. She thought of Ricardo…and of the fact that Alix had been in and out of her shop a few times now and no one seemed to have picked up on it. Maybe it would be okay. Maybe the skeletons in her closet wouldn't jump out to bite her.

She forced a smile. 'Okay.'

CHAPTER SIX

'EARTH TO ALIX...HELLO? Anyone home?'

Alix blinked and looked at his friend and chief advisor, Andres, who had flown in from Isle Saint Croix to meet him. Andres was Alix's secret weapon. Devoutly loyal to getting Alix back on the throne, he was also working as a spy, of sorts, in the current regime in Isle Saint Croix. He was the reason Alix was going to get reinstated as King.

'Have you heard a word I've said?'

Alix knew he hadn't. His head had been consumed with soft silky skin. Long dark hair. Huge green eyes like jewels. Soft gasps and moans. The heady rush of pleasure when he—

Damn. He jerked up out of his chair. This was ridiculous.

Leila was like a fever in his blood. He couldn't concentrate.

He went and stood at the window, and then after a few seconds turned back to his friend and said, 'I've met someone new.'

Andres made a small whistling sound, his boyishly handsome face cracking into a wry grin. 'I know you move fast, Alix, but this is your fastest ever. Usually you leave at least a week between switching partners. This is good, though—when will we see pictures hit the press?'

Alix folded his arms and scowled at his friend's exaggeration. And then he thought of what Leila had said about wanting to avoid press intrusion. And, as much as he needed it right now, suddenly the thought of paparazzi hounding her was very unpalatable. It made him feel almost...*protective.*

There had to be a solution. His brain seized on an idea and it took root. And the more it did so, the more seductive it became.

'Our supporters on the ground are aware that we are conducting a campaign of misdirection, aren't they?'

Andres nodded. 'Absolutely. They know that you're primed and ready to return, no matter what the press says.'

'Then if I was to leave and go to my island in the Caribbean for ten days it could only work in our favour?'

Andres huffed out a breath. 'Well, sure… I mean, you're just as contactable there as here… And if there are photos emerging of you frolicking in the sun with some leggy beauty the opposition will be taken completely by surprise when we pull the rug right out from underneath them.'

Alix smiled, sweet anticipation flooding his blood. 'My thoughts exactly.'

Andres frowned. 'But, Alix, you do know that your island is totally impenetrable by the outside world? No paparazzi have ever caught you there. It's too far—too remote.'

Alix's smile faded as he got serious. 'Which is why you're going to arrange for one of my most trustworthy staff on the island to take long-range grainy photos—I'll let you know when is a good time. Enough to identify me, but not Leila. He can email them to you, and you can send them out to whoever you think should get them for maximum beneficial exposure. I want this controlled.'

Alix felt only the smallest pang of his conscience and told himself he'd still be protecting her identity.

Andres's eyes gleamed with unmistakable interest at the lengths his friend was willing to go to for a woman, but Alix cut him off before he could say anything.

'I don't want to discuss her, Andres, just set it up. We'll fly out tomorrow.'

* * *

'You want to take me *where*?'

The blinds were down in Leila's shop and she'd just closed up for the evening when Alix had appeared, causing a seismic physical response. She hadn't heard from him since that morning, when they'd arrived back from Venice, and she didn't like to admit the way her nerves had stretched tighter and tighter over the day, as she'd wondered if she'd hear from him again. In spite of what he'd said.

And now he was here, and he'd just said—

'I have an island in the Caribbean. It's private…secluded. I've cleared my schedule for the next ten days—I need to take a break. I want you to come with me, Leila. I want to explore this with you…what's going on between us.'

Leila felt sideswiped, bewildered, along with an illicit flutter of excitement. 'But…I can't just *leave*! Who'll look after my shop and business? The last thing I can afford now is to close up.'

Smoothly Alix said, 'I can hire someone to manage the shop in your absence. They won't have your knowledge, obviously, but they'll be able to cover basic sales till you get back.'

Leila opened her mouth to protest, but the truth was she wasn't really in a position to take orders for new perfumes until she found some factory space, so all she was doing in essence was selling what they had. She could mix perfumes on a very small scale, which was what she'd done for Alix. So she was dispensable.

Weakly, she protested. 'But we've only spent one night together. I can't just take off like this.'

Alix raised a brow. 'Can't you? What's stopping you?'

Leila felt irritation rise. 'Not everyone lives in a world where you can just take off to the other side of the earth on a whim. Some of us have to think of the consequences.'

But right then Leila knew she wasn't thinking of financial or economic consequences—she was thinking of more emotional ones. Already.

Then Alix did the one thing guaranteed to scramble her brain completely. He came close and slid his hand around the back of her neck, under her hair, and tugged her towards him.

He said softly, 'I'll show you the consequences.'

His scent reached her brain before she even registered the effect it was having on her. Her blood started fizzing, and between her legs she was still tender but she could feel herself growing damp.

An acute physical reaction to desire. To this man.

Hunger, ravenous and scary, whipped through her so fast she couldn't control it. And when Alix lowered his mouth to hers she was already lost. Already saying yes, throwing caution to the wind. Because the truth was that dealing with him in this environment was scarier—so maybe going to the other side of the world would keep them in fantasy land. And when it was over she'd come back to normality. Whatever normal was...

When the kiss ended they were both breathing heavily, and Leila was pressed between the counter and Alix's very hard body. They looked at each other.

Shakily, Leila said, 'This is just... It won't last.' She didn't even frame it as a question.

Something infinitely hard came into Alix's eyes and he shook his head. He almost looked sad for a moment. 'No, it never lasts.'

Leila drew in a slightly shaky breath. One more step over the line couldn't hurt, could it? She was doing this with her eyes wide open. No illusions. No falling in love. She was not her innocent, naive mother.

'Okay, I'll come with you.'

Alix just smiled.

* * *

'There it is—just down there.'

Leila looked, and couldn't quite believe her eyes. She'd never seen such vivid colours. Lush green and pale white sand, clear azure water. Palm trees. It was like the manifestation of a dream she wasn't even aware she'd had.

She couldn't actually speak. She was dumbfounded. This was the last in a series of flights that had taken them from Paris to Nassau and now in a smaller plane to Alix's private island, which was called Isle de la Paix—Island of Peace.

And it looked peaceful from up here. They were circling lower now, and Leila could see a beautiful colonial-style house, and manicured grounds leading down to a long sliver of beach where foamy waves lapped the pristine shore.

She was glad she'd agreed to come here—because she knew this experience would help her to keep Alix in some fantasy place once their affair was over.

They landed, bouncing gently over a strip cut into the grass in a large open, flat area. Leila could see a couple of staff waiting outside and an open-top Jeep.

When they left the plane the warmth hit Leila like a hot oven opening in her face. It was humid—and delicious. She could already feel the effects sinking through her skin to her bones, making them more fluid, less tense.

The smiling staff greeted them with lilting voices and took their bags into a van. Alix led Leila over to the Jeep, taking her by the hand. When he'd buckled her in, and climbed in at the other side, he looked at her and grinned.

Leila grinned back, her heart light. He suddenly looked more carefree than she'd ever seen him, and she realised that he'd always looked slightly stern. Even when relaxed. But not here.

'Would you like a brief tour of the island, madam?'

'That would be lovely,' Leila responded with another grin.

They took off, and Alix drove them along dirt tracks through the lush forest that skirted along the most beautiful beaches she'd ever seen. The sun hit them and the Jeep with dappled rainbows of light, bathing them in warmth. Leila tipped her head back and closed her eyes, revelling in the sensation.

When the Jeep came to a stop she opened her eyes again and saw that they were on the edge of a small, perfect beach.

Leila leant forward. The smell of the sea was heady, along with the sharper tang of vegetation and dry earth. She itched to analyse the scents but the view competed. It was sensory overload. And the most perfectly hued clear seawater she'd ever seen lapped the shore just yards away.

Alix jumped out of the Jeep and came around, expertly unbuckling her belt and lifting her out before she could object, strong arms under her legs and back. He walked them down to the beach. It was late afternoon, and still hot, but the intense heat of the sun had diminished.

He put her down and looked at her, raising a brow. 'Have you ever skinny-dipped?'

Leila's mouth opened and she blustered, 'No, I certainly have *not*!' even as she felt a very illicit tingle of rebellion.

Alix was already pulling off his clothes. He'd changed on the plane before they'd got to Nassau, into a polo shirt and casual trousers. Leila gaped as his body was revealed, piece by mouthwatering piece.

She'd only seen him naked in the dimly lit confines of the Venetian *palazzo*, and now he stood before her, lit by the glorious sun against a paradise backdrop.

He was stunning. Not an ounce of fat. Hewn from rock. Pure olive-skinned muscular beauty. And one muscle in particular was twitching under her rapt gaze.

Leila's cheeks flamed and she dragged her gaze up.

She sounded strangled. 'I can't—we can't! What if someone comes along?' She glanced behind her into the trees.

But then Alix was in front of her, his hand turning her chin back to him. She looked at him helplessly and he said, 'Listen. Just listen.'

Leila did—and heard nothing. Not one sound that didn't come directly from the island itself. No sirens or traffic or voices. Just the breeze and the trees and birds, and the water lapping near their feet.

'It's just us, Leila. Apart from a handful of staff at the house, we're completely alone.'

A sense of freedom such as she'd never felt before made her chest swell and lightness pervade her body. She felt young and carefree. It was heady.

'Now, are you coming into the water willingly? Or do I have to throw you in fully clothed?'

Leila started to shrug off her jacket, and said, mock petulantly, 'Fine, Your Majesty.'

Alix watched her, stark naked and completely blasé. 'That's more like it.'

His eyes got darker as Leila self-consciously took off her shirt and trousers, very aware of their chain-store dullness.

When she was in her bra and pants she hesitated, and Alix growled softly, 'Keep going.'

Leila fought back the memory of that other woman and reached behind her to undo her bra, letting it fall forward and off. The bare skin of her breasts prickled and her nipples tightened. Avoiding Alix's gaze now, she pulled down her pants with an economic movement, stepping out of them and laying them neatly on her pile of clothes.

She was naked on a beach, in a tropical paradise with an equally naked man. The reality was too much to take in, so with a whoop of disbelief and sheer joy Leila ran for the sea, feeling the warm, salty water embrace her. And then she dived deep under an oncoming wave before she exploded into pieces completely.

Leila wandered through Alix's house dressed in nothing but one of his oversized T-shirts, her hair in a tangled knot on top of her head. She'd never been so consistently undressed in her life, and after her initial self-consciousness she'd realised to her shock that she was something of a sensualist, relishing the freedom. Much as she'd exulted in the feel of her naked body in the sea on that first day.

Since they'd arrived at his house after skinny-dipping three days before, damp and salty from the sea, they'd barely left his bedroom. He'd retrieved food from the kitchen at intermittent intervals, and they'd gorged on each other in a feast of the senses. Leila's inexperience was fast becoming a thing of the past under Alix's expert tutelage.

When Leila had woken a short time before it had been the first time Alix hadn't been in bed beside her, or in the shower, or bringing food back to the bedroom. So she'd come to find him.

And now she was taking in the splendour of his house properly for the first time. It was luxurious without being ostentatious. Mostly in tones of soothing off-white and grey. Muslin drapes billowed in the soft island breeze through open windows. It truly was paradise, and Leila felt a pang that her mother was gone and couldn't experience this.

Little *objets d'art* were dotted here and there—tastefully. Leila stopped before a small portrait that hung in the main foyer area and her jaw dropped when she realised she must be looking at an original Picasso.

A soft sound from nearby made Leila whirl around, and her face flamed when she saw an attractive middle-aged, casually dressed woman looking at her with a warm smile on her face.

The woman put out a hand. 'Sorry to startle you, Miss Verughese. I was wondering if you'd like some lunch? I'm Matilde—Alix's roving housekeeper.'

She had an American accent. Leila forced an embarrassed smile. She hadn't seen any staff yet. She gestured to her clothes—or lack of them. 'Sorry, I was just looking for Mr Saint—that is…Alix.'

Matilde smiled wider. 'Don't worry, honey, that's what this island is all about—relaxation. You'll find Alix in his study, just down the hall. Why don't I prepare a nice lunch for you both on the terrace? It'll be ready in about half an hour.'

Leila smiled back at the woman, who was clearly friendly enough with Alix to be on first-name terms. 'Please call me Leila—and that sounds lovely.'

The woman was turning away, and then she turned back suddenly and said, *sotto voce* to Leila, 'You know, he's never brought a woman here before.'

And then, with a wink, she was disappearing down the corridor, leaving Leila with a belly full of butterflies. She hated it that it made her so happy to know this wasn't routine for him.

Leila wandered down the hall, with its gleaming polished wooden floors. She heard a low, deep voice and followed it into a room to see Alix, bare-chested, sitting at a desk with a laptop open before him. He was on the phone. And he was frowning.

The room was as beautiful as the rest of the house, with floor-to-ceiling shelves filled with books. Books that looked well used.

He looked up and saw her, and some indecipherable expression crossed his face before he said something Leila couldn't hear and put down the phone. He closed his laptop.

Leila felt as if she'd intruded on something and put out a hand. 'Sorry. I didn't mean to disturb you.'

Alix stood up and Leila saw that he was wearing only low-slung, faded jeans. Her insides sizzled. He looked amazing in a suit and tuxedo, but like this…he was edible.

'You're not disturbing me. Sorry for leaving you…'

He came and stood before her and Leila imagined she could feel the electricity crackle between them.

'I bumped into Matilde,' she babbled. 'She seems lovely. She's making us lunch and it'll be on the terrace in half an—'

Alix put a finger to Leila's mouth and quirked a sexy smile. 'Half an hour?'

Leila nodded.

Alix took his hand away and scooped Leila up into his arms before she knew what was happening. He was soon climbing up the stairs and Leila hissed, 'She's making lunch, Alix. We can't just disappear—'

They were at the bedroom door by now, and the sight of the tumbled bed made Leila stop talking. Apparently they *could*.

When they finally did make it down to the terrace, much later that day, Matilde was totally discreet and delivered a feast of tapas-like food. Salads and pasta. American-style wings and ribs. Seafood—spicy fish and rice, crab claws with garlic sauce. Lobster. Chilled white wine.

Leila had wondered if they would even make a dent in the feast laid before them, but just when she was licking her fingers after eating spicy fish she caught Alix's amused gaze.

'What?'

He leant forward. 'You have some sauce on the corner of your lip.'

Leila darted out her tongue and encountered Alix's finger, because he'd reached out to scoop it up. Immediately a wanton carnality entered Leila's blood and she moved so that she could suck Alix's finger into her mouth, swirling her tongue around the tip, much as he'd shown her how to—

She let his finger go with an abrupt *pop*, aghast at how easily she was becoming a slave to this man and her desires.

She found herself blurting out the first thing that came into her head to try and diffuse the intensity. 'Is it true that you've never brought a woman here?' She immediately regretted her words. Damn her runaway mouth!

Hurriedly she said, 'It's okay. You don't have to answer that—it doesn't matter.'

Alix's voice was wry. 'I should have known Matilde couldn't resist. She's a romantic at heart after all—as I think are *you*, Leila.'

She looked at Alix, horror flooding her at the thought that he might think— She shook her head. She forced all the boneless, mushy feelings out of her body and head and said firmly, 'No, I'm not. I'm a realist, and I know what this is—a moment in time. And I'm fine with that—believe me.'

Alix looked at Leila in the flickering candlelight. The island was soft and fragrant around them. *Like her.* Apparently he didn't need to be worried that she'd got the wrong idea from Matilde, and he wasn't sure why that thought wasn't giving him more of a sense of comfort. What? Did he *want* her to be falling for him?

She had her profile towards him and he was stunned all over again at her very regal beauty. Totally unadorned and all the more astounding because of it. In the last couple of days her skin had lost its pale glow and become more rich. Her Indian heritage was obvious, giving her that air of exotic mystery. Her green eyes stood out even more.

He felt a pang of guilt when he recalled the conversation he'd had with Andres to set up the photo opportunity.

It would be a far less intrusive photo than most of those he'd had taken with other women, so why did he feel so uncomfortable about it? And guilty...?

It didn't help to ease his conscience when Leila looked at him then and he couldn't read the expression on her face or in her eyes. It irritated him—as if she'd retreated behind a shield.

'Do you think you'll ever regain your throne in Isle Saint Croix?'

Alix blinked, jerked unceremoniously back to reality. Immediately he was suspicious—but then he felt ridiculous. She wasn't some spy from Isle Saint Croix, sent to find out his movements.

Even so, Alix had kept his motivation secret for so long that he wasn't about to bare his soul to anyone—even her.

He shrugged nonchalantly. 'Perhaps some day. If the political situation improves enough for me to make a bid for the throne again... But there is a lot of anger still—at my father.'

Leila had turned more towards him now, and put her elbows on the table, resting her chin on one hand. The diaphanous robe she was wearing made it easy to see the outline of her perfect braless breasts and Alix was immediately distracted. He had to drag his mind out of a very carnal place.

'What was he like?'

The question was softly, innocently asked, and yet it aroused an immediate sense of rage in Alix. He felt restless, and got up to stand at the nearby railing that protected the terrace and looked down over the lawns below.

He heard Leila shift in her seat. 'I'm sorry. If you don't want to talk about it...'

But he found that he did. Here in one of the quietest corners of the earth. With her.

He didn't turn around. Tightly he said, 'My father was

corrupt—pure and simple. He grew up privileged and never had to ask for anything. It ruined him. His own father was a good ruler, but weak. He let my father run amok. By the time my father married my mother—who was an Italian princess from an ancient Venetian family line—he was out of control. The country was falling apart, but he didn't notice the growing poverty or dissent. My mother didn't endear herself to the people either. She spent more time gadding around the world than on the island—in Paris, or London, or New York.'

Alix turned around and leant back against the railing. He looked down into his wine glass and swirled the liquid. When he looked at Leila again she was rapt, eyes huge. It made something in Alix's chest tight.

'My father took mistresses—local girls, famous beauties, it made no difference. He had them in the castle whether my mother was there or not. I think her attitude was that once she'd given him his heir and a spare she could do what she wanted.'

Leila said softly, 'You had a younger brother...?'

Alix nodded. 'Yes—Max.'

He went on.

'One day, both my parents were in residence—which was a rare enough occurrence. A young local girl was trying to see my father, holding a baby, crying. Her baby was ill and she needed help. She was claiming that it was his—which was quite probable. My father had his soldiers throw her and the baby out of the castle...'

Alix's mouth twisted.

'What he didn't realise was that a mob had gathered outside, and when they saw this they attacked. Our own soldiers were soon colluding with the crowd and they turned on my father and mother. They shot my parents and my brother, but I got away.'

Alix deliberately skated over the worst of it—made it sound less horrific than it had been.

He drank the rest of his wine in one gulp.

Leila's eyes shone with what looked suspiciously like tears. It had a profound effect on Alix.

'Your brother…were you close to him?'

He nodded. 'The closest. Everything I do now is to avenge his death and to make sure it's not in vain.'

He knew instantly that he'd said too much when Leila frowned slightly. Clearly she was wondering how his living the life of a louche royal playboy tallied with avenging his brother's untimely death.

She didn't know, of course, of the charitable foundations he headed that supported the families of people who'd lost relatives in traumatic circumstances. Or the amount of times he'd gone on peace and reconciliation missions all over the world, observing how it was done so he'd be qualified to apply it to his own country when he returned.

Leila looked at Alix, so tall and brooding in the moonlight. Her heart ached for him—for the young boy he'd been, helpless, watching his own parents destroy their legacy—and taking his younger brother with them.

She thought of how she'd lied about her father being dead and it made her feel dishonest now, after he'd told her what had happened to him.

'Alix,' she began, 'there's something I should—'

But he cut Leila off as he moved, coming over to the table. He put his glass down. His eyes were blazing and she could see they'd dropped to her breasts, unfettered beneath her thin gown. Instantly heat sizzled in her veins and she forgot what she'd wanted to say.

'I think we've talked enough for one evening. I want you, Leila.' And then, almost as an afterthought, he said, 'I need you.'

I need you. Those three words set Leila's blood alight.

She sensed that he needed to lose himself after telling her what he had. So she stood up, allowing him to see all of her, thinly veiled. He might have said he needed her, but she knew that this was about *this*.

And as Alix led her inside and up to the bedroom she reassured herself once again that that was fine.

'Who would have thought you like to read American *noir* crime novels?' Leila's voice was teasing as she lay draped across Alix's chest on a large sun lounger in his garden.

He lowered his book and looked at her, arching a brow. 'And that *you* would like Matilde's collection of historical romance novels covered with half-naked Neanderthals and long, flowing blonde hair?'

Leila giggled and ducked her head, and then looked up again. 'It was my mother's fault. She devoured them and led me astray from a young age.'

'You must miss her.'

Leila unpeeled herself from Alix and sat up, pulling her knees to her chin and wrapping her arms around them. She looked out over the stunning view from their elevated height in the garden at the back of the house, where the pool was.

Quietly, Leila said, 'I miss her, of course. It was always just the two of us.'

Leila was afraid to look at Alix in case he saw the emotion she was feeling. A mix of grief and happiness. And gratitude to be in this place. To be with this man and yet to know not to expect more. Even if her heart *did* give a little lurch at that.

Alix came up on one elbow beside her, his long half-naked body stretched out in her peripheral vision like a mouthwatering temptation.

'The man you were with before—what did he do to you?'

Leila glanced at him. *Damn.* She'd forgotten that she'd

mentioned Pierre, even in passing. She shrugged. 'He was a mistake. I was naive.'

'How?'

Leila bit her lip, and then said, 'It was just after my mother died—I was vulnerable. He paid me attention. I believed him when he said he just wanted to get to know me, that he wouldn't push me. But one night he came up to my apartment and said he was tired of waiting for me to put out. He tried to force himself on me—'

Alix sprang upright in one fluid move and caught Leila's arm, turning her to face him. Anger was blazing from his eyes. 'Did he hurt you?'

Leila was shocked at this display of emotion. 'No. He… he tried to, but I had some mace. I threatened to use it on him. So he just insulted me and left.'

'*Dieu*…Leila…he could have—'

'I know,' Leila said sharply. 'But he didn't. Thank God. And I was proved a fool for believing that he—'

Alix's hand tightened on her arm. 'No, you weren't a fool. You just wanted reassurance and some attention.'

Words trembled on Leila's lips. Words about how much she'd wanted to believe that love and security did exist. *Could* exist. But she couldn't let them spill. Not here, with this man. He'd made no promises. He was offering her this slice of paradise—that was all and if she'd been fool-ish before she'd be triply so if she started dreaming about anything more with a man like Alix.

He urged her gently back down onto the lounger and pushed their books aside. Tugging her over his chest again, he cupped the back of her head, fingers threading through her hair. 'The man was an idiot, Leila.'

He brought her mouth down to meet his and they luxu-riated in a long and explicit kiss. Leila felt emotional—as if Alix was silently communicating his gratitude to her for trusting enough in him to let him be the one to take her innocence.

The kiss got hotter, more desperate. Alix's free hand deftly untied the strings of her bikini and she felt the flimsy material being pulled from between their bodies. Then his hand was smoothing down her back, cupping her buttock and squeezing gently, and then more firmly, long fingers covering the whole cheek, exploring close to where the seam of her body was wet and hot.

Obeying the clamouring of her blood, Leila moved over Alix so that her legs straddled his hips, breasts pressed to his broad chest. With an expert economy of movement, barely breaking their connection, mouths and body, Alix managed to extricate himself from his shorts and disposed of Leila's bikini bottoms too. Now there were no barriers between them.

Leila had got so used to their privacy being respected that she felt completely uninhibited. Her legs were spread and she could feel him, hard and potent, at her buttocks. Alix moved so that his erection was between them, and Leila luxuriated in moving her body up and down, her juices anointing his shaft, making him groan…making them both want more.

Until she couldn't stand teasing him any more and rose up, biting her lip as Alix donned protection, and then letting her breath out in a long hiss as he joined their bodies and he was deep inside her. Nothing existed in the world except this moment. This exquisite climb to the top of ecstasy.

CHAPTER SEVEN

ALIX HAD HIS HANDS in his pockets and he was looking out over one of the back lawns to where Leila was deep in conversation with his head gardener. He smiled and realised that in spite of the fact that he was standing on the precipice of possibly the most tumultuous period of his life he'd never felt so calm...or content.

The last ten days had been unlike anything he'd ever experienced. He'd never spent so much time alone with a woman. Not even the woman he'd thought he'd lost his heart to all those years ago. That had been youthful lust mixed up with folly and arrogance and hurt pride.

Leila was easy to talk to. *Disturbingly* easy to talk to. He'd told her things that he'd never discussed with anyone else. Not even Andres.

And their chemistry was still white-hot. Alix frowned. He knew he had to let Leila go. Within days the news was going to break that Alix's people had voted for him to return to Isle Saint Croix. His life would not be his own any more. And he couldn't return to the island with a mistress. It would undo all his hard work. He had to return alone, and then find a wife.

He felt heavy inside, all of a sudden. And then Leila looked up and spotted him, a smile spreading across her face. She said something to the gardener and shook his hand. The old man looked comically delighted with himself and Alix shook his head. *The Leila effect.* Yesterday he'd found her in the kitchen, showing Matilde how to make a genuine hot Indian vegetarian curry.

She hurried towards him now with a box in her hand, dressed for travelling in slim-fitting trousers and a sleeveless cashmere top. He drank her in greedily…something elemental inside him growled hungrily. He wasn't ready to let her go—and yet how could he keep her?

'I'm sorry. I didn't mean to keep you waiting.'

Alix smiled even as an audacious idea occurred to him. 'You didn't. Was Lucas helpful?'

Leila smiled. 'Amazingly! He's even given me some flower cuttings to take home in special preservative bags. I've never smelled anything like them. If I can just distil their essences somehow—' She broke off, embarrassed. 'Sorry—we should get going, shouldn't we?'

Alix's chest felt tight. 'Yes, we should. The plane is waiting.'

'I'll just get my handbag.'

Leila moved to go inside, but then stopped beside Alix and looked up at him. Her voice was husky. 'Thank you… this has been truly magical.'

He reached out and cupped her jaw, running his thumb across the fullness of her lower lip. 'Yes, it has,' he agreed.

And right then he knew that he wasn't ready to let Leila go, and that whatever it took to keep that from happening, he would do it.

'Stay with me tonight?'

Leila looked at Alix across the back seat of his chauffeur-driven car. It was very late—after midnight—and the rain-wet streets of Paris were like an alien landscape to Leila. She realised she hadn't even missed it. And she also realised that, in spite of her best intentions, she wasn't ready to say goodbye to Alix.

She nodded jerkily and said, 'Okay.'

The Place Vendôme was empty when they arrived, and they were escorted into the hotel with discreet efficiency. It gave Leila a bit of a jolt to see how the staff fawned over Alix, and how he instantly seemed to morph into someone more aloof, austere. She'd forgotten for a moment who he was.

When they entered his suite, low lamps were burning. Alix took off his jacket and Leila walked over to the window, feeling restless all of a sudden. She could see her shop, dark and empty, and a faint prickle of foreboding caused her to shiver minutely.

Then she saw Alix in the reflection of the window. He was looking at her. She turned around. The air shimmered between them. He came towards her and in a bid to break the intensity Leila glanced away, still a little overwhelmed by how much he made her *feel*.

And then something caught her eye on a nearby table, and when it registered she let out a gasp. 'Oh, *no*!'

Alix had spotted what Leila had spotted just a second afterwards and he cursed silently and vowed to have whoever had left the papers here sacked.

It was a popular French tabloid magazine and there was a picture on the front. A picture of Alix and Leila on a beach. They'd gone there the day before. They were sprawled in the sand, their swimwear leaving little to the imagination, but they were not naked, thankfully. Her face was turned away, up to his, so she wasn't identifiable—but he was.

Leila had already picked it up, but Alix whipped it out of her hands and threw it away. He said urgently, 'They didn't get your face...it's okay.'

She was pale, shocked. She looked up at him. 'You *knew* about this?'

Alix's conscience stung so much it hurt. Funny, he'd never considered himself to have much of a conscience. *Before.*

'My assistant sends me updates on any news coverage.'

Leila looked wounded. 'Why didn't you tell me?'

Alix gritted his jaw. 'Because I was hoping you wouldn't see it.'

Leila waved an arm. 'Well, the whole of France has seen it now.' She looked down to where the magazine was on the floor and read out, '"*Who is the exiled King's latest mystery flame?*"'

Alix caught her chin and moved it towards him. He felt her resistance. When she was looking at him he said, 'They don't know who you are and I'll make sure they won't. Please—trust me.'

Something moved across her face—some expression that Alix didn't like. Eventually she said, 'This has to end after tonight, Alix. I'm not made for your world and I don't want to be dragged through the papers as just another one of your women.'

Alix rejected everything she said, and a sense of desperation rose up inside him—that need to make her *his*. But he couldn't articulate it. So instead he used his mouth, moving it over hers, willing her to respond—and she did, because she was as helpless against this as he was.

The following morning when Leila woke up it took her a long time to orientate herself. She was in a massive bed, with the most luxurious coverings she'd ever felt. She was naked and alone. And her body ached. Between her legs she was tender.

And then it all flooded back. Alix had led her in here last night and stripped her bare, as reverently as if she was something precious. Then he'd laid her down and subjected Leila to what could only be described as a sensual attack.

An attack that had been fully consensual.

It was as if everything he'd taught her had been only the first level, and his lovemaking last night had shown her that there could be so much more. Alix hadn't been tender or gentle. He'd been fierce, bordering on rough, but Leila blushed when she thought of how she'd revelled in it, meeting him every step of the way, exulting in it, spurring him on, raking her nails down his back, begging hoarsely for more, harder, deeper…

Even the fact that her picture had been in that magazine, albeit not identifiable, had faded into the background now.

She had a vague memory of finally falling asleep around dawn, with Alix's arms tight around her. Leila frowned as another memory struggled to break through her sluggish thought processes. Alix had kissed the back of her head and said, 'You're not going anywhere…this isn't over…'

Leila frowned. *Had* she heard that? And what could it mean? The prospect that Alix had decided that something more permanent might come out of what they had made her silly heart speed up.

She needed to talk to him.

Leila got out of bed and made her way to the opulent bathroom that her small apartment could have fitted into twice over. Once showered and dressed, she made her way to find Alix, hearing his low, deep tones before she saw him.

She smiled. Even his voice made heat curl in her belly as she recalled the way he sounded in bed—all earthy and husky and desperate… Maybe, just *maybe*, there was something different between them? The fact that she wasn't like his usual women—

Leila stopped in her tracks outside the door when she heard her name.

Alix spoke again. 'Leila's perfect, Andres. She's beautiful, accomplished, intelligent, refined.'

Leila blushed to find herself eavesdropping like this— and to hear herself being spoken of this way.

But Alix sounded a little angry when he spoke next. 'The very fact that she didn't want to be seen with me is a point in her favour. She's totally different to any other woman I've ever been with.'

Leila frowned minutely. *A point in her favour?* It sounded as if she was being graded.

She went to move forward, to let him know she was there, but when she got to the doorway she saw he was standing with his back to her, looking out of the window. So he didn't see her.

And when he spoke again his tone had the little hairs standing up on the back of her neck.

'To be perfectly honest,' he went on, 'I couldn't have possibly engineered this to go better if I'd planned it to happen. We're on the brink of a referendum that will return me to the throne and the ruling party haven't a clue. They probably think I'm still sunning myself with her on a beach in the Caribbean. Everything is falling into place at just the right time.'

Leila stepped back through the doorway, out of sight, horror coursing through her, her skin going clammy with shock.

Alix laughed and it was harsh. 'Since when has *love* had any relevance when it comes to the wife I will choose? The important thing is that she's falling in love with *me*—I'm sure of it. This will be nothing like my parents' marriage... toxic from the inside out.'

He continued, oblivious to the devastation taking place just outside the door as the full import of what he was saying sank into Leila.

'How do I know? She was a *virgin*, Andres...a woman doesn't give that up easily. To return to power with a fiancée by my side will put me in a much stronger position. Leila will make a great queen, I'm sure of it. She's the right choice.'

He was silent again, and then he spoke in a low voice.

'No, I've no doubt that she'll say yes. If I need to reassure her that I love her too, to achieve my aims, then so be it. It won't be a hardship. And the sooner we have children the better—an heir will be the strongest sign of stability for Isle Saint Croix. A sign of hope and things moving on.'

Leila's heart was pounding so hard she thought she might faint. Sweat was breaking out on her brow.

She was a virgin...a woman doesn't give that up easily. If I need to reassure her that I love her too...then so be it.

For a moment a sharp pain near her heart almost caused her to double over. What Alix was proposing to do made her feel sick. He would embark on a life with her based on lies and falsehoods just so that he could present the whole package to his precious island. An island that he was on the brink of regaining after he'd let her believe that it was a far distant possibility—not imminent. He'd lied to her face! And he would father a child purely to further his own political aims!

The irony was like a slap in the face—her own father had rejected a child for the same reasons. But Leila was in no mood to appreciate that dark humour now.

All their conversations took on a sinister glow now. His questions about her opinions on politics—had that been to make sure she wasn't some kind of raving anarchist? His questions on her opinions on anything had just been an interview.

And the intensity of their lovemaking—had that been to make sure Alix felt she could sustain his interest long enough for him to father an heir?

What broke her out of her shock was the fact that Alix had stopped talking. Feeling sick, Leila walked to the door, silent on the carpet. He was still standing at the window with his hands in his pockets. Master of all he surveyed—including, as he obviously believed, his innocent, gullible lover. A ruthless man who saw her only as a vehicle to help him regain his throne.

Leila felt the slow burn of an anger so intense it made her tremble. She only wanted one thing: to walk away from Alix and forget that she'd ever met him, forget that she'd repeated the sin of her mother: falling for the first man to seduce her.

* * *

Alix's brain was still whirring after the phone call. Had he really told Andres that he was prepared to make Leila his wife? His Queen?

Yes. He waited for a sense of regret, panic or claustrophobia. But even now it felt right. He'd never met anyone like her. She was sweet, innocent...and yet not so innocent any more. His body tightened as he recalled how quickly she'd learned, her shyly erotic, bold moves in bed, how she'd taken him in her mouth and tasted him a few short hours ago.

His body went still. A familiar figure walking quickly across the square came into his line of vision and his breath caught.

It was Leila, and she was carrying her holiday bag— the only woman he'd ever known not to travel with twelve pieces of luggage. Where was she going? His skin prickled uncomfortably when he recalled the phone conversation— was there a chance she'd overheard him?

But if she had why was she walking away? What woman would walk away from the prospect of a man like him making their union permanent?

A small voice whispered: *A woman like Leila.*

Alix was about to follow her when his phone rang again. He picked it up and said curtly, 'Yes?' He could see her now, disappearing into her shop, and he didn't like the flare of panic in his gut. The feeling that if he didn't follow her he'd never see her again.

'Your Majesty, are you there? We need to discuss plans for when the result of the referendum is announced tomorrow.'

Tomorrow. Tomorrow was when his life would change for ever. That reminder was a jolt to Alix. A jolt that told him he was in danger of losing focus when he needed it most. Over a woman. Even if she *was* the woman he'd chosen to be his Queen, she was still just a lover, a woman, peripheral to his life.

Alix pushed the insidious feeling of something slipping out of his grasp out of his head and concentrated on the call. For half an hour. When it was finally over he went to look out of the window again, and when he took in the view, every muscle in his body locked tight.

Leila was across the square, closing the door to her shop. The blinds were down and she was dressed in jeans, sneakers and a jacket. With a wheelie travel bag.

And as he watched she hitched up the handle on her bag and started to walk swiftly away from the shop, the bag trailing behind her.

Leila was almost at the corner of the street when Alix caught up with her, catching her arm. She didn't turn around and he felt the tension in her body.

'How much did you hear?' He directed the question to the back of her head.

She turned around then, and Alix steeled himself for some emotion, but Leila's face was expressionless in a way he'd never seen before. It sent something cold through him—along with a very uncomfortable sense of exposure.

'Enough. I heard enough, Alix.' She pulled her arm free and said, 'Now, if you'll excuse me, I have a train to catch.'

Alix frowned. Just a couple of hours ago he'd left her sated and flushed from their lovemaking in his bed. He'd whispered words to her—words he'd never thought he'd hear himself say to any woman. That sense of exposure amplified.

'Where are you going?'

Leila looked surprised. 'Oh, didn't I tell you? I've got to go to Grasse to discuss sharing new factory space with an old mentor of my mother's.'

Alix felt panic and he didn't like it. 'No, you didn't tell me.'

Leila looked at her watch. 'Well, I must have forgotten to mention it—'

She went to walk around him but he stopped her with a hand on her arm again. It felt slender under his hand.

Leila looked expressively at his hand. 'Let me go, please.'

'You had no plans to go anywhere until you overheard that conversation.'

Her eyes blazed into his. 'Don't you mean your royal decree?'

Alix was aware that they were drawing interest from passers-by and he saw the glint of something in the distance that looked suspiciously like the lens of a paparazzi camera.

He gritted his jaw. 'We need to talk—and not in the street.'

Leila must have seen something on his face, because she looked mutinous for a second and then pulled her arm free again and started back towards her shop.

Alix took her case from her hand, although she held on to it until she obviously realised it would end up in a tug of war. She let him take it and the incongruity of the fact that he, Alix Saint Croix, was tussling over a case in the street with a woman was not lost on him.

When she'd opened the door to her shop they stepped inside and she shut it again. Alix fixed his gaze on her pale face. 'Why were you leaving?' *And without saying goodbye*... He bit back those words. Women didn't say goodbye to him—he said goodbye to *them*.

She folded her arms across her chest. She was mad at him—that much was patently obvious. 'I was leaving because I need to sort my business out. And also because your arrogance is truly astounding.' She unlocked her arms enough to point a finger at herself. 'How dare you assume that I'm falling in love with you? We've only known each other for two weeks. Or did you think that because I was a virgin I had less brain cells than the average woman and would fall for the first man I slept with?'

Alix felt something violent move through him at the implication that there would be more men and that he'd just been the first.

Now she looked even angrier. 'You told someone called Andres I was a virgin. How dare you discuss my private details with anyone else?'

Alix gritted his jaw harder. 'Unfortunately the life of a royal tends to be public property. But it wasn't my right to divulge that information.'

Leila huffed a harsh-sounding laugh. 'Well, that's a life I have no intention of ever knowing anything about, so from now on I'd appreciate it if you kept details of our affair to yourself. You can rest assured, *Your Majesty*, I'm not falling in love with you.'

Alix told himself she wouldn't have run like that if something about overhearing that phone call hadn't affected her emotionally.

His eyes narrowed on her. 'So you say.'

'So I *mean*,' Leila shot back, terrified that he'd seen something else on her face. 'I've saved you the bother of having to pretend that you feel something for me, so I'll save you more time with the undoubtedly fake romantic proposal you had in mind...the answer is no.'

Alix lifted a brow. 'You'd say no to becoming a queen? And a life of unlimited wealth and luxury?'

Leila's stomach roiled. 'I'd say no to a marriage devoid of any real human emotion living in a gilded cage. How can you, of all people, honestly think I'd want to bring a child into the world to live with two parents who are acting out roles?'

Alix's eyes were steely. 'You weren't acting a role this morning.'

Immediately Leila was blasted with memory: her legs wrapped around Alix's waist, fingers digging into his muscular buttocks. What had she turned into? Someone unrecognisable.

She huffed a small unamused laugh. 'Surely you don't mean to confuse lust with love, Alix? I thought you were more sophisticated than that?'

His face flushed at that but it didn't comfort Leila. She felt nauseous.

'Look,' Alix said tersely, 'I know that you're probably a little hurt. The fact is that the woman I choose to be my Queen has to fulfil a certain amount of criteria. We respect each other. We like each other. We have insane chemistry. Those are all good foundations for a marriage. Better than something based on fickle emotions or antipathy from the start.'

Something dangerously like empathy pierced Leila when she thought of what he'd told her about his parents' marriage.

And then she thought of his assessment of her being a *little* hurt, and the empathy dissolved. The hurt was all-encompassing and totally humiliating. The last thing she wanted was for him to suspect for a second how devastating hearing that conversation had been.

'You never even told me you were so close to regaining your throne,' she accused.

Alix's jaw was hard as granite. 'I couldn't. Only my closest aides know of this.'

'So everything—the whole trip to your island—was all an elaborate attempt to throw your opponents off the scent? And what was I? A decorative piece for your charade? A convenient lover in the place of the last one you dumped so summarily?' Leila laughed harshly and started to pace. '*Mon Dieu*, but I was a fool, indeed. Two times in a row now.'

Alix sounded harsh. 'I am *not* like that man, and you were *not* a fool.'

Leila's gaze snapped back to his, but she barely saw him through her anger. 'Yes, I was. To have believed for a second that a trip like that was spontaneous.' She recalled something else about the conversation she'd overheard and gasped. '*You* had someone take those pictures of us, didn't you?'

Alix flushed. He didn't deny it.

Leila shook her head and backed away from him. The tender shoots of something that she'd been frantically trying to ignore finally withered away. She'd thought they'd been sharing intimate moments alone...he'd led her to believe they were alone on the island. She'd bared her body and soul to this man and he'd exploited that. She had to protect herself now.

She needed to drive him away before he saw how fragile she really was underneath her anger.

She affected nonchalance. 'To be perfectly honest, Alix, I used *you*.'

I used you. Alix reacted instantly, with an inward clenching of his gut. Pain.

An echo of the past whispered at him—another woman. *'I used you, Alix. I wanted back into Europe and I saw you as a means to get there and restore my reputation.'*

He went cold and hard inside. 'Used me?'

Leila nodded and shrugged lightly. 'I wanted to lose my virginity but I'd never met anyone with whom it was a palatable prospect...until you walked into the shop.'

Her eyes were like hard emeralds.

'It was only ever about that for me, Alix. And excitement— I won't deny that. My mother was over-protective, but now

I'm finally free and independent, and I'm not about to shackle myself to some marriage of convenience because you deem me a suitable candidate for being your bride and the mother of your precious royal heirs.'

A mocking expression came over her face.

'I'm annoyed that you used me for your own ends, but that's the extent of any *hurt*. And surely you don't think you're the first rich man to invite me up to his suite for a private consultation?'

She didn't wait for a response.

'Well, you weren't the first, and you probably won't be the last.'

Alix's vision blurred for a moment at the thought of Leila going into another suite, smiling at some man, taking out her bottles. *Getting under his skin.* Concocting the perfect scent for him like a sorceress. Sleeping with him.

Darkness reared up inside him. She'd used him. Just as he'd been used before. He'd vowed never to let it happen again. Yet he had. The evidence of such weakness made him feel bilious. He'd been prepared to woo her into becoming his bride. He'd been prepared to take her into his life, parade her as his Queen. Prepared for her to bear his children. The heirs of Isle Saint Croix.

One thing broke through his mounting rage. 'You could be pregnant.'

The thought was repugnant to him now, when a couple of hours ago he'd thought it might be something used to persuade her to agree to marriage.

Leila went a little paler, but then her chin lifted. 'I'm not.'

Alix wanted there to be no doubt. None. 'How do you know?'

'I got my period this morning.'

Alix smiled humourlessly. 'And I suppose you'd have

me believe that if you were pregnant you wouldn't come after me for everything you could?'

Alix was aware of her arms dropping and her hands fisting at her sides. *He* felt nothing, though. Only a desire to lash out.

'Your cynicism really knows no bounds. And now I have that train to catch. Please leave.'

Alix took a step back and forced himself to be civil when he wanted to swipe a hand across the nearest glittering shelf covered in glass bottles and bring them all crashing to the ground. To crush Leila under the burning anger in his gut, forcing her out of this hard obduracy. Force her to be soft and pliant again.

The desire made him feel disgusted with himself.

He turned and walked out of the shop.

It wasn't until Alix reached his suite in the hotel that his brain cleared of its dark haze.

He couldn't even accuse Leila of avariciousness. There were a million other women who would have heard that conversation and used it to inveigle their way into his life, take everything he offered and more. But not her.

The dark irony mocked Alix.

He saw the rumpled sheets on the bed out of the corner of his eye—and something else. He strode into his bedroom and picked up the House of Leila perfume bottle, containing his signature scent.

An image came to him of Leila in the bath, after they'd made love for the first time. He saw it as clearly as if she was in the room right now. The small sensual smile that had played around her mouth, her hand on her breast, a nipple trapped between her fingers. That smile scored his insides now like a knife. She'd looked *satisfied.* Mission accomplished. *I used you.*

Acting on a rising tide of rage, Alix lifted his arm and hurled the bottle at the nearest wall, where it smashed into a million tiny shards and scattered golden liquid everywhere. And that smell reached into his gut and clenched hard.

He lifted the phone and gave curt instructions that he and his entire team were to be moved to another hotel. And just after that call he got another one from Andres. The man was excited.

'The polls are in and they're all suggesting a landslide victory. The government is panicking but it's too late. This is it, Alix. It's almost time to go home. When you return with Leila on your arm—'

Alix cut him off coldly. 'Do not mention her name again. Ever.'

There was silence on the other end of the phone before the man recovered with professional aplomb and went on as if nothing had happened.

Alix listened with a grim expression.

When the conversation was finished, staff appeared, scurrying to do his bidding. Alix cursed himself for overreacting. Leila Verughese was just a woman. A beautiful woman. And it had been lust that had clouded his judgment. Just lust. Nothing more. If anything, it was a timely and valuable lesson.

By the time Alix was getting out of his car and entering his new temporary home, Leila Verughese wasn't a recent or even a distant memory. She had been excised from his mind with the kind of clinical precision Alix had used for years to excise anything he didn't want to think about. Women…the death of his brother.

His destiny was about to be resurrected from the ashes like a phoenix, and that was the most important thing in the world.

It was only when the train had left Paris far behind that Leila felt some of the rigid tension seep out of her locked muscles. Her jaw unclenched. The ache in her throat eased slightly.

She sent up silent thanks for the old friend of her mother's who would let her stay for a while with her in Grasse. There was no meeting about sharing factory space, but it would get her out of Paris until Alix was gone.

And then the pain started to seep in from where she'd been blocking it out. The pain that told her it had taken more strength than she'd thought she had to stand in front of Alix and pretend he'd meant nothing to her. That she'd used him.

He'd used her. Thank God the press hadn't discovered her identity.

Her naivety made her want to be sick. And that reminded her of the slightly nauseous feeling she'd had for the last few days—not strong enough to cause concern, but there in the background. She'd put it down to Matilde's rich food.

She'd lied to him about her period. It hadn't come yet. But she'd wanted him gone. If he'd thought there was the slightest chance... Horror swept through her at the prospect.

She put her hand on her belly now and told herself fiercely that she *wouldn't* be pregnant, because the universe wouldn't be so cruel as to inflict the sins of the mother on the daughter. It couldn't.

If she *was* pregnant she didn't want to contemplate Alix Saint Croix's reaction. After their last conversation he would advocate only one thing to protect his precious ascent to power: termination. Because Leila Verughese had just comprehensively ruled herself out of the suitable bride stakes.

CHAPTER EIGHT

Seven weeks later

ALIX LOOKED OUT over the view from where his office was situated in the fortress castle of Isle Saint Croix. It was at the back, where the insurmountable wall of the castle dropped precipitously to the sea and the rocks below. The most secure room.

The window was open, allowing the mildly warm sea breeze to come in, bringing with it all the scents of his childhood that he'd never forgotten: earth, sea, wild flowers. And the more exotic scents of spices and herbs that always managed to infiltrate the air were coming from the main town's market.

It had been a tumultuous few weeks, to say the least, but he was still here and that was something.

Leila. She was a constant ghost in his mind. Haunting him. Tormenting him. As soon as he'd returned to Isle Saint Croix on a wave of triumph the perfume of the island had reminded him indelibly of her. Of the perfume she'd made for him.

Was she sitting in a luxurious hotel suite right now, with her potions arrayed before her? Smiling at some hapless man? Enthralling him? *Witch.*

He still couldn't believe she'd turned her back on the opportunity to become his Queen. Or that her rejection had smarted so badly. He told himself it was a purely ego-based blow. He'd chosen Leila because he'd genuinely believed she had the necessary attributes. Plus he'd had the evidence that they got on well, and he'd felt she had integrity and that he could trust her.

Not to mention the insane chemistry between them.

And all along she'd had her own agenda.

An abrupt knock at the door interrupted his brooding and made him scowl. 'Come in.'

It was Andres, looking worried. Holding a tablet in his hand. When he got to Alix's desk he was grim. 'There's something you need to see.'

He turned the device around and Alix looked down to see rolling news footage. It took a second to compute what he was looking at, but when he did his entire body tensed and a wave of heat hit him in the solar plexus.

It was a picture of him and Leila, arguing in the street that day seven weeks ago. He had his hand on her arm and she looked angry. And beautiful. Even now it took his breath away.

The headline read: '*Want to meet the very fragrant mystery lover of the new King of Isle Saint Croix? Turn to page six...*'

Alix looked at Andres. 'Do it.'

Andres scrolled through and stopped. Alix read, but couldn't really take it in. Words jumped out at him:

*Illegitimate secret daughter of Alain Bastineau...
next President of France?
Pregnancy test...positive...royal heir?
Does King Alix know if he's the father?
Scandal and controversy don't seem to want to leave
this new King in peace...*

Leila was still in shock. It hadn't left her system yet even though she'd had since yesterday to come to terms with the news. She'd had it confirmed, after weeks of trying to deny the possibility when one period hadn't materialised and then the next one. She was pregnant—approximately eight weeks, according to the doctor she'd gone to see after doing three home tests: positive, positive, *positive*.

Pregnant and without the father. Just like her mother.

A sense of shame and futility washed over her. It was genetic. She'd proved no less susceptible to a gorgeous man intent on seduction. The only difference being that this time around the father would have been quite content to marry the mother of his child.

Leila smiled, but it was mirthless. Perhaps that was progress? Maybe by the next generation her child would manage *not* to get pregnant and would avoid dealing with the prospect of rejection and/or a convenient marriage?

Oh, God. Leila clutched her belly. Her child. A son or daughter. With this legacy in its past. How pathetic. Bitter tears made her eyes prickle.

A furious pounding on the door of the shop downstairs made her jerk suddenly upright. She heard a clamour of voices. She was late opening up, but her clientele hardly arrived in droves, so desperate to get into the shop that they'd pound on the door like that.

Momentarily distracted out of her circling thoughts, Leila hurried down to the shop, thinking that perhaps an accident had happened.

More banging on the door…urgent voices. Leila fumbled with the lock and swung the door wide—only to be met with a barrage of flashing lights, shouting voices and people pushing towards her.

It was so shocking and unexpected it took a moment for what they were saying to sink in, and then she heard it.

'Is it true you're pregnant with Alix Saint Croix's baby?'

'Are you getting back together?'

'How long have you been seeing him?'

'Why did you fight?'

'Are you in touch?'

'Does he know about the baby?'

The voices morphed into one and Leila finally had the presence of mind to slam the door shut again before someone got their foot in the door. Just before she closed it, though, someone threw in a newspaper and it landed at her feet.

She bent down to pick it up. Emblazoned across the front page was a picture of her and Alix arguing in the street that day all those weeks ago, his hand on her arm, her face tilted up to his: angry. *Hurt, humiliated.* She cringed now to see her emotions laid so bare. So much for believing she'd been in control.

And the headline: *'Leila Verughese, secret lover of Alix Saint Croix and the even more secret daughter that Alain Bastineau never wanted you to discover.'*

They knew about her father.

Leila's back hit the door and she slid down it as her legs turned to jelly. She barely noticed the pounding on the door, the shouting outside. She just knew that however bad she'd believed things to be just minutes before… when she'd known she was pregnant and it had still been her secret…they were about to get exponentially worse.

From somewhere came a persistent and non-stop buzzing noise. Leila dimly recognised that it was the phone. On hands and knees she crawled over to where the device sat under the counter. She picked it up.

Somehow she wasn't surprised to hear the familiar authoritative male voice. It caused her no emotion, though. She was numb with shock.

It told her that in one hour Ricardo would be at the back lane entrance of her property with a decoy. She was to let him in. In the meantime she was to pack a bag, and then leave with him when instructed.

The shock kept Leila cocooned from thinking too much

about these instructions, or the baying mob outside. And in just over an hour she let Ricardo in, with a girl who looked disconcertingly like her... Leila didn't think twice about letting them borrow one of her coats for the girl, nor about the fact that he sent the girl out through the front. The baying mob reached fever pitch and then suddenly died down again as she heard vague shouts of, *'She's getting away!'*

Ricardo was saying urgently, 'It won't be long, Miss Verughese, before they realise she's not you. Where is your bag? We need to lock up and go—now.'

And then Leila was being escorted into the back of a car with blackened windows and they were racing through the streets of Paris. At one point Ricardo must have been concerned by her shocked compliance and pallor as he asked if she was okay. She caught his eye in the mirror and said numbly, 'Yes, thank you, Ricardo.'

The shock finally started dissipating when they pulled up outside one of Paris's most iconic and exclusive hotels. It seemed as if a veritable swarm of black-suited men appeared around the car, and one of them was opening her door.

Leila looked at Ricardo, who'd turned around to face her.

'It's okay, Miss Verughese, they're the King's security staff. They have instructions to bring you straight to him.'

The King. He was a king now. Leila blanched. 'He's here?'

Ricardo nodded. 'He flew in straight away. He's waiting for you.'

The man almost looked sympathetic now, and that galvanised Leila. No way was she going to be made to feel that she was in the wrong here. Her life had just been torn to pieces and it was all *his* fault.

The wave of righteous indignation lasted until she was standing outside imposing doors on one of the top floors of the luxurious hotel and the bodyguard escorting her was knocking on the polished wood.

Indignation was fast being replaced with nerves and trepidation and nausea. *She was going to see him again.*

She wanted to turn and run. She wasn't ready—

A voice came from inside the suite, deep and cold and imperious. 'Come.'

The bodyguard opened the door with a card and ushered her in. Leila all but fell over the threshold to find herself in a marbled lobby that would have put a town house to shame.

It was circular, and doors led off in various directions. For a second she wanted to giggle. She felt like Alice in Wonderland.

And then a tall, broad shape darkened one of the doorways. *Alix.* He looked even bigger than before, dressed in a three-piece suit. His hair was severely short and he was clean shaven. Leila immediately felt weak and hated herself for it.

She fought it back and lifted her chin. 'You summoned me, Your Majesty?'

Alix's face darkened. A muscle pulsed in his jaw. He didn't rise to her bait, though, just stood aside and said, 'We need to talk—please come in.'

Leila moved forward and swept past him with all the confidence she could muster, quickly moving into the enormous room with its huge windows looking out over the Place de la Concorde, with the Eiffel Tower just visible in the distance.

She'd tried not to breathe his scent as she passed, but it was futile. She found herself drinking it in…it seemed to cling to her…but she couldn't find any of the notes she'd made for him. It was the scent he'd had *before*. She felt a pang of hurt. He wasn't wearing her scent any more…

She looked out of the window and folded her arms over

her chest, wishing she felt more presentable. Wishing she wasn't wearing the same old dark trousers, white shirt, flat shoes. Hair up in a neat ponytail for work. No make-up.

'Is it true? Are you pregnant?'

Leila fought the urge to bring a hand down to cover her belly protectively, as if she could protect the foetus from hearing this conversation.

'Yes, it's true,' she said tightly.

'And it's mine?'

She sucked in a breath and turned around. 'Of course it's yours—how dare you imply—?'

Alix held up a hand. He looked cold and remote. She'd never seen him like this apart from at that last meeting.

'I *imply* because *I* come with quite a considerable dowry.'

Leila bit out, 'Well, if you remember, you have come to me—not the other way around.'

Alix dug his hands into his pockets. 'And would you have come to me?'

Leila opened her mouth and shut it again, a little blindsided. But she knew that her fear of how Alix would have reacted would have inhibited her from telling him—at least straight away.

She avoided answering directly. 'I've only just found out for sure. I haven't had much time to take it in myself.'

That was the truth.

Alix looked so obdurate right then that it sent a prickle of fear down Leila's spine. 'I'm not getting rid of it just because I'm not suitable wife material any more.'

He frowned. 'Who said anything about getting rid of it?' His frown deepened and then an expression came over his face—something like disgust. 'You suspected you might be pregnant that day, didn't you?'

Leila's face got hot. She glanced down at the floor, feeling guilty. 'I *hadn't* got my period.' She looked up again. 'But I didn't want to say anything. I had no reason to believe it wasn't just late, and I was hoping that...' She stopped.

'That there would be no consequences?' Alix filled in, with a twist to his mouth.

Leila nodded.

'Well, there are. And rather far-reaching ones.'

More than fear trickled down her spine now. But before she could ask him to clarify what he meant he moved towards her. He stopped—too close. She could smell him, imagined she could feel his heat. She wanted to step back, but wouldn't.

'You lied to me.'

Leila frowned. 'But I only just found—'

'About your father. You said he was dead.'

Leila felt weak again. She'd conveniently let that little time bomb slide to the back of her head while dealing with this.

She glared at Alix. 'You lied too. You lied about the fact that you were poised to take control of your throne again and just using me as a smokescreen.'

Alix appeared to choose to ignore that. He folded his arms. Eyes narrowed on her. 'Why did you lie about your father?'

Leila turned away from him again, feeling like a pinned insect under his judgemental gaze. He came alongside her. She bit her lip. He was silent, waiting.

Reluctantly she said, 'It was my mother. It was what she always said. *"He's dead to us, Leila. He didn't want me or you. And he only wanted me to prostitute myself for him. If anyone asks, he's dead."*'

Alix stayed silent.

'I was aware of who he was—his perfect life and family. His rise to political fame. Why would I ever admit that he was my father? I was ashamed for him. And for myself. It's one thing to be rejected by a parent who has known you all your life, but another to be rejected before they've even met you.'

She and her mother had seen both sides of that coin.

Alix's tone was arctic, he oozed disapproval of her messy past. 'We found out that the press sat on the story of your identity in order to dig into your past and see if they could find anything juicy. And they did. Your father is already doing his best to limit the damage, claiming these reports are spurious—an attempt to thwart his chances in the election.'

Leila hated it, but she felt hurt. Another rejection—and public this time. 'I'm not surprised,' she said dully. And in front of Alix. Could this day get any worse?

Apparently it could. From beside her he said briskly, 'The press conference will be taking place in an hour's time. I've arranged for a stylist and her team to come and get you ready.'

Leila turned to look at Alix. 'Press conference? Stylist? What for?'

Alix turned to face her. His expression brooked no argument. 'A press conference to announce our engagement, Leila. After which you'll be leaving with me to come back to Isle Saint Croix.'

For some reason Leila seized on the most innocuous word. 'Back? But I've never been…' Her brain felt sluggish, words too unwieldy to say.

A sharp pinging noise came out of nowhere and Alix extracted a sleek phone from his pocket, holding it up to his ear. He took it away momentarily to say to Leila, 'Wait here for the stylist. I'll be back shortly.'

And he was walking out of the room before she could react.

When she did react, Leila felt red-hot lava flow through her veins. The sheer arrogance of the man! To assume she'd meekly roll over and agree to his bidding just because he had a King Kong complex!

Leila stormed off after Alix, going down seemingly endless corridors that ended in various plush bedrooms and sitting rooms, and a dining room that looked as if it could seat a hundred.

She eventually heard low voices from behind a closed door and without knocking threw the door open. 'Now, look here—what part of *I don't want to marry you* didn't you understand the first time I said it?'

Leila came to an abrupt halt when about a dozen faces turned to look at her. There were two women in the group, scarily coiffed and besuited. Alix was in the middle, looking stern, and they were all watching something on the television.

A man around Alix's age detached himself from the group and came over to Leila, holding out a hand. 'Miss Verughese—a pleasure to meet you. I'm Andres Balsak, King Alix's chief of staff.'

Leila let him take her hand, feeling completely exposed.

Andres let her hand go and urged her in with a hand on her elbow. 'We're watching a news report.'

The crowd parted and Leila was aware of their intense scrutiny. She avoided looking at Alix's no doubt furious expression.

The news report was featuring a very pretty town full of brightly coloured houses near a busy harbour. An imposing castle stood on a lushly wooded hill behind the town.

A reporter was saying, 'Will King Alix be able to weather this scandalous storm so early into his reign? We will just have to wait and see. Back to you—'

The TV was shut off. Alix said, 'Everyone out. *Now.*'

The room cleared quickly.

The reality of seeing that report, as short as it had been,

brought home to Leila the stark magnitude of what she was facing.

She turned to Alix. 'What exactly is it that you're proposing with this press conference and by bringing me to Isle Saint Croix?'

Alix looked at Leila. She could have passed for eighteen. She was pale and even more beautiful than he remembered. Had her eyes always been that big? The moment he'd seen her standing in the foyer, his blood had leapt as if injected by currents of pure electricity.

And when she'd passed him, her scent had reminded him of too much. How easily he'd let her in. How much he still wanted her. How much he'd trusted her. Would she even have come to him to let him know about the baby? He had a feeling that she wouldn't, and his blood boiled.

Damn her. And damn that sense of protectiveness he'd felt when she'd revealed the truth about her father. He couldn't think of that now.

'You'll come because you're carrying my heir and the whole world knows it now.'

Leila looked hunted, her arms crossed tightly over her chest again, pushing the swells of those luscious breasts up. They looked bigger. Because of the pregnancy? The thought of Leila's body ripening with his seed, his child, gave him another shockingly sudden jolt of lust. A memory blasted—of taking a nipple into his mouth, rolling it with his tongue, tasting her sharp sweetness—he brutally clamped down on the image.

Leila was pacing now. 'What is the solution here? There *has* to be a solution…' She stopped and faced him again. 'I mean, it's not as if you're *really* intending to marry me. The engagement is just for show, until things die down again…'

She looked so hopeful Alix almost felt sorry for her.

Almost. Her reluctance to marry him caught at him somewhere very primal and possessive.

'No, Leila. We *will* be getting married. In two weeks. It's traditional in Isle Saint Croix to have short engagements.'

Leila squeaked, 'Two weeks?' She found a chair and sat down heavily. She looked bewildered. 'But that's ridiculous!'

Alix shook his head. 'It's fate, Leila. Our fate and our baby's. The child you're carrying is destined to be the future King or Queen of Isle Saint Croix. It will have a huge legacy behind it and ahead of it. Would you deny it that?'

Leila's arms uncrossed and her hands went to her lap, twisting. Alix had to stop himself from going over and lacing his fingers through hers.

'Well, of course not—but surely there's a way—?'

'And would you deny it the chance to grow up knowing its father? Surrounded by the security of a stable marriage? You of all people?'

Leila paled and stood up again. 'That's a low blow.'

Alix pressed on, ignoring the pang of his conscience *again.* 'We have a child to think of now. Our concerns are secondary. If you choose to go against me on this I will not hesitate to use my full influence to make you comply.'

'You bast—'

Alix spoke over her. 'There's not only our child to consider, but the people of Isle Saint Croix. Things have been precarious, to say the least, since I won back the throne. We are at a very delicate stage, and we desperately need to achieve stability and start getting the country back on its feet. Everything could descend into chaos again at a moment's notice. This scandal is all my enemies need to tip the balance. Would you allow that to be on your conscience?'

Leila thought of the pictures she'd just seen on the TV of the pretty town, the idyllic-looking island.

She swallowed. 'That's not fair, Alix. I'm not responsible for what happens to your people.'

'No,' he agreed. 'But I am, and I'm taking full responsibility for *this* situation.'

In the end it was the weight of inevitability and responsibility that got to Leila. And the realisation that she'd suspected all along that this might happen. Either this or Alix would have asked her to get rid of the baby. And the fact that he hadn't...

She put her hand over her belly now, that newly familiar sense of protectiveness rising up. She'd felt it as soon as the doctor had confirmed her pregnancy beyond all question. Along with a welling of helpless love. So this was what her mother had gone through... It put a whole new perspective on her mother, and how brave she'd been to go it alone.

And Leila wasn't even facing that. She was facing the opposite—a forced marriage to someone who pretty much despised her after she'd told him she'd used him. In a pathetic attempt to save face, to hide how hurt she'd been.

And now she'd have to live with that. But as long as she remembered Alix's phone conversation she wouldn't lose her way. He'd never intended this to be anything but a means to an end. And at least he hadn't fooled her into thinking he'd fallen for her.

Her child would not suffer from the lack of a father as she had done. Feeling rejected. Abandoned. Unwanted. Alix might want this baby purely for what it represented: continuity. But it would be up to Leila to make sure it never, ever knew how ruthless its father was.

'There, Miss Verughese, see what you think.'

Leila smiled absently at the stylist who'd been waiting with a rail of clothes when Alix had escorted her back through the suite like a recalcitrant child. Someone had also been there to do her hair and make-up.

She looked in the mirror now and sucked in a breath. She looked totally different. Elegant. She wore a fitted long-sleeved dress in soft, silky material. It was a deep green colour, almost dark enough to be blue. It was modest, in that it covered her chest to her throat, but it clung in such a way that made it not boring. It fell from her hips into an A-line shape, down to her knees.

Her hair was up in a chignon, showing off her neck. Her eyes and cheekbones seemed to stand out even more. She put it down to the artful make-up, and not the fact that her appetite had waned in the last month.

She was given a pair of matching high heels. And then Alix appeared. He'd changed suits and was now wearing one with a tie that had colours reflecting those in Leila's dress. She reeled at the speed with which he'd reacted to the news and been prepared.

'Please leave us.'

Once again the room emptied as if by magic. Alix's cool grey gaze skated over Leila and she felt self-conscious. This man was a stranger to her. But a stranger who made her body thrum with awareness.

He held out a velvet box and opened it. Inside was a beautiful pair of dangling emerald and gold earrings. Ornate—almost Indian in their design.

She looked from them to him. 'They're beautiful.'

Alix said, 'They're part of the Crown Jewels. They were protected by loyalists to the crown while I was in exile. Put them on.'

Leila glared at him.

'Please,' he said.

She lifted them out, one by one, and put them on, feeling their heavy weight dangling near her jaw.

'I have something else...'

Alix was holding out a smaller velvet box. Her heart thumped hard. She'd dreamed of this moment, even though she'd never have admitted it to herself—but not like this. Not with waves of resentment being directed at her.

Alix opened it and she almost felt dizzy for a moment. Inside was the most beautiful ring she'd ever seen.

Five emeralds—clearly very old. Set in a dark gold ring. It was slightly uneven, imperfect.

Leila reached out a finger and touched it reverently. 'How old is this?'

Carelessly Alix said, 'Around mid-seventeenth century.'

She looked at him, horrified. 'I can't accept this.'

Alix sounded curt. 'It matches your eyes.'

Something traitorous moved inside her to think of him choosing jewellery because it matched her eyes. That he'd thought about it rather than just picking the first ring he saw.

Alix took the ring out of the box and took up Leila's left hand.

Immediately her body reacted and she tensed. Alix shot her a look before sliding the ring onto her ring finger and Leila held her breath. It was as if the fates and the entire universe were conspiring against her, because it fitted her perfectly.

Alix's hand was very dark next to her paler one, his fingers long and masculine. Hers looked tiny in comparison.

He didn't let her go and she looked up, confused.

Alix's expression was unreadable. 'There's one more thing.'

'More jewellery? I really don't need—'

But her words were cut off when Alix's head lowered and his mouth slanted over hers. She was so shocked she didn't react for a second, and that gave Alix the opportunity to coax open her mouth and deepen the kiss.

When Leila recovered her wits she tried to pull away,

but Alix had a hand at the back of her head and stopped her from retreating. Everything sane in Leila was screaming at her to push him away, but her body was exulting in the kiss, drinking him in as if she'd been starved in a desert for weeks and had just found life-restoring water.

His scent intoxicated her, and before Leila could stop herself she was clutching at Alix's jacket and pressing her body closer to his.

A sharp rap at the door broke through the fog and Alix broke contact. Leila didn't have time to curse him or herself, because Andres was popping his head around the door and saying, 'They're ready for you.'

Alix said abruptly, 'We'll be right there.'

Andres disappeared and Leila realised she was still clinging onto Alix's jacket. He was barely touching her. She took a step back. He was looking at her almost warily, as if she might explode. And she *had* almost exploded—in his arms. It was galling.

'What was that in aid of?' Her tongue felt too large for her mouth.

'The world's press are waiting for us downstairs. We need to convince them that this was a lovers' tiff and we are now happily reunited. That the pregnancy is the happy catalyst that has brought us back together.'

The speed and equanimity with which Alix seemed to be reacting to this whole situation, not to mention his attention to detail—*that kiss*—just confirmed for Leila how ruthless he was. And how she'd never really known him.

She wanted to kick off her heels and run as fast as she could for as long as she could. But she couldn't. Together they had created a baby, and that baby had to come first. Exactly as Alix had said.

She smoothed clammy hands down her dress and drew her shoulders straight. 'Very well—we shouldn't keep them waiting, then, should we?'

Alix watched Leila walk to the door and open it. Her spine was as straight as a dancer's and her bearing was more innately regal than any blue-blooded princess he'd ever met. Something like admiration mounted inside him, cutting through the eddying swirl of lust that still held his body in a state of heightened awareness and uncomfortable arousal.

He'd tried to block out the effect she had on him, telling himself it couldn't possibly have been as intense as he'd thought. But it had been *more*.

CHAPTER NINE

THE PLANE THAT was taking them to Isle Saint Croix was bigger than the plane Alix had used before. The fact that Leila had only ever travelled on private jets was something she should have found ironically amusing, but she couldn't drum up much of a sense of lightness now.

The press conference had passed in a blur of shouted questions and popping cameras. Leila had just about managed to lock her legs in place so they hadn't wobbled in front of everyone.

Andres had sent someone to retrieve her most important and portable possessions from her apartment and they were in a trunk in the hold.

Alix's staff, whom she'd seen in the suite in Paris, were all down at the back of the plane now, including Andres, and she and Alix were alone in the luxurious front. There was a sitting room, dining room and bedroom with en-suite bathroom. Stewards had offered dinner, but Leila had only been able to pick at it. Her stomach was too tied up in knots.

She thought of how Alix had responded to a question about her father at the press conference.

He'd said curtly, 'If Alain Bastineau is so certain he is not my fiancée's father, then let him prove it with a DNA test.'

Huskily Leila said now, 'When they asked about my father…you didn't need to respond like that.'

Alix looked at her. 'Yes, I did. Any man who rejects his own child is not a man. You're to be the Queen of Isle

Saint Croix and I will not allow you to be speculated about in that way.'

Immediately Leila felt deflated. He'd only stood up for her because of concerns for his own reputation. She'd been stupid to see anything else in it, however tenuous.

'You need to eat more—you've lost weight.'

Alix was looking at her intently and Leila cursed herself for having drawn his attention. She felt defensive and, worse, self-conscious.

'Apparently it's common to lose weight when you're first pregnant.'

Alix's voice was gruff. 'We'll arrange for you to see the royal doctor as soon as you're settled. We need to organise your prenatal care.'

Leila was surprised at the vehemence in Alix's voice and had to figure that all this meant so much more to him than the fact of a baby. She and the baby now represented stability for the island's future.

She frowned then, thinking of something else. 'How did they find out?'

Alix was grim. 'I told you—they had that picture of us in the street and they sat on it, wanting to know more about you. Also, as I had just been crowned King again, they knew there was potentially a much bigger story in the offing. They were keeping an eye on you, Leila. We think someone went through your bins and found the home pregnancy tests you did.'

Leila instantly felt nauseous and put a hand to her mouth. She shot up out of her chair and made it to the bathroom in time to be sick. She knew it wasn't necessarily what Alix had just said—her bouts of nausea hit her at different moments of the night and day.

To her embarrassment, when she straightened up in the small bathroom she saw Alix reflected in the mirror, looking concerned. No doubt concerned for her cargo.

Weakly she said, 'I'm fine—it's normal.'

'You look as pale as a ghost. Lie down and rest, Leila. You'll need it.'

Alix went out into the bedroom and pulled back the covers. Leila kicked off her shoes and avoided his eye as she sat down. Then she thought of something else and looked up at him, panicked. 'What about my shop?'

Alix was grim. 'We can arrange for someone to manage it in the short term. It'll probably be for the best if you sell it. You'll be busy with your duties as Queen and as a mother.'

Furious anger raced through Leila's blood, galvanising her to stand, all weariness gone. 'How dare you presume to take my livelihood away from me just like that?' She snapped her fingers.

'Leila, look—'

'No, *you* look.' Leila stabbed a finger towards Alix, the full tumult of the day catching up with her. 'That business is my own family legacy. It's a vocation, making perfumes, and I will *not* be giving it up. If you insist otherwise then I won't hesitate to leave Isle Saint Croix on the first return flight out.'

She folded her arms tight across her chest.

'Or are you telling me that you'll incarcerate me like some feudal overlord? I'm sure the tabloids would love to hear about *that*!'

Alix's mouth was a thin line, and a muscle jumped in his jaw. Finally he said, 'Fine. We'll discuss how you can incorporate it into your life.'

And just as suddenly as the anger had come, it faded away, leaving her bone-weary again. Leila sat down on the side of the bed. Alix stood in her vision, huge and immovable.

Leila lay down and curled away from where he stood, eyes shut tight. Maybe when she woke up this would all be a bad dream...?

* * *

Alix stood looking down at the woman on the bed, seeing how her breath evened out and her muscles grew slacker. Her back was to him and that only compounded the frustration still rushing through his system. He knew he'd been out of line to suggest that Leila sell her business, but he found it hard not to operate from some base place when she was in front of him.

He'd noticed the minutely perceptible thickening of her waist. Her hand had rested there just now, as if to protect the child within. And suddenly an almost dizzying sense of protectiveness rose up within him.

He thought of those paparazzi hounding Leila, and recalled that when Andres had shown him the news footage, his primary instinct had been to get to her and keep her safe more than to confront her about the pregnancy.

It made him feel exposed.

Alix finally backed away from the bed and out of the room. When he sat down again he asked for a shot of whisky from the hovering attendant.

He swirled the dark amber liquid in the heavy crystal glass for a long moment. He'd always thought that having a child would be something he'd feel quite clinical about. Not entirely unemotional, of course. He would be as loving as he could be. But how could he be something he knew nothing of? A loving parent?

Alix had only ever really loved one person: his brother. And the pain he'd felt when his brother had been murdered had nearly killed him too. He would never forget that raw chasm of rage and grief. And he never wanted to feel it again.

Except now his gut was churning with dark emotions that felt far too close to the bone.

When he'd first contemplated making Leila his Queen it had felt like a relatively uncomplicated decision. He liked

her. Liked talking to her, spending time with her. Liked
that he'd been her first lover. *Just* that memory alone was
enough to have Alix's body hardening.

His mouth twisted. Their intense mutual chemistry had
told him that there would be no issues in the bedroom.

For someone who had always known that his choice of
bride would be strategic above all else, it had felt like a
very logical choice. A beautiful bride…a queen he would
have no hardship creating a family with.

Until she'd rejected his offer outright.

And now she was pregnant with his child and he had
no choice but to make her his wife. He was being mocked
by the gods for his initial complacency.

Alix willed down the heat in his body and the darkness in his gut. He'd believed that Leila was falling for
him when evidently she hadn't been.

He ignored the intensifying of the tightness in his chest
and told himself that this would only make things easier.
No emotion on either side. No illusions. This was about the
baby and the future of Isle Saint Croix, and while Leila was
not the bride Alix would choose if he had a choice right
now, he *would* make this work. For the sake of his people
and for the sake of his legacy into the future.

When they arrived in Isle Saint Croix it was after midnight. Too late for any kind of formal reception, much to
Leila's relief. She was still feeling a little hollowed out and
overwhelmed. Her sleep on the plane had been populated
with scary dreams of her running and a tall, menacing
figure trying to catch her. She didn't have to be a genius
to figure that one out.

Her first impressions of the island were of warm, damp
heat. Warmer than she'd expected. Stars populated the
clear night sky. There was the zesty sea-salt freshness of

the ocean nearby. And something much more exotic and intriguing.

On the journey to the castle Leila caught glimpses of small pretty villages and a bigger town down near the sea, lights twinkling in the harbour. Then they rounded a bend, and there on a hilltop in the distance stood the floodlit castle.

She couldn't hold in a gasp of pure awe. On the TV it had looked like a toy…now she could see just how massive and imposing it was. As if it had been hewn directly out of the rock of the mountainside.

Its influence was clearly Moorish, with its flat roofs and long walls and what looked like lots of quadrangular buildings. Something about it called to Leila—something in its stark beauty.

'That's the castle. Our home.'

Our home. It was surreal. Leila felt overwhelmed again and said, 'I don't even know what language you speak…'

Alix turned his head. 'It's a colloquial mixture of Spanish and French and Arabic. But the official language is French, thanks to the fact that the French were our longest colonisers until the mid-eighteenth century.'

'There's so much I don't know.'

'I'll arrange for Andres to find a tutor for you.'

The car was descending now, down winding steep roads into a sort of valley. Leila could see the lights of a town nearby—presumably the capital. And then they were bypassing it and climbing again, up towards the castle, in through ornate gates and up a long driveway.

When they arrived in a huge stone courtyard with a bubbling fountain in the centre the car drew to a stop. Leila could see through the tinted windows to where a large handsome woman was waiting for them.

When they were out of the vehicle Alix led Leila over to her and said, with evident fondness in his voice, 'This is Marie-Louise, the castle manager. She and her husband risked their lives to protect some of my family's oldest artefacts, including the Crown Jewels.'

Leila's engagement ring winked at her in the moonlit night. 'That was very brave of you.'

The woman beamed and then ushered them inside to where the castle spread out into what seemed to be a warren of imposing stone corridors and inner courtyards.

Alix spoke to the woman in his own seductive tongue. He was obviously telling her goodnight, because she walked away from them.

He let Leila's hand go and indicated for her to precede him down a long corridor. It was lit by small flaming lanterns and for a moment Leila had the sensation that they might have slipped back in time and nothing would have changed.

They were approaching a wall that held a huge wooden door, ornately carved. The guard there stood aside and bowed as Alix opened the door and led them through.

'These are the royal family's private apartments.' He stopped outside another door and opened it. 'And these are your rooms.'

Leila felt a kind of giddy relief mixed with disappointment. She looked at Alix. 'We won't have to share a room?'

Alix saw that vaguely hopeful look on Leila's face and it made him feel rebellious. He desisted from telling her that his own parents had not shared rooms. That it would be considered perfectly normal if they had their own suites.

He shook his head. 'This is just until we're married—to observe propriety.'

Leila's hopeful look faded and became something else—something cynical, hunted. She gestured to her belly. 'It's not as if people don't *know* we've already consummated our relationship.'

Alix had to battle the urge to remind her of just what

that consummation had felt like. The magnitude of the fact that Leila was here under his roof, pregnant, was hitting him in a very deep and secret place.

He ruthlessly pushed it down and walked into the suite. 'I hope you'll find the apartment comfortable.'

Leila had followed him in and was looking around with big eyes. He saw it as if for the first time again: the understated luxury that the ruling regime had seen fit to keep for themselves. It was a little shabby now, but still with shades of its former opulent glory.

A glory that would be fully restored.

With his wife by his side.

With that in mind Alix forced out all emotion and said, 'The sleeping quarters are accessed back through the main hall. I have instructed that you are to have everything you might need.'

Leila looked at him and he could see the faint shadows under her eyes. Like delicate bruises.

The fact that she didn't want to be here sat like a dense heavy stone in his chest. He ignored it. She wouldn't have that power over him.

'I've made an arrangement for a scan at the hospital to-morrow—apparently you're due one about now.'

Leila's mouth twisted. 'To check on the cargo? Make sure that it's all looking good before you commit?'

Alix gritted his jaw at the sudden urge he had to go over and slam his mouth down on hers, making those mutinous lines soften.

'Something like that.' He moved towards the door. 'You should rest, Leila. The next few days will be busy.'

And then he left, almost afraid that she'd see something of the lack of control he felt.

Leila watched Alix leave. She was barely aware of the beauty of her surroundings, only vaguely aware that they'd walked through an open-air courtyard to come into the living room.

She felt numb with tiredness, delayed shock and the lingering effects of adrenaline.

Exploring back through the main hall, she found a bathroom off the bedroom. It was massive, with a grand central sunken tub. The dressing room was a more modern room, luxuriously carpeted and filled from floor to ceiling with clothes. A central island held hundreds of accessories in various shelves and drawers—and underwear. Underwear that made her cheeks grow hot.

She hurriedly shut those drawers, knowing how wasted the lovely underwear would be—because clearly Alix felt no desire for her any more, despite that kiss earlier, which had just been for appearances. He'd looked at her since as if he could hardly bear to be in the same room as her.

She ignored the pain near her heart and found the least skimpy nightwear she could find. Silk pyjamas. After conducting a rudimentary toilette and carefully putting the jewellery away in a drawer, she climbed into a bed that might have slept a football team and tried not to be too intimidated by the grandeur.

For a long time she looked up at the ceiling. Leila couldn't stop thinking about the fact that if Alix didn't desire her any more, then what glue could possibly hold their union together beyond duty and a shared responsibility for their child?

The following early afternoon Leila was pacing in the sitting room of her lavish suite. Marie-Louise had appeared that morning with a meek-looking girl who apparently was to be Leila's personal maid. When Leila had protested she'd been ignored and all but marched into a small dining room, where a delicious breakfast had been laid out. Her stomach had still been in knots, so she hadn't eaten much.

She'd explored thoroughly now, and had discovered the beautiful open-air atrium had a small pool, with glittering mosaics on the bottom and brightly coloured fish darting back and forth.

There was also a terrace outside her bedroom doors, and a balcony that overlooked the town far below with its brightly painted houses and the harbour.

Smells had tickled her nostrils, making her tip her head back to breathe deep. Earth, flowers, the sea, a distant wood… And then she'd realised why Alix had reacted so strongly to the scent she'd made. She'd somehow managed intuitively to recreate the scents of this island without having ever been there before.

Hating it that she felt so hurt because he obviously didn't wear the scent any more, Leila focused on checking herself in a nearby mirror. She'd had to pick a dress from the vast array of clothes in the dressing room as her own clothes hadn't appeared yet. She'd chosen a simple wrap dress in a very deep blue, and matching shoes.

She plucked at the material now, feeling that it was gaping over her breasts, which were sensitive and felt inordinately swollen.

She put a hand on her belly, knowing that it hadn't grown perceptibly in size, but feeling a telltale bloatedness.

'How are you today?'

Leila jumped and whirled around to see Alix behind her, hands in his pockets, dressed in a simple dark suit and white shirt. Every inch of him exuded pure masculine power and sensuality. And that new reserve tinged with disapproval.

The carpet must have muffled his steps. She hated it that he'd caught her in a private moment like that. And that her body had immediately zapped to life in his presence, nerve endings tingling.

She lifted her chin. 'Time to confirm all is well with your precious heir?'

His eyes glittered, as if he was angry at her insolence. 'The doctor is waiting for us at the hospital.'

Alix stood back to let Leila precede him from the room and she prayed he wouldn't see how brittle her sense of control was.

They walked down another seemingly unending labyrinth of imposing stone corridors and Leila had much more of a sense of the grandeur of the castle. She had to admit it: she was *impressed*. It was a little overwhelming, to say the least.

As was the display when they got to the entrance of the castle and about a dozen bodyguards jumped to attention. Alix opened the passenger door of a Jeep for Leila and after she was in got in the driver's side.

She watched him take the wheel with easy confidence, the guards preceding them and following them.

Slightly nervously, Leila asked, 'You said things were precarious here—is there any danger?'

Alix flashed her a look and she saw his jaw tighten before he said, 'I would never put you or the baby in danger. We are being protected by the best security firm in the world.'

Leila was slightly taken aback at his vehemence and said, 'I didn't mean to imply that you'd put me—*us*—in danger.' She'd realised, of course, that Alix probably couldn't care less if she was in danger. It was the baby he cared about.

She saw his hands tighten on the wheel and then relax. 'Forgive me. But you don't have to worry. The opponents to the throne are small in number, and weakened after years of not living up to their promises to build an egalitarian society. They have no real power. I've made sure of that. Still, I would never take anything for granted—hence the protection until Isle Saint Croix is on a much more solid footing economically.'

They were driving through the town now, and Leila could see its charm up close. She could also see that it was badly in need of sprucing up, with a general sense of neglect pervading the air.

A few people waved at their Jeep and Alix waved back. He said now, 'It's going to take time for the people to adjust to having their King back. They're not sure how to deal with me yet.'

Leila asked, with a feeling of something like disappointment, 'And do you really want them bowing and scraping to you?'

Alix looked at her again, slightly incredulous. 'God, *no*. I couldn't imagine anything worse.'

He looked back to the road, one hand on the wheel, the other on his thigh. Which Leila found very distracting, as she remembered how those thighs had pushed hers apart so that he could sink deep—

'I want to live side by side with my people. To move among them as an equal. I don't want pomp and ceremony. But equally I want to be their leader and protector. To provide for them.'

Leila jerked her gaze up. Alix's voice was quiet but his words had a profound effect on her. He sounded so… *protective*.

Before she could truly analyse how that made her feel she saw that they were driving into a car park outside a beleaguered-looking building.

Alix grimaced slightly as he pulled to a stop. 'The hospital doesn't look like much, but it houses some of the best consultants in the world. I've personally put many of our medical students through college for this very purpose— to bring them home to work and teach others. We're in the process of building a new hospital on a site nearby, and this one will be pulled down once it's built.'

Once again Leila was surprised to discover the depth of Alix's commitment to his island. And to discover how little she really knew him.

He got out of the Jeep along with a flurry of movement from the cars before and behind them, and as Alix solicitously helped her out she saw staff lining up to greet them.

Alix kept hold of her hand and Leila figured that of course he'd want to project a united front. Promote the fairy tale that they were in love.

She was introduced to the staff and the doctor who would be taking care of her prenatally—a genial older man. And then she was whisked away to be prepped for the scan, leaving Alix behind talking to the staff. The nurse was shy and sweet, and Leila did her best to put her at ease even though her own nerves were jumping.

What if they found something wrong?

When she was dressed in a gown and lying on a bed the doctor came in with Alix. He was chatty and warm, but Leila couldn't help her nerves mounting as cold gel was spread on her belly.

She glanced at Alix, but he was looking intently at the monitor where the doctor was focusing his attention as he moved the ultrasound device over Leila's belly.

She winced a little as he pressed in hard and almost reached for Alix's hand—some reflexive part of her was craving his solid strength and support. Instead she curled her hands into fists and looked at the monitor too. Her mother had done this alone. And even though Leila's baby's father was beside her she might as well have been alone too, for all the emotional support he was offering.

Suddenly a rapid beat filled the room, and it took Leila a second to figure out that it was the baby's heartbeat.

The doctor smiled. 'He—or she—is strong, that's for sure.'

A shape was appearing on the screen now, like a curled-over nut. The head was visible. And the spine. So delicate and fragile, yet there. Growing. Becoming someone. A son or a daughter.

Emotion suddenly erupted in Leila's chest and she had to put a hand to her mouth to stop a sob escaping. The love she felt, along with a fierce protectiveness, made her dizzy. Up to now it had been largely an intellectual thing. But this was visceral and all-consuming. *Primal.*

The doctor was saying reassuringly, 'Everything looks fine to me. We'll have you back in another few weeks, to see how things are progressing, but for now just eat well, take some gentle exercise and get lots of sleep.'

Leila just nodded at the doctor, too emotional to speak. He patted her hand, as if he saw this every day—which he probably did.

When Leila felt a little more composed she looked at Alix. But even steeling herself didn't prepare her for seeing the closed-off expression on his face. His eyes were unreadable. He certainly wasn't feeling the same depth of emotion Leila was experiencing, and it was like a physical blow.

His gaze was still fixed on the screen, and then he seemed to come out of the trance he was in and he said curtly, 'So everything is fine, then?'

'Yes, yes...nothing to worry about.'

'Good.'

He didn't look at her. His jaw was hard, resolute. They'd established that the baby was well. That was all he cared about. Leila was far too emotional to deal with Alix's smug satisfaction now, and she welcomed the distraction of the nurse coming to help her change back into her clothes.

The doctor and Alix left, and Leila did her best to ignore the ache in her throat and the hollow hole in her chest. She'd never really imagined what this experience would be like, but even if she had she would have expected the father of her child to be slightly more interested.

This had obviously just been a clinical experience, as far as Alix was concerned. And she was a fool to have had even the minutest impulse to seek anything from him.

That protectiveness that had assailed her moments ago surged back at the thought of Alix being so distant once the baby was born.

Once she emerged into the corridor her ire increased when she saw Alix pacing up and down, on his phone. As if they'd *not* just established that their baby was well. He saw her and gestured to say that they were leaving. She had to almost trot to keep up with his long-legged stride, and with each step she felt angrier and angrier and more *hurt*.

Alix terminated his phone call once they were in the Jeep and silence reigned. Leila was determined not to break it, feeling far too volatile and emotional. She knew Alix was sending her glances, but she resolutely ignored him, looking at the pretty scenery but not taking it in.

When they pulled up outside the castle she opened her door and got out before he could do it—or anyone else. She all but ran back into the huge stone fortress and blindly made her way down corridors, hoping she was headed in the right direction.

Everything was bubbling up—her hurt, her unwelcome desire for Alix and the need to get far away from the man who had turned her world upside down.

She heard steps behind her. 'Leila, what the—? *Stop!*'

She did stop then, breathless and hopelessly lost. She turned to face Alix, who was glowering. Fresh anger bubbled up, and again that fierce protectiveness. She felt the walls of the massive building crowd in on her, squeezing her chest tight. But biggest of all was the *hurt*.

She put a hand on her belly. 'You didn't feel a thing in

that scan room, did you? Except maybe a sense of satisfaction that your precious heir is fine.'

Alix looked at Leila. She'd never been more beautiful. Her cheeks were flushed with colour, eyes sparkling
with anger. And with something else that he didn't want
to identify.

He saw movement in his peripheral vision and, aware
of staff nearby, strode forward, taking Leila's arm in his
hand. 'Not here.'

He looked around and saw a doorway, recognised what
it was. He opened it and brought a resisting Leila in, shutting the door behind him.

She ripped her arm free of his hand and moved away,
looking around, her cheeks flushing even more and her
eyes going wide as she took in the lavish surroundings.

'What is this place?'

Leila's voice was shaky and Alix hated the fact that it
twisted his guts. He strode forward into the room. It was an
opulent stone chamber with a raised marble platform. Al-
coves around the edges of the room held sinks and drains.
The ceiling was domed, and inlaid with thousands of mosaic mother-of-pearl stars that glittered.

'It was the women's *hammam*. And the harem is in this
section of the palace too.'

Leila sent him an incredulous look. 'A harem? I thought
we were still in the civilised west—not some medieval
desert kingdom.'

Alix pushed down his irritation. 'The harem hasn't been
in regular use for some time.'

Leila let out a laugh. 'Wow, *that's* reassuring. But
maybe you're contemplating starting it up again? Taking
additional wives just to fulfil your royal quota of children?'

Alix's jaw was so tight it ached, and yet he couldn't stop
a series of images forming of Leila being stripped, massaged, washed and dressed by an army of women. And of

him coming here to these secret and sensual rooms to find her waiting for him. Supplicant.

He wanted her so badly right then that he shook with it. He curled his hands into fists and said, 'Want to discuss what that was all about?' He couldn't even articulate himself properly. This woman tied him into knots.

She folded her arms over her breasts and it only served to remind Alix that he kept noticing how much fuller they were. The wrap dress she wore accentuated every womanly curve. He'd found it near impossible not to look at her bared belly in that room in the hospital, his control feeling far too flimsy.

'I'm talking about the fact that you might as well have been looking at a weather report in the hospital… Did seeing our baby on that screen affect you at *all*?'

CHAPTER TEN

ALIX LOOKED AT HER. *Did seeing our baby on that screen affect you at all?* His mind reeled. It had affected him so much he'd almost doubled over from the rush of pride, mixed with love and an awful bone-numbing sense of terror. Terror that something would happen to that fragile life that wasn't even born yet. Terror that something would happen to Leila. Terror at the surge of an emotion he'd never expected to feel again.

Leila didn't wait for him to speak. 'You were so cold... impervious. I will *not* bring a baby into a marriage where there is nothing between us except a sense of responsibility and duty. It's obvious you feel nothing for this baby beyond valuing it for the fact that it will inherit—'

Alix put up a hand, stopping her. Her words scored at his insides and yet he couldn't let it out—it was too much. And all he could see was *her*. So beautiful, so vital, and *here*. In front of him. Pushing his buttons.

Suddenly Alix wanted all the turmoil he felt to be consumed by fire. He moved closer to her and was gratified to see the pulse grow hectic at the base of her neck. Her breasts swelled with her breath.

'You say there's nothing between us?'

She nodded her head jerkily. Not so sure of herself now. 'There isn't. You only pursued me to distract people from your plans. You used me. You don't want me—you just want a vessel for your heirs. And it's not enough—for me or the baby.'

Alix was so close to Leila now he could smell her scent. Her unique brand of musk and sweetness.

'You're wrong, you know.'

Something flared in her eyes—something that once again he didn't want to identify.

'How?' she asked defiantly.

Alix reached out and took a lock of long, dark, glossy hair, winding it around his finger, tugging her gently towards him. She resisted.

'There *is* something between us and it's enough to bind us together for ever.'

He saw Leila swallow. He tugged her hair again and she jerked forward slightly, almost against her will.

'You see, I *do* want you. I wanted you the moment I saw you. I have ached with wanting you for the past seven weeks. And I am afraid that I will never stop wanting you, no matter how much I have of you—*damn you.*'

And with that Alix's control snapped and he hauled Leila into his arms, driving his mouth down onto hers, crushing her soft abundant curves to his body that was aching with need to be embedded in her tight, hot warmth.

Leila's brain fused with white-hot heat and lust. For long seconds she felt only intense relief as Alix's mouth crushed hers and he finally relaxed enough to allow the kiss to deepen and become a real kiss.

Then Leila's brain finally cleared enough to recall his words: *I have ached with wanting you*. Just like her. And now that ache was finally being assuaged.

Alix's big hands were roving over her back and waist, finding her hips, squeezing. Cupping her bottom, lifting her against him so that the hard ridge of his erection slid against her...just *there*.

She moaned into his mouth, rubbing herself against him, wanting more. She was incoherent with lust. Warning bells telling her to stop and think about what they'd just been saying to each other were being drowned out, and Leila knew that she was complicit in this.

She also knew that she was proving some point for Alix—and it wasn't necessarily a point she wanted to prove. But it was too late. She needed him too badly. She needed *this*. Physicality. No words or confusing emotions or hurt. Just the satisfaction of needs being met. Transcending everything.

Alix broke the kiss and drew back. He yanked aside the material of her dress to expose her breast, encased in lace.

Leila bit her lip to stop herself from begging. She was only still upright because one of Alix's arms was around her. Her legs were like jelly. And now he was pulling down the lace cup of her bra, freeing her breast and thumbing her nipple, then squeezing it gently.

She was so sensitive there that she almost screamed, circling her hips against Alix, utterly wanton.

He looked at her, his eyes flaming dark silver with need. A need that resonated within her too.

In a swift move he lifted her into his arms before she knew what was happening. Her shoes fell off as Alix strode out of the main *hammam* room and deeper into the harem. It was dark and shadowy. Mysterious. Rooms led off the corridor all in different colours.

He shouldered open one door and Leila's eyes went huge when she took in an enormous circular bed, dressed in blood-red silks and satins. The walls were covered with murals and it took a second for it to sink in that the murals depicted *Kama Sutra*–like explicit drawings.

A courtyard filled with wild blooming flowers was visible through French doors and a brightly coloured bird flew away from a water fountain. It was as if this was some kind of fairy tale and these rooms had been suspended in time all these years.

And then Alix laid Leila down on the bed and she knew

this was no fairy tale. He was too intent...serious. Focused. And she knew she should care...should be getting up, walking away...but she couldn't move. And, worse, she didn't want to.

If this was all they had then she wanted it as fiercely as he did. Somehow, here, with Alix stripping off his outer urban layer, Leila could pretend that nothing else existed. For a moment.

When Alix was naked he lowered himself over Leila on his arms and dropped his head, his mouth feathering hot kisses along her jaw and neck down to where her pulse beat like a drum, sucking her there and biting gently. As if he wanted to leave his mark on her.

She reached for him, groaning with deep feminine satisfaction when she found his hard muscles, the defined ridges of his abdomen. And she reached down further, to where his erection jutted proudly from his body. Hot and hard. Silk over steel.

She wrapped a hand around him, suddenly more confident than she'd ever been before. She stroked him, loving how the muscles in his belly tightened at her touch.

Then he put a hand over hers and drew it away. 'I'll explode if you keep touching me like that. I need you—*now*.'

Suddenly Leila was frantic with the same urgency, and aware that she was still fully dressed—albeit with her dress gaping open and her bra pulled down.

Alix undid the tie of her dress and Leila wriggled out of it. Her bra was dispensed with and Alix pulled her panties and tights down and off.

He stood back for a moment and just looked at her. Waves of heat made her blood throb and her skin feel tight. And then he came over her again, nudging her legs apart. He lavished attention on her breasts, sucking her nipples into his mouth and making them wet and tight with need.

Then he trailed his mouth and tongue down over her belly, where their baby was nestled in her womb.

He seemed to linger there for a second, and Leila felt a rush of emotion, but she bit her lip to stop it coming out, afraid of what she'd say. And then she couldn't think, because Alix's mouth was moving lower, and so was he, hitching her legs over his shoulders and gripping her buttocks as he put his mouth on her *there*.

At the hot, wet seam of her body where she couldn't hide how much she wanted him.

She felt utterly exposed, but couldn't stop him as he stroked her with his tongue, opening her up to his ministrations, and then he found that cluster of cells and licked and sucked until she was gripping his hair and bucking towards his mouth, and his tongue was thrusting deep inside her.

And even though she'd climaxed, right into his mouth, it wasn't enough. She was panting, almost sobbing as he rose up like some kind of god. Her legs flopped wide and Alix moved his erection against her. After an enigmatic second of silent communication he thrust deep into her core. And her world shattered into pieces for a second time.

She became pure sensuality—engulfed in a never-ending moment of bliss. Alix moved within her, deeper and harder with each thrust. She was boneless, and yet she couldn't help the rising tide of another climax. Even after the last two.

She caught a glimpse of something above them and looked up. The ceiling was mirrored glass. Old and dark. But she could see Alix's sculpted and muscular buttocks moving in and out of her body, her legs wrapped around him, ankles crossed over the small of his back.

And it was as she saw his huge, powerful body flexing into hers with such beauty and strength that she fell apart for the third time, her orgasm so intense that she barely felt the rush of Alix's hot release, deep in her body, as he jerked spasmodically with the after-effects of his own climax.

When Leila woke she was completely disorientated. She was alone on the huge circular bed and the covers were pulled up over her chest. She could see herself reflected in the ceiling and her hair was spread around her head. Images came back... The sheer carnality of their union. The humiliating speed with which she'd capitulated.

'You're awake.'

Leila tensed and lifted her head. Alix stood by the open French doors of the room. It was dusk outside and birds called. The scent of the flowers was heady. Leila had to block out the immediate instinct she had to assimilate the smells.

She pushed herself up on her elbows, noting that Alix was in his trousers, but still bare-chested. 'Yes, I'm awake.'

She felt as if she'd been turned inside out. She tried to claw back her sense of anger from earlier, but it was hard when she felt as if someone had drained every bone from her body and injected her with some kind of pleasure serum.

She saw her dress at the end of the bed and sat up, holding the sheet to her as she reached for it. She put it on awkwardly, aware of Alix's intense regard, and tied it around her, sitting on the edge of the bed.

'You asked me earlier if it affected me, seeing the baby today?'

Leila went still and nodded.

'Of course it affected me. What kind of man would I be if I couldn't see my own child and feel something?'

Leila stood up, hoping her legs wouldn't fail her. She needed to move away from the bed—the scene of where she'd lost control so spectacularly. She saw a chair nearby and sank onto the edge.

'Why didn't you say something?'

Alix was terse, tense. 'Because I couldn't. It was too much all at once.'

Leila felt a very fragile flame of hope light within her. 'That's how I felt too. But when I looked at you, you were so closed off—as if you were just checking something off a list. I'm afraid that you won't love this baby. That it'll just be a means to an end for you.'

Like this marriage.

Alix looked as if he'd prefer to eat nails than pursue this conversation, but eventually he said, 'I should tell you about my brother.'

Leila frowned. 'You told me he was killed—with your parents.'

Alix nodded. 'Max was handicapped. A lack of oxygen to the brain when he was born prematurely. He wasn't severely disabled, just enough not to be able to keep up with kids his age. I was five when he was born. He spent a lot of time in hospital at first, in an incubator. My parents weren't interested, so I spent most of my time with him.'

Leila's heart lurched. She could imagine Alix as a serious, dark-haired five-year-old, with both his parents God knew where, keeping an eye on his brother.

'It was obvious to our father that he'd never become King, so he had nothing to do with him after that.'

Leila hid her shock. 'And your mother?'

His mouth twisted. 'She barely knew *I* existed, never mind Max.'

'He must have loved you very much.'

If anything Alix looked grimmer. 'He did, the little fool, following me everywhere… But I couldn't give him what he needed most: our parents' care and love.'

Leila sensed his reluctance to talk, even though he'd brought it up. But she needed to know this—because if they were to have a life together she couldn't bear for him to shut their children out.

'What happened the day he died?'

'They murdered him...' Alix moved a hand jerkily. 'Not just the actual murderers, but my parents. *They* were the ones who made sure I was protected so the precious line would go on, and *they* kept Max with them, knowing that he would die, hoping that seeing him would distract the soldiers enough to let me get away. The last thing I remember hearing was Max, screaming for me. He couldn't understand why I wasn't coming to get him, to take him with me—and I couldn't go back...they wouldn't let me. One of the men taking me away had to knock me out. I came to on a boat, leaving the island behind.'

He looked at Leila.

'It nearly killed me, knowing that I'd left him behind. I had nightmares for years. Sometimes they still come...'

Leila stood up. 'Oh, Alix...I'm so sorry.'

She could understand in an instant how something must have broken inside him that day when he'd lost his home and his beloved brother. She was going to walk over to him, but something in his expression stopped her.

Alix was harsh. 'Don't give me your pity, Leila, that's the last thing I want or deserve. I've told you this because you need to know that I wasn't unaffected today. But I won't lie to you. I have always envisaged myself keeping an emotional distance from my Queen and any children. My role as King is a *job*, and as such I need to avoid distraction. Focus on what's best for the country and the future. But when I saw the scan today it all came back— the love I felt for Max and the awful grief when he died.'

Alix shook his head.

'It terrifies me that I'll be unable to control how I feel about my own child in case anything happens. I couldn't survive that grief again.'

A gaping hollow seemed to open up in Leila's chest. What could she say? Wasn't every parent terrified of their child being hurt or worse? Terrified that they wouldn't be able to protect it from every little thing? What Alix didn't understand yet, and what she only had an inkling of herself, was that he wouldn't be able to control it.

He walked over to her then, and Leila tried desperately to call up some sense of defence. She felt raw with this knowledge, not sure what it meant now.

'I want you, Leila, and I want our baby. I will do my best to serve you both well—and any other children we may have.'

Leila went still. Nothing had changed. Not really. Even though he'd opened up to her his main concern was the baby. Not her. And she should be feeling relieved that he'd admitted he wanted this baby as much for itself as for its role as heir. That he would not shut it out.

Alix reached a hand out then, but Leila stepped back jerkily. If he touched her now she'd break into a million pieces.

She forced herself to sound far more calm than she felt. 'I'm quite tired now. I'd like to go back to my rooms, please.'

Alix still felt raw from the mind-blowing sex and what he'd just revealed about his brother. But he hadn't been able to bear the thought that Leila really believed he'd felt nothing for their baby. And she deserved to know the truth. That he wasn't prepared to go through that emotional wasteland again. Having lost everything.

His hand was out to touch her, but she'd stepped back out of his reach. His first instinct was to move closer…but something stopped him. If he touched her again who knew what else he might feel compelled to reveal?

His hand dropped. He'd never wanted a woman so badly that he wanted her again as soon as he'd had her, but right now he really could see no end in sight to this constant craving.

The lush surroundings of the old harem didn't help. And the fact that *she'd* been the one to step away made something prickle inside him. She had control when he was in danger of losing it.

He was terse. 'Okay, let's go.'

Alix put on the rest of his clothes and watched Leila step into her panties, sliding them up her slim thighs. Thighs that had been wrapped around him only a short time before, her inner muscles clasping his shaft with spasms so strong he'd almost climaxed twice in quick succession.

Damn.

She picked up her shoes on the way out and Alix was forced to feel a measure of shame. They were like teenagers, sneaking off to the nearest private space to have sex. He was a *king*, for God's sake. Not a randy schoolboy.

'What are you going to do with this place?' Leila asked as she walked out through the main door.

He watched as she went past him, his eyes tracking down her body and up to her tangled hair. Lust was sinking its teeth into him all over again.

'I had thought of getting rid of it, but now I'm not so sure.'

She looked at him, and before she could say anything he stepped up to her, so that there were just centimetres between their bodies. 'It won't be for more wives, Leila, it'll be for us alone,' he said.

Her cheeks coloured at that. 'But that's…outrageous. A whole *hammam* and harem, just for two people?'

Alix quirked a smile at the mix of expressions on her face: slightly scandalised, and yet interested at the same time.

'It'll be purely for your pleasure and mine, Leila. You're

to be my Queen, and I will want to make sure that you are satisfied.'

The colour faded from her cheeks and she said, 'I'll be satisfied when you don't shut our child out, Alix. Sex is just sex.'

Alix felt her words like a physical blow to his chest. He watched as she stepped out from where he had her all but caged against the wall and started to walk down the corridor. *Sex is just sex.*

'Leila,' he called out curtly.

She stopped and turned around with clear reluctance.

'It's this way.' He pointed in the opposite direction and watched as she came back down the corridor and past him, head held high. He had to stop himself from hauling her back into the harem to show her that he knew *exactly* that sex was just sex.

The irritating thing was he didn't *need* Leila to tell him sex was just sex. So why did he suddenly feel a need to prove that to her—and himself?

Leila wasn't sure how she made it back to her rooms with Alix behind her, boring holes in her back with the intensity of his gaze. She thought of that harem, existing just for carnal pleasure... She'd almost melted on the spot when he'd said that it would be solely for their use.

Sex is just sex—ha! Who was she kidding when she felt upside down and wrung out?

It had brought up all the emotions she'd been feeling the morning after they'd returned from Venice, when she'd felt so perilously close to believing she'd fallen for him.

There was no 'falling'.

The truth hit her like a slap in the face. She was in love with Alix and had been for some time, if she was honest with herself. And that last bout of *just sex* had left her no-where to hide.

She almost sobbed with relief when she saw their door appear and the guard standing outside.

When they reached her room she was about to escape inside when Alix said, 'Wait.'

Leila turned around, schooling her features. No way would Alix know that what had just happened had been cataclysmic for her.

'Yes?' Reluctantly she looked at him, and saw his eyes were like grey clouds.

'We're having an engagement party at the end of this week. It's a chance to introduce you to society here, and there will be some international guests.'

Immediately nerves assailed Leila. She was a perfumer, a shop manager—not someone who walked confidently among the moneyed classes. Royalty!

But she needed space from Alix to process everything that had happened so she just nodded nonchalantly and said, 'Okay—fine.'

And then she slipped into her room and leant back against the door, letting out a long, shuddering breath.

She was in love with a man who had admitted to her that he was averse to love—based on the fact that he'd suffered so much pain due to losing his beloved brother. She could understand his trauma—and he would have felt it that much more keenly, being young and impressionable. But who was she to say to him that he wouldn't be able to control who or how he loved?

And yet he was willing to do his best for the sake of their child. Clearly that would have to be enough—and it should be. Everything Leila did now was for the sake of this baby. Her own personal needs and desires were not important.

Yes, they are, you'll wither and die in this environment with no love, whispered a rogue voice.

Leila pushed herself fiercely off the door and ignored

the voice. As much as she longed for a different life from
the one she'd had with her mother, she'd be an absolute
fool to hope, even briefly, that some kind of fairy tale
might be out there.

She stripped off her clothes and stepped into a hot
shower and tried not to think of how it had felt to have
Alix surging between her legs, touching her so deeply that
it had made a mockery of the words she'd spouted at him.

Sex is never just sex, crowed the same rogue voice.

She shut it out and blinked back the prickle of weak
tears.

On the evening of the engagement party Leila was a bag
of nerves. It didn't help that she'd barely seen Alix since
their last conversation. But she'd welcomed the space—
especially in light of what had happened. She'd been having lurid erotic dreams of the harem all week.

Alix had sent her messages and notes, explaining that
he was caught up with political meetings and getting everything prepared for the wedding.

And Leila had been kept busy with lessons about the
history of the island, along with etiquette classes, instruction on how she would be expected to behave as Queen.
And with wedding dress fittings.

The magnitude of how radically her life was changing
was overwhelming.

The last thing she needed was to see Alix and have him
guess just how brittle she was feeling.

Her personal maid, Amalie, was just finishing dressing
her now, and Leila winced a little at the increased sensi-
tivity of her breasts—which only made her think of how
it had felt to have Alix's mouth on her there.

Amalie obviously misread Leila's discomfort. 'Are you
too hot, *mademoiselle*? Shall I open the doors?'

Leila shook her head quickly. 'No, I'm fine—honestly.'

She forced a smile and looked at herself in the mirror, not really recognising the sleekly coiffed woman in front of her and feeling a moment of insecurity that Alix would take one look at her and feel nothing but disappointment with his inconvenient bride.

Alix stood in the doorway, unnoticed for the past few minutes, and watched as Leila was transformed from beautiful to stunning. His breath caught in his throat. She wore a cream strapless dress with a ruched bodice that clung to her full breasts before falling in delicate chiffon layers to the floor. Her dark hair was coiled into a complicated-looking chignon at the back of her head. Make-up subtly enhanced her eyes and that lush mouth.

Alix's body reacted with predictable force. A force he'd spent the week avoiding by keeping busy at all costs. Like some kind of yellow-bellied coward. He'd stood face to face this week with one of the men who had shot his parents and his brother, and he hadn't felt half the maelstrom he was feeling now.

As if sensing his regard, Leila turned her head and saw him. Her cheeks flushed and Alix gritted his jaw to stop his body reacting even more rampantly. He felt like a Neanderthal. He wanted to throw her over his shoulder and carry her back to the heart of that harem, to sink himself so deep he'd never have to feel or think again. He wanted to lock them in there for a month.

He stepped into the room with a velvet box in his hand, vaguely aware of the young maid curtseying and disappearing.

Leila looked from the box to him. 'More jewellery?'

She said it as if it was a poisoned chalice, and bleakly he had to realise that perhaps that was what this marriage was for her.

Alix curbed his irritation. 'Yes, more jewellery.'

He came closer to Leila and opened the box, watching her eyes widen at the sight of the exquisite gold necklace and matching earrings. He put it down and lifted the necklace, already knowing it would look stunning on her flawless olive skin. It was faintly geometric in design, and circular. He opened it and placed it around her neck, burningly aware of her body so close to his. Of his straining erection.

Leila put a hand to it as he took his own away and stepped back. 'It's beautiful. I don't mean to sound ungrateful. I'm just not used to...*this*. I feel like I'm not qualified.'

Alix saw her insecurity and was amazed at how little she was aware of her own beauty and power. *Over him.*

Gruffly he said, 'You're just as qualified as anyone else ever was. Most of the Queens in this family were slave girls, transported from northern Europe on ships, taken by pirates.'

Leila looked at him, a rare spark of humour in her eyes. 'That's one part of your history I *didn't* particularly relish learning about.'

Alix handed her the earrings and watched as she slid them into her ears. *Dieu.* He even found that erotic.

Feeling compelled, he said, 'I'm sorry I left you alone all week. I had things to attend to.'

It sounded so lame now. Pathetic. No woman had ever made him feel as if he wasn't in complete control. Except for this one.

He forced his mind back from the brink and stepped back. 'Ready?'

She nodded and he saw how she swallowed nervously. Instinctively he reached for her hand and led her out of the suite and into the corridor, aware of her tension and wanting to soothe it. Reassure her. Alien concepts for Alix.

They were coming close to where the sound of over two hundred guests could be heard and she stopped in her tracks. He looked at her and his chest squeezed at the fear on her face. *He'd* done this to her. He'd never contemplated having a wife who wouldn't just take this in her stride.

Her eyes were huge. 'What if I can't do this? I'm not a princess…'

Alix couldn't stop himself from reaching out and putting a hand to her neck, massaging her muscles with his fingers, feeling them resist and then relax. Her eyes were all he could see: huge pools of green. Her skin was so soft under his hand, and then he couldn't resist tugging her into him and lowering his mouth to hers.

They sank into each other, mouths open and tongues tangling, their kiss growing hotter and deeper before he had a chance to claw back some control. They were in the corridor. About to face guests. And he was ready to lift her against the nearest wall and thrust into her tight sheath.

Alix pulled back, feeling dizzy. Leila looked equally disorientated. Mouth pink and swollen.

Somehow he managed to grit out, 'You'll be fine. Just follow my lead.'

Leila wasn't sure how she was able to make her feet move at all after that kiss, but somehow Alix's words and his hand anchored her—although she had to figure that the kiss had been a somewhat calculated move to make her look suitably starry-eyed before they faced his public.

And then suddenly they were standing at the top of the stairs at the entrance to the majestic ballroom and Leila's nerves were back. It was filled with portraits of his rather fearsome-looking ancestors. The crowd started to hush as people noticed them. Alix took her hand and placed it on his arm.

A man in an elaborate Isle Saint Croix uniform struck a tall staff on the ground. It made an impressive booming noise and then he shouted out, 'May I present to you the King of Isle Saint Croix, Alixander Saul Almaric Saint

Croix, and future Queen and mother of Isle Saint Croix, Leila Amal Lakshmi Verughese.'

Leila felt absurdly emotional at being called the mother of Isle Saint Croix as Alix led her down the stairs. She took a deep breath as they reached the bottom, and suddenly it was organised chaos as Andres appeared and led them around the room, introducing them to everyone.

CHAPTER ELEVEN

WHAT FELT LIKE aeons later, Leila wondered if her mouth would stay in a rictus smile for ever. Her cheeks ached and her feet were burning in the too-high heels. Thankfully the crowd had dissipated somewhat now, and she felt as if she could breathe again.

Alix's conversation with a man whose name Leila couldn't recall ended. He turned to her, looking genuinely concerned. 'Are you okay? You probably shouldn't be on your feet for so long.'

Leila had to stop her silly heart from lurching and forced a smile. 'Don't be silly—I'm pregnant, not crippled.' But in fact she *was* feeling a little hot and weary.

Alix was gesturing to a member of staff, giving him some kind of signal, and then he was leading Leila out to a secluded open courtyard off the main ballroom.

Leila sat down on a wrought-iron chair with relief, slipping off her shoes for a moment to stretch her feet. She caught Alix's look and said ruefully, 'Okay, my feet *were* beginning to kill me.'

The staff member appeared again, with a tray of hors d'oeuvres and some sparkling water. Alix sat down too and tugged at his bow tie, loosening it a bit.

More touched than she liked to admit, and surprised at this show of concern, Leila said, 'You don't have to wait out here with me. I just need a moment.'

Alix popped an olive into his mouth and shook his head. 'I could do with a break myself. The French ambassador was beginning to bore me to death.'

Leila smiled and felt a moment of extreme poignancy, imagining that it could be like this—this sense of communion, sneaking out to take a break during functions. She quickly slammed the door on those thoughts. It was heading for dangerous fairy-tale territory again.

She helped herself to a vegetarian vol-au-vent and savoured the flaky pastry and delicate mushroom filling, more hungry than she'd like to admit.

'You need to eat more.'

She looked at Alix and grimaced. 'I'm still nauseous sometimes, but the doctor said it should ease off soon.'

Alix stood up then and looked out at the view. Something about his profile seemed so lonely to Leila in that moment—it was as if she might never truly reach him or know him. She found herself wondering if anyone ever had, and didn't like the sharp spiking of something hot and dark. *Jealousy.*

She forced her voice to sound light. 'Have you ever been in love, Alix? I mean with a lover.'

He tensed, and Leila found herself holding her breath.

'I've thought I was in love once before, but it wasn't love. It was only a very wounded youthful ego.'

Swallowing past the constriction in her throat, Leila asked, 'Who was she?'

Alix turned around to face her, leaning back against the wall. His expression was hard. 'I met her in America when I was a student. I thought she only knew me as Alix Cross. I was trying to stay under the radar and I believed that she was attracted to me for myself—not who I was...'

He leaned his hands on the stone wall.

'She was English. She'd come to America to escape the public scandal of her father gambling all their money away. They were related to royalty. She was looking for a way to get back into Europe and restore her reputation via someone else. Namely me. I was young and naive. Arrogant enough to believe her when she said she loved me. But the truth was that she just used me to get what she wanted. And clearly I wasn't enough for her, because I walked into her room one day and found one of my undercover bodyguards giving it to her a lot rougher than I ever could or wanted to.'

Leila looked at Alix's hard expression. *She just used me.* Her own words that she'd thrown at him came back to her like a slap on the face. *I used you.* She felt sick.

Then Alix said, 'I've already told you Max was the only person I've loved. I was brought up knowing any marriage would be a strategic alliance, all about heirs. I saw no love between my parents. Love was never part of the equation for me.'

That was what he'd said on the phone to Andres that day in Paris.

'I *can* promise to honour you and respect you, Leila. You did well this evening, and I have no doubt you'll make a great queen. And mother of our children. But that will have to be enough, because I can't offer any more.'

There it was—the brutal truth, sitting between them like a squat ugly troll. Dashing any hopes and dreams Leila might have had.

'Well,' she managed to say, as if her heart wasn't being lacerated in a million different places, 'at least we know where we stand.'

In a desperate bid to avoid Alix looking at her too closely, seeing the devastation inside her, she stood up too. She thought of what he'd said about being used and her conscience smarted. She really didn't want to do this, but his honesty compelled her to be honest too.

She went to the wall and mirrored his stance. 'I owe you an apology.'

'You do?'

Leila nodded and avoided his eye. 'That day in Paris… when I told you I'd used you just because I wanted to get rid of my virginity…I lied.'

She turned and looked at him, steeling herself not to crumble.

'The truth is that I *was* humiliated and hurt. I lashed out, not wanting you to see that.'

Something like a flash of horror crossed Alix's face.

Before he could say anything she cut in hurriedly, 'Don't worry. I wasn't falling for you... It was wounded pride. That's all.'

His expression cleared and Leila felt a monumental ache near her heart to see his visible relief.

'Look,' she said, putting a hand over her belly, 'all I want is to go forward from this moment with honesty and trust between us. At least if we have that we know where we stand, and it might be something we can build on. I won't deny that this marriage won't give me all that I need and want emotionally, but I'm doing this for our baby, and I'll try to make you a good queen.'

Alix looked at Leila and felt flattened by her words when only a moment ago he'd been feeling relief that she hadn't fallen for him.

This marriage won't give me all that I need.

And her admission rocked him. The fact that she hadn't meant those words, *I used you.* It ripped apart something he'd been clinging on to since he'd seen her again. As if as long as he had that he'd be protected.

She humbled him, this woman who had walked out of a shop and into a world far removed from anything she'd known, and she'd captivated the entire crowd this evening, behaving with an innate graciousness that he hadn't even known she possessed. She was putting everyone around her to shame.

Including him.

He felt like a fraud. He felt for the first time as if he was taking something beautiful and tarnishing it. He should let her go—but he couldn't. They were bound by their baby.

He owed her full honesty now.

'There's something you need to understand. When I met you I was consumed with nothing more than you. I never set out to use you as a smokescreen. There was no agenda. When we took that trip to Isle de la Paix it *was* spontaneous in that I planned it once you'd mentioned you didn't want any press intrusion. But I *did* see an opportunity, and I *did* arrange for someone to take that photo, seizing the chance to keep attention diverted.'

Alix sighed heavily.

'I had no right to exploit you for my own ends. And I'm sorry for that. Ultimately it led them straight to you. But when I pursued you it was because I wanted you— pure and simple.'

His admission made Leila feel vulnerable. If anything it just made things harder to know that he *hadn't* ruthlessly used her from the start.

She said, as breezily as she could, 'Well, it's in the past, and we're here now, so I think we just have to keep moving forward.'

Terrified he'd read something in her eyes, or on her face, she stepped around him and walked back into the ballroom.

She spent the rest of the evening avoiding him, in case he saw how close to the surface her emotions were. Emotions that she'd denied she felt right to his face.

She knew they'd agreed to be honest, but there was such a thing as taking honesty too far. And Leila hated how this new accord made her feel as if they'd taken about ten steps forward and twenty back.

She realised that if she was to negotiate a life living with a man who could never—*would* never—love her, she was going to have to develop some hefty self-protection mechanisms.

'She's a natural, Alix. If you'd seen her... The kids loved her. The nurses and doctors are in awe of her. She's possibly done more for Isle Saint Croix in one visit to the children's ward of the hospital than you could have done in six months. No offence.'

Alix grimaced as he recalled his recent meeting with Andres. Of course he hadn't taken offence at the fact that apparently his fiancée was indeed bound to be as perfect a queen as he'd expected her to be. When he'd believed she was falling for him. The fact that she'd assured him she *hadn't* been was like a burr under his skin now.

In the past few days, since the engagement party, Leila had thrown herself into doing as much as she could to learn about her new role. Alix had gone to her rooms at night to find her sleeping, and as much as he'd wanted to slide between the sheets and slide between her legs, something had held him back.

The same thing that had held him back the night of the party, when he'd left Leila at her door. He'd wanted her so badly, but after everything they'd said he had been almost afraid that if he touched her something would spill out of him—something much deeper than a mere climax. Some truth he wasn't ready to acknowledge yet.

'Your Majesty? Your fiancée is here to see you.'

Conjured up out of his imagination to taunt him?

He turned around. 'Show her in, please.'

Leila walked in and Alix felt that all-too-familiar jolt of lust mixed with something else. Something much more complex.

She looked pale.

Alix frowned, immediately concerned. 'What is it?' He cursed softly as he came around and held a chair out for her. 'You've been doing too much. I told Andres that you're busy enough with wedding preparations—'

She put up a hand and didn't sit down. 'No, I'm fine. Honestly. I enjoyed the visit to the hospital.'

Alix smiled. 'You were a big hit.'

She blushed and ducked her head, and Alix felt a pang near his heart. Her ability to blush and show her emotions was one of the things that had made him fall for her...

Alix went utterly still as the words he'd just thought sank in—and dropped like heavy boulders into his gut.

Alix was so quiet that Leila looked at him. The smile was gone from his face and he was deathly pale. She put out a hand. 'Alix...are you all right? You look like you've seen a ghost.'

He recoiled from her hand and a look of utter horror came over his face. Leila flinched inwardly. But, if anything, this only confirmed for her the reason why she needed to talk to him. She had to do this to protect herself.

At least over the past few days she'd discovered a real sense that perhaps she *could* be a queen, that she could relatively happily devote her life to the people of Isle Saint Croix and her children.

But in order to survive she needed to create a very firm boundary where Alix was concerned.

The fact that he hadn't made any attempt to sleep with her in the past few nights had left her feeling frustrated and relieved in equal measure. She knew physical intimacy without love would eventually crack her in two—or that she'd end up blurting out how much she loved him, and she couldn't bear to see that horror-struck look on his face again.

Alix retreated around the desk—as if he needed to physically put something between them. Leila tried not to feel hurt.

She steeled herself. 'I wanted to talk to you about something. About us. And our marriage.'

Alix sat down, still looking a little shell-shocked. Leila sat down too, twisting her hands in her lap.

'Go ahead.' Alix sounded hoarse.

'I am committed to doing my best to be a queen that you can be proud of, and I will love our child—and children, if we have more. I do believe that we can have a harmonious union, and that's important to me for the sake of those children—I expect you will want more than one.'

Alix frowned. 'Leila—'

She spoke over him. 'But apart from with our children, and promoting a united front for social occasions or events, I would prefer if we could live as separately as possible. I don't want to share rooms with you. And I would prefer if any intimacies were to be only for the sake of procreating. I will understand if that's not enough for you, but I would just ask that you be discreet in your liaisons, should you feel the need.'

Alix's face was getting darker and darker. He stood up now and put his hands on the desk. Leila tried not to move back, or be intimidated.

'Let me get this straight. You want to maintain a separate existence in private and we'll only share the marital bed for the purposes of getting you pregnant? And if I'm feeling the urge in the meantime I'm to seek out a willing and discreet lover?'

Leila nodded, telling herself that it hadn't hurt so much or sounded so ridiculous when she'd thought it all through in her head. But this was the only way she felt she could survive this marriage, knowing he didn't love her.

At least if she could create a family then she would have some purpose in her life—love and affection.

But all at once she realised that that was the most selfish reason in the world for creating a family.

Alix's mouth was a thin line. 'My father paraded his many mistresses around the castle and did untold damage to this country. I vowed never to repeat his corrupt ways—so, no, I don't think I'll be taking you up on your helpful suggestion to maintain a discreet mistress.'

He came around the desk and towered over Leila. She stood up.

'And, no,' Alix continued, 'I don't believe I *do* agree that we should maintain separate existences. I believe that you will share my bed every night, and I expect intimacies to be many and varied. Are you *really* suggesting that I am going to be forcing myself on a reluctant wife?'

Leila had to stop a slightly hysterical laugh from emerging. Of course he wouldn't have to force himself on a reluctant wife. Even now she felt every cell in her body straining to get closer to him. But, standing so close to Alix now, she realised that she'd actually completely underestimated her ability to survive even if she could maintain some distance from Alix. And of course he wouldn't agree to her admittedly ridiculous terms. What had she been thinking?

A sense of panic made her gut roil. 'Then I don't think I can do this, Alix. I thought I could, for the sake of the baby...but I can't.'

She felt weak, pathetic, selfish.

'What are you saying, Leila?'

She forced out the words. 'I'm saying that I want more than you can offer me, Alix. I'm sorry...I thought I could do this, but I can't.'

Terrified she'd start crying, Leila turned and hurried out of the room.

Alix looked at the door that had just closed and reeled. He had to recognise the bitter irony of the fact that Leila had more or less just outlined the kind of marriage that he'd always believed he wanted.

Space between him and his wife. She would be his consort in public and mother to his children. She wouldn't infringe upon his life in any other more meaningful way.

He might have laughed if he hadn't still been consumed by the terrifying revelation that made his limbs feel as weak as jelly. The rush of love he'd felt while watching that scan had been for Leila as much as for the baby. He'd just been blocking that cataclysmic knowledge out.

She had just said she wanted more. And the even more ironic thing was that *he* wanted more too. He suddenly wanted the whole damn thing—and it was too late.

The gods weren't just mocking him…they were rolling around the floor, laughing hysterically.

Leila was aware of the bodyguards, standing at a discreet distance, and was doing her best to ignore them. Her chest ached with unexpressed emotion. She had taken a Jeep and driven away from the castle, needing some space and time to breathe. She should have expected that she wouldn't be able to move without triggering a national security alert.

And even the stunning view from this lookout point high on the island was incapable of soothing her.

The sound of another vehicle came from the narrow road and Leila heaved a sigh of frustration. She turned around. Really, this was getting ridiculous.

But her breath stopped in her throat when she saw Alix getting out of the driver's seat. He looked grim and went over to the bodyguards. After a couple of seconds they all got back into their vehicles and left.

When they were gone he looked at her for a long moment, and then came over. He stood beside her and gestured with his head to the view.

'On a clear day, with good binoculars, you can see both the Spanish and African coasts from here.'

Leila looked away from him. 'It's beautiful.'

'There are hundreds of shipwrecks around the island. It's my plan to use them as an incentive to get people to come wreck-diving. Part of the tourism package we're putting together.'

Leila's heart ached. 'The island is magical, Alix. You won't have a problem getting people to come.'

He turned to face her and said quietly, 'And what about

getting people to stay? I wonder what incentive I could offer for that…'

Your love, Leila thought bleakly.

But she had to come to terms with the futility of her position and she said, 'I'm sorry. I overreacted just now. Of course I won't be leaving. I can't. Our baby deserves two parents, and a stable foundation. It was just…hormones, or something.'

Alix didn't say anything for a moment, and then he held out a hand. 'Will you come with me? I want to show you something.'

Leila hesitated a moment, and then slipped her hand into his, hating how right it felt even as a gaping chasm opened up near her heart.

Alix brought her over to the Jeep and she got into the passenger side. She watched him walk around the front, her gaze drawn irresistibly to his tall, powerful form.

He drove in silence for about ten minutes, and then drove off the main road down a dirt track. They weren't too far from the main town, and Leila could just make out the castle in the distance.

After about a mile Alix stopped and got out. Leila got out too and looked around, but could see nothing of immediate interest. Alix led her over to where a vast area looked as if it was in the process of being cleared and levelled, even though there were no workmen at the site today.

'What's this?'

Leila looked at Alix when he didn't say anything immediately. He was so handsome against the sunlight it almost hurt. She could see that he truly belonged here, in this environment. And that somehow she was going to have to belong here too. And weather the emotional pain.

'It will be your new factory.'

Leila blinked, distracted. 'My new…*factory*?'

Alix nodded. 'The area is being cleared and I've lined

up architects to meet with you and discuss how you want it designed and built. There's also room for a walled garden, so you can cultivate and grow plants and flowers. We have a huge range on the island, including a rare form of sea lavender. There's room for a greenhouse too, if you need it. You'll know more than me what you need.'

Leila looked around, speechless. The area was massive. And in this environment she could grow almost anything. What Alix had just said was almost too much to take in. She turned around and saw the island falling away and the sea stretching out to infinity. She was simply stunned.

Alix said worriedly, 'You don't like the site? It's too small?'

Leila shook her head and blinked back tears, terrified that once the emotion started leaking out it wouldn't stop. 'No, no—it's lovely…amazing.'

When she felt more in control she looked at him.

Her voice was husky. 'I thought you said I'd have other priorities—the baby, my role as Queen?'

Alix looked serious. 'Leila, you inhale the world without even realising you're doing it—it's part of you. You're led by your nose. I want you to be happy here. And I hope that this will make you happy. I know you want more… you deserve so much more…'

A slightly rueful expression crossed his face.

'And I need you to make me more of that scent, because I destroyed the bottle you gave me in Paris. I destroyed it because I was angry and hurt.'

Leila's heart gave a little lurch. 'You weren't hurt. Your ego was wounded because I dared to say no to you.'

Alix nodded. 'That's what I believed. That it was my ego. Except it was a lie that I told myself and kept telling myself, even when I saw you again. The truth is that it wasn't just my ego—it was my heart. And I didn't have the guts to admit it to myself.'

He took her hands in his.

'It hit me today, Leila. Like a ton of bricks. I've been falling for you from the moment I saw you in your shop. When we were leaving Isle de la Paix I knew I had to let you go, but I didn't want to. I think I came up with the idea of proposing to you because it was the only way I could see to make you stay...'

Leila looked at Alix. She said a little dumbly, 'You're saying you *love* me?'

He nodded, looking wary now.

For a second Leila felt a dizzying sweep of pure joy— and then a voice resounded in her head: *Silly Leila...there's no fairy tale.* The joy dissolved. She had thought the chasm in her chest couldn't get any bigger, but it just had.

She pulled her hands free. 'Why are you doing this? I've told you I'm not leaving.'

Alix frowned. 'Doing what? Telling you I love you? Because I do.'

Leila shook her head, those damn tears threatening again. 'I can't believe you'd be this cruel, Alix. Please don't insult my intelligence. I tell you that I want to go, that I don't think I can marry you, and now suddenly you're claiming to love me? You're forgetting I heard your conversation on the phone that day: *"If I have to convince her I love her then I will."'*

Alix ran his hands through his hair, his frustration palpable. Leila folded her arms.

'Why would I do this now? Pretend?'

Leila felt ill. 'You've made a very convincing case for persuading me that you're incapable of love, and now I'm suddenly supposed to believe you've had some kind of epiphany? It's three days to the wedding, Alix, and I know how important it is for you and for Isle Saint Croix, but I never thought you'd be unnecessarily cruel.'

Alix looked as if she'd just punched him in the gut, but Leila steeled herself.

He opened his mouth, but she said with a rush, 'Please don't, Alix. Look, I appreciate what you're trying to do—and all this...' She put out a hand to indicate the site for the factory. 'It's enough—it really is.'

It'll have to be. At least he didn't know that she loved him. It was her last paltry defence.

She turned away and started to walk back to the Jeep, fiercely blinking back tears. She didn't see the way Alix's face leached of all colour as he watched her go. She also didn't see the look of grim determination that settled over his features.

Their journey back to the castle was made in tense silence. When they arrived Leila jumped out of the Jeep, but Alix moved faster than her and her hand was in his before she could react.

He led her into the castle, and when she tried to pull her hand free Alix only tightened his grip and looked at her, his face more stern and stark than she'd ever seen it.

'We have not finished this conversation, Leila.'

She had to trot to keep up with his punishing pace, and only recognised where they were when he opened a door.

Immediately Leila dug her heels in and pulled furiously on Alix's hand. 'I am not going in there.'

Alix looked at her and said tauntingly, 'Why, Leila? Sex is just sex, after all—isn't it?'

They were in the impressive *hammam* room before Leila could object and the door was closed. Alix stood in front of it, arms folded. She hadn't even registered him letting her hand go.

'You know, I never thought you were a coward, Leila.'

Leila's mouth opened, and she finally got out, '*Coward?* I am not a coward.'

Alix stepped away from the door and towards her. She eyed the door, wondering if she could make a run for it, and then his words sank in.

She couldn't run. So she rounded on him. 'What's that supposed to mean?'

He walked around her now, looking at her assessingly, and she had to keep turning, getting dizzy.

'You're a coward, Leila Verughese. An emotional coward. And I know because I was one too.'

Something like panic was fluttering in Leila's belly now. 'That's ridiculous. I'm not a coward and you're a liar.'

He arched a brow and made a low whistling sound. 'That's harsh. I told you I love you and you call me a liar?'

Leila changed tack. 'Why are you doing this? I've told you I'm happy to stay. You don't have to sweeten it up for me.'

Alix almost sneered now. 'You're "happy to stay"— like some kind of martyr? The days of pirates kidnapping European slaves and forcing them into marriage are over. When we marry it'll be because you want it as much as I do. Because you love me too—except you're too much of a coward to admit it. Why else would you want us to maintain a distance while we're married?'

Leila felt her blood draining south. Her last defence was crumbling in front of her eyes. 'I don't love you,' she lied.

'Liar.'

Alix stalked closer, tension crackling between them.

'If I'd been more honest with myself sooner I would have recognised it the day we left here—when you said sex is just sex. That was the key. Sex has *always* been just sex for me. Until you. That's why I haven't touched you since we were in here—because as soon as I touch you I'm not in control, and I was afraid you'd see it. And I think it's the same for you. *Dieu*, Leila,' he spat in disgust. 'You'd really want me to take a mistress?'

Leila could feel her insides tearing apart. 'But you don't love me—you can't. You said it.'

She sounded accusing now. The fairy tale was like a shimmering mirage, and she knew that the moment she committed herself to trusting, believing, it would disappear and she'd be left with less than she had even now.

Alix was ruthless. 'I can—and I do. You brought me to my knees and showed me that anything less than total surrender to love and all its risks is a life not worth living. It terrifies me, because I know how awful it is to lose someone you love, but I've realised that it's impossible to live in constant fear of that. I want more too—and I want it with you. No one else.'

Leila shook her head, tears making her vision blurry. It hit her then. Alix was right—she was a coward. Terrified to trust. Terrified that the dream didn't exist. Her mother's ghost whispered to her even now that it couldn't. She hadn't had it, so why should Leila?

Alix stepped right up to her. 'Say it, Leila.'

She shook her head. 'Please, don't make me…'

She had a terrifying vision of telling him she loved him only to see him go cold and shut down, satisfied that his convenient wife had surrendered to him completely.

Alix wrapped a hand around her neck. 'Then we do it this way… You're mine, body, heart and soul, and I will leave you nowhere to hide.'

Alix's head dipped and his mouth settled on hers like a scorching brand. Leila resisted. *This* was what she was afraid of, and suddenly speaking the words didn't seem so scary— what was far worse was the honesty he would wring from her now, because she literally would have nowhere to hide.

But it was too late for resistance. And Leila was weak. And again he was right. She *was* a coward.

She sobbed her anguish into his mouth as his tongue stroked hers and the flames licked higher and higher.

This time there was no way they could make it to the harem bedroom. Leila felt herself being lowered onto the raised platform of smooth marble. Their movements were not graceful or measured. There was a feral urgency to their coming together.

Clothes were ripped off. Alix's hands were rough, his mouth hard, teeth nipping and tongue thrusting deep into the slick folds of her sex. Leila's back arched. Her hands clenched in Alix's hair. His hands clasped her so tightly she knew she'd be bruised, but she revelled in it.

He was her man and she loved him.

And now he loomed over her, huge and awe-inspiring, face flushed and eyes glittering intensely. She saw the need on his face, making his features stark. She saw the uncertainty even now, in spite of his bravado, and her heart ached.

He sank into her body with slow and devastating deliberation, watching her. Demanding that she expose herself utterly.

Leila had nowhere to hide. He was true to his word. She wrapped her legs around him and finally broke free of the bonds of fear. He touched her so deeply she gasped and caught his face in her hands, the words spilling from her lips in a rush of emotion.

'Of course I love you, Alix. I love you with all my heart and soul. You're mine, and I'm yours, for ever.'

An expression of pure awe broke over his face. A look of fierce male satisfaction. And *love*.

Leila's heart soared free, and then the delicious dance of love started. And when Leila arched her back in the throes of orgasm and looked up, all she could see were thousands of glittering mosaic stars above their heads. And finally she believed in his love—deep down in the core of her body, where Alix had broken her apart and now put her back together.

EPILOGUE

LEILA HURRIED FROM the Jeep into the castle, greeting staff as she went in. Happiness and fulfilment were things that she felt every day now, but she didn't take them for granted for a second.

In the seventeen months since she'd married Alix, in a deeply emotional ceremony, they and the island had undergone seismic changes.

The island was thriving and growing stronger every day. Her factory had opened a few months ago and it, too, was beginning to flourish as she started to manufacture perfumes again. Her apartment in Paris was now an office over the shop, and she went back about once a month to keep an eye on proceedings.

She'd been stunned to get a call one day from her father's daughter—a half-sister. He'd been put under immense public pressure to do the DNA test which had proved his paternity of Leila and consequently ruined his political career. Leila's half-sister, Noelle, had confided that her and her brother's life had been blighted by his numerous affairs and their mother's unhappiness.

She'd already come to Isle Saint Croix to meet Leila, with a protective Alix by her side, and their relationship was tentatively flowering into something very meaningful.

But the real heart and centre of her life was right here in the castle. Everything else was a bonus.

When Leila walked into Alix's office she couldn't help a grin spreading across her face at the scene before her, featuring her two favourite people in the world. Alix and their dark-haired eleven-month-old son, Max.

Max was bouncing energetically on Alix's knee, simultaneously slapping his pudgy fists on the table while trying to cram what looked like a very mushed up banana into his mouth.

Alix had a big hand firmly around his son and was typing with one hand on his open laptop, safely out of destruction's way.

Then they both caught sight of her at the same time—two pairs of grey eyes, one wide and guileless, the other far more adult and full of a very male appreciation and love.

'Mama!'

Small arms lifted towards her and Leila plucked Max off Alix's knee. But before she could move away Alix's arm snaked around her waist and pulled her onto his lap. Max was delighted—clapping his hands, bits of banana flying everywhere.

Leila chuckled. 'I was trying to help you.'

Alix slid Leila's hair over her shoulder and pressed a kiss to her exposed neck.

She shivered deliciously and asked a little breathlessly, 'Where's Mimi?'

'I gave her the afternoon off. We were lonely without you—weren't we, little man?'

Max gurgled his agreement. Leila stood up and found a wet wipe to clean her son as much as possible, before putting him into his playpen and watching him pounce on his favourite cuddly toy.

She turned to face Alix, eyes sparkling, voice dry, 'I was in the factory for three hours and you got *lonely*?'

Alix stood up and took Leila's hand and drew her over to a nearby couch, pulling her down with him so she ended up sprawled on his lap again—this time in much closer proximity to a strategic part of his anatomy.

'I get lonely the minute you leave my sight,' he growled softly.

Leila's heart swelled. 'Me too.'

The playpen was suspiciously quiet, and Leila checked quickly to see their son sprawled on his back, thumb in his mouth, cuddly toy clamped to his side, fast asleep. Worn out.

She leaned back against her husband. 'I have something for you.'

He arched a brow and moved subtly, showing her that he had something for her too. 'Do you, now?'

She nodded and took a bottle from the pocket at the front of her shirt dress. The label read *Alix's Dream*. It was the perfume she'd first made for him. And one that was so personal she never sold it to anyone else.

He kissed her, long and slow and deep. 'Thank you.'

'Mmm,' she said appreciatively. 'I'll have to make it more often if that's the sort of response I'll get.'

Alix shifted so that she slid into the cradle of his lap. Leila groaned—half in frustration, half in helpless response. 'Alix…'

'I'm going to make a secret passage from here to the harem,' he grumbled.

Leila blushed to think of their very private space, which had been completely refurbished. The *hammam* was in use again too, and was open to local women and the women of the castle.

Leila loved going there amongst them and hearing their stories. It was one of the things that had earned them both the love and respect of their people—their unaffected ways and their wish to be considered as equal as possible.

Alix teased a strand of Leila's hair around his finger. 'Andres said you went to the hospital today? Another visit to the new children's wing?'

Leila nodded—and then the excitement bubbling inside

her couldn't be contained any more. 'Yes, but I also had an appointment to see Dr Fontainebleau.'

Alix immediately tensed at the mention of the royal doctor. 'Is there something wrong?'

Leila shook her head and took his hand, placing it over her belly. 'No, everything is very okay…but we'll be a little bit busier in about eight months.'

The colour receded from Alix's face and then rushed back. His arms tightened around her and then he lowered her down onto the sofa. His formidable body came over her, his happiness and joy palpable.

When he spoke his voice sounded a little choked. 'You do know that you've made me the happiest man in the world, and that I love you to infinity and beyond?'

Leila blinked back emotional tears and wound her arms around her husband's neck, drawing him down to her.

'I know, because I feel exactly the same way. Now, about that secret passage to the harem…do you think we could get it done before the baby arrives?'

* * * * *

'I'm not sleeping with you!'

Zachim tugged the horse blanket over the top of them. 'No, you're not. You're sleeping *next* to me. There's a big difference. We need to share body heat to keep warm. Relax and this will be a lot easier.'

Relax? Farah couldn't have been more tense if she'd tried. It had been a long time since she had been physically close to anyone, and all this bodily contact was messing with her head.

'This isn't right.'

'But kidnapping your Prince is fine?'

'Must you always have the last word?' she grumbled.

'I was going to ask the same of you.'

Not wanting to find him at all amusing, Farah curled herself into a tight ball to try and put distance between them. Self-sufficiency was a prized trait in the harsh desert climate, and Farah was proud that she could survive on her own if she had to. She wanted to point this out to the Prince, but that would involve speaking to him and she'd much rather pretend he wasn't there. She'd much rather pretend she was in her own bed than on the cold, hard ground, wrapped in the strong arms of her father's number one enemy.

With two university degrees and a variety of false career starts under her belt, **Michelle Conder** decided to satisfy her lifelong desire to write and finally found her dream job. She currently lives in Melbourne, Australia, with one super-indulgent husband, three self-indulgent (but exquisite) children, a menagerie of over-indulged pets, and the intention of doing some form of exercise daily. She loves to hear from her readers at michelleconder.com

Books by Michelle Conder

Mills & Boon Modern Romance

Prince Nadir's Secret Heir
The Most Expensive Lie of All
Duty at What Cost?
Living the Charade

The Chatsfield

Russian's Ruthless Demand

Dark, Demanding and Delicious

His Last Chance at Redemption

Scandal in the Spotlight

Girl Behind the Scandalous Reputation

**Visit the Author Profile page at
millsandboon.co.uk for more titles.**

HIDDEN IN THE SHEIKH'S HAREM

BY

MICHELLE CONDER

MILLS & BOON

Published in Great Britain 2015
by Mills & Boon, an imprint of Harlequin (UK) Limited,
Eton House, 18-24 Paradise Road, Richmond, Surrey, TW9 1SR

© 2015 Michelle Conder

ISBN: 978-0-263-25081-7

Printed and bound in Spain
by CPI, Barcelona

HIDDEN IN THE
SHEIKH'S HAREM

For my family, with love. Always.

And to Bobo, shokran!

CHAPTER ONE

PRINCE ZACHIM BAKR AL-DARKHAN tried not to slam the door as he left the palace apartment his half-brother was using for his brief visit but it wasn't easy. Nadir was being a cranky, stubborn hard-ass, refusing to take his rightful place as the next King of Bakaan, which left Zach in line for the job.

'Everything, all right, Highness?'

Damn; he was so preoccupied with what had just gone down he hadn't even sensed the elderly servant he'd known all his life waiting in the shadowed recess of the arched windows.

But, no, everything was not all right. Every day that passed without a leader made their people more and more uneasy. His father had only been dead for two weeks but already there were whispers of some of the more insurgent tribes gathering for 'talks'.

Yeah, like the Al-Hajjar tribe. Once their families had been rival dynasties, but two centuries ago the Darkhans had defeated the Hajjars in a brutal war, creating resentments that still remained. But Zach knew that the current leader of the tribe—Mohamed Hajjar—hated his father, not only because of their history, but because he held his father responsible for the death of his pregnant wife ten years ago. And probably his father had been partly respon-

sible because, Allah knew, he had been responsible for
the death of Nadir's mother for entirely different reasons.

The fact was their father had been a miserly tyrant
who'd ruled through fear and had been ruthless when he
didn't get his own way. As a result Bakaan was stuck in
the dark ages, both in its laws and infrastructure, and it
was going to be an enormous challenge to pull it into the
twenty-first century.

A challenge that his brother was better suited to take
on than Zach. And not just because Nadir was politically
savvy with finely honed boardroom instincts, but also because it was his rightful place as the eldest son. With Nadir
taking charge it would also free Zach up to do what he did
best—creating and managing change at street level where
he could do the most good.

Something he'd already started doing after his delicate
mother had begged him to come home five years ago when
Bakaan had been on the brink of civil war. The cause of
the unrest had stemmed from a rogue publication started
by someone in one of the mountain tribes detailing his father's failings and calling for change. There wasn't much
in the publication Zach could argue with, but he'd done
his duty and settled the unrest in his father's favour. Then,
appalled at the state his country was in, he'd set aside his
Western lifestyle and stayed, working behind the scenes
to do what he could until his increasingly narcissistic and
paranoid father had either seen sense or died. Death had
come first and the only thing Zach felt was hollow inside. Hollow for the man who had only ever seen him as
the spare to the throne, and not a very worthy one at that.

'Highness?'

'Sorry, Staph.' Zach shook off the memories he didn't
want to delve into and started striding towards his own
private wing of the palace, Staph quickstepping to keep

pace with him. 'But, no, everything is not all right. My brother is proving to be stubborn.'

'Ah, he does not wish to return to Bakaan?'

No, he did not. Zach knew Nadir had good reason for not wanting to, but he also knew that his brother was born to be king, and that if Nadir could get past the bitterness he felt for their father, he would want to rule their small kingdom. Realising that Staph was having trouble keeping pace with him, Zach slowed. 'He has some other considerations to think of right now,' he hedged.

Like an infant daughter he hadn't known about and the mother he was set on marrying. Now, there had been a revelation to shock the hell out of Zach. Out of the two of them it was he who believed in love and marriage, while Nadir thought the concept had been created by the masses to counter boredom and a lack of productivity. Zach didn't believe that. He knew that one day he'd have a family who he'd treat a lot better than their old man had treated his.

In fact, he'd nearly proposed to a woman once; right before he'd been called home. Amy Anderson had ticked all his boxes—sophisticated, polished and blonde. Their courtship had gone smoothly and he still didn't know what had made him pull back. Nadir had been no help at the time, claiming that Zach had a tendency to choose women who were all wrong for him so that he didn't have to make a commitment at all.

Zach bid Staph goodnight and strode into his apartment. As if he'd ever take relationship advice from a confirmed bachelor. Or confirmed *ex*-bachelor, so it seemed.

Shedding his clothes on the way to the shower, he doused himself in steaming hot water before lying on his bed and willing himself to sleep. He'd agreed to meet his brother the following lunchtime so that Nadir could abdicate in front of the council but Zach was hoping he would see sense way before then.

When a message pinged into his phone, he immediately reached for the distraction and saw it was from a good friend he used to race superboats with, Damian Masters:

Check email for party invite. Ibiza. Also, just relented and gave Princess Barbie your private email address. Hope that's okay. D

Well, well, well. Zach wasn't one for all that 'signs and destiny' rubbish but he'd just been thinking about Amy—or 'Princess Barbie' as his friends had unhelpfully nick-named her—and now here she was.

Clicking onto his email list, he found hers and opened it.

Hi Zach, Amy here.
Long time, no chat. I hear you're going to Damian's party in Ibiza. I really hope to see you there. Catch up on old times perhaps??
Love Amy xxx

A wry smile crossed his face. If those question marks and kisses were any indication she wanted to do more than "catch up" on old times. But did he?

He laced his hands behind his head. He might not have thought of her much over the last five years, but what did that matter? It would be interesting to see her again and see how he felt. See if he still thought she should be the mother of his future children.

Almost distractedly he sent a short reply indicating that if he went to the party they would talk, but instead of feeling better he felt worse.

Sick of the thoughts batting back and forth inside his head and the restlessness that had invaded his usually up-beat attitude, he gave up on sleep, flung on jeans and a shirt, and headed out to the palace garage. Once there he jumped into an SUV and waved his security detail off as he turned the car towards the vast, silent desert beyond the city. Before he even knew he was thinking about it, he turned the car off-road and sped down one enormous sand dune after another, lit up in peaks and shadows by the light of the full moon.

Feeling his agitated mood ebb away, he let out a primal roar and pressed the accelerator flat to the floor.

Two hours later he disgustedly tossed the empty jerry can into the back of the car and swore profoundly. He hadn't realised how long he'd been out or how far he'd come and now he was stranded in the desert without any juice and no mobile phone reception.

No doubt his father would have put his impulsivity down to arrogance and his cavalier attitude to life. Zach just put it down to stupidity. He knew better than to head into the desert without a backup plan.

Hell.

Just then the soft whisper of movement had him turning as a dozen or so horsemen appeared on the horizon. Dressed all in black, with their faces covered by traditional *keffiyehs* to keep the sand out of their mouths and noses, he couldn't tell if they were friend or foe.

When all twenty of them lined up in front of him and sat motionless without saying a word, he thought probably foe.

Slowly, he walked his gaze over the line up. Probably he could take ten of them, given that he had a sword and a pistol with him. Probably he should try diplomacy first.

'I don't suppose one of you gentlemen has a jerry can full of petrol strapped to one of those fine beasts, do you?'

The creak of a leather saddle brought his attention back to the thickset stranger positioned at the centre of the group and who he had already picked as the leader. 'You are Prince Zachim Al Darkhan, pride of the desert and heir to the throne, are you not?'

Well, his father would probably argue with the antiquated 'pride of the desert' title, and he wasn't the direct heir, but he didn't think now was the time to quibble over semantics. And he already knew from his tone that the stranger with eyes of black onyx had figured out who he was. 'I am.'

'Well, this is fortuitous,' the old man declared and Zach could hear the smile in his voice even if he couldn't see it behind the dark cloth.

The wind picked up slightly but the night remained beautifully clear, full of stars and that big old moon that had beckoned him to leave the palace and burn up some of his frustrated energy on one of his favourite pastimes.

The old stranger leaned towards one of the other men, who then dismounted slowly from his horse. Of medium height and build, the younger man squared off in front of Zach, his legs braced wide. Zach kept his expression as impassive as he'd held it the whole time. If they were going to try and take him one at a time, this was going to be a cakewalk.

Then the other eighteen dismounted.

Okay, now that was more like it. Pity his weapons were in the car.

Farah Hajjar woke with a start and then remembered it was a full moon. She never slept well on a full moon. It was like an omen and for as long as she could remember she was always waiting for something bad to happen. And it had once. Her mother had died on the night of a full moon. Or, the afternoon of one, but Farah had been unable to sleep that night and she'd railed and cried at the moon until she'd been exhausted. Now it just represented sadness—sadness and pain. Though she wasn't twelve any more, so perhaps she should be over that. Like she should be over her fear of scorpions—not the easiest of fears to overcome when you lived in the desert where they bred like mice.

Rolling onto her side to get more comfortable, she heard the soft whinny of a horse somewhere nearby.

She wondered if it was her father returning from a weeklong meeting about the future of the country. Now that the horrible King Hassan was dead it was all he could talk about. That and how the dead king's son, the autocratic Prince Zachim, would probably rule the country in exactly the same way as the father had. The prince had led a fairy-tale existence, if the magazines Farah had read were true, before moving back to Bakaan full-time five years ago. As nothing had really changed in that time, she suspected her father was right about the prince—which was incredibly demoralising for the country.

Yawning, she heard the horses gallop off and wondered what was going on. Not that she would complain if her father would be gone for another day or two. Try as she might, she could never seem to get anything right with him, and Allah knew how hard she had tried. Tried and failed, because her father saw women as being put on the earth to create baskets and babies and not much else. In fact, he had remarried twice to try to sire a son and discarded both women when they had proved to be barren.

He couldn't understand Farah's need for independence and she couldn't understand why he couldn't understand it, why he couldn't accept that she had a brain and actually enjoyed using it. On top of that he now wanted her to get married, something Farah vehemently did not want to do. As far as she could tell there were two types of men in the world: those who treated their wives well and those who didn't. But neither was conducive to a woman's overall independence and happiness.

Her father, she knew, was acting from the misguided belief that all women needed a man's protection and guidance and she was fast running out of ways to prove otherwise.

She sighed and rolled onto her other side. It didn't help

that her once childhood friend had asked if he could court her. Amir was her father's right-hand man and he believed that a marriage between them was a perfect solution all round. Unfortunately, Amir was cut from the same cloth as her father, so Farah did not.

To add insult to injury, her father had just banned her from obtaining any more of her treasured Western magazines, blaming them for her 'modern' ideas. The truth was that Farah just wanted to make a difference. She wanted to do more than help supply the village with contraband educational material and stocks of medical supplies. She wanted to change the plight of women in Bakaan and open up a world for them that, yes, she had read about—but she knew she had zero chance of doing that if she were married.

Probably she had zero chance anyway but that didn't stop her from trying and occasionally pushing her father's boundaries.

Feeling frustrated and edgy, as if something terrible was about to happen, she readjusted her pillow and fell into an uneasy sleep.

The sense of disquiet stayed with her over the next few days, right up until her friend came racing up to where she was mucking out the camel enclosure and made it ten times worse.

'Farah! Farah!'

'Steady, Lila.' Farah set aside her shovel while her friend caught her breath. 'What's wrong?'

Lila gulped in air. 'You're not going to believe this but Jarad just returned from your father's secret camp and—' She winced as she took in another big breath of air, lowering her voice even though there was no one around to hear her but the camels. 'He said your father has kidnapped the Prince of Bakaan.'

CHAPTER TWO

FEELING HORRIBLY GUILTY that she had been enjoying her own time while her father was away, Farah raced to the ancient stables and saddled her beloved white stallion. If what Lila said was true then her father could face the death penalty and her heart seized.

As if he could sense her turmoil, Moonbeam whinnied and butted his head against her thigh as she saddled him. 'It's okay,' she said, knowing she was reassuring herself more than the horse. 'Just go like the wind. I don't have a good feeling about this.'

Riding into the secret camp a short time later, she reined in Moonbeam and handed him off to one of the guards to rub down. As it was dusk the camp was getting ready to bed down for the night, the tarpaulin tents shifting and sighing with the light breeze that lifted her *keffiyeh*. The camp was set up with mountains on one side and an ocean of desert on the other and she usually took a moment to appreciate the ochre tones in the dying embers of the evening sun.

Not tonight, though. Tonight she was too tense to think about anything other than hoping Lila was wrong.

'What are you doing here?' Amir asked curtly as she approached her father's tent, his arms folded across his chest, his face tense.

'What are you?' She folded her arms across her own

chest to show him she wasn't intimidated by his tough guy antics. He'd been her friend once, for Allah's sake.

'That's not your concern.'

'It is if what I just heard is true.' She took a deep breath. 'Please tell me it isn't.'

'War is men's business, Farah.'

'War?' The word squeaked out of her on a rush of air and she let out a string of choice words under her breath. Amir looked at her with the disapproving frown he wore ever since he had asked her father for her hand in marriage; the boy she had once played with, and who had taught her to use a sword when she'd been twelve and full of anger and despair over the death of her pregnant mother, seemingly long gone. 'So it's true.' Her voice dropped to barely a whisper. 'The Prince of Bakaan is here?'

Amir's lips tightened. 'Your father is busy.'

'Is he in there?'

She'd meant the prince but he'd misunderstood. 'He won't want to see you right now. Things are…tense.'

No kidding. You could have cut the air in the camp with a knife. 'How did this happen?' she demanded. 'You know my father is old and bitter. You're supposed to look out for him.'

'He is still leader of Al-Hajjar.'

'Yes, but—'

'Farah? Is that you?' Her father's voice boomed from inside the tent.

Farah's insides clenched. As much as her father's controlling and chauvinistic ways chafed—a lot—he was all she had in the world and she loved him. 'Yes, Father.' She swept past a disgruntled Amir and entered the plush interior of her father's retreat, lit from within by variously placed oil lamps.

The roomy tent was divided into sleeping and eating areas with a large bed at one end and a circle of cushions at the other. Worn rugs lined the floor to keep out the night-time chill and silk scarves were draped from the walls.

Her father looked tired as he sat amongst the cushions, the remnants of his evening meal set on a low table before him.

'What are you doing here, girl?'

Looking out for you, she wanted to say but didn't. Theirs had never been an overly demonstrative relationship even when her mother had been alive. Then, though, at least things had been happier and she'd tried so hard to get that feeling back in the years since.

Frown lines marred his forehead and his hands were clasped behind his broad back, his body taut. If she'd been a boy she would have been welcomed into this inner sanctum but she wasn't and maybe it was time she just accepted that. 'I heard that you have the Prince of Bakaan here,' she said in a 'please tell me it isn't true' voice.

He stroked his white beard, which she knew meant he was thinking about whether to answer her or not. 'Who told you?'

Farah felt as if a dead weight had just landed on her shoulders. 'It's true, then?'

'The information needs to be contained. Amir, see to it.'

'Of course.'

Not realising that Amir had followed her in, she turned to him, her eyes narrowing as she noticed that one of his eyes was blackened. 'Where did that come from?'

'Never mind!'

Farah wondered if it was from the prince and turned back to her father. 'But why? How?'

Amir stepped forward, his jaw set hard. 'Prince Zachim arrogantly assumed he could go dune driving in the middle of the night without his security detail.'

Ignoring him, Farah addressed her father. 'And?'

'And we took him.'

Just like that?

Farah cleared her throat, trying not to imagine the worst. 'Why would you do that?'

'Because I will not see another Darkhan take power and he is the heir.'

'I thought his older brother was the heir.'

'That dog Nadir lives in Europe and wants nothing to do with Bakaan,' Amir answered.

'That is beside the point.' She shook her head, still not comprehending what her father had done. 'You can't just… *kidnap a prince!*'

'When news gets out that Prince Zachim is out of the picture, the country will become more and more destabilised and we will be there to seize the power that has always been rightfully ours.'

'Father, the tribal wars you speak of were hundreds of years ago. And they won. Don't you think it's time to put the past to rest?'

'No, I do not. The Al-Hajjar tribe will never recognise Darkhan rule while I am leader and I can't believe my own daughter is talking like this. You know what he stole from me.'

Farah released a slow breath. Yes, the king's refusal to supply the outer regions of Bakaan with basic medical provisions, amongst other things, had inadvertently led to the death of her mother and her unborn brother—everything her father had held dear. Farah tried not to let her own misery at never quite being enough for her father rise up and consume her. She knew better than anyone that wanting love—relying on love—ultimately led to pain.

Her father continued on about everything else the Darkhans had stolen from them: land, privileges, freedom. Stories she'd heard at her bedtime for so long she sometimes heard them in her sleep. Truth be told, she actually agreed with a lot of what her father said. The dead King of

Bakaan had been a selfish, controlling tyrant who hadn't cared a jot for his people. But kidnapping Prince Zachim was not, in her view, the way to correct past wrongs. Especially when it was an offence punishable by imprisonment or death.

'How will this bring about peace and improve things, Father?' She tried to appeal to his rational side but she could see that he had a wild look in his eyes.

Her father shrugged. 'The country won't have a chance of overthrowing the throne with him on it. He's too powerful.'

Yes, Farah had heard that Prince Zachim was successful and powerful beyond measure. She had also heard he was extremely good-looking, which had been confirmed by the many photos she'd seen of him squiring some woman or another to glamorous events. Not that his looks were important on any level!

She rubbed her brow. 'So what happens now? What was the Bakaan council's response?'

For the first time since she'd walked in, her father looked uncertain. He rose and paced away from her, his hands gripped behind his back. 'They don't know yet.'

'They don't know?' Farah's eyebrows knit together. 'How can they not know?'

'When I am ready to reveal my plans, I will do so.' Which told Farah that he didn't actually have a plan yet. 'But this is not something I am prepared to discuss with you. And why are you dressed like that? Those boots are made for men.'

Farah scuffed her steel-capped boots against the rug. She'd forgotten that she still wore old clothes from working with the camels, but seriously, they were going to discuss her clothing while he held the most important man in the country hostage? 'That's not important. I—'

'It is important if I say it is. You know how I feel.'

'Yes, but I think there are more…pressing things to discuss, don't you?'

'Those things are in play now. There is nothing that can be done.'

A sudden weariness overcame him and he flopped back onto the cushions, his expression looking suspiciously like regret. Farah's heart clenched. 'Is he…is he at least okay?' She cringed as visions of the prince beaten up came into her head. She knew that would only make things worse— if that was even possible.

'Apart from the son of a dog refusing to eat, yes.'

'No doubt he thinks the food is poisoned,' she offered.

'If I wanted him dead, I'd use my sword,' her father asserted.

'How very remiss of him.' Fortunately her sarcasm went over his head, but it didn't escape Amir, who frowned at her. She rolled her eyes. She knew he thought she overstepped the boundaries with her father but she didn't care. She couldn't let her father spend his last years in prison— or, worse, die.

'Perhaps that is the answer,' Amir mused. 'We kill him and get rid of the body. No one could pin his death on us.'

Farah gave him a fulminating glare. 'I can't believe you said that, Amir. Apart from the fact that it's completely barbaric, if the palace found out, they would decimate our village.'

'No one would find out.'

'And no one is going to die, either.' She shoved her hands on her hips and thought about how to contain the testosterone in the room before it reached drastic levels. 'I will go and see him.'

'You will not go near him, Farah,' her father ordered. 'Dealing with the prisoner is a man's job.'

Wanting to point out that her father was doing a hatchet job of it if the prince was refusing to eat, Farah wisely kept her mouth shut. Instead she decided to take matters into her own hands.

'Where are you going?'

She stiffened as Amir called out to her in a commanding tone. Slowly she pivoted back around to face him. 'To get something to eat,' she said tightly. 'Is that okay?'

He had the grace to look slightly uncomfortable. 'I would like to speak with you.'

She knew he was waiting on her answer as to whether she would accept his courtship but she wasn't in the mood to face his displeasure when she told him no. 'I don't have anything to say to you right now,' she informed him.

His jaw tensed. 'Wait for me outside.'

Farah smiled sweetly. Like that was going to happen!

Quickly stepping out of the tent, she took a moment to pull her headdress lower and bent her head to shield her eyes against the setting sun. The air temperature had already dropped and the nearby tents flapped in the increasing wind. She looked for signs of a storm but found nothing but a pale blue sky. That didn't mean one wasn't coming. In the desert they came out of nowhere.

Deciding not to waste time on food, she stomped off to the only tent that had a guard posted outside, anger rolling through her. Anger at her father for his outrageous actions and anger at the prince himself—the lowly offspring of the man who had inadvertently caused her mother's death and changed her once-happy life forever.

She tried to get her emotions under control but it felt like she was fighting a losing battle. Still, she needed to remain calm if she was going to work out a way to get her father out of this mess before he did something even more insane—like listen to Amir!

CHAPTER THREE

ZACHIM SHIFTED HIS hands and feet and felt the ropes chafe his wrists and one of his ankles where it had slipped beneath his jeans. His stomach growled.

Ordinarily he wouldn't say he was a man who angered easily. Three days in this hellhole at the hands of a bunch of mountain heathens had ensured that his temper not only festered, but also boiled and blistered as well. And it wasn't just directed outwards. It had been stupid to drive so far from the city without alerting anyone as to where he was going.

He rubbed the ropes binding his wrists against the small sharp stone hidden in his lap. He'd picked it up when he'd 'fallen' during a toilet break the day before. Since refusing to eat, his ropes had not been checked, which was to his advantage, because it had taken that long to work through the thick layers, but he was just about there. Once his hands were free it would be a simple matter to untie his ankles and get the hell out of there.

He leant his head against the solid wooden post he was secured to by a length of rope circling his waist. It allowed him enough room to lie down on the dusty ground but that was it. What he wouldn't give for the comforts of his soft bed back at the palace. Ironic when he considered that three days ago he'd been looking for a way to leave the stifling walls of the place.

Be careful what you wish for, he thought grimly.

He wondered what had happened in his absence and how his brother was dealing with the fallout from his disappearance. He also wondered why he hadn't heard any search helicopters fly overhead.

Flexing stiff muscles that had been bound for too long, he tried to ignore the fact that his stomach was trying to eat itself. He'd been in worse situations during his stint in the army, though he wouldn't wish that on anyone. Okay, maybe he'd wish it on Mohamed Hajjar and his pompous second-in-command who thought himself mightier than a prince.

The sound of footsteps pausing at the entrance of his tent brought his head up and he shoved the sharp rock beneath him. When the flap was raised he feigned sleep, hoping that whoever had arrived would leave quickly so he could get on with sawing at his bindings. If they were checked now there was no way the person wouldn't notice what he'd been up to.

With his senses on high alert, he listened to the sound of the soldier's footfalls. A lightweight, he decided. About one hundred and twenty pounds. Someone he could take easily if it came to that. Unable to smell food, he wondered what the soldier wanted. It was too soon for a toilet break so he kept his features impassive. Whoever it was had gone a few too many rounds with a camel, by the smell of them.

'I know you're not asleep,' a low, sexy voice murmured, sending ripples of awareness across his skin. Hell, that was some voice the soldier had, and he slowly peeled his eyes open, curiosity getting the better of him. He took in black steel-capped boots and combat trousers and moved up the slender figure from the dusty midthigh-length tunic that covered a small pair of breasts plumped up by rigidly folded arms. His gaze lifted to an unsmiling but feminine face that was shadowed by the tribe's traditional red-checked *keffiyeh*. Not a guy, then—a relief, given his body's instant reaction to the voice.

'And I know you're not a man even though you're dressed like one. I didn't know Hajjar allowed women in his army of rebels.'

She stiffened slightly. 'Who I am is not important.'

Zach leant his head back against the pole and watched her. She was quite petite overall and was probably less than one twenty, now that he got a good look at her. Maybe one ten, he assessed with the clinical precision left over from his army days.

The taut silence lengthened between them but he knew it wouldn't take her long to break it. Her energy was twitchy despite her outwardly cool composure.

'I want to make a deal with you,' she finally said.

A deal?

The rage he'd been feeling earlier that had been eclipsed momentarily by curiosity returned with full force. He controlled it but barely. 'Not interested.' He knew Nadir would be looking for him—and if he didn't get here soon he had his own escape plans—and then he'd bring hell down on Mohamed Hajjar for holding him like this.

The girl's eyes flashed darkly before she subdued them. 'You haven't heard what I'm offering yet.'

'If you wanted to gain my attention you should have worn less.' He raked her body with his impassive gaze. 'A lot less. Possibly nothing at all, although even then I'm not sure you have what it takes to hold my interest.'

A lie, because for some reason she already had it. But his taunt had hit its mark if her little gasp was anything to go by.

'My father is right. You're a lowly dog who doesn't deserve to rule our country.'

'Your father?'

Farah Hajjar? Mohamed's daughter? Well, well, wasn't

that interesting? His gaze raked her again and he nearly smiled when he caught the self-disgusted look that crossed her face at her mistake. He hadn't expected the old guy to send his daughter to do his bidding. Was he hoping Zach would somehow be seduced into making a deal? If he was, he was going to be disappointed because, despite his reaction to her voice, Zach had never been attracted to Bakaani women. A shrink would no doubt tell him that it was because of the amount of arranged marriages his father had tried to foist on him. But Zach just preferred blondes. 'I didn't think your father considered himself a part of Bakaan but it's nice to know that he still does.'

'He…' She stopped and Zach could see she was trying to rein her temper in. She took a deep breath and slammed her hands on her hips, drawing his attention to their feminine curve. *Not going to help, sweetheart.*

'If you agree to let our region formally separate from Bakaan,' she said, 'I'll let you go.'

'*You'll* let *me* go?'

He laughed and she paced away from him, her stride long, and he realised she wasn't as small as he'd first assumed: maybe five-seven, five-eight. She stopped abruptly, facing him. 'Your family has suppressed our people for long enough.'

Now that was something he couldn't argue with. He didn't condone how his father had ruled Bakaan, and he'd even considered launching a coup against him himself, but his mother would have been devastated. 'I haven't done anything to the people of Bakaan.' But he couldn't allow her tribe to secede from the kingdom because others might follow and the country would get picked over by their neighbours, seeking to secure Bakaan's oil reserves for themselves.

'You haven't done anything *for* them either,' she countered, 'even though you've been back and have controlled the army for the last five years.'

'And when was the last time that army attacked any of your people, or any other country, for that matter?' Zach bit out, surprised that her attitude had got to him.

'You're saying you're responsible for peace?' She scoffed.

'I'm saying that, for all your big talk, your father has potentially instigated a war by his current actions. Not me.' Her face paled at that and his eyes narrowed. 'Something to think about, *sweetheart*, before you run off at the mouth with your uneducated accusations!'

'You only think they're uneducated because I'm a woman. I know more than you think, *Your Highness*.'

She loaded his title with as much derision as she could muster, which was a pretty impressive amount. But her spunk only irritated him more. 'A woman?' he taunted. 'I've known skunks that smell better than you. I would advise against marketing the scent. It's not all that appealing.'

Her eyes flashed darkly in the dying light. 'As if I would want to appeal to you,' she returned scathingly.

Zach nearly laughed at her haughty tone. He'd yet to come across a woman who didn't want to appeal to him. Good genes, a good bank account and what sounded like a good title went a long way to impressing the female population. He raised his hands in the air and cocked an eyebrow. 'Untie my hands, little heathen, and I'll soon change your mind.'

He almost heard her teeth grind together from across the room at his suggestive tone and, just as she was about to launch into what he could only imagine was another cutting admonition of his character, the tent flap was once again pushed aside and Hajjar's second-in-command sauntered in, bearing a dish of food. The smell hit Zach instantly and made his stomach curl in on itself.

Obviously surprised to see Mohamed's daughter, he pulled up short. 'What are you doing here?' he bit out.

Zach saw her chin snap up and her eyes shoot daggers. 'I can handle this, Amir,' she murmured icily.

'No, you can't.'

She responded in hushed tones and Zach avidly followed their furiously whispered interaction. She clearly had a personal relationship with the soldier and for some inexplicable reason he was disappointed.

Not wanting to dwell on why that was, he focused on the soldier's face. He wasn't at all happy with whatever it was she was saying but he clearly lacked the *baydot* to do anything about it. Idiot. All she needed was a sound kissing and she'd see reason.

A sound kissing?

He nearly chocked at the absurdity of the thought. His ancestors might have behaved that way, but since when did he think kissing a woman into submission was an acceptable mode of conduct for a man? And who would want to kiss this smelly little spitfire anyway?

Disgusted with his interest in their argument, he drew up his knees and used their distraction to work at his bindings.

Too soon the woman won and took the bowl of food from the soldier's hands. Needing more time alone, Zach goaded him by asking where he'd misplaced his *baydot*. The soldier stiffened. So did the spitfire.

She whirled on him, all fire and ice. Maybe 'spitfire' was too tame a word to describe her. She was more like a wild little cat with her dark, almond-shaped eyes and pursed lips.

'Come, Farah.'

The girl rounded on the other man and, for all that Zach didn't like him, he felt himself wince for the guy. 'He's just trying to rile you,' she bit out.

Not stupid, then, Zach mused with reluctant admiration.

'He is dangerous,' the soldier returned. And he should know, since it had taken six of them to subdue him.

'And tied up,' she pointed out impatiently. 'Which I have no plans to change.' But Zach did and he felt another coil of rope give as he put more pressure on it.

'What *are* your plans?'

Fascinated by the changed tension in the air, Zach stilled his movements. He sensed there was more behind that question than met the eye. The girl obviously did, too, but her scrunched brow indicated that she didn't understand the meaning behind his question.

He wants in your pants, sweetheart, if he hasn't been there already.

She released a slow breath. 'Just give me five minutes here. I'll meet you in the dinner tent.'

Slightly mollified, the soldier nodded tersely. He sneered at Zach before stalking out of the tent, letting the flap drop back loudly into place.

She stared at it, brooding.

'Trouble in paradise, little cat?' Zach offered, as if they were old friends taking tea together.

His question snapped her out of her reverie and she marched back to him. 'Be quiet. And don't call me that.'

'I thought you wanted me to speak.'

She glanced down at the small metal bowl in her hand and frowned. 'What I want is for you to eat.'

Zach's stomach agreed with her. 'I'm not hungry.'

She scoffed. 'What is the point of starving yourself? You'll die.'

'So nice of you to care.'

'I don't.'

Her condescending attitude and lack of respect annoyed the hell out of him and he was starting to get some inkling as to the reasoning behind his ancestors' methods of subduing a woman. He wouldn't mind having this one bow down at his feet and acknowledge his superior position to hers. 'You know, your father might want to send someone with better interpersonal skills to plead for leniency next time,' he suggested testily.

Damn, but the urge to have this man bow and scrape at her feet was so strong Farah nearly pulled her small dagger out from inside the hidden pocket in her tunic and made him do it. His attitude was truly irritating.

As were those piercing golden eyes. Lion's eyes. They said so much and nothing at all, just stared back at her as if he knew something that she didn't. With the few days' worth of beard growth covering his angular jaw, those implacable eyes made him seem harshly masculine and deeply imposing even though he was sitting on the ground. The tightly coiled energy he emanated made her think of a cobra about to strike. Or an eagle about to take flight and rip its prey to shreds. He wore a dusty black shirt that stretched across broad shoulders and jeans that hugged what looked to be powerful thighs, the muscles bunching periodically when he looked at her.

She'd known he was incredibly good-looking from the magazine pictures she'd seen, but with his aristocratic features, wide mouth and pitch-black, neatly cropped hair, he was something else in the flesh. Not that she cared.

'I have not come to plead for leniency,' she assured him.

'Lucky.' His eyes trapped hers in a challenging stare. 'Because when I get out of here I have no intention of giving it.'

Her mouth twisted. 'Perhaps you need a little longer to think about your position,' she suggested, glancing pointedly at his bound hands.

'Perhaps I do,' he drawled carelessly.

Oh, but he was getting under her skin! She stared him down for another few minutes and then gave up. This wasn't a contest, even though he seemed determined to turn it into one. 'Nevertheless...' she began, pausing when his hands clenched in his lap yet again. She made a mental note to check his bindings before she left. The last thing she needed was to return him damaged. It would only fare worse for her father. 'You are not going to die on my watch.'

'And there I was thinking that our plans weren't in alignment.' He smiled and Farah felt an unfamiliar jolt of heat deep in her belly. His teeth gleamed whitely against his dark stubble and she scowled to cover her unexpected reaction. The man was dangerous; his cavalier attitude in the face of his imprisonment was proof enough of that even before one took in the breadth of those shoulders.

Determined not to be intimidated, Farah crouched down in front of the high and mighty Prince of Bakaan. She watched as he blatantly worked his gaze over her from head to toe and for a moment she couldn't move; a horrible urge to arch her spine and thrust her breasts out for his inspection making her nipples pull tight.

Rocked to her core by the inclination she noticed his eyelids had lowered to half-mast making her feel both hot and cold all over, her sense of danger heightened like never before.

The silence between them lengthened and Farah became aware that her breathing was shallow and that her clothing felt rough against her skin. She couldn't seem to drag her eyes away from his perfectly proportioned mouth and, as if he sensed her inner turmoil, one corner of it tilted knowingly. More annoyed than ever, she shifted her weight to the balls of her feet, slowly raised the bowl between them and offered it to him.

He didn't look at the food. Instead his golden eyes held hers in such a way that made her discomfort levels hit an all-time high. 'If you're so interested in getting me to eat, then you feed me, my feral little cat.'

Feral little cat? The shock of those soft words had Farah rocking back on her heels as feminine pride kicked in. She might not look her best but she was hardly feral! And as for feeding him... She felt steam rising out of her ears. Even tied up and at her mercy he assumed the superior position. 'I have no intention of feeding you,' she snapped.

He gave a soft, deep chuckle that took up residence in the pit of her stomach. 'Well, there goes that fantasy.'

Farah's mouth tightened at the taunt. He'd already made it clear he thought she was lacking in the female department so his comments could only be to try and throw her off. Though to what end, other than to rile her, she didn't know.

It was obvious he didn't believe she would take him up on his challenge to feed him—and normally she wouldn't even think of doing so, but there was something about this insolent prince that rubbed her up the wrong way. Plus, she'd dealt with dusty, stubborn camels her whole life so one dirty, scruffy male would be no different. Involuntarily her eyes dropped to his body. It was difficult to see the full extent of his physique in his current position but there was no doubt he emanated a masculine power she hadn't come across before. Or had never noticed.

She glanced at his hands and the rope around his waist that kept him tethered to the post. The sense of menace and danger that cloaked him made her think twice about her next actions while the wicked glint in his eyes goaded her on. But it wasn't as if he could actually do anything to her, tied as he was.

A shiver went through her anyway and she lifted her chin. 'If I feed you, will you eat?'

One dark eyebrow lifted lazily and dense ebony lashes lowered slowly to shield his eyes. 'You'll need to get closer to find out.'

Farah ignored the sudden leap of her pulse at his words. Better just to get this over and done with and she'd have one thing accomplished. And wasn't it true that a man with a full stomach had a better disposition than one with an empty one? Maybe then he'd be more amenable to seeing reason.

Besides, she had something to prove. This was nothing more than a classic power play and she would not let him see that he intimidated her. Not that he did, exactly; it was just that any animal handler knew that you approached an un-known beast with caution. Particularly a large, predatory one.

Deciding that, like cleaning the privy, thinking about the deed was worse than actually doing it, Farah clenched her jaw and dug the tips of her fingers into the fragrant meat dish. She had to shuffle even closer to him and his male scent rose to mingle with the food. Logically he should have smelt like a pair of damp old socks. He didn't. He smelt of man and sweat and heat.

Heat?

What did heat even smell like?

That was about as relevant to her current objective as the shape of his mouth. Quickly, before she could change her mind, she scooped out a portion of meat and rice, care-ful to keep the bowl close to catch any drips, and leaned forward onto the balls of her feet before raising her fin-gers to his mouth.

In this position she was almost straddling him and she flushed hotly as unexpected images of the two of them naked and entwined came into her head. A year ago she'd seen a sexy magazine spread of a man and a woman pre-tending to make love. She'd felt a momentary jolt of cu-riosity at seeing them but it was nothing compared to the jolt she was feeling now. She'd always viewed sex as a means of procreation, not pleasure. So why had her mind transplanted the skimpily clad models in the magazine with the two of them? It was so clear she could almost picture the prince's powerful body lying beneath her own; she could almost see herself sitting astride him; could almost feel the press of his ribs against her inner thighs. She squeezed them together unconsciously and heat bloomed there, catching her off guard.

The walls of the tent seemed to draw in around her as she fought to contain her body's visceral reaction to her thoughts and she frowned as the prince's firm lips remained resolutely closed. Exasperated, she lifted her eyes to his, the angry tirade she was about to unleash on him dying on her tongue as he chose that moment to lean forward and draw the rice and meat—and her fingers—inside his warm mouth.

As soon as her fingers slipped inside his lips, his tongue curled around them to claim the food. She felt its warm, thick moistness and shuddered at the rush of liquid heat between her legs and the tingling sensation that caused her nipples to tighten. She'd never experienced anything like this and she couldn't tear her eyes from his.

Dimly aware that she was all but panting, she was completely mesmerised by the way he licked and sucked on her fingers, some deep part of her consciousness trying to tell her that her fingers were now well and truly clean. Still she allowed him to linger, another part of her consciousness urging her to replace her fingers with her mouth. It was so overpowering it was all she could do not to lean in and…

Realising she was about to topple into him, she felt a fire rise up to consume her face and jerked back. Before she could remove her fingers, however, he gripped her wrist and stroked his tongue in between the webbing.

'I think I missed a bit,' he murmured in a rough voice that worked like a sanding tool over her sensitive skin. His tongue flicked back and forth, back and forth, in a purely sensual exploration, before gently biting down on her sensitive palm.

A small whimper escaped her lips and her fingers curled against his beard-roughened face, her body swaying toward his. Almost absently she was aware that a warning voice had started clanging inside her brain but his hand was pressing hers closer. His hand that was…that was…

By Allah! Farah's eyes flew to his as it finally registered that his hands were free, only to find him staring into hers with a knowing gleam. Immediately she tried to wrench herself free and the small metal bowl hit the dirt as she valiantly pushed against him. Unfortunately he was on her quicker than lightning could fork into the ground and she was on her back before she had time to blink.

Slightly winded from the way he tossed her onto the ground, Farah twisted away from him to scream, but the back of her head hit the dirt as his large hand clamped over her mouth. 'Oh, no, you don't. There will be no calling the cavalry just yet, sweetheart.'

Farah squirmed beneath the weight of his upper body and knew it was futile to push against him. He was too strong. And it wasn't just from lean, hard-packed muscle either. One look into his furious face and she could see that he'd leashed his rage so successfully she hadn't realised how deep it ran. Although she *should* have, and perhaps she *would* have, if she hadn't been stupidly distracted by his masculinity and her own rioting hormones.

Knowing she could never throw him from this angle, she tried desperately to get her hands beneath her tunic to her hidden dagger that had saved her skin a few times in the past. Admittedly those times had been from snakes and scorpions, but hadn't she already noted that this man was just as dangerous as any predator? Having learnt how to use a dagger and to fight with a sword when she was younger, Farah knew just where to threaten him with it so that he'd let her go. But it was as if he could read her mind because he caught her wandering hand in his and brought it over her head.

Frantic at the ease with which he contained her, she desperately curled her fingers towards his skin in the hope of causing some damage but he pressed the hand against her mouth more firmly and brought her eyes to his.

'Scratch me, little cat, and I'll scratch you back,' he growled close to her ear.

Farah paused at the menace in those words but then she realised that he would have to let her go to scratch her so she didn't care. She kicked out, catching his shin with the solid point of one boot, and scratched at his wrists at the same time.

'Damn it to hell!' He cursed softly and stretched her arms high to breaking point, pinning her legs down with one of his. Farah moaned behind his hand. She was struggling to draw oxygen into her lungs and was thankful when he adjusted his palm a little to ease her growing dizziness.

'Follow my instructions and I won't hurt you,' he promised.

Ha! As if she believed that. His family had been hurting the people of Bakaan for centuries and tyranny ran in his veins as surely as the blood she'd just drawn on his wrist.

The weight of him felt like an anvil slowly crushing her chest and Farah was just wondering how she could lever her legs to help dislodge him when she felt him go still above her.

'Damn it, keep still.'

His rough tone compelled her to stop fighting him and she was completely unprepared when he flipped her onto her stomach. Before she could pull in another breath, he had her hands wrapped in the same rope that should still have bound his own.

Sand coated her eyelashes and filled her nose and she tried to turn her head before she suffocated. It was then that she felt his hand smoothing over her bottom and fear turned her as cold as stone. Surely he wasn't going to... going to...?

'Easy, little spitfire.' He brought his hand up to the side of her face and she felt the cool blade of her dagger flat against her cheek. 'Quite a nice little piece. I could have used this a couple of days ago,' he said mockingly. 'Do you even know how to use it?'

Trust him to think that she wouldn't be able to handle a knife. Her eyes flashed with annoyance but she wasn't going to tell him anything. Not that she could with his hand pressed against her mouth. But she could still make sounds, she realised, and although she couldn't hear anyone walking outside she knew there was a guard nearby. If he heard something, he'd come running.

Squirming beneath him, she tugged against the rope and screamed behind his hand.

Immediately his thumb and forefinger pinched her nose and her ears popped as she tried to force the sound out of her lungs. She thrashed her head from side to side even though she knew it was futile.

'This is how it's going to go,' he murmured when she finally exhausted herself. 'I'm going to take my hand away from your mouth and you're going to stay quiet.'

Farah listened but she knew there was no way she was going to follow his orders.

'If you don't, you'll surely bring the guard in from outside and I'll be forced to kill him with *your* dagger.'

Fear kept her immobile. It was one thing to risk her own life but she'd never risk another person's.

Roughly he pulled her to her feet. 'Nod if you're going to comply.'

CHAPTER FOUR

FOR A MOMENT Zach thought he was going to have to knock her out cold and he didn't want to do that. In order to get out of the camp, he needed her to lead him to the horses without drawing too much attention to them.

Fortunately she had no idea how important she was to his escape and she nodded curtly. Slowly Zach drew his hand back and she immediately pressed her lips together as if he'd hurt them. Probably he had. She'd fought like a little wild thing and he was surprised at how strong she was. He was surprised at how slender and soft she had felt beneath him as well, and at how beautiful her face was—oh, not classically, like the faces of many of the women he'd dated, but there was something about the slant of her cheekbones and those bottomless brown eyes that made him want to sink into them. Her smooth skin and sexy-as-sin mouth didn't hurt, either.

With her *keffiyeh* having come off during their struggle, he ran his eyes over her heart-shaped face and down the long dark plait that rested just above small jutting breasts. She was dishevelled and in need of a bath, her proud little chin tilted upwards as if she wanted to tell him to go to hell, but still he wanted to hear her make that soft little hitch in her voice she'd made when he'd sucked on her fingers.

Hell of a time to get a hard-on, oh mighty pride of the desert.

He looked her over. 'Do you have any other weapons, my little Zenobia?' he asked dulcetly, unwinding the rope from her slender wrists.

She rubbed at them and, even though it was nearly completely dark inside the tent, he could still read her fury and the desire to best him in her eyes. 'As if I'd tell you that.'

'If you don't, I'll be forced to search you.'

'No!' The sharp little word sprang from her lips like an Olympian off the starter's block. 'I don't.'

Zach nearly laughed at the desperation behind her words and wondered if she was afraid of him or afraid of the unexpected chemistry that had ignited between them.

Chemistry he needed to ignore.

'Come.'

Her chin shot up again and she tossed her head like a mare that was being pulled too hard at the bit. 'I'm not going anywhere with you.'

Zach smiled grimly. 'You are. You're about to walk me out of here and take me to the horses. If anyone stops us, you will tell them that you are taking me to your father. You'll then lead me by this rope that will look like it is binding my hands until we get there.'

He could almost hear her thoughts running wild, trying to take an alternate route. He yanked her against him and ignored her shocked gasp and the way his palm fit snugly around the curve of her bottom. He had a moment of questioning his decision, of second-guessing his plan, but he really had no other option. And he'd let her go as soon as they got to the horses. In the meantime, she needed to know that he wasn't about to cop any attitude from her. 'Sound the alarm and I'll kill anyone who stops us.'

The desert was already freezing and he could hear the rising wind beating at the sides of the tent and making a hell of a racket. He had no idea how far Mohamed Hajjar's camp lay from civilisation but he knew it was going to be a long night.

Bending down, he retrieved a length of rope and coiled it around his wrists. He knew an observant guard would notice that his ankles were no longer bound but he was hoping the closing darkness would prevent anyone from noticing that before they got to the horses. Of course, he'd much prefer a high-powered vehicle to climb into, but in the three days he'd been held hostage he hadn't once heard the sound of an engine.

Zach positioned Farah just to the side so he could observe her expression. 'Okay, my little warrior queen, let's go.'

'I'm not your anything.' She kept her face averted but he saw the betraying tremble of her lower lip. For all her attitude, she was afraid of him. Not something he was going to allay even though he had never hurt a woman in his life. Of course, he'd never had cause to before now. Women loved him and he loved them—a much more desirable arrangement than this one.

'Move.' He positioned himself slightly in front of her but, rather than her grabbing his hands, he grabbed hers, laying the small dagger against her inner arm so that she knew who was in charge. 'And don't rush it.'

When she lifted the tent flap he blew out a relieved breath that her boyfriend didn't appear to be in the vicinity.

The nearby guard was, though, and he immediately came to attention when he saw them. He asked Farah if everything was okay and when she hesitated Zach pressed the tip of her sharp dagger against her wrist.

'Fine,' she said through clenched teeth.

'We'll have to brush up on your acting skills but good enough for now,' Zach whispered against her ear and got another whiff of camel. He grimaced and wondered whether she'd been rolling around with them.

'You can't get away. There's a storm brewing.'

Zach had already clocked the incoming storm and his eyes scanned the camp. Many of the men were still filling their stomachs around the campfire and the remaining ones were busy securing the tents against the rising wind. 'I know. Perfect cover.'

She stopped and he nearly ran into her. 'I won't do it,' she hissed out of the side of her mouth.

'Your father will mourn your death, no doubt.'

'You won't kill me.'

Zach crowded her from behind. 'It would be a mistake to underestimate what I would or would not do right now. Have you forgotten who my father was?'

'Pig.' The word was spat towards the sand.

Exactly. Zach urged her forward. 'I'm glad we understand each other. Now, walk and none of your men will die. Hopefully.'

Farah brushed at the strands of her hair that had come loose from her struggles with the prince and which now blew uncontrollably around her face. She was so angry with herself for being duped, she could spit. No doubt this would reinforce for her father that women were best left to domestic chores and had no place getting involved in the business of men. Right now she had to agree because it was her own stupidity that had got her into this mess. As if reading her mind, the hateful prince leaned in close again, his warm breath stirring the loose strands of hair at her temple. 'Don't feel bad about aiding my escape. If it had been anyone else, I would have been forced to kill him.'

That thought gave her little comfort. She had made a mistake and didn't know how to fix things. And she always knew how to fix things. It was her calling card. Everyone in the village came to her when there was trouble. And now she'd caused the trouble—or at least exacerbated it before a solution could be found.

Focusing on the biting cold wind against her face, she willed one of the men around her to notice that something was amiss. Other than a cursory glance, they didn't question her. They trusted her. Trusted her, and she was about to let them down. A well of emotion rose up in her throat and self-pitying tears filled her eyes.

'Stop here.'

The prince's words were low and with a start Farah realised they had already reached the horses. As if sensing her presence, her big stallion trotted over.

'By Allah, he's a monster,' the prince murmured appreciatively.

One of the men had put him in a halter and blanket to ward off the cold and as soon as he reached them he stretched his nose out to her, as if seeking a treat.

'Yours?'

She knew from the tone of his voice that he was going to steal him and she shoved at Moonbeam's muzzle to try and push him away.

At the same time a cry went up from across the camp. It was Amir calling her name; the prince tensed. Relief flooded Farah and she pushed harder at Moonbeam to get him to go. Typically male, he didn't listen so she yelled at him.

More shouts rung out around them and Farah could hear the heavy sound of feet pounding the sand as her father's men rallied. Giving up all pretence that he was still captured, the prince shoved her through the gate, her scream lost on the driving wind. Then suddenly hard hands spanned her waist and her eyes snapped back to the prince's. She saw a moment of indecision cross his face, then she was being lifted, and she instinctively raised her leg to swing it over Moonbeam's neck before she thought better of it.

Seconds later the prince vaulted on behind her and kicked her stallion into action. Being herd animals, the remaining horses fretted and the prince used this to his advantage, wheeling around behind them and forcing them out of the gate.

Before she knew it they were in full flight and all Farah could do was grab Moonbeam's mane as the prince reached around her for the halter and raced them straight into the dark heart of the incoming storm.

Hours later, wet, filthy and exhausted, the prince stopped the now plodding horse. Farah would have slipped from Moonbeam's back if the man behind her hadn't tightened his arm around her waist, the steel-like muscles bunching beneath her breasts as they had so often done over the past few hours.

Some time ago, when the storm had hit hard, he had stopped and pulled off his shirt to tie around Moonbeam's eyes and nose to shield him from the worst of the swirling dust. He'd then cut the bottom of her tunic to make two coverings to keep as much of the sand off their faces, as well.

Feeling wretched, with sand coating every part of her cold, wet body, Farah could have cried with relief when she glanced up to see a rocky incline in front of them.

Jumping down from the stallion's back, the prince reached up and tugged her off, unceremoniously dragging her and her horse under the shelter. It wasn't much, just a narrow crevice really, but it was facing away from the wind. When he released her arm, she swayed and he held her while her legs worked to keep her upright.

Carefully she unwrapped her makeshift headdress and shook it out. She tried to brush some of the sand from her body but she was so wet it only made her cold fingers sting. Instead, she used the torn fabric to brush over Moonbeam's legs to offer him some relief. She could hear the prince shaking out fabric and presumed he had taken his shirt from around the stallion's head. She knew his skin must be sore from where he'd been pelted by the storm.

'Thank you,' she said stiffly.

'For what?' His deep voice sounded beside her and she jumped because she hadn't heard him move and couldn't see a thing in the blackness.

'For protecting my horse.'

'If he had died, so would we,' he bit out.

Okay, so that cleared up any notions she'd had about him being thoughtful. About to move as far away from him as possible she let out a shriek when he put his hands on her shoulders and worked them down to her waist.

Incensed at the invasion of her person, Farah slapped his hands away. 'I told you I don't have any more weapons.'

'Where's your mobile phone?'

Feeling small and helpless compared to his size and strength, she shoved at his wide chest, thankful that it was now covered in fabric. 'Why would I have a mobile phone when our village doesn't have coverage?'

He cursed and moved away from her. Farah let out a pent-up breath and gave a hollow laugh, her arms coming around her body to ward off the chill. 'Swearing won't help, and you only have yourself to blame, because your father refused to spend money on anyone but himself.'

He ignored the jab and once again she heard the rustle of fabric.

'What are you doing?' she demanded as he pulled Moonbeam's blanket off.

'We need this more than he does.'

'You can't just take it off. He'll freeze.'

'He will not freeze. He has a thick coat of hair and he's mostly dry. We are not.'

As if on cue, another huge shiver wracked her body and she rubbed her arms. The wind howled outside their rocky respite but at least it didn't cut right through her any more. Too tired to argue, she dropped to her knees on the hard ground.

'You're too close to the opening there. Come here.'

How he knew her location was beyond her. 'I'm fine.'

'That wasn't a request,' he growled so close to her she jumped again.

'I'm too tired to argue with you' she snapped. 'Just let me be.'

'The way your father let me be?'

Farah closed her eyes. She didn't want to think about why they were in this predicament because she knew her father had been wrong to do what he'd done, even if he did think his reasoning was solid. 'Did I not just say I was too tired to—hey! Put me down!'

'I too am tired, I'm also hungry and angry, so I would advise you not to test the limits of my patience because that ran out three days ago when your father refused to release me. He hasn't had the courage to face me since.'

'My father is not a coward!'

'No?' He placed her on the ground more gently than she expected, given the roughness of his hold. 'So you condone his actions? Or perhaps you assisted him.' When he sat beside her Farah automatically scooted sideways to get away from him but he grabbed her arm and yanked her back. Then he anchored her with his forearm and pulled her backwards until she was lying on her side with him plastered along her back, his knees pressing into the backs of hers.

'I'm not sleeping with you!'

He tugged the horse blanket over the top of them. 'No, you're not. You're sleeping *next* to me. There's a big difference, *habiba*, and believe me you would not be invited to do the former.'

Farah felt her blood boil at his arrogance.

'But there is only one blanket,' he continued, shifting

her even closer. 'And, given that you can't stop shaking, we need to share body heat to warm up. Relax and this will go a lot easier.'

Relax? Farah couldn't have been more tense if he'd pointed a loaded gun at her head. It had been a long time since she had been physically close to anyone and all this bodily contact was messing with her head. 'This isn't right.'

'But kidnapping your prince is fine.'

'Must you always have the last word?' she grumbled.

'Must you?'

Not wanting to find anything remotely amusing about him, Farah curled herself into a tight ball to try to put distance between them. Self-sufficiency was a prized trait in the harsh desert climate and Farah was proud that, although she was female, she could survive on her own if she had to. She wanted to point this out to the prince but that would involve speaking to him and she'd much rather pretend he wasn't there. She'd much rather pretend she was in her own bed than on the cold, hard ground wrapped in the strong arms of her father's number one enemy.

Finally she fell asleep. Thank Allah. Once her trembling had subsided, she'd squirmed around trying to get comfortable to the point that Zach had needed to place a staying hand on her hip to stop her from rubbing her bottom against his burning erection one more time. It was bad enough he even had one let alone her knowing about it.

Realising that his hand was still gripping her hip, he eased it away. He knew his reaction to her was based on his recent bout of celibacy and little else. Maybe the way danger heightened the senses, as well. Whatever it was, he had no intention of acting on it. He wasn't the type to lose his head over anything and one slender spitfire wouldn't change that.

Sighing, he shifted to get comfortable. The little spitfire whimpered in her sleep like a small kitten having a bad dream. He didn't doubt she was and he wondered if it featured a jail cell and the span of twenty years. That brought a small smile to his lips, one that was quickly supplanted by a scowl when she burrowed closer to his warmth. He briefly thought about putting his arm beneath her head to offer his biceps as a pillow but then dismissed the idea. What did he care about her comfort? She might have offered him food earlier and… Damn. Just the thought of her crouching over him and bringing the food to his lips was enough to have his mind spiralling back to what she would look like naked. He'd noticed the telltale flush of arousal on her face when he'd drawn her fingers into his mouth and laved them with his tongue, the way her eyes had glazed with desire. She'd been turned on and, damn it, so was he. Again.

Absently he wondered if she was intimate with the arrogant soldier who had argued with her. He clearly wanted her. Not that Zach cared, but there was definite tension between the two of them. The man was clearly a moron, though, to have left her alone with him. If she had been his woman there was no way he'd have let her have her own way in a dangerous situation. She would be his to take care of. His to protect. And thank Allah she wasn't.

He felt her shiver and curl into a tighter ball. She must still be cold; he damned well was. Cold, hungry, angry and his arms and torso felt like they were covered in a thousand tiny pinpricks from where the sand and rain had pelted him in the storm.

He let out an aggrieved sigh. Farah Hajjar better not give him any trouble in the morning because he was very far from his cool, controlled self.

CHAPTER FIVE

'WAKE UP, ZENOBIA. Time to hustle.'

Hustle?

Groggily Farah came awake and realised the prod in her bottom had been the Prince of Bakaan's foot. Her teeth ground together at the way he mockingly referred to her as a warrior queen from the Roman era. Some warrior she was, allowing him to get the better of her. 'Only if you'll give me back my dagger so I can do to you what she did to Probus.'

She sat up and rubbed the grit from her eyes but still caught the look of surprise on his face. 'Oh, sorry,' she simpered. 'Am I supposed to play the part of the village idiot who isn't anywhere near as learned as the high and mighty prince with his first-class degree?'

He didn't move but she felt his eyes on her like a hot brand. 'Two degrees, actually.'

'Oh, well, excuse me.' She glanced at Moonbeam so she wouldn't have to look at him.

'So you're educated?'

'Self-educated, no thanks to your family's reign.' She flicked him a scathing look. 'But, as much as your father tried to keep us all in the dark, we're a little more resourceful than you might think. Especially when—'

She stopped, suddenly realising she was about to tell him that there was someone on his staff who was supplying the outer tribes with contraband medical and educational goods.

Great going, Farah, she admonished herself. *What a way to get a man fired—or, worse, killed.*

His eyes narrowed. 'When what?'

She brushed sand off her legs. 'Never mind. Why did you kick me?'

'I didn't kick you. I nudged you.' His deep voice made her insides feel unsteady. 'And I wouldn't be Probus in your little fantasy. I'd be Aurelian.'

Aurelian, who had captured Zenobia and ended her reign as queen. She made a rude noise at his arrogance. 'You wish,' she muttered, half under her breath.

He stopped in front of her and she stared at his dusty boots and the way his jeans—so foreign in her part of the world and yet so sexy in the way they moulded to his legs—hung over the top. 'I captured you, didn't I?'

Instant annoyance hit her at his words and she threw her head back to glare at him—only something black and alive dropped to the ground beside her and she let out a blood-curdling scream. The scorpion took off into a nearby crevice and Farah went from paralysed inertia to violently brushing at her clothing in seconds.

Suddenly large hands grasped her upper arms and lifted her to her feet. 'Keep still.' The prince scoured the ground for the offending visitor and released her. 'It's gone.'

Something crawled across her shoulder and she nearly hit the cave roof. 'More! There's more.'

'No, there's not.' The prince's voice seemed to come from far off before he gripped her arms again and shook her gently. 'It's your imagination.'

'My hair,' she gasped. 'They're in my hair.' It was one of those irrational fears she'd struggled to master since her mother's death all those years ago.

With an exaggerated sigh, the prince gently knocked her hands away from her head and turned her around.

Zach's eyes swept over dark chestnut tresses that a bird would think twice about before nesting in. It was long, thick and matted with sand, half of it still in the braid that hung down her back.

Carefully he scanned it for anything moving. 'There is nothing.'

'There is. I can feel...' She shivered and turned towards him. Her eyes were huge in her face and moist from where she held tears at bay. She was afraid he realised; truly petrified. Something inside his chest pulled tight and before he could question the move he dug his fingers into her hair. She stood stock-still but he caught the small tremors of fear racing through her and the need to comfort her overwhelmed everything else.

Smoothing her hair back from her face, he moved behind her to unwind her plait. The dark waves parted beneath his fingers and he found himself studying the lightly tanned skin of her neck. It looked smooth and supple, not unlike the body he had curved around the night before.

Reminding himself that she was as bloodthirsty as her father, he ignored the underlying silky texture of her hair as he combed his fingers through it. Again his body responded to the fact that he was touching her, which only elevated his already soaring stress levels. He should be focused on getting home, not on saving a woman he couldn't care less about from desert insects.

Roughly he turned her back to face him. 'You're clear.'

She stared up at him with those guileless chocolate-brown eyes and he felt a jolt go right through him. Bedroom eyes, he decided, his gaze automatically dropping to her slightly parted lips. Bedroom eyes and soft, kissable lips...

Time seemed to stop as he imagined doing all sorts of unholy things to those lips, starting with his mouth and ending with… The hair on his forearms stood on end and it wasn't the only thing that did.

Hell.

He stepped back and took himself in hand—metaphorically speaking.

Farah stiffened as the prince moved away and grabbed hold of Moonbeam's halter.

She shook off the lethargy that had invaded her limbs as soon as he had touched her, as soon as he had looked at her mouth—as if it were the ripest peach and he couldn't wait to sink his teeth into it. For a tense moment she had thought he might kiss her, and she was ashamed to admit that she had wanted him to. But how could she when he was the kind of man she had vowed to avoid? A man who walked all over others in order to further his own interests. Not to mention the reason behind the situation they were in. 'He needs water,' she muttered, knowing it must be true because her lips were as dry as the desert itself.

'Water and food,' he agreed shortly. 'But unless you can divine it from these rocks he isn't going to get any here. Nor are we.' He patted the stallion. 'He's an impressive animal. What's his name?'

'Moonbeam.'

The laughter that followed her announcement was both warm and strong. 'You should have just gelded him when you named him. It would have been easier on him.'

'Oh, you're hateful.'

'When I want your opinion, I'll ask for it.' He sobered and threaded his fingers together to form a platform. 'Give me your foot.'

'I'm not coming with you!' He had to be mad to suggest it, the hateful, arrogant—

'Fine.' He straightened and vaulted onto Moonbeam as if the stallion was no bigger than a Shetland.

Hold on. 'What are you doing?'

'Leaving.'

'Not on my horse.' She grabbed onto the halter. He couldn't just leave her here without any way of getting home. 'Damn it, why did you have to come into my life?'

He stared down at her. 'I've been asking myself the same question. Now, get on or I'll leave you to become buzzard food.'

Farah thought about telling him to go to hell but knew that she couldn't. Yet. 'This time I'm riding on the back.' No way was she going to be made to feel small and helpless by having his arms wrapped around her again.

'I don't care if you ride on your head. Just move it.'

Knowing this was probably a mistake, but aware that she really had little option, Farah stomped to his side. He'd wrapped part of her dark tunic around his head again and, even though he was as dusty and as unkempt as she was, he managed to look regal and magnificent atop her snorting stallion. When their eyes connected she refused to let herself be swayed by his looks and injected as much venom into her gaze as she could.

Stony-eyed, he reached out his much larger hand for her to take. As soon as she placed hers in it he yanked her up behind him as if she weighed little more than a pillow.

Unfortunately, riding behind him didn't make her feel any better than riding in front, because she was forced to hold tightly to his lean hips as he urged Moonbeam to get them to safety.

Which came in the form of a nearby tribal village some hours later, just when she thought she might expire. The tribe was a fair distance from her own so she knew they had covered a lot of ground the night before, desperation and adrenaline pushing them on. She didn't know anyone in the village, not having much cause to leave her own, and was surprised when their leader bought the prince's charming 'lost in the storm with one of his servants' scenario.

Servant!

Oh, how she wished she could contradict him but the consequences weren't worth it.

With a promise that Moonbeam would be housed until he could return, the prince ate down a mountain of food before borrowing a battered jeep and driving them through most of the afternoon and night, with only the occasional rest for a power nap. Farah didn't know how he kept up the pace and after a night of little rest, slept most of the way.

Awakening just before dawn her eyes were riveted to the changing landscape and the size of the city of Bakaan as they approached the following morning. She'd visited once or twice as a child but she'd forgotten how large it was—and how busy. Even this early the streets were filled with cars, bicycles, oxen and camels with a mass of people dressed in all styles of clothing filling the pavements. Built into a hillside, the Shomas Palace towered over the city in all its golden glory and Farah secretly admired its opulent beauty as Zach identified himself to the guards and drove through the iron gates.

'What do you intend to do with me?' she asked, proud of the way she managed to keep the tremor out of her voice.

Ignoring her question, he jerked the old car to a stop in front of a set of massive stone steps; heat shimmered off the pale sandstone walls of the palace, turning them white. The courtyard they were in was already a hive of activity with a procession of servants rushing around. Farah returned her gaze to the prince's as he rested his hands on the steering wheel, his lion's eyes scanning her face to the point of discomfort.

She raised her chin as if his perusal was nothing more than an irritant. She was hoping he was going to tell her that, now that he was back home, he was going to let her go. That he was going to let the whole thing drop and forget it had even happened. She knew she'd like to. 'Well?' She stared him down. 'Are you going to tell me or not?'

'Yes, I'm going to tell you.' He smiled but it was grim in his hard, beautiful face. 'I'm going to use you as bait.'

Farah fumed as the prince all but dragged her along opulent hallways and past closed doors, servants and guards bowing one after the other as they proceeded; none of them showing an ounce of shock at seeing their prince pulling a woman along roughly by the arm. If possible the interior of the palace was grander than the exterior and Farah's mind buzzed at the wondrousness of the wide hallways and soaring ceilings stencilled in blue, green and gold fretwork prevalent in the Moorish period, the ancient artworks that were framed under bright lights, and the solid marble floor that shone to a high gloss from the sunshine streaming in through high arched windows.

Realising she was letting herself become awestruck, she dug her heels into the polished floor. 'You can't do this.'

Of course he didn't respond to her outraged cry but stopped before an enormous carved door. Ignoring her, he turned towards two guards who had rushed to follow them. 'No one comes in here, no one goes out—is that clear?'

'Yes, Your Highness,' they said in unison.

'I won't let you use me this way,' Farah asserted as he shoved her into the room.

When he gave a short, sharp laugh she stared at him belligerently. 'You have no grounds to hold me.'

The prince turned cold, menacing eyes on her and for the first time she noticed the deep brown ring that bordered all that gold. 'I don't need a reason.'

'Right. Your word is law, is that it?' Farah tossed her filthy hair which she'd replaited after the prince had sifted his fingers through it back over her shoulder.

He stepped into her space and brought his face level

with hers. 'That is it, yes. An eye for an eye. Isn't that what your father believes in?'

Her father did unfortunately hold to that cynical view of the world but Farah didn't.

Dismissing her, he turned towards a maid she hadn't noticed slip into the room behind them. Only half listening to what he was saying to the girl, Farah took in the scope of the opulent room for the first time. And what she saw made her gasp out loud.

'Oh, my…is this the harem?'

'What gave it away?' the prince drawled lazily. 'The cherub motifs on the wall or the large sunken marble tub in the middle of the room?' He walked over to it and raised his foot to rest on the curved edge like the insolent sheikh that he was.

Farah told herself not to react but it was no good. There was something about him that pushed all reason out of her brain and replaced it with…with something she did not want to identify. 'I'm not staying in here.'

'No?' He raised a brow. 'Admittedly the soft furnishings are quite old but it's about to be renovated. Perhaps the updated version will be more to your liking.'

'I won't be around long enough to see it,' she promised.

'Don't be so sure.' He straightened and headed back to her. His nose twitched. 'See that she has a bath,' he said to the maid, although he didn't take his eyes from hers.

See that she… Farah's gaze narrowed into angry slits. If he thought she would just fall in with his plans he was wrong. There was no way she was going to wait around in this horrible room for her father to show up. If she could somehow escape and get back to him she would.

Her silence must have spoken volumes because he cast her a condescending smile. 'I can almost hear your mind ticking over, and if you're thinking of trying to leave I would advise against it.'

Farah angled her chin up and suddenly their faces were

only inches apart, his gaze fixed on her mouth. It was impossible not to be aware of him, and for one—no, two—erratic heartbeats she thought he was going to kiss her and her breath backed up in her lungs. Then he moved away. Slowly.

Incensed that she had stood there like a besotted idiot instead of pushing him away, she lashed out in a show of rash pride. 'Fortunately for me, I don't have to take your advice.'

He regarded her with a cool look that said he knew exactly what he did to her. 'Just try it and see how far you get.'

Oh, she wanted to. She wanted to do that and more. And the feeling only grew worse when he reached the main door and turned back, his gaze raking her from head to toe and making her tingle with hot, impotent fury.

'And burn those clothes she's wearing,' he instructed the maid. 'There's no soap in the world that will kill that smell.'

Striding from the room, Zach was wondering what the hell he was going to do with the spitting she-cat who was more trouble than she was worth when Staph rushed towards him.

'Highness, I just heard of your return. We were all so worried about you.'

Zach grimaced. He needed to bathe, to burn his own clothing and to find his brother in that order. 'I'm back now.' He set off in the direction of his private wing. 'Where's Nadir?'

'Preparing for his wedding.'

That stopped him in mid-stride. 'His what?'

'His wedding, Your Highness. He is marrying mistress Imogen today.'

Today!

Well that at least explained the extraordinary amount of activity he'd noticed in and around the palace.

Hell. Talk about bad timing.

Forgetting all about a shower for now, he left Staph and trawled the palace for Nadir, eventually finding him holding a small dark-haired infant that could only be Zach's new niece. Gazing into her wide-spaced gray-blue eyes, Zach felt something uncurl inside his chest. How was it that his brother had what he had always wanted for himself, while all he could do was think about bedding some woman who was wholly unsuitable for him? The irony of the situation wasn't lost on him. He thought of the email he'd received from Amy, but it wasn't her face that filled his head—it was Farah Hajjar's.

'Where the hell have you been?' his brother barked at him. 'You have a lot of explaining to do.'

Nadir's curt words brought Zach's attention back to the present. '*I* do?' He raised a dust-covered eyebrow. 'Thanks for the concern and the belated rescue team.'

Nadir frowned. 'You look like hell. What happened?'

Knowing now wasn't the time to go into detail, Zach shrugged. 'The short version is that I had an unfortunate run-in with one of the less welcoming tribes in the mountains.'

'Hell. For a while I thought you were holed up with a woman.'

Zach laughed, a ripple of discomfort running through him as he thought about the feel of Farah's surprisingly strong arms wrapped around his belly as they'd raced across the desert on horseback. It had surprised him how alive he had felt—possibly because he'd been imprisoned for three days—and how connected to the desert he'd felt for a change. He'd been surprisingly connected to those soft little breasts nuzzling against his back, as well. 'I suppose technically you could say that I was, but it wasn't by choice, and she's more like a spitting she-cat than a woman. One who is currently locked in the old harem.'

He grimaced as Nadir's eyebrows shot skywards. 'Not the most convenient situation on your wedding day, but then I didn't know it was your wedding day until a moment ago.'

Nadir stared at him as if he had two heads. 'You have a woman locked in the harem?'

'Farah Hajjar, to be exact,' Zach growled, his words laced with disgust.

'Mohamed Hajjar's daughter!'

'One and the same.'

Nadir swore. 'Hajjar will have your head for that.'

Zach's gaze turned wry. 'They both very nearly did.'

'For the love of...' Nadir's gaze narrowed. 'You didn't compromise her, did you?'

Zach gave a sharp bark of laughter. 'A wild boar couldn't compromise that woman, and nor would it want to.' Which should have been the truth, and would be, now that he was back home and out of danger. 'I take it this is my niece?'

'You're changing the subject.'

'I am.' He smiled at her. 'She's beautiful.'

'I know.' He could see that Nadir wanted to ask him more but then he shook his head. 'I don't have time to get the details now, but you're okay?'

'No thanks to you,' he teased his big brother, as he used to when they were boys.

'Ever heard of the boy who cried wolf?' Nadir arched a brow. 'That will teach you for playing so many tricks as a kid.'

Zach grinned. 'Come chat while I get cleaned up.'

'I can't.'

'Why not? The wedding isn't for hours yet.'

'No, but...' Nadir shook his head, clearly distracted by something. 'Here, take your niece and get acquainted.'

He handed the wide-eyed child to him and Zach took her easily. She immediately gazed up at him and he nestled her close. He caught his brother's expression and grinned. 'Hey, don't look so surprised. I'm okay with babies. They're like women and horses—handle them with the utmost care and don't do anything to rub them up the wrong way. Isn't that right, *habibti*?'

Zach immediately thought about the woman he'd left

in the harem. He hadn't exactly handled her with care but
then he hadn't exactly been in the mood to. Then there was
the fact she was more street urchin than woman—except
for those breasts and that mouth.

'Don't let her cut herself on that, and if she cries take
her to Maab.'

Zach smiled down at his niece, who was patting the
scruff on his face. Hell, he must smell terrible, as well.

'Where will you be?' he asked, but Nadir had already
taken off up a flight of stairs and Zach had a feeling he
knew precisely where he was headed. He was about to
call out that it was bad luck to see the bride on his wedding day but let it go.

The baby in his arms gurgled and looked a little uncertain now that her father had disappeared but he gave
her a reassuring smile. It was true what he'd said, horses
and women loved him, and he saw no reason why a baby
would be any different. He bounced her gently in his arms
and stared into her big eyes. 'So, kid, your parents are getting married?' She stared back and he laughed. 'A big step.
Are you happy about it?'

She touched his face again and made a litany of garbled
sounds.

'Great. Then I am, too.'

He wandered around with her for a bit longer and then
sought out Maab when she started fussing.

'I think she's hungry,' he told the elderly woman.

She smiled and cooed at his niece. Then she wrinkled
her nose at him.

'I know, I know.' He backed away, 'I smell like death
warmed up.' He could also do with some more food.

Heading back to his private apartment, he organised a
light meal to be sent up for after his shower and wondered
if the spitfire in the harem was hungry. Then he grimaced.
He'd known immediately that Nadir wasn't happy about

the situation and neither was he. He really didn't have a firm plan as to what he was going to do with her but involving the local police wasn't something he intended to do on his brother's wedding day.

No, she would just have to wait, and perhaps that would be a good thing. His fight wasn't with her but with her father. He had no doubt the old man would be furious that he'd taken Farah, but if Mohamed was prepared to trade himself for her, Zach would let her go.

An eye for an eye.

That was his father's way, not his, yet he was so damned angry right now he didn't care. Fury replacing rational thought. But then being kidnapped, riding through a sandstorm and driving for nearly twenty-four hours would do that to a man. As would wanting to put his hands all over Mohamed Hajjar's spitfire of a daughter. He wondered if she had already completed her bath. Wondered how she would smell when the stink of camel was cleaned from her body. An X-rated fantasy started playing out in his head. A fantasy that entailed both of them wet and naked while he tasted every delicious inch of her.

By Allah, she wasn't even his type.

He scrubbed a wet hand over his face, twisting the shower nozzle to full-on hot, and soaped the stink from his own body. Maybe he'd find a woman he could spend the night with at the wedding. Doubtful, he knew, since he had no idea whether there would be any European women invited, but maybe he'd get lucky. Maybe there would be someone there who was interested in a night of pleasure and relaxation. And Zach was not being immodest in knowing he could give it to her. He was thirty-two and he enjoyed a healthy libido. A healthy libido he'd unhealthily left unattended for too long if his earlier lust for Farah Hajjar was any indication.

He shut off the shower and shook the water from his

hair. There would be no reason for him to have to see Farah Hajjar again after this so it was time to put her from his mind altogether. Something he was very happy about, he mused as he pulled on a clean robe and turned his mind to his brother's wedding.

Dressed and ready to go, Zach was surprised to find Staph knocking on his door. The old man twisted his hands together, his face marred with concern. Immediately Zach wondered if something had happened to Farah. Had she hurt herself? Had someone hurt her?

'What is it, man?' he snapped, uncharacteristically curt. 'Speak up.'

'It's your brother, Your Highness. He has called off the wedding and asked that I send all the guests home.'

Zach shook his head. So much for relaxing once he got home.

Not wasting any time on niceties when he found Nadir seated behind his father's desk, he strode into the room. 'What are you doing?'

His brother looked up at him and smiled as if there was nothing wrong. Which told Zach that something was drastically wrong. 'Working. You look better.'

'It's amazing what a shower and a shave will do.' Zach parked himself in the chair opposite the desk. 'Why are you working? You're getting married in a few hours.'

His brother tried to stare him down but Zach was a master communicator who had always been sensitive to the nuances of others. He was also doggedly determined to get to the bottom of the problem before Nadir completely closed off and made a hash of everything.

Thirty minutes later he'd managed to talk his brother down from the ledge. 'I know you think you're pretty clever,' Nadir said. 'But frankly I wouldn't wish this sick feeling in my gut on anyone.'

Zach shook his head. 'I would love to care for a woman

as much as you do yours,' Again he thought of Amy Anderson and again Farah's face annoyingly intruded. Frustrated that he didn't seemed to have any control over his thoughts, he gritted his teeth. 'Instead,' he began, forcing a lightness into his tone he didn't feel, 'I have to figure out how to stop myself from being shackled to a living, breathing fire-eater who would as soon run me through with a *kanjhar* than look at me.'

'I doubt her father will push it. He hates our family.'

'It's fine.' Zach waved away Nadir's concern, hoping he'd given his brother the right advice. He could think of nothing worse than a man spilling his guts to a woman only to have her politely reject his advances.

Of course there would be nothing polite about Farah Hajjar's rejection...and why the hell was he still thinking about her? 'I can deal with Farah and her insane old man,' he assured his brother. 'You just do us both a favour and go get your woman.'

'Prince Zachim!' At the sound of Staph's breathless cry and harried appearance in the doorway, Zach frowned. Surely he wasn't about to tell him that the sky had fallen in? 'You need to come quick.' Staph drew in another life-saving breath and Zach thought about reminding him that he was too old to be running around the palace like a man half his age. 'The woman you put in the harem has disappeared.'

Zach immediately stilled. 'Disappeared?' He frowned. 'That's impossible. I've put an experienced guard on the door.'

'Yes, my lord,' Staph panted. 'He can't find her.'

Stunned, Zach let off a list of expletives that would have caused his delicate mother to faint if she'd heard him. Surely a slip of a woman like Farah couldn't have bested him?

His brother made a comment but Zach didn't hear it. Within minutes he had rounded up his most trusted guards and was halfway to the harem.

CHAPTER SIX

FARAH STOPPED INSIDE a shadowed doorway to collect herself and get her bearing amidst the labyrinth of busy city streets and buildings. Initially she'd thought there would be no chance of escaping the arrogant prince but in the end it had been remarkably easy.

A workman's forgotten extension ladder in the garden had provided the necessary equipment for her to scale the high wall, and the preparations for some big celebration at the palace had added the perfect cover. In her freshly laundered *abaya*, Farah had looked like any other servant going about her business, or ending her shift with a bunch of others as they headed out of the palace grounds.

Now, standing on a busy street corner, her only goal was to get as far away from the prince as she could and back to her father. First, though, she had to navigate the hot, noisy, dusty city. Glancing at the position of the sun she decided to head north and started zigzagging her way through the moving sea of bodies around her.

She knew that asking for help wasn't an option. She had a feeling if she tried to hitch a ride from a passing motorist he'd probably take her to the police. And what would she tell them—that the Prince of Bakaan planned to use her as bait to bring her father out to charge him with kidnapping? Not going to happen.

Glancing left and right, Farah hurried down a narrow

walkway with high buildings on either side and found herself in a large, quiet square that gave off a bad vibe. She kept the scarf on her head pulled firmly forward and moved with purpose in case anyone tried to stop her.

'Hot afternoon for a stroll, Miss Hajjar.' That deep, taunting voice she had grown to hate had her swinging round towards a nearby alley. Squinting into the shadows she could just make out the prince's imposing shoulders before he stepped into the sunshine. 'I have to confess I usually prefer to stay indoors when it's this hot.'

Farah's body temperature just grew a little hotter. He'd found her! How was that possible? She was sure no one had noticed her leave and as far as the maid was concerned she was planning to have a sleep. Frustration zinged through her as he leant one shoulder lazily against the sandstone wall of a building, as if they were two friends meeting at a planned rendezvous. But they weren't. They were sworn enemies and this time she was ready for him. This time she would not be caught off guard by the shape of his horrible mouth that looked even more sinfully seductive in his cleanly shaven jaw.

Oh, dear Allah, but he was attractive!

Her lower body clenched alarmingly, her breathing erratic, and she knew it wasn't just from the adrenaline speeding through her body at the presence of danger. It was him. He did things to her, stirred things up inside her, she didn't want to think about.

Pushing that aside, she forced her attention away from her body and back to the tautly honed male that she knew was tensed to strike despite his relaxed stance. He was dressed in a black *dishdasha*, his freshly shaven jaw doing nothing to make him look more civilised than the unshaven version. In fact he looked even more ruggedly handsome, every inch the powerful male in control of his surroundings. He drew her like the devil himself and a frisson of helpless fear went through her as he silently surveyed her.

The feeling made her so angry she drew the sword she gripped tightly in the folds of her dress before she could think better of it. 'If you take another step, you'll regret it,' she warned.

He glanced at her weapon and raised an amused eyebrow. 'Is that so?'

By Allah, his insolence was insulting and she unconsciously shifted into a purely combative stance. She wasn't stupid enough to think that she could win a real contest with him—he dwarfed her in height and breadth—but maybe, just maybe, she could take him by surprise and land him on his backside long enough to dash through the maze of streets that led back to the busy souk. There she could blend with everyone else and disappear in the sheer volume of human bodies.

As far as plans went, it wasn't much of one, but since giving up wasn't an option either she held her ground.

'Did you know,' he drawled, inspecting his fingernails as if every one of his senses wasn't attuned to her slightest movement. 'There are at least twenty-five ways to kill a person with your bare hands?'

No, she hadn't known that. 'Right now, I'd settle for just one.' She held the sword tighter and waited for him to come at her. Instead he threw his head back and laughed.

The sight and sound of his amusement disconcerted her because she'd been serious!

'Put the sword away, Farah,' he instructed softly, all pretence at relaxation over.

Farah's fingers flexed around the hilt. The way he said her name in that rough, sexy voice sent a sharp, sweet ache straight to her pelvis but she ignored it. 'No.'

His eyebrows climbed his forehead. 'I was starting to

think that you were smart, my little Zenobia. Are you about to prove me wrong?'

She had trained with a few of her father's respected bodyguards before he had put a stop to it. They'd soon see who wasn't very smart. 'I escaped, didn't I?' she taunted.

A muscle ticked in his jaw. Good. An angry man made more mistakes than a rational one.

'My guards found you.' His eyes fell to the glint of the sun shining off the sharp blade of her rapier.

Farah curled her lip. 'Your guards are incompetent. I doubt they could find a particle of dust in a sandstorm. Perhaps they are poorly trained.'

The muscle flickered again in his jaw and a small smile threatened to curve her lips at how easily she got to him. He'd been lucky when he'd grabbed her at her father's camp. He wouldn't be so lucky this time.

'It's not a good idea to prod an angry lion,' he drawled as he pushed away from the wall. 'They tend to bite.'

A shiver snaked down Farah's spine at the warning implicit in that drawl; his voice was deep and melodious, as if he were paying her a grand compliment. 'I think you got lucky coming upon me now,' she challenged. 'If your men had truly found me, why didn't they take me?'

'They were ordered not to.'

'Why?' Farah tensed as he took another step toward her, the overhead sun highlighting his chiselled features.

The square behind her was deathly quiet but she didn't take her eyes off the prince to find out why. Nothing was more dangerous to her right now than this man. She raised her sword in preparation to strike, sweat making her palms slippery. 'Were you afraid they'd get hurt?'

'No.' He circled to her right and she pivoted on her slippered feet to follow him. 'I was afraid you would.'

His black robes billowed as he prowled around her and

she knew beneath the soft trousers his strong thighs would be tensed to spring at her.

'Put the sword down. You won't win this battle.'

Farah didn't say anything but her keen eyes caught movement on the rooftop above him so she knew that they weren't alone. She let her lip curl into an insolent sneer. 'Need help to bring in one woman, Prince Zachim?'

'Oh, I think I've already proven that I don't need help bringing you in, little cat.'

'Ha!' She was scornful. 'You got lucky the first time. You caught me by surprise.'

'Really?' His teeth sank into his fleshy bottom lip as his gaze dropped to her mouth, telling her more than words that he knew exactly what had distracted her the first time. 'Who's to say it won't happen again?'

'Me,' she snapped, humiliated by her own weakness where he was concerned. Why, oh, why did her body find his so damned fascinating? It made no sense at all.

The cumbersome *abaya* dragged around her legs as she shifted to keep him in sight. If she got the chance she was going to have to toss modesty to the wind and lift her skirts to try and outrun him. 'I know you have a sword on you.' She lifted her chin. 'Draw it or get out of my way.'

'I'm not going to fight you.'

'Afraid?' she challenged.

He smiled. 'Give it up. We both know you have no chance of beating me.'

Farah stilled. His voice was so controlled, so knowing. He was calling her bluff, damn him, and a deep desire to do the opposite, a deep desire to *show* him, turned her muscles hard. For a brief moment she indulged in the reckless fantasy of besting him, of being the one to bring the mighty Prince of Bakaan and his monumental ego to his knees. Could she do it?

'I can take you,' she said, twisting the sword in a few

expert loops, testing it for weight and balance. It wasn't a great piece of craftsmanship but it was better than nothing.

A slow smile spread across his face. 'Now, that I'd like to see.'

Oh! She caught the not so subtle innuendo in his tone and lunged at him, hoping to catch him off guard, realising too late that that was exactly what he'd wanted her to do.

Moving with impressive speed for a man his size, he dodged her blade and she heard the hiss of metal against leather as he unsheathed his own. Adrenaline raced through her veins and charged her body. This was what she needed—a good bout of sparring to rid her of all the tension, fear and worry that threatened to swallow her whole.

She charged him again and brought her sword crashing down against his as hard as she could. She didn't let up and the clash of steel was the only sound ringing in the small empty square around them. Although, as to that, a thousand spectators could have been watching and she wouldn't have noticed.

The adrenaline seemed to give her added strength, but even so she couldn't detect any weakness in him that would give her an advantage.

'Cease this, Farah,' he ordered, using his sleeve to wipe the sweat from his brow.

Distracted by the sight of his muscular forearm it was she who was caught off guard when his sword unexpectedly came down over hers with so much force her teeth rattled.

It was as if he'd only been using half his strength before, and irritation that he would go easy on her gave her a burst of energy and she rushed him, both exhilarated and appalled when she heard the rip of fabric.

Absolute shock held them both immobile and, horrified, Farah watched as bright red blood bloomed from the dark sleeve of his robe.

Oh, dear Allah… She hadn't really meant to hurt him…
Her appalled gaze rose to his. Instinct finally kicked in at
his ferocious expression and she dropped the sword before
taking off towards a nearby alley.

Sweat and fear made her more clumsy than usual and
she screamed when she felt a hand grab hold of her head-
scarf. Fortunately the fabric gave and Farah shot into the
alleyway.

The pounding of his footsteps behind her alerted her as
to how close he was right before his arm reached around
her and yanked her back against him.

Incited by real terror, Farah fought him with all her
might but it seemed to take him only seconds to subdue
her and have her pinned face first against a rough wooden
door, her hands stretched above her head and his hip angled sideways as he forced her legs apart to hold her lower
body still.

Completely powerless, Farah leaned her hot face against
the rough cool wood and listened to her heart hammering
inside her chest.

Zach steadied his uneven breathing as he held the little
wild cat hard against the door, his eyes shifting to the cut
on his arm. It stung but he knew it wasn't deep because
he'd felt her pull back at the last second. Really he should
have disarmed her straight away but he'd been enjoying
sparring with her too much. She was good—no match for
his strength, but she was nimble and he'd felt that same
exhilarating spark he had felt riding with her in the desert. It had been a long time since he'd felt this energised,
this *alive*, and he wondered how much of it was the sense
of danger or the woman before him.

As if sensing his distracted thoughts, she suddenly
bucked against him to try and dislodge him and Zach
pressed her harder against the wood. It occurred to him

that she might have more weapons on her and that he'd need to pat her down before he released her. The thought brought an image of his hands drifting over her lithe body, shedding her of her clothes as he went, and he hardened in anticipation. He cursed silently. For some reason her body acted like a lure for his and he was fast running out of plausible explanations to justify it. As far as sex went, he usually had to like a woman to want her.

He eased back slightly and barely fought the urge to shift his stance so that his erection could nestle against her rounded backside. By Allah, that would feel good, soft and warm, and if he bent his knees a little he could push himself against the apex of her thighs. With his attention so acutely consumed by her femininity, he thickened even more, aching with a need he was hard-pressed to remember feeling before.

He unconsciously breathed in her sweet scent from the oils used in her bath and he felt a sharp sting against his shin for his efforts. The little wild cat had kicked him and even managed to get a hand free as his hold had unconsciously slackened. By Allah, he needed to get a grip.

Restraining her once more, he leaned in close. 'You would have done better if you'd used that agile little body against me for pleasure, Farah, rather than trying to fight me,' he goaded.

Cocoa-brown eyes rounded, sparking with a mixture of fear and anger. And something else. *Hunger? Need?* He drew in a sharp breath. What would she do if he just said to hell with it and kissed her until she was moaning in submission as he'd wanted to do earlier in the harem, moaning for him to take her and pleasure her as no man ever had before?

'I would rather boil myself in oil than try and entice you,' she spat.

Normally Zach had no trouble controlling his libido—

his *emotions*—but this woman could incite a monk to forget his vows. 'Liar,' he said against her skin. He wanted to turn her so that he could feel her curved into him and before he could think of all the reasons why that wasn't a good idea he had her in his arms and his mouth slanted over hers.

He kissed her hard and mercilessly and he didn't stop when she hissed a noise against his lips and thumped his shoulders. He didn't stop as she squirmed to get away from him and he didn't stop when the voice of reason rang out a warning inside his head.

This thing between them had started the minute she'd put those slender fingers in his mouth, maybe even before, and he was uncaring that this was something he would normally never do—uncaring about anything but having her surrender to him. Of having her wind those long legs around his hips so he could satisfy the primal need that owned him and made him want to own her.

When she moaned as if he was hurting her, it penetrated the fog of surging testosterone and he raised his head to look down at her. Her cheeks were flushed bright pink and strands of her silky hair clung to her neck. Her eyes looked too large for her face and her lips were moist and swollen from where he had ravished them. She looked wild and wanton and with every panting breath she took her breasts rose temptingly against his chest.

Shaken by the strength of his reaction to her, Zach thought about releasing her right up until the moment her pink tongue stole out of her mouth and swiped his taste from her lips. It was then he realised she was no longer struggling against him and that her eyes were trained on his mouth in a way that said she wanted more. And, by Allah, so did he.

With a pained groan he lowered his head and once more touched his lips to hers, only gently this time. He wanted to take his time to savour her lips, to feel their texture and taste their unique flavour. He wanted to feel her meet him halfway and he made a guttural sound deep in his chest when she tentatively rose against him in an innocent quest for more. Zach couldn't remember a kiss ever feeling so intimate, so good, and he fell against her, pressing her back into the door.

Thick lashes came down to shield her eyes as if the sensation was too much to bear, as if she could only focus on one thing at a time. He felt her lips give beneath his own, opening wider as he took the kiss deeper, the sensations shaking him to his core. Without even knowing it, he released her hands and wound his through her lush hair, cradling the back of her skull as he positioned her to take his tongue.

He growled as she melted against him, her tongue gliding shyly against his, and his world shrank to encompass only this. Only her. He pulled her in tighter, hitching her higher. She gave a soft, feminine whimper, her fingers clenching at his shoulders as she quivered against him. Zach cursed the amount of clothing between them, unable to stop himself from grinding his erection against the juncture of her thighs. He swallowed the catch in her breath and chased her tongue into her mouth, his hands restless in her hair, restless on her body, as he sought to pull the blasted *abaya* up and over her head so he could get to her body.

Dimly he became aware that they weren't alone. A couple of his senior officers had gathered at the entrance to the alleyway to ensure his safety and were at this moment watching him make love to his little prisoner. It wasn't the best behaviour he'd ever modelled and it took every ounce of willpower he had to let her go and step back from her.

When he did she slumped against the doorway, her eyes

wide, her lips swollen and wet. She looked beautiful. Wild
and untamed and just as shocked as he was.

It was the shock that finally brought him to his senses.
'What the hell was that?'

A surfeit of emotions charged across her face, wounded
pride being one of them. 'That was you being a bully,' she
accused hotly.

Zach felt as if he'd been slapped. His father had been
a bully; he wasn't, and as for forcing her, her body had
been primed for his kiss from the moment they met. 'You
wanted everything you just got,' he snarled. 'And if you
try to tell me otherwise I'll strip you naked and prove
you wrong.'

'Oh!'

Zach placed a hand on her shoulder and turned her to
precede him. 'Consider yourself warned.'

Oh? *Oh?* That was all she could come up with after he'd
kissed her into a stupor and then insulted her?

Oh?

By Allah, she could come up with a hundred responses
now and if he were here she'd give him every last one of
them.

Pacing the lavish harem she'd been locked back up in,
with two guards posted *inside* the room, she spun around
when she heard the lock turning in the door.

She eyed Prince Zachim with open hostility as he stood
in the doorway, flanked on either side by the two maids
she'd sent away earlier.

'I see your arm is still attached to your body,' she said,
still feeling a little guilty at having hurt him, even though
he had completely deserved it. 'What a pity.'

'Yes. No thanks to you.' He stepped into the room, his
two lackeys shuffling to keep up. 'I believe I left specific
instructions for you to dress.'

She felt her body tense as she took in his wide-legged stance. He was no longer wearing the black robes that had made him look like a menacing pirate earlier, but now wore a regal white one, the colour emphasising his swarthy skin and the deep amber tones of his eyes.

By all that was holy, she still couldn't believe the way she had responded to his kisses back in the alley, and her fingers curled into her palms in an attempt to stave off the memory.

She'd never been kissed like that before. Certainly Amir had never tried to kiss her. In fact she'd only ever been kissed once before, by a youth from a neighbouring country who hadn't had the sense to be afraid of her father. It had been rushed and impossibly chaste compared to the Prince of Bakaan's kisses, which she was not going to think about any more.

'I am dressed,' she said, knowing that he was referring to the purple silk gown that had been brought to her earlier and which she hadn't touched.

His lips quirked. 'So you are. Unfortunately your current outfit will not work for my brother's wedding.'

'What do I care about your brother's wedding?'

'Nothing. Obviously. But I find myself uncomfortable with the notion of leaving you alone again.'

Farah crossed her arms over chest. 'Am I supposed to feel sorry about that?'

'No, my bloodthirsty little heathen, but given your recent behaviour I have no wish to be sitting at my brother's wedding, wondering what plans you're hatching down here in my absence.'

Farah tried not to be pleased at causing him some measure of discomfort. 'Just leave me with your guards. I'm sure we can find some way to occupy ourselves.'

'No doubt,' he murmured. 'But I have no wish to have to discipline any more of my men.'

'Am I really so dangerous, Prince Zachim?'

His mouth kicked up into that crooked grin that made her heart trip just a little. 'More like troublesome.'

'My father won't take the bait, you know,' she asserted, hoping that it was true.

'We'll see.'

Farah gnashed her teeth together at his cavalier attitude. He was so cool as to appear almost bored, but why wouldn't he be? It wasn't his life hanging in the balance.

'In the meantime, Isla and Carine are here to prepare you to be my guest at the wedding.'

Farah's eyes cut to both the women and for the first time she noticed that they were carrying towels and drawstring bags that held goodness knew what.

'And you will cooperate this time.'

The prince's insolent drawl brought her eyes back to his. He looked hard and unyielding, as if she had no choice in the matter. 'There is no—'

'Way you're going to attend?' He flicked his hand in her direction as if she were an irritating insect. 'Yes, I know.' He walked towards her and raised his hand to stay the women, who immediately obeyed. Farah's eyes narrowed and she forced herself to remain rigid as he took the last two steps into her personal space. 'But you will. And you will behave.'

As she was about to tell him to go to hell, he shook his head slowly. 'I can of course just lock you in a cell. Or perhaps it would be better to chain you to your bed. I'd hate you to be uncomfortable.'

The air between them grew thicker, making it harder for her to breathe, and Farah automatically stepped back from him. 'It would be better than having to endure your company for the night.'

She heard one of the women gasp. The prince's eyes

narrowed. 'But who said anything about you being alone in that big *harem* bed?'

A dark, thrilling desire rose up inside of Farah as her head filled with all sorts of debasing images of her shackled to a bed with the prince gloriously naked and aroused in front of her. On top of her. *Inside* of her. Because he would be glorious naked; he would be... Farah clamped down on the thoughts running amok inside her head and tried to think straight.

'What if I apologise on behalf of my father?' she gushed, finally prepared to humiliate herself and bow and scrape for this man if it meant she could get her father out of trouble and her life back to normal. 'What if I make up for what he did in some way?'

He leaned back against the cabinet behind him, his fingers tapping a lazy beat against the curved wood. 'What did you have in mind, *habiba*?'

Farah glanced at the maids. 'I could work for you. I could cook or clean or—'

'I already have enough staff in my employ.'

She bit her lip. 'I could...' She wracked her brain to come up with something else. Surely there was something? 'I could train your horses. Your camels.'

'The palace no longer keeps camels and my horses are well taken care of.'

'Damn it, surely there is something you need?'

His gaze ran over her body, lighting a fiery path as it went. 'Keep going, I'm sure you'll hit on something mutually agreeable at some point.'

Farah frowned. Did he mean...?

You wanted everything you just got...and if you try to tell me otherwise I'll strip you naked and prove you wrong.

Farah's face flamed hotly as his words in the alleyway came back to her. 'Not that!' she cried. '*Never* that!'

'Then we have nothing to discuss,' he said in a bored tone.

'You are every bit the tyrant your father was,' she accused, turning away from him.

Embarrassment and despair swamped her. If she had been a man, this whole situation would never have happened. She would have been by her father's side when he'd come upon the prince's SUV and been able to talk sense into him. And she certainly would never have given into this man's challenge and tried to feed him. What had she been thinking?

About his mouth, a little voice reminded her. *You were thinking about his dreamy mouth.*

Self-disgusted, she was about to stalk over to her bedroom when the prince grabbed her and swung her back to face him, his fingertips digging into her upper arms.

'Dammit, you know how to push my buttons but your father took me hostage for three days before I escaped. If you think that will go unpunished, you're sadly mistaken.' He glowered down at her. 'Now get dressed. And if you cause either of these women another problem you won't find me so lenient next time.'

Farah swallowed hard, determined to show zero emotion in the face of his fury, while inside her whole being was quaking. Watching him stride from the room she waited for the resounding echo from the slammed door to pass before she turned to the two wide-eyed maids, who had probably never said a cross word to the prince in their lives. 'I will bathe myself, is that understood?'

'Yes, my lady.'

CHAPTER SEVEN

'STOP FIDGETING,' the prince whispered out of the side of his mouth for about the fifth time.

Farah dropped her hands to her side once more and pretended to focus on the gorgeous wedding ceremony taking place in front of her. 'This dress doesn't fit,' she complained under her breath.

'It's perfect,' he growled.

It wasn't perfect. It was tight across the bodice, the slender straps exposing her arms and upper chest. The stiletto-heeled shoes she'd been given to wear were also surely torture devices with the way they made her feet ache. In the magazines they had always looked so glamorous and beautiful. On the feet they felt like pincers.

'And smile.'

Tired of his instructions—'no sneering, no balled fists and no attacking anyone at the wedding'—Farah pinned a wide smile to her lips. 'Like this?'

The prince's Adam's apple bobbed as he looked at her. 'Better,' he mumbled, followed by something that sounded like, 'I'd hate to experience the real thing,' before turning back to the proceedings.

Farah surreptitiously studied him in his royal white robes and headdress. He was so virile and masculine and so utterly charming when he wanted to be that she almost believed he was as nice as he seemed.

Except that he'd been grouchy towards her ever since he'd picked her up from the harem and she had no idea what she'd done to prompt his ire again other than exist. Earlier, after he'd stormed out, she had done everything that had been asked of her, intending to lull him into thinking that she would cooperate from now on. She'd let the women apply her make-up, dress her and brush her hair until it gleamed, pinning it up at the front and letting it fall down around her shoulders. When she'd finally looked in the mirror she had barely recognised herself. In fact, she'd thought she looked quite pretty until the prince had taken one all-encompassing glance at her and scowled—just like her father had, over her boots! She didn't know why the prince's bad opinion of her affected her so much but it did and the realisation had set her on edge all over again.

She wondered if he believed her when she'd agreed to the truce he'd requested before marching her from the harem and decided that it didn't matter right now. His brother was in the middle of marrying a Western woman so lovely that Farah had no wish to spoil things. There was just something so utterly romantic about the way Sheikh Nadir gazed at his bride that was totally riveting for Farah.

What would it be like to have a man look at her that way?

Debilitating, a little voice reminded her. It would place her in a life of servitude where her wishes would be overlooked or overruled. It certainly wouldn't make her happy.

She shifted her weight into her heels to relieve the pressure on the balls of her feet and felt Prince Zachim tense. Given his importance in the ceremony, they were standing at the front of the glamorously packed ballroom that was overflowing with white and pastel-pink flowers and deep-green foliage with softly lit candles on every available surface.

She had felt the imprint of a thousand curious eyes on

her as she had made her way slowly to the front of the guests but she hadn't recognised a single face who could help her.

A loud cheer went up in the crowd and Farah realised that the ceremony was over, the glowing couple smiling brightly, the groom totally besotted as he took their daughter from a male guest who hadn't stopped beaming the whole time.

Moving slowly, they stopped in front of Farah and the prince, accepting their congratulations. When the little girl reached out and patted Prince Zachim's jaw, he laughed and murmured to her tenderly, leaning forward to kiss her cheek. Farah was so surprised by the action her whole body went still. He really was the most confounding man, she thought a touch tetchily—one minute hard and ruthless and the next charming and...devastatingly male. Confused and feeling too many emotions at once, she was glad when they hung back and let the procession of guests precede them from the stately room.

Testing her weight on her toes, Farah gingerly stepped forward, trying not to feel as though she was walking on stilts.

'Take smaller steps,' the prince advised roughly.

Farah's head came up. 'Smaller steps?' She stared at him. 'Have you seen the things on my feet?'

Yes, he had, and they were beautiful. She was beautiful, standing there scowling at him, and he wondered how a woman who had never genuinely smiled at him, who had never been anything but defiant in his presence, managed to drive him half-crazy to the point that, even now, he was contemplating taking her to bed regardless of who she was or who he was.

Would she be amenable to the idea? No, not likely, but he knew she'd been as lost in their interlude in the alleyway as he had been, and it probably wouldn't take much effort to return her to that state of stupefied, delirious lust. It sure as hell wouldn't take him long.

He saw a flash of vulnerability cross her delicate features as he continued to eat her up with his eyes and he realised she was nervous. A pang different from lust went through him.

'These are not shoes,' she said indignantly, raising the hem of her gown to reveal delicate stiletto sandals designed with lingerie and sex in mind. 'I have no idea why women wear them.'

Zach swallowed heavily but it did nothing to dislodge the gravel from his voice. 'They elongate the leg and highlight a woman's calves.' And she had sensational legs that went on forever. A sheen of sweat rose up along his hairline. *Absolutely sensational.*

She scowled. 'I think they are meant to control women. Next you'll ask me to darn your socks.'

'I throw away my holey socks.'

'Rich *and* wasteful. It figures.'

She lifted her nose at him and he ground his teeth. 'That's some opinion you have of me, sweetheart.'

'Are you saying I'm wrong?'

'Yes, you're wrong.' She sniffed as if he was a servant who had just offered her substandard fare. 'And not only that but you're prejudiced.'

That snapped her out of her holier-than-though repose. 'I am not,' she declared hotly.

The scent of jasmine and honey entwined together and invaded his senses: his favourite. He sighed, not wanting to fight with her. 'Take my arm.'

She cocked an eyebrow. 'Where would you like me to take it?' she asked sweetly. 'The garbage?'

He bit back a laugh and noticed her own lips twitching. So she had a sense of humour. Who knew? 'As long as you don't take a sharp object to it again, you can take it wherever you like.'

Surprise showed on her face at his rejoinder and then she laughed, a dead sexy, full-on, throaty chuckle he thought he could listen to forever.

Finally she stopped and he lifted his gaze to hers. 'You can lean your weight on me until you get used to the heels,' he offered gruffly.

She hesitated before releasing a long breath and reluctantly placed her hand on his arm as if she were touching dynamite.

Zach lifted her hand off his forearm and placed it in the crook of his elbow. When he felt her fingers curl into the fabric of his robe and cling, he felt as if a heavy object had been placed on his chest. He rubbed it but the sensation remained. So did the memory of the way she had fit in his arms earlier; the heat of her response to his kisses.

He swore under his breath and she glanced at him from beneath kohl-rimmed eyes, her long hair falling forward over one shoulder. Whether she was dressed to the nines as she was now, or wearing combat trousers and an old tunic with her hair matted against her head, she was more beautiful than any woman he'd ever seen in his life. Which couldn't be right. Surely Amy's classically cool beauty had touched him more than Farah's exotic dark looks?

He knew bedding the woman at his side would probably put an end to the hunger he felt for her but that wasn't an option. She was the daughter of his enemy and wanting it to be otherwise was just a fool's errand.

'Why are you looking at me like that?'

The words could have come from a petulant teenager to a parent and he shook his head. 'Because I didn't expect to find you so beautiful.'

A pink flush rose along her cheekbones and she dampened her lips. By Allah...

'You're just saying that to try and lull me so that I won't try to escape again,' she said.

No, he hadn't been, he thought grimly, but now he knew that she intended to do so—even though he had trusted her when she'd agreed to cooperate with him earlier—and he felt like an idiot. 'You know that gold sash draped so artfully around your waist?' he asked.

She raised her pointy little chin at him. 'What of it?'

He leant in so close her scent filled him. 'You take one step in the wrong direction tonight and I'll wrap it around your elegant throat and use it as a leash.'

Oh! Farah felt like screaming. One minute she was enjoying his company and the next she hated him again. But his comment had been a good reminder that she was not, in fact, his guest at this wedding, but his prisoner, and she had her own agenda: escape!

Smiling dutifully at the little group they had joined, she watched the covetous glances the women—the very *married* women—gave the prince. Instinct no doubt told them that the reason he was so completely at ease in his own skin was because he was a man who had known pleasure—and had given it.

A hot flush swept up her neck and she raised her hand to mask it. What she wouldn't give to be back in her little hut and arguing with her father about why she didn't want to get married. It seemed so much more simple than parading around with a man who disturbed her on so many levels.

'I said stop fidgeting.' He cupped her elbow as he directed her away from the avid faces of their small group. 'How are your feet?'

'Hobbled. Yours?'

He chuckled. 'You're delightful.'

She scowled. 'I'm not trying to be.'

'I know. Dance with me.'

Not expecting that request, she wasn't ready when he slid a hand to her lower back, his gaze hot on hers when she glanced up at him. 'I don't dance.'

He considered her for a long moment. 'Don't or can't?' he asked shrewdly.

Farah felt another flush heat her cheeks. 'I...' she began, only to stop as he cast her a crooked grin.

'Can't, then,' he concluded, turning her towards him. 'Don't look so outraged, *habiba*, I will teach you.'

A shiver went through Farah as he moved in closer, his warmth hitting her like a wall. Then his spicy scent made her head foggy. This was so not a good idea. Especially when he was right: she couldn't dance. She'd never thought about learning before, preferring to watch from the sidelines. She hadn't thought about sex much, either, but since meeting the prince it was the single most dominating thought that occupied her time. If he'd been an ordinary man in her village or a neighbouring one, who was considerate of her needs, she might have thought about exploring the chemistry that made her stomach flutter and her insides feel liquid, but he was Zachim, Prince of Bakaan, and he was cut from the same controlling cloth as their fathers.

'Not interested,' she said, trying to ignore the little voice in her head that said dancing with him would be fun. Riding Moonbeam full pelt through the desert was fun. Sitting by the fireside dreaming up impossible adventures with her friends was fun. Dancing with Prince Zachim would not be fun. It would be out-and-out dangerous.

As if reading her mind, he gave her a devastating half smile. 'Come on. You know you want to.'

And there was that innate arrogance of his popping up at the right moment to remind her why she disliked him so much. 'No.'

'Just follow my lead.'

His grin widened as she flashed him a look. 'Do you even understand the word *no*?'

'You never know, Farah, you might enjoy it.'

And wasn't that half the problem? She knew that maybe she would enjoy it. Too much.

Before she could rally her defences against him, he raised his left hand. 'Right hand in mine.'

Farah froze so he reached down and clasped her hand in his. 'Now, left hand on my shoulder.'

Again she froze and again he took control and did it for her.

'Now what?' she asked, her whole body taut as she tried to remain impervious to this nearness.

'Now I put my hand here.' He placed his left hand lightly against her hip and Farah's spine lengthened as she registered the heat of his touch.

Her lips felt dry and she mashed them together. He watched her like a hawk zeroing in on its prey. 'And now?'

'Now we move together.' He smiled, clearly amused by her stoicism. 'It's called a waltz. When I lead with my right leg, you move your left leg back. No, not like that—smaller steps, remember, and slower. My leg is supposed to slide against yours so that it looks like we're moving as one.'

A lone sitar player filled the dance floor with a gentle, teasing ballad and Farah desperately focused on the music as the prince's muscular body lightly brushed her own.

'Close your eyes.'

Her eyes flew to his and she moved her face back when she realised how close they were. 'Why? What are you going to do to me?'

'Nothing you don't want me to.'

Time seemed to grind to a halt as those gravelly words grazed along her nerve endings. She felt her pulse race. Those blasted magazine images wove into her consciousness and heat made her dizzy. Then she realised she was holding her breath and let it out.

'Closing your eyes might help you feel the music,' he suggested, watching her closely.

It might help her forget about how devastatingly handsome he was as well, so she did. On some level it made her awareness of him even more intense, but on another it did help, and before she knew it she could feel herself moving much more gracefully than she would have thought possible.

'You're a quick study,' he murmured against her ear. 'How are the feet now?'

Farah shivered and opened her eyes. She'd forgotten all about her feet but now she could feel the balls of them throbbing. 'Not great.'

He pulled her indecently close. 'Lean against me,' he said roughly.

She wanted to say no, she wanted to move away, but gremlins had invaded her body and suddenly her lids drooped closed and she entered some dreamy realm where her body took over. She wouldn't have said exactly that she was dancing because they were barely moving but it felt lovely. She could feel him against her, hard and so solid. His body was so different from her own and it amazed her how they fit together—as if they were made for each other.

When the music changed tempo her eyes drifted opened and she was embarrassed by how lost she had been in the moment. Her heart beat double time and she was shocked to realise how aroused she was just by dancing with him.

It used to be that her body was more like a machine that did her bidding: arms, legs, hands, feet. Now she was aware of useless things, like her breasts, the hollow space between her thighs, the prince's hand on her hip and a tingling weakness at the back of her knees. Sensations that made her feel fragile and defenceless. And then she wondered if it was the same for him. Did men feel weak and defenceless when lust overtook them? Did Prince Zachim feel that right now, for her? It seemed impossible and yet more shocking was how much she wanted him to want her—she, a village girl, with all the sophistication of a desert mouse. Why, he must have had the most sophisticated lovers in the world. Women like the ones that peppered the wedding and gazed at him with a deep longing. A deep longing Farah never wanted to feel for anyone.

Suddenly feeling claustrophobic, she surprised them both by pulling out of his arms. Wanting Prince Zachim was a betrayal to her father and to everything she wanted for herself: self-sufficiency, independence. *Self-respect.* 'I need to use the bathroom,' she said, furious all over again.

'I'll take you.'

Of course he would, and it was a welcome reminder that she wasn't really a wedding guest but a captive. And she no longer cared about his threats if she tried to escape.

Inside the bathroom there were no windows or back doors so she finished up quickly and returned to the ballroom with him, alert now to where the guards were.

A few men dressed in Western attire came over and talked to the prince and he turned to engage in conversation. Farah half listened and smiled politely, as if she were part of the group when she wasn't. She noticed a small knot of women standing close by and realised they were the partners of the men talking and she was the only woman in this group—a lone gazelle in a pride of male lions.

She didn't bother getting the prince's permission before making her way over to them. Let him stop her if he dared. It wasn't for her to decide how long the leash was and, although earlier she had not doubted he'd tie her dress cord around her neck as punishment for defying him, she knew now that he wouldn't jeopardise his brother's wedding by causing a scene. He wasn't *that* uncivilised.

When one of the women she was only half listening to complained she was hot, Farah could have hugged her.

Taking charge, she suggested they walk on the terrace. Lush gardenias and roses scented the warm evening air but Farah was only interested in where the exit points were.

Cursing the torture devices on her feet, she realised she would have to leave them behind, Cinderella-like, if she got a chance to escape. Only she would be leaving both behind and she didn't want the prince to come after her. Ever.

Making her apologies to the women, she quickstepped down the stone steps as if she knew exactly where she was going and skirted the plethora of plants in the verdant garden. Clearly water restrictions did not apply inside the palace—another black mark against the Darkhan family.

A large stone wall covered in a passion-fruit vine loomed in front of her and she paused to get her bearings.

'The gate is about fifty metres to your left,' the prince drawled from behind her.

Farah groaned softly and expelled all the air in her body. 'I got hot.'

'Really?' His eyebrow rose. 'And I thought that was only while we were dancing.'

Oh! 'A simple enough mistake to make for a man with your sized ego.' She smiled sweetly, giving up all pretence of cooperating with him. What did it matter? He wouldn't let her get away from him now.

His eyes gleamed, no doubt taking her response as some sort of challenge. 'You had goose bumps.'

She hated that ring of confidence in his voice. 'Maybe I was cold,' she retorted.

He grinned. 'Now, we both know that's not true.'

His suggestive tone grated along every one of her nerve endings. 'Oh, to be so sure of yourself.'

'You know,' he began conversationally. 'I almost want

you to make a run for it so that I can use that cord on you after all.'

Farah's hand strayed to her neck. 'You wouldn't dare.'

'Oh, I'd dare, Miss Hajjar. Remember, I'm a barbarian prince.'

'Your brother—'

'Is about to leave with his new wife.'

Farah swallowed. He moved in closer and the urge to take flight warred with a deep-seated determination to stand her ground.

'Your skin looks almost luminescent in the moonlight.' He reached out and stroked his hand down the side of her face. Farah reeled back and would have scratched herself on the vine if the prince hadn't grabbed her elbow. 'Careful, you could hurt yourself.'

Only by giving into the pull of attraction between them, she thought wildly, her heart racing as she fought to maintain control over her senses. 'I'll take my chances with a spiky plant any time,' she threw at him.

Ignoring her smart comment, he drew her inexplicably closer. 'You don't like being told what to do, do you?'

Sensation zipped through her as his hands dropped to her hips and splayed wide. 'Not by men like you, I don't,' she bit out scathingly. Anything to put him off.

'Men like me?' His eyes narrowed dangerously. Soft music and the tinkling conversation from the ballroom drifted over them. 'You need taming, my little Zenobia,' he whispered, taking full advantage of the tilt of her chin to nuzzle his way down her throat. 'And I'm the man to do it.'

The hands she intended to shove against his shoulders slipped and she nearly groaned as her fingers slid along the top of his robe and grazed the ends of his thick hair.

A fierce expression crossed his shadowed face and one of his own hands cupped the nape of her neck, holding her firm. It seemed like forever that they stared at each other,

silent and intense, the only sound that of their harsh, uneven breaths and the pounding of her heartbeat she was
sure he could hear as loudly as she could.

She felt his hand sift through her hair before he slowly
wound its length around his fist. She could feel the tug
of each loop at her scalp and she couldn't tear her eyes
from his.

'Tell me you want me, Farah.'

His lips slid along her jaw, feather-soft, as he breathed
her in. Farah's head fell to the side, unconsciously offering
more of her neck to his sinful lips, offering more of herself.

He was going to kiss her. She knew it and she wanted
him to. She wanted to feel the moist thrust of his tongue
again and lose herself in his dark taste. She wanted him
to crush her against him and ease the unbearable ache that
throbbed low in her body. Just imagining it had her knees
giving out. He took her weight effortlessly, his free hand
skimming up the sides of her torso, stealing her thoughts
like a sexy cutpurse filching goods from an unprotected
market stall. Then, ever so slowly, he brought his other
hand down and skated his thumbs lightly along the underside of her breasts until her throbbing nipples were so
tight they ached for his touch. Ached for his...

'I wouldn't go there if I were you, Zach.'

Shocked and dazed by the voice at her side, Farah
whipped her head around to find Sheikh Nadir scowling at them.

'Her father is here.'

It took a moment for the sheikh's words to penetrate her
desire-fogged brain but when they did she gasped.

Here? As in, the palace *here?*

'What?' Zach's tone echoed her own disbelief.

'Yes. And he's after blood—yours, to be precise. I told
you this would happen.'

Told him what would happen?

The prince released her and stepped back, a victorious, snake charmer's grin on his face. 'He'll get blood, but it won't be mine.'

A lightning streak of fear shot through Farah. 'What are you going to do to him?'

Ignoring her, Zach raised a hand and a nearby guard materialised at his side. 'Take Miss Hajjar to the harem.'

She grabbed his forearm. 'I want to see my father.'

'Don't let her out of your sight,' he continued as if she hadn't spoken. 'Not even for a second.'

Nadir stayed the guard before he could move. 'Unfortunately I told her father I would bring her.'

'Why would you do that?' the prince snapped at him.

Nadir's brow rose and Farah wasn't sure if it was with censure or surprise. 'He wants to see her for himself.'

'I don't care.'

'I do.' This time the look was definitely censure. 'This is my wedding night, Zach,' he said grimly. 'You need to take care of this quickly and smoothly before Imogen realises something is amiss.'

The new king's care of his bride made Farah's stomach clench. Men did not put their women first, in her experience.

'Fine,' the prince growled. 'Let's get this over with.'

Farah tensed at the ominous ring in those words. In Bakaan, the prince wouldn't need a court order to have her father imprisoned or put to death, and desolation overtook her as she realised that, despite all her efforts, there was next to nothing she could do to save him now.

CHAPTER EIGHT

FARAH'S HEART CAUGHT in her throat as she saw her father standing proud and tall in what looked like a private office. Amir was beside him, four palace guards surrounding them both.

Her father's eyes fell on her and widened before turning to the prince. 'What have you done to my daughter?'

Farah felt the prince's barely leashed anger. 'Greetings to you, too, Hajjar,' he drawled insolently. 'How good of you to grace us with your presence.'

Her father's eyes narrowed. 'Just answer the question, cur.'

Farah nearly groaned at her father's rudeness. Now was not the time to challenge the man he had kidnapped.

'You will not be making demands here, Hajjar,' the prince said with grim certainty. 'You are in my realm now.'

Her father raised his head. 'I'm sure you will do your worst, but not to my daughter.'

'I'll do what I like.'

'Gentlemen.' Sheikh Nadir stepped between them. 'I urge you to keep this civil.'

'This is not one of your boardrooms, Nadir,' the prince overrode his brother. 'I intend to see justice done.'

'Justice?' Her father spat. 'You wouldn't know justice if it jumped up and bit you in the backside. You're just like your father.'

'Careful, Hajjar.' Sheikh Nadir's tone was unmistakably deadly. 'This is my wedding day and you did kidnap my brother.'

'I don't deny it. But he took my daughter and spent two nights with her alone in the desert. That is a slur against her good reputation and he should be forced to make amends.'

Amir shifted forward. 'Did you touch her?' he bit out.

Farah's eyes flew to his. A muscle jumped in his jaw as he eyeballed the prince.

'That's none of your business.' Prince Zachim's piercing gaze cut from Amir's to hers and Farah felt her face turn brick red as she recalled every time he *had* touched her and how much she had secretly enjoyed it. A spark of awareness simmered behind the prince's eyes, as if he knew exactly what she was thinking, as if he too could still feel the press of his blunt fingertips against the underside of her breasts. An unexpected shaft of hunger tightened every one of her nerves, as if in anticipation of that touch, and she released the shaky breath she'd been holding for too long. She knew she should be saying something but she couldn't move under the weight of that unmistakably sexual look; couldn't *think*.

'By Allah!' Her father's righteous bellow filled the room and Farah shook off the sensual malaise that threatened to consume her. 'If this cur has compromised my daughter's honour then he will marry her.'

Marry her?

'No!' Farah's automatic response was nearly drowned out by Prince Zachim's insulting laugh and Amir's horrified shout of disapproval.

'If you think you can use this to get out of justice being served, Hajjar, you're wrong,' Zach stated menacingly.

'At least I admit what I did,' her father spat, as if that completely exonerated him from his crime. 'You…you take my daughter and dress her up as your…your *whore* and expect me to say nothing?'

Even though she knew her father hadn't meant to insult her quite so badly, Farah still felt the sting of his disapproval like a sharp slap. The prince stilled beside her. 'Retract that insult to your daughter immediately,' he warned quietly. 'Or I will do it for you.'

Farah stiffened with shock at his instant and unequivocal defence of her. It felt as if no one had been in her corner since her mother had died and a sweet spear of pain lanced her heart.

'Do you deny the charge?' her father demanded.

'I am not beholden to you or anyone else,' the prince stated grimly.

'But you are beholden to the laws of this country and you have wronged my daughter by taking her from her home and then spending the night with her. And something happened between you,' her father asserted. 'My daughter is in shock.'

An understatement, Farah thought, her mind reeling at all that had been said, including the ludicrous statement that the prince should marry her. Her father had to be mad to even suggest it.

'Zach?' Nadir's quietly controlled voice broke into the emotion swirling around them and something passed between the two brothers that she couldn't read.

Prince Zachim growled low in his throat and stabbed a hand through his jet-black hair, the lethal glitter in his amber gaze pinning her to the spot. Power throbbed from every one of his muscles and the sexual chemistry that thrilled her as much as it appalled her ratcheted up a notch. 'I did not compromise this woman,' he said with deliberate slowness.

'Easy enough to say,' her father snarled.

'Tell him, Farah,' the prince ordered roughly, her name husky on his lips.

Tell me you want me, Farah?

'Tell him that nothing happened between us.'

Nothing?

She blinked up at him. She supposed in his world the way he had touched her and kissed her had meant nothing to him and, no, he hadn't compromised her in the way her father meant. But he had made her aware of the sensual nature of her body for the first time in her life and it had changed her in a way she couldn't yet explain. Worse, it had made her want him on a level she had never wanted another man. Was that nothing?

Appalled to find herself close to tears, she stared at the floor to gather her wits but as soon as she heard Amir's swift intake of breath she realised that the men had interpreted her hesitation as an admission of guilt.

A clock she hadn't noticed before ticked loudly in the deathly silence right before both her father and Amir erupted, gesticulating wildly. Within seconds the palace guards surrounded them, guns drawn.

Farah saw Prince Zachim stiffen as he stared at her, his expression one of outraged astonishment. Sheikh Nadir swore under his breath.

'By Allah, you will marry my daughter,' her father bellowed, 'or you will bring the wrath of all the mountain tribes down on your head.'

The sheikh swore again.

So did the prince this time.

'Father, listen, I—'

'Stay out of this, Farah.'

Stay out of it! Farah nearly choked as her own temper rose to the surface.

Then Amir spoke, further tightening the screws of tension in the elegant room. 'I will marry Farah.'

Farah groaned. 'Amir, don't.'

His brown eyes were fierce as they met hers. 'I don't care if you have lain with him. I will have you for my own.'

'Over my dead body.' The prince hadn't moved a muscle but he seemed to dominate the space.

Farah's head throbbed as her mind scrambled to fix what was happening.

'Zach. A word.' Nadir's commanding tone brooked no argument. Farah glanced away as the prince gave her a loaded stare before following his brother to the other side of the room.

Sighing heavily, she rounded on her father. 'Father—'

'Don't argue.' He folded his arms across his massive chest. 'That dog will do the honourable thing by you if it's the last thing he does.'

'But I don't want to get married,' she asserted.

Her father waved her claim away as if her desires were inconsequential. 'Every woman wants to get married.'

Well aware of his chauvinistic views, Farah tried another tact. 'At least let me choose who I marry, because the prince was telling the truth—*nothing* happened.'

'You should have listened to me,' her father stated as if she hadn't even spoken. 'When I told you to stay away from him.'

'Like you're listening to me now?' she retorted.

'I told you to stay away, too.' Amir interrupted, clasping her clammy hands between his. 'I knew it would lead to trouble.'

So this was her fault?

She felt so utterly infuriated she didn't trust herself to speak. And she supposed this *was* her fault, in a way. She *had* defied her father in her misguided attempt to fix everything but, damn it, she had only wanted to help. She had only wanted to prevent things from getting worse for her father. Next time he wanted to go rampaging she'd make sure she stayed home!

She stared down at Amir's hands holding hers, his thumb stroking her skin in a soothing gesture, and she wondered how much more this night would deteriorate when the high and mighty Prince of Bakaan refused to marry her.

'Zach, you don't have to marry her.'

Zach heard Nadir's quiet words but his attention was riveted to the tableau across the room. Their body language spoke volumes. Farah's face flushed with her ardent displeasure; her bearing was nothing short of regal, her father holding himself aloof like an imperious ass, and his second-in-command…had just taken hold of her hands.

Zach's eyes narrowed. An unexplainable rage welled up inside him. Were they secret lovers? It wasn't unheard of, even though a woman was supposed to come to her husband's marriage bed a virgin. Would she come to his in that untouched state? Or had she already given herself to the idiot who was about to lose his hand—at best!

His jaw clenched. 'Idiot.'

'Sorry?'

'Not you.' Zach briefly thought about bypassing his hand and going straight for his neck. He, the master communicator—well, there was nothing like a broken neck to get a point across, he supposed. 'But, yes, I do have to marry her.'

Nadir's expression grew stern. 'Bloody hell. I believed you when you said you hadn't slept with her. I should have known when I saw you in the garden—'

'That was nothing.'

'Nothing? Two more minutes and you would have ripped her clothes off.'

Zach drew his eyes away from Farah and regarded his brother. 'More like one, but that's not why I have to marry her. And I didn't lie. Nothing has actually happened between us.' Well, nothing if you ignored the unexpected make-out session in the alleyway or his subsequent fantasies in the shower. Not to mention what he'd been about to do to her in the garden. 'I have not slept with her. Not in the biblical sense, anyway.'

'Then we'll get you out of this.'

Zach could see Nadir readying himself to go into problem-solving mode but Zach's attention was elsewhere. Which was why he only vaguely heard the mention of war, peace and love. And he knew his brother wasn't doing a book review.

He swung back to Nadir. 'What about love?'

Nadir sighed impatiently. 'You said that was the only reason you would marry—if you were in love.'

Yeah, that was what he'd said once. But honour and integrity were just as important and he wasn't about to let this little spitfire who knew obscure facts about Roman history, and who intrigued him and made him laugh as no other woman ever had, take that from him. 'Excuse me,' he said to his brother, crossing the room before he'd even registered his intention.

His icy gaze went to the idiot's, his hand to Farah's elbow. 'This meeting is over,' he informed the tense trio.

Of course, she tried to pull away from him. 'I told my father—'

'I will marry your daughter.' He spoke over the top of her, clasping her elbow more firmly.

'Never thought I'd see the day a Darkhan would do the right thing,' the old man preached.

'Only because you probably don't recognise the gesture.'

Farah's knight-errant cleared his throat. 'I don't—'

Zach turned on Amir as he squared off against him and was clearly about to spill his guts. 'You are about to lose your head if you're not careful,' he bit out. 'Guards, put them in prison,' he ordered softly.

At the mention of prison his newly acquired fiancée came to life once more. 'No!'

She pulled out of his hold and rushed to stand in front of the two men like Joan of Arc facing off against the English at Orleans. 'You can't send them to prison.'

Any other time her loyalty might have impressed him. Just not this time. 'And just how do you propose to stop me?'

'Zach…' He heard his brother's cautioning tone but ignored it.

'Not even you could lock up your own father-in-law,' she announced belligerently.

Her father stiffened. 'That's enough, Farah!' he scolded. 'I don't need you to fight my battles for me.'

Zach stared at the woman in front of him, all willowy and beautiful, a touch of vulnerability in her eyes most would probably have missed. He'd noticed it earlier as well, when her father had insulted her, and it had made him want to protect her then, as it did now.

Unable to stop himself, he reached out and ran the back of his knuckles down the smooth line of her cheek. Her breath hitched and he didn't miss that, either. 'So tough, my little spitfire,' he murmured. 'So passionate.'

She knocked his hand away. 'About things I care about, yes.' Her voice was husky and made his body ache to have her.

'Hell.' His brother's low curse spoke volumes. 'She has a point, Zach, and I need to get back to Imogen. I'll let you go, Hajjar,' his brother informed the older man. 'But you put one foot out of line and I'll haul you into prison so fast your head will spin.'

A lead silence filled the room.

'Come, Farah,' her father finally said with a regal dignity that made Zach want to laugh. 'I will take you home.'

'No, you won't,' Zach found himself saying. He smiled. 'Your daughter is now my fiancée and that means she's mine to do with as I please.'

CHAPTER NINE

WITH THE RUSH of adrenaline behind him, Zach was seriously starting to question his sanity. He'd just committed himself to marry a woman he barely knew. A woman he didn't even like!

He stormed down the corridor with said woman in tow. How had this happened? One minute he'd been celebrating not only his brother's wedding but also the fact that Nadir had agreed to take the throne and the next he was…he was…getting married? Any minute now and he was sure doctors in white coats were going to come rushing around the corner looking for him.

The cause of his immense irritation tugged against his hold. 'I'm tired of you dragging me around like this.'

Zach tightened his grip. 'Not as tired as I am of having to do it.'

Especially when they were in this predicament because she hadn't spoken up and admitted that nothing had happened between them.

Nothing? his conscience mocked.

A growl rose up in his throat. A few kisses did not require a marriage proposal. In the West they might not, but in Bakaan a man didn't trifle with a woman unless he was serious.

But marry Farah Hajjar?

Zach inwardly cursed himself. All his life he'd ignored

the exotic Bakaani girls who had thrown themselves in his path with one purpose in mind. All his life, until this one. And she hadn't even thrown herself at him. No. She'd done something much worse: she'd kidnapped him. Or her father had.

He still didn't know why the old man had done it, although he could guess. With Zach's father gone, Hajjar had probably hoped to destabilise the country and attempt a coup. The thought was as ludicrous as his suggestion that Zach marry his daughter. And then another possibility hit him and his whole body went still.

Farah squeaked as she nearly ran into him from behind. Zach stared at her. Was that why Hajjar had done it? To get the two of them together so that they were forced to marry and get a Hajjar on the throne any way possible? His rational side discounted the idea as absurd—the Hajjars had hated the Darkhans since the dawn of time—but he'd underestimated Farah once before and had the scar on his arm to show for it. Had he underestimated her father, as well?

'We need to talk.' He pushed open the door to his apartment.

Farah glanced up at him as she swept past. 'I couldn't agree more.'

Dismissing his guards with a nod, Zach followed her inside. He bypassed his sofas, headed straight for his wet bar and grabbed a crystal decanter half filled with whisky. 'Drink?'

She eyed the offer disparagingly. 'I thought you wanted to talk.'

He downed a finger of Scotch. 'I'd like to dull the pain first.'

'We're not really getting married, you know.'

'We're not?' He added ice to the glass this time before leaning back against the bar, taking in her rigid stance.

'That whole thing was just an act back there? Damn, I wish I'd known. I would have organised party music.'

Her soft lips pinched together. 'Don't you know that sarcasm is the lowest form of wit?'

'It's fitting, then,' he drawled. 'Since I can't remember feeling this low before.'

'You and me both,' she said on a rush, sinking down onto one of the sofas and removing her heels; her sigh of pleasure hitting him exactly where he didn't need it to right now.

'You know, if you drop the kidnapping charges I could probably get my father to withdraw his demands that we marry.' Her pleading look was one of innocence and hope and for a fleeting moment he had to fight the urge to go and comfort her.

Clearing his head with another dose of alcohol, he cast her a cynical smile. 'Oh, I'm sure you'd like that,' he bit out. 'But it's not that simple any more.'

'I don't see why not.'

'Because your lack of a convincing denial that I have *dishonoured* you has set something bigger than the two of us in motion. But then, maybe you knew that all along,' he added softly.

'Knew what?'

Zach paced to shake off the adrenaline that surged through him. Her puzzled expression was either genuine or a good act. His money was on the latter. 'Marrying me has enormous benefits.'

'Like what?' She gave a derisive snort. 'Being close to your *enormous* ego?'

Unable to remember another woman who had dared to speak to him with such disdain, he stopped in front of her, forcing her to have to look a long way up to meet his gaze. 'Money. Power.' He gritted his teeth. 'A Hajjar potentially on the throne one day.'

Instead of being intimidated by him, she just looked annoyed. 'If you're implying that my father *wanted* this to happen...' She wrinkled her nose. 'That's ludicrous. He loathes your family.'

'He loathes that my family is on the throne, and now we're to be married. A bit opportune, don't you think?'

'No, I don't think that at all, and if you thought about it logically you'd know it's not true. My father is stuck in the past and thinks that all women need a man to take care of them. That's the only thing that's going on here.'

It wasn't the only thing going on here but perhaps he should have stopped at one whisky because what she said made sense. Not that he wouldn't put it past Hajjar to capitalise on a situation that had arisen as a result of his own poor judgment in lifting her onto that horse in the first place.

Zach crushed an ice block between his teeth. 'Unfortunately I don't feel particularly logical right now. And your father gets to go free with you as the sacrificial lamb.'

Her face paled. 'No, there has to be another way.'

'Why, so you can go off and marry your boyfriend, the knight, instead?' he asked silkily.

She frowned. 'Amir?' she finally said. 'No, I don't want to marry Amir or anyone, and given your reputation I'd think you would feel the same way.'

Zach stilled. 'My reputation?'

'We get magazines in the mountains,' she said loftily. 'And I think the amount of different women you've been photographed with speaks for itself.'

He gave a rough bark of laughter. 'You're making me out to be the bad guy here?'

'Are you saying you want to get married?'

'As a matter of fact, I was nearly married once.' Or at least he'd contemplated asking Amy to marry him, which was close enough for the purposes of putting this little heathen in her place. 'So, yes, I do want to get married—just not to you, Miss Hajjar.'

Her face went even paler before flooding with colour and he felt like an ass.

'I suppose it doesn't matter to you because you can have a hundred wives if you choose.'

'I admit that I have great stamina in the bedroom,' he drawled. 'But even I would struggle with a hundred women. But, regardless, that law is about to be repealed.'

Farah's eyes climbed her forehead. 'It is?'

'Yes. It's time Bakaan entered the twenty-first century and my brother and I intend to see that happen. By the look on your face, you don't agree.'

'No. I mean, yes, of course I agree.' She hesitated. 'I just didn't expect…'

'That I would think that way?' he finished when her words tapered off. 'Possibly it's not just your father who is stuck in the past.' And why her poor opinion of him rankled was beyond him.

'I am not stuck in the past.' She thrust her hands on her hips righteously.

Zach eyed her appreciatively as she stood before him in a full snit. 'Hit a chord did I?'

Yes, he had hit a chord, because she was a forward-thinking person, not a backward-thinking one. But she was so confused right now. His declaration that he'd been nearly married once before, and his adamant statement that he would never want to marry her, had somehow rocked her and she had no idea why. 'No, you have not hit a chord,' she denied hotly, staring into his too-cocky, too-handsome face. 'But I want to hit you and I'm a non-violent person!'

'So says the woman who attacked me with a sword.'

'Okay, fine—generally I'm a non-violent person. And

I'm sure if you could just reach into your heart and forgive my father and let this go—'

'Let bygones be bygones, you mean?'

'Yes, exact—'

'No.'

'Would you stop cutting me off?' She angled her chin at him. 'Can't you see that showing forgiveness puts you in the powerful position? If my father continues to act out against you unprovoked, then everyone is likely to turn on *him*.'

'Remind me which fairy story you derived that bit of whimsy from.'

Having him mock her made Farah grit her teeth together. 'Just because you don't believe in non-violent methods of communication doesn't mean you have to belittle ideas that have worked before. Ever heard of Martin Luther King? Ghandi? *Mother Teresa?*' She lobbed the names of some of her heroes at him. 'Perhaps if you open your mind up a bit more you might learn something.'

The look he gave her was ferocious. 'You have some nerve coming to me about non-violent methods of communication. Someone in your village started a publication five years ago that nearly incited a civil war. If I hadn't come home and settled things—in a *non-violent* manner, I might add—who knows how many people would have died?'

'I didn't mean to incite anything,' she countered.

'I didn't say you did, I said—' He stopped and stared at her. 'You started that provincial publication?'

Farah was instantly flooded with heat at his condescension. 'My magazine was not provincial, thank you very much!' She bit her tongue to stop herself from calling him every name she could think of, digging her toes into the soft pile rug beneath her feet.

'That's not possible,' he said, the incredulity in his voice beyond insulting. 'You would have only been a child when that was done.'

Farah's hands shot to her hips. 'I was seventeen!'

He shook his head, a frown on his face. 'There were a lot of sharp observations in that paper.'

'If you're expecting me to thank you for saying so, you'll be waiting a long time.' Like, forever. 'And I hardly think it's important.'

'Not important,' he growled, seemingly as angry as she was. 'It's the reason I had to return to Bakaan!'

'Something you obviously didn't want to do, by your tone.'

'Not when I had to give up control of my company and end my racing career, no.'

'I'm so sorry,' she simpered. 'How thoughtless of us— your people—to need you.'

'Yes, it was.' His voice lowered an octave and the skin on the back of her neck prickled with awareness. 'Although, I'm not completely unhappy that *you* need me.'

Attempting to ignore the suddenly charged atmosphere he was deliberately creating, she lifted her chin. 'I need you to install medical centres in our villages and provide educational materials so we don't have to sneak them from across the border or—' She stopped, suddenly aware that yet again he'd got her so incensed she was about to divulge sensitive information to him.

'Or what?' he asked softly. 'Get them from a secret source inside the palace?'

He knew about that! Farah tried to act nonchalant because she had no doubt that whoever had sent those items to them over the past couple of years would be punished. 'I don't know what you're talking about. But what I want to know is how we get out of this marriage.'

'We're not.'

The conviction in his tone chafed her already raw nerves. 'But we have to.'

'I don't know why you're fighting this so much. Your life is about to improve out of sight.'

'Improve?' She laughed, because what else could she do? 'That's because you're nothing but an arrogant, egotistical, high and mighty prince whose shoe size is larger than his IQ.'

His slow smile told her that her insults had landed on fallow ground. 'Careful, *habiba*, or I might start to think that you like me.'

Oh, but he had a way of pushing her buttons. 'That will never happen,' she assured him loftily.

'No?'

'No.'

'But you like my touch.' He came towards her all long, lean and muscular. 'Don't you, Farah?'

She swallowed hard. 'No.'

He paused and cocked his head. 'Have you forgotten what I said would happen the next time you denied you wanted me?'

'You know you're redefining the term "egotistical," don't you?'

He laughed. 'And you're redefining denial. But I find myself wondering why I'm denying myself something I've already been accused of taking.'

Farah's hands came up to ward him off, a thrilling sort of fear coursing through her as he kept coming until she was forced up against a wall, his towering body just inches from hers. He planted his hands by both sides of her head, caging her in. 'Give me one good reason, *habiba*, *one* good reason why I shouldn't unwrap you from that pretty dress and give you exactly what we both want?'

Feeling as if she'd just run a marathon, Farah could barely breathe let alone speak. All she wanted to do was smooth her hands up over his wide chest and finish what he had started back in the garden. The urge was almost overwhelming but she knew there would be no going back after that and she definitely wasn't ready for that.

'Tell me,' he said softly, 'How far did you and the knight go?'

Not sure what he was asking, she frowned, and then she caught the suggestive glint in his eyes and she knew. Struggling to get her thoughts in order with him this close, she frowned again. 'We haven't… I've never…'

A slow smile spread across his face. 'He didn't touch you.' He shook his head as if in wonder.

Knowing there was in insult buried in that look, she pushed at his chest, relieved when he let her pass. 'I won't do it,' she muttered, 'I refuse to marry you.'

'You have to.' His gaze turned implacable. 'Have you forgotten that my honour and your reputation are at stake?'

'No, but I don't care about my reputation!' she cried. Her vision of a future in which she directed her own life was falling away from her before her very eyes. If she couldn't do anything about it, she was going to be married, and she couldn't think of anything worse. Well, her father dying in a prison cell was worse, and perhaps never experiencing the prince's hot kisses again… But, no, how could that be worse?

'Well, I care about my honour,' he said coldly. 'Especially at a time when I need the support of our people. And let's not forget your father's small threat of war.'

'But—'

'Enough. I find I am exhausted from all the *excitement* of the past week, not to mention tonight. We will be married, Farah. Perhaps it is fate.'

A sense of inevitability stole over her at his words. She had always known there would be a price to pay for her father's actions; she just hadn't expected that price to be her marriage.

Shaking her head, she swallowed past a lump in her throat that extended all the way to her stomach. 'I've never liked fate,' she said dully.

The prince gave her a faintly mocking smile. 'While I have never believed in it. But it won't be all bad.' His tone softened. 'I will be gentle with you, *habiba*.'

Heat bloomed across her cheeks as she realised how exactly he was going to be gentle with her. 'I don't want you to be gentle with me,' she blazed. 'I don't want you to be anything with me.'

He smiled as if he knew better than she did. 'We'll see.'

CHAPTER TEN

THREE DAYS LATER Zach found himself a married man. Something he should have felt worse about, given that he wasn't in love with his bride, but didn't.

The wedding had been small, nothing like his brother's extravaganza, but everyone had said it was romantic, the way the prince had fallen in love with the daughter of his father's archenemy thus uniting what had once been the two biggest tribes in the country. Zach hadn't thought of it that way at the time it was going down, but the advantages were obvious on a political level. On a personal level his mother seemed to take great delight in the 'love match' so he had remained silent about the real reason behind their union.

A union he'd had the power to prevent when Nadir had informed him that he'd come up with a plan to extricate him from it. Zach knew it would have been what Farah wanted. Hell, it was what *he* wanted. So why hadn't he done it? Especially with his brother about to become the next king; it would have meant total freedom for him, which he had now firmly denied himself.

Nothing made sense, not the churning feeling in his gut, nor the way Farah made him feel so hungry for her. As if she was the last woman in the world for him.

Well, she is, his conscience reminded him, *and you will be the first man to touch her.*

Something he found himself increasingly impatient to do. Probably he should be a little worried about his eagerness to bed a woman who so obviously didn't like him, but he wasn't. They might not have started this marriage in a conventional way but he had no doubt that she would please him. As he would please her once she stopped being so prickly about everything.

She was an intriguing personality, his new wife—headstrong and handy with a sword, as well as brave and fiercely loyal, with a keen intelligence all tied up in one delectably feminine package he was straining to unwrap.

Nadir's comment about his deliberately choosing the wrong women in the past came back to him. Was it possible? He never would have said so before but he also knew that Amy had never stirred the level of feeling in him that Farah did.

Scanning the milling crowd he easily located Farah across the room talking with his mother. She looked striking in a long-sleeved cream gown that skimmed her slender frame and ended at the floor. A whiff of something far more insidious than desire curled through him as he watched her. It gave him pause and, as if sensing the swirl of emotion coursing through him, his lovely bride glanced at him from beneath her long lashes.

Her eyes flared briefly as he took her in and Zach could almost feel the shudder that went through her. As much as she might not like to admit it, she wanted him just as much as he wanted her. His blood heated, driving everything else out of his head except bedding her.

'Drink, little brother?'

Cursing under his breath, Zach arched a brow at his brother. He knew Nadir felt sorry for him. He knew he wasn't in love with Farah and since finding love himself he'd turned into some sort of agony uncle. But he didn't want a drink. He didn't want anything to dull his senses for his wedding night to come. 'No, I'm good.'

Was it too early to leave? He glanced at his watch. They'd been at the reception for an hour; surely that was long enough.

'Imogen was wondering where you intend to go for your honeymoon.'

Honeymoon? Interesting question and one he hadn't even considered. He'd spent the last three days in back to back meetings trying not to think about sex before marriage. Now he realised that a honeymoon would be the perfect excuse to take Farah away from the worries of Bakaan and the reason behind their marriage. A chance to start fresh.

But where to go? Paris? New York? The Seychelles? No, wrong time of year for— Suddenly Damian's birthday invitation swung into his mind. *Ibiza?* Could he take her to Ibiza?

'I wouldn't recommend it.'

Not realising he'd spoken out loud until Nadir replied, Zach frowned. 'Why not?'

'It's a bit…wild. But why would you— Ah…' His brother smiled. 'Offshore racing.'

Zach shrugged. 'I am still the team owner,' he pointed out. 'But it's Damian's birthday. I should be there.'

Nadir's brows rose. 'You're going to spend your honeymoon at a mate's birthday party?'

'Of course not,' Zach grated; he wasn't that selfish. 'The party is one night and we'll have the whole week. What's wrong with that?'

Nadir held up his hands at Zach's aggrieved expression. 'You're the expert on women, not me.'

'Glad you finally admit it,' Zach growled. Ibiza was the perfect idea: fun, carefree and totally different from Bakaan. What could possibly go wrong?

* * *

'The wedding was beautiful and you look especially lovely in your wonderful dress.'

'Thank you.' Farah automatically murmured the rote response she had given most of the well-wishers at the wedding even though the gentle woman who had just joined her was now her mother-in-law. The fact was her brain was operating in some sort of a fog. She kept reminding herself that she was doing this for her father but that didn't always feel like the truth and that worried her just as much as being married did.

'I hope you don't mind about the orchid.'

'The orchid?'

'A wedding gift from my private nursery. I had it delivered to your apartment in the palace. It's very rare but also very hardy. It represents love and fertility.'

Farah forced a smile at her words. Earlier Zach had asked her not to reveal the reason behind their marriage to his mother. She didn't know why, other than to stroke his massive ego, but she had agreed to go along with it. Now she felt like a phony as his mother beamed up at her. 'My son always said he would marry for love, and I am so glad he has, because he deserves it.'

Love? Farah never would have imagined that her new husband would be motivated by such a deep emotion and it made her wonder if he had been in love with the woman he had almost married. And if he had been in love then, was he still? She clutched her stomach, feeling a little ill at the thought. Or was that just the bubbly drink she'd consumed? Imogen had warned her to go easy on it but it was so sweet and refreshing she kept forgetting. She took another sip and realised that her mother-in-law was waiting for her to say something.

Wondering if 'thank you' was even mildly appropriate, she was almost glad when Zach approached them.

'I hope my mother is not making your ears bleed, *habiba*?' He smiled down at her like any indulgent new husband who was indeed in love with his wife.

'Not at all,' she said a little breathlessly, trying to remember how much she disliked his handsome face.

She noticed the loving look he bestowed on his mother and suddenly wondered if his wish to keep his mother in the dark about their union had less to do with his ego and more to do with real caring. She'd lived on a diet of her father's prejudices against this man and his family for so long it was difficult to differentiate fact from fiction where he was concerned. His comment that perhaps her father wasn't the only one living in the past returned but she shook it off. She absolutely did not live in the past.

Grumpily, she watched his mother return his smile as if the sun shone out of him and Farah felt a pang that her own mother wasn't present. Probably if she had been, then Farah wouldn't have been here because her father would not have been bitter enough to kidnap the prince.

She glanced across the room to where her father was talking with a group of men, seeming to have forgotten the events that had led them to this night. He was the only person from her village present because Farah hadn't wanted to invite anyone else. It wasn't as if this was a real celebration and now she wished she had at least invited her good friend, Lila. She could do with the moral support, if not some advice about her wedding night to come.

The thought of sleeping with the prince caused a riot of mixed emotions to take flight in her stomach and she sipped her drink to subdue them. Should she be looking forward quite so much to joining with a man she didn't like? And would it be as good as kissing him was, or would it be a let down, as she'd heard other women tell of it? Somehow she knew that it wouldn't be and she shivered.

'Cold, *habiba*?' Zach leant closer to her and she shook her head. She wasn't cold, she was hot. Too hot.

As if he was completely attuned to her innermost thoughts, his hand splayed possessively across her hip. 'I'm afraid we have to leave you, Mother. We have a honeymoon to get to.'

'Oh, how romantic. Make me lots of babies.'

Honeymoon? Babies? Farah's stomach fluttered again. All this talk of love and seeing Imogen and Sheikh Nadir's obvious adoration for each other was making her think strange, unwanted thoughts about things she'd once steadfastly declared she did not want, things that would make her just as beholden to a man as any other Bakaani woman. Things that had her earlier panic about marriage return tenfold.

Before she could tell him she had no desire to go on a honeymoon like a real married couple, his nose grazed the top of her head. 'You smell delicious,' he murmured huskily. 'What scent did you bathe in?'

Farah didn't want to remember her bath. Four women had come to prepare her for his pleasure and it had been like negotiations in a war room as they'd massaged and plucked and waxed her body into submission. Farah had determinedly refused to allow them to touch the hair between her legs and they'd clucked and tsked like old hens trying to establish the pecking order. The prince would not approve, they'd said. Good, she'd replied, much to their consternation. Now she wondered if he would approve and she hated the feeling of weakness that underscored that thought, hated the desire that she wanted to please him at all. She didn't. She didn't care what he thought of her.

She lifted her chin. 'Poison.'

'Then I will die a happy man tonight.'

His husky chuckle made her nerves tighten and Farah raised her half-empty glass to her lips. 'One can only hope.'

But he wasn't listening, instead he was frowning at her glass. 'Perhaps you should think about switching to water.'

'But I like this very much.' She tilted the glass to her lips in what she knew was a childishly defiant gesture and drained it. 'What is it called again?' She felt slightly dizzy from the rush of alcohol as it hit her stomach, but it was worth it to see him scowl.

'Champagne.' His frown deepened. 'Have you even had it before?'

'Loads of times. We distil it in the hut behind my father's.'

His eyes narrowed and Farah widened hers innocently. Then he completely surprised her by shaking his head and laughing softly. 'Okay, I deserved that.'

And there he went again, throwing her off just when she thought she had him all worked out.

'Come, Farah, we should go.'

Oh, yes, the honeymoon.

Suddenly nerves attacked her. She'd been deliberately not thinking about the end of the evening and what would come next. 'I think it would be rude to leave so soon,' she said, aiming for cool and knowing she'd missed by a mile when his lips twisted in sympathy. *Sympathy!*

'Actually, it's quite late.'

Heat raced through her, making her feel even dizzier than she already was.

'Where are we going?'

'So suspicious, wife.' He smiled. 'We are going to Ibiza.'

'Ib… Where?'

'It's a small, ruggedly beautiful island off the coast of Spain. You'll love it.'

She raised an eyebrow. She had always wanted to travel to faraway places but had never imagined she'd ever get the chance. 'Because you say I will?'

She hadn't realised she'd raised her chin until he gripped it and tugged it down, his thumb resting on the curve of her lower lip. Her nerves were so raw even that small contact made her insides fizz.

'I know you want another argument but I'm not going to give you one,' he said. 'It's time to make love, Farah, not war. Wouldn't you prefer that?' His voice was a rough caress against her ear and before she could tell him that, actually, she was quite happy with war, he placed his hand firmly against the small of her back. Her breath caught and a delicious tingle of anticipation followed his fingers as they slid upwards to grip the nape of her neck. It was a blatantly possessive hold and spoke of domination and ownership. Farah, who had never imagined wanting to experience either of those things, felt every one of her bones turn to water.

Half an hour later they were ensconced on the royal plane and she was trying not to ogle the sleek luxury of the streamlined jet. 'Where are all the seats?' she asked, taking in the well-spaced leather chairs and small tables.

'This is a private plane. You'll need to take a seat when we take off. After that you can walk around the cabin. There's a bedroom in the back and two bathrooms. Are you okay?'

'I'm not sure.' Her hand went to her head. 'I think I have a headache.'

'Already?' His smile was faintly mocking. 'I've heard it takes wives a little longer to start producing that ex—'

'Oh…' Farah moaned and must have turned as green as she felt because Zach forced her head down between her knees. 'Oh, that's worse.'

'It's the champagne.'

She waited for the nausea to pass and then sat up slowly. 'How can something that tastes so lovely make me feel so ill?'

'You're meant to drink it in small doses.'

'Small doses, like small steps,' she hiccuped.

'Exactly.' She heard the smile in his voice but kept her eyes closed.

'I think I'm okay now.'

'Just lie back.'

The plane chose that moment to accelerate down the runway and Farah's stomach revolted as they were lifted into the air. 'Oh, no I— Oh!'

Before she registered what was happening, she was in Zach's arms and then she was bent over a toilet bowl and emptying the contents of her stomach—which was thankfully very little, since she'd been too nervous to eat during the reception.

'I think I hate champagne,' she mumbled, so wretched she couldn't even muster any embarrassment.

His soft laugh was vaguely reassuring. 'I thought you loved it.'

'Not any more.'

'Unfortunately, you're likely to feel even worse tomorrow.'

'Please feel free to shoot me if I do.'

'I don't want to shoot you, *habiba*,' he said so softly she almost didn't catch it.

She took the glass of water he offered and drank deeply. When she was finished, she was only vaguely aware of him lifting her and carrying her to a cool, flat surface. She buried her head against something warm and firm. A pillow?

She felt her hair being released from the confines of her twist and moaned softly when he threaded his fingers through it.

'I love your hair.'

She frowned but didn't open her eyes. 'You do?'

'Yes. And your eyebrows.' He swept a finger over each one. 'Like the wings of a raven in full flight. And your nose—'

'My nose is too prominent.'

He ran his finger down the fine blade. 'It suits your face. And your mouth…'

Farah yawned and snuggled further into the pillow that smelled just like the prince. For some reason she felt completely relaxed and safe, as if she didn't have anything in the world to worry about. It was such a novel experience she let it wash over her. 'What about my mouth?' she asked, her mind drifting toward sleep.

'Your mouth.' He paused. 'Let's just say your mouth keeps me up nights.'

'Mmm, that's nice.'

He chuckled. 'I'm glad you think so.'

He stoked her hair and Farah floated into another realm, trying to cling on to whatever it was the prince was saying, but quite unable to do so.

When she finally regained consciousness she was instantly flooded with alarm. She should be helping to get water down by the well; she should be fixing breakfast. Then the softness of the bed she was in permeated her hazy state and she opened her eyes and saw floaty white curtains across the room being ruffled by a gentle breeze. Used to gaging her surroundings by scent, she breathed in deeply. The air was humid rather than dry and held a tinge of brine to it. A balminess.

Her mind started recollecting all the moments that had led to this one but there was a gaping hole between her throwing up on Zach's luxuriously appointed plane to lying in a bed that was as big as her whole room growing up.

And where was he? Because she could already tell that he had not slept beside her last night. Rising up on her elbows, she gingerly shifted her head from side to side to test the headache. Fortunately it didn't hurt but her mouth felt like she'd stuffed cotton into it and she was thirsty. Which was probably why she'd woken up thinking about water.

Pushing the linen sheet aside, she frowned when she realised she was only wearing her underwear. Did that mean Zach had undressed her last night or did he have an army of servants in this place, as well?

Flicking the bathroom light on against the gray haze of early morning, she was surprised to see that she looked pretty normal, except for the smudge of kohl around her eyes and her mussed hair. Wiping away the make-up, and brushing her teeth with the new toothbrush that stood in a small gold jar on the marble sink, she set about trying to tidy her hair. Deciding it was impossible, she was about to leave the room when she caught sight of herself in a full-length mirror. The underwear she'd been given for the wedding was pure white and as delicate as a finely spun spider's web. The bra was demi-cup, the panties cut high on her hips and completely sheer, somehow making the dark curls they hid look tempting and erotic. Shaking off the unnerving spark of arousal that thought caused, she truly hoped a servant had undressed her and not Zach.

Really? A little voice taunted.

No… She grimaced at the battle inside her head, grabbed a white robe she spied hanging from the back of the door and belted it tightly around her waist. She didn't hope that. Much to her chagrin, part of her hoped that Zach had undressed her and that he'd liked what he'd seen.

But where was he?

Asleep on the deep divan in the adjoining room, as it turned out. His large frame was sprawled on his back, his bare feet hanging over the edge. At some point he must have changed because he was no longer wearing his wedding robes but low-riding sweatpants and nothing else… And, oh, but he was built.

Farah stilled, taking him in. She wanted to go to him and run her hands all over his gloriously golden-brown skin, petting the dark pelt of hair on his chest right where it arrowed down the centre of his lean torso like a tempting trail. Of course, she didn't. She couldn't think straight enough to unglue herself from the doorway for a start.

'You're awake.'

Farah's eyes flew to his. So was he.

Obviously.

She swallowed, feeling vulnerable at having been caught staring at him. 'Yes.'

He stifled a yawn. 'It's early.' His eyes held hers, gleaming in the faint light.

'I'm sorry did I...did I wake you?'

'Not really. This sofa isn't the most comfortable to sleep on.'

'Oh, you should have...' She gestured vaguely to the bedroom behind her. He was her husband. He would be sleeping with her from now on. Yesterday the thought had been horrifying but right now she couldn't muster that same sense of dread.

'Did you undress me?' Her face flamed as soon as the words left her mouth. What was wrong with her? 'I mean—'

'Yes, I undressed you.'

'Oh.' She gripped the lapels of her robe together and glanced around, only vaguely aware of the beautifully appointed room cast in morning shadows. 'I thought maybe you had servants.'

'No.' He swung his feet to the floor and stood up. Farah's eyes returned to his large frame and her heart took off. 'No servants here.'

Had he been that tall yesterday? That imposing? She suddenly felt very thirsty again. 'Oh, well.' She waved a hand around aimlessly. 'I didn't mean to wake you.' *Especially not when you're only half-clothed.*

'I already said that you didn't wake me.'

Right. So he had.

'How's the head?'

It took her a minute to realise he was referring to her drunken episode on the plane. 'Um, good.' His gaze dropped to the belt on her robe and she realised she was fidgeting with it. 'So, thank you for taking care of me last night.'

A muscle knotted in his jaw. 'My pleasure.'

The softness of his tone thumped into her breastbone, his tone full of sensual promise and a decadent passion she was finding harder and harder to resist.

But for some reason it seemed imperative that she did resist, some deep awareness warning her that it was too much. That he made her feel too much. And as if to prove her own point her nipples peaked beneath her robe as if he were already touching her, the delicate fabric of her bra chafing like sandpaper, yet not rough enough to ease the ache. Would his hands be able to do that? His mouth? Involuntarily her eyes lifted to his.

A gruff sound broke the heavy silence between them and Farah realised that her husband was no longer standing stationary across the room. He was moving, towards her, his long, panther-like strides eating up the space between them.

Farah didn't move. She couldn't. She just waited, and if she'd thought her breathing shallow before, that was nothing compared to now. When he reached her he stopped and tucked a strand of her hair behind her ear.

The gesture tugged at her heartstrings. 'Do you...do you want coffee?' she asked on a nervous rush, her whole body taut with equal parts desire and dread.

'Coffee?' He shook his head. 'No, my beautiful bride, I do not want coffee.' He forked his fingers into the loose tumble of her hair. 'I want you.' He eased her forward until all that separated them was the thick cloth of her robe and his sweats. 'Naked.' She shuddered, completely mesmerised by the hunger burning in his eyes. 'Untie the robe.'

Like someone in a daze, Farah fumbled with the knotted belt until the lapels hung straight down. She saw his nostrils flare and a thrill raced down her spine.

'Now open it,' he urged roughly.

Slowly, feeling as if she was in a hot whirlpool about to go under, Farah did, and then she was hard up against him, the tips of her breasts crushed against the solid wall of his chest. She made a sound, more like a whimper, and her knees gave out.

'Yes,' he growled right before he dragged her mouth up to his and kissed her.

CHAPTER ELEVEN

IT MIGHT HAVE been because of the mystical aspect of the predawn morning or it might have been because of the state of her nerves—probably it was just him—but Farah gave up all thought of resisting. Instead she opened to him, lost in the mindless passion that he had started inside her.

Raising her arms she wound them around his neck and arched into his rough, restless hands as they skated over her back and met at her bottom, lifting her onto her toes.

He growled low, the sound rough and exciting. Her body answered it with a flood of moisture at her core. Fevered, Farah clutched at his shoulders, lifting herself higher, her body searching for that perfect alignment with his, that perfect amount of pressure that would ease the ache. Oh, there it was, right there! 'Zachim!'

He swallowed his name with his kiss and brought both hands up to cup her breasts. Farah nearly died as pleasure knifed through her. She arched more fully against him, seeking more, wanting—oh, yes, wanting—him to lightly pinch her nipples. Her body bowed toward his, seeking more. Had anything ever felt this good, this perfect? She nuzzled her nose against his neck, planting open-mouthed kisses along his jaw, his cheek, wherever she could reach.

He turned his head, his mouth capturing hers again, his hands squeezing her gently, his fingers teasing, one muscled thigh wedged between hers, stroking the flames higher.

Suddenly his touch on her breasts wasn't enough and she nearly whimpered with ecstasy as his hand trailed over her stomach and curved between her legs. She felt like she was standing on some kind of tightrope, her whole body like a finely tuned instrument waiting for the master player to stroke the correct parts, her focus completely centred on the heat of his palm cupping her.

He hitched her higher, one arm hooked below her bottom as he bent forward and took her nipple into his mouth, sucking hard. Farah cried out and clutched at him to hold him close.

'So beautiful. So…sweet.' He rolled her nipple between his teeth and then drew on her rhythmically, his fingers playing with the lace of her panties between her legs. Dimly she thought that she should stop him and then her brain reminded her that they were married. That he was allowed to touch her like this. That she was allowed to lift her hips towards his hand and widen her stance to make it easier for him to… She groaned long and low and her head hit the wall when his fingers slid beneath the lace.

Which was when she remembered, and her head snapped forward. 'I didn't— That is, I'm not—' She clamped one hand over his to stay his exploration.

'You're not what, *habiba*?'

His finger moved along the folds of her most private place and she completely forgot what she was or what she wasn't. Nothing mattered except the delicious sensations he evoked as he stroked her and pressed deep.

With her eyes blissfully closed, Farah was completely unprepared when Zach dropped to his knees and ripped her flimsy panties from her body.

Her eyes flew to his. 'Oh. I… You…'

'Shhh,' he whispered, lifting one of her thighs and draping it over his shoulder, opening her to him. 'I need to taste you.'

Lost in a rush of liquid heat Farah gripped his hair as his tongue lapped at her, part of her wanting to pull him away and another, much more wanton part, wanting to pull him in closer.

The wanton part won out and he rewarded her with long firm strokes of his tongue. 'That's it, *habiba*, let yourself go.' His lips latched on to a part of her that made her body tighten with anticipation and she no longer knew exactly what he was doing to her or what part of himself he was doing it with, every cell in her body assaulted by a kaleidoscope of sensation it was stretching to reach. 'You taste so good,' he crooned between licks. 'Hot and sweet.'

'Zachim, Zach—please, please, I…' She didn't know what she was asking him for but suddenly she screamed as sensation ripped through her body, holding her for one brief, paralysing moment before tossing her into a maelstrom of pleasure that had her falling, falling…

'I've got you.' Dimly she was aware of his hand between her legs, of his fingers pushed up inside her, locking her into place, absorbing the shudders that wouldn't seem to stop while he held her against him.

She could hear her own harsh breathing but she couldn't stop it. Couldn't… 'What did you just do to me?'

His mouth lingered on hers, easing her back down to earth. 'I gave you an orgasm.' Masculine satisfaction coated each word.

'Oh.' Farah licked her lips. She could taste him there and also herself.

'Good, yeah?'

She felt her already hot cheeks catch fire.

'It's okay, sweetheart. I want to do that again—have you come in my mouth. I want— Hell.' He swore and muttered something about a bed before scooping her up in his arms.

'What's wrong?'

'I just remembered that you haven't done this before.

I don't know how I forgot.' He twisted the doorknob and shouldered open the door. 'I'm sorry if I scared you.'

Farah buried her head against his shoulder and inhaled his male scent. He hadn't scared her, exactly. 'It was nice.'

'Nice? That was more than nice.' He placed her on the bed and slipped off her bra. Completely naked now, Farah stared up at him. A muscle flicked in his jaw.

'You're exquisite.' He came down over the top of her and lashed the tip of her naked breasts with his tongue. The sensation was so piercing Farah nearly shot off the bed. 'Oh. Oh. Do that again. Please…'

'With pleasure, *habiba*,' he purred against her aroused flesh. 'With pleasure.'

Her tiny little panting breaths were going to be the end of him, Zach decided as he tried to keep from yanking off his sweats and driving straight into her nude body. Especially with her squirming beneath him like she was.

He placed a hand on her hip to stay her, wanting to draw out the moment, wanting to memorise every dip and curve of her silky skin. Wanting to feast on her tight little nipples that were now the colour of dark berries from where he'd sucked them—and they were just as sweet. As was every part of her; he wanted to lick and kiss her all over, starting with her mouth and ending with his face buried deep between her thighs again. The way she had come apart before, the shock widening her chocolate-brown eyes as she'd reached the absolute pinnacle of pleasure for the first time, would stay with him always.

'Zachim?' Her voice was soft, questioning, and he realised he was staring at her.

He drew a lazy circle around the swells of her breasts. 'What do you want, sweetheart?' He lapped at her. 'More of this?'

'Yes, oh, yes!' she gasped. 'But I want… I want to see you. To touch you.'

He'd be damned if he didn't want that, too. 'I'm all yours.' He sat up and stilled when he felt her small hands lift to his chest. She smoothed them over him, testing the firmness of his muscles, the springiness of his chest hair. He worked out regularly, so he knew he was in shape, but watching her avid face as she took him in was a pleasure all by itself. Who would have known?

Her movements grew bolder as she worked her hands over his shoulders and down his arms, then back up to stroke them down his happy trail. Every muscle in his body tensed as she stopped at his sweats riding low on his hips. His erection was so hard he was surprised he hadn't burst a seam.

Unable to wait any longer, he came over the top of her. She looked up at him, her eyes questioning. 'I want to make this last,' he said thickly, bending his head and nipping at her lips. She opened instantly and Zach moaned, settling his weight on top of her.

She wound her arms around his neck and he widened her legs and gently slid a finger along her damp curls to test her readiness. She was still hot and slick and he had to bite back a low groan, pleased when a whimper escaped her lips and she raised her hips to meet his gentle thrusts. 'You like that?' He inhaled her aroused scent. 'You like it when I touch you?'

'Yes, oh, yes.' She widened her knees even more and Zach slipped another finger inside her tight sheath, preparing her for his possession. Sweat broke out over his forehead and his muscles shook with the effort to hold himself back.

He watched her eyes glaze over and felt masculine pride that he could get her so close to the edge again so quickly. She was his. All his. Her dark hair was a messy cloud around her head, her slender limbs quivering for more. So he gave it to her, bending his head to tongue her nipple while circling her clitoris with his thumb. She nearly came off the bed and he growled his appreciation and took the tight bud deeper. He went from one to the other until she was writhing and moaning on the bed.

'Zachim, I need more. Please. I want—'

'Me,' he finished for her. 'Only me.'

Rearing up, he quickly stripped the sweats from his legs and noticed her eyes widen at the sight of him. 'Don't worry, *habiba*, we will fit together.'

She swallowed. 'I don't know how.'

Zach smoothed her sweat-dampened hair from her face. 'I'll make it good for you. Open your legs for me, Farah,' he instructed after she had closed them at the sight of him.

Gently nudging her knees wide with his own he settled his hips between her thighs. She was so wet the tip of his erection slid a little way into her without him meaning to. She lifted against him and he stilled. 'Easy, *habiba*, I don't want to hurt you.'

He felt her muscles clamp down around him and his body shuddered as it fought for control. Barely holding back he leaned down to kiss her. When he felt her attention absorbed by his mouth, he slid in a little deeper, gritting his teeth as her soft heat surrounded him. By Allah, but going slow was torture. 'Sweetheart, *habiba*, just relax a little more for me.'

Sweat slicked his skin as she shifted beneath him and it was all he could do not to drive into her with one wild, brutal thrust home.

'Zachim...'

She lifted against him and it was Zach's undoing. 'I'm sorry, sweetheart, but I have to—' He slid deep and heard her gasp.

He stilled, waiting for her to push him away. Instead

she stroked his slick shoulders, his back, reaching down to cup his buttocks.

Zach pulled out a little way and pushed back in. She was hot, wet and so soft beneath him. So responsive. 'How are you? Does it hurt?'

'No, I... It feels like you're filling me up.'

'I am, sweetheart.' Zach withdrew and plunged into her a little more roughly. 'I'm all the way in.'

She gasped his name and something primal uncoiled inside him. Something unsettling, like a whispered warning. Tensing he tried to catch the essence of it but Farah lifted to him, trying to match his rhythm, and he stopped thinking and helped her, guiding her, learning her, his brain focused on only one objective.

He could feel the slight tremors of her contractions and sense the urgency of her impending orgasm as her body pushed up to meet his. The pleasure was so intense he lost all sense of control, his body driven by an ancient instinct that threw them both over the edge into a place he'd never known was possible.

For a long time afterwards, Zach lay staring at the ceiling, Farah asleep at his side, wondering if he'd ever experienced anything like what had just happened. Wondering if the world had ever stopped at the point of his joining with a woman before. Wondering if he had ever felt this sense of completion before, this happy.

It seemed like a ludicrous emotion to have in bed. Satisfaction, yes. Pleasure, a given. But completion? Joy? *Possessiveness?*

He turned onto his side and tucked a silky strand of her hair behind her ear. She sighed and curled closer. Zach rubbed his chest, too tired to think let alone analyse what he was feeling. What did it matter anyway? It was what it was. Farah was his wife and there was no going back now.

* * *

Blinking against a room filled with light, Farah slowly opened her eyes and listened to the distant street noises that told her she should have been up hours ago. Then she remembered why she wasn't in such glorious, technicolour detail that she wasn't sure if she should feel appalled or delighted. Certainly she'd never experienced that kind of pleasure in her life before.

She pulled a face as she recalled every one of her whimpers, moans and cries for more. Then there was the way she had stroked the downy line of hair that covered Zach's rocky abdomen... She'd been out of control. Internal muscles ached in agreement and she wondered how she was going to face him this morning. For a woman who claimed she hadn't wanted to get married or have a man in her life, she'd put up very little resistance.

Actually, a little voice pointed out helpfully, *you put up none.*

Great. Even better.

Showering and washing her hair quickly, she dried off and then realised she had nothing to wear. Hearing a noise in the next room, she cast around and saw her folded wedding dress on a chair against the wall. She'd feel silly putting that on. Then she noticed a T-shirt draped over the back of a chair.

It was red and had a white image of a bird of prey in full flight on the front. It smelt of Zach and she inhaled deeply, her internal muscles softening even more. She frowned. Should she be thinking of sex again so soon? Was this even normal?

Determined that she would not turn into one of those clingy women who lived only to serve her husband, Farah pushed her thick hair back over her shoulder and opened the bedroom door, hoping at least that Zach had more clothes on than earlier.

Unfortunately not; she inwardly groaned. He was standing, half-turned away from her, slicing something at the kitchen bench and wearing low-riding denims, his hair slightly damp as if he, too, was not long out of the shower; his torso and feet were bare.

The leap in her pulse was instant and she drew in a deep breath, the scent of bacon and coffee making her stomach rumble. Hearing the embarrassingly loud noise, Zach turned towards her, his leonine eyes raking her from head to toe in that intense way that made her body burn.

He cursed, a swift, harsh sound, before he brought the side of his thumb up to his mouth.

Realising what had happened, she rushed to his side. 'Oh no, did you just cut yourself?'

She took his hand in hers, examining the line of blood that appeared as soon as he stopped sucking on it. 'You need to wash this under running water so we can see how deep it is.'

'It's not deep.'

But he complied and Farah tested the skin around the cut. He was right. It wasn't deep. 'It will still need a plaster. Do you have one?'

'No idea.' His eyes darkened as he watched her. 'Don't you think it's strange that I always seem to bleed around you?'

'That only happened once before,' she said indignantly. 'And you can hardly hold me responsible for this incident.'

'You walk in wearing nothing but my T-shirt, what do you expect? It's more of a weapon than the damned sword.' His eyes drifted over her again. 'Please tell me you at least have panties on underneath.'

Her skin felt hot under his eyes. 'You ripped them.' Right about the time he'd fallen to his knees.

He stilled and she knew he was remembering the same

thing that she was. 'So I did.' He drew her into the circle of his arms. 'How are you feeling this morning?'

Embarrassed. Confused. *Wanton*… 'Good,' she said gruffly, unsure what the post-sex etiquette was with a man who was still a virtual stranger to her.

'You're not sore?' His eyes scanned hers. 'I wasn't exactly as gentle as I had promised for your first time.'

Farah knew she was blushing and hated the way he so effortlessly undermined her self-possession while he remained so composed. It hardly seemed fair. 'Not sore at all,' she lied blithely. If he was unaffected by her, then she was equally unaffected by him.

About to pull away and ask for a coffee, she gasped as his hands skimmed up her waist and cupped her breasts. Her eyes flew to his as her hands manacled his wrists, her breathing uneven. 'Zach?'

He strummed his thumbs across her nipples. 'How about here? Was I too rough here?'

He knew he hadn't been. He knew right now she was so turned on she was about to melt at his feet. 'I… I… What about your finger?'

He lifted her onto the bench and stepped between her legs. 'My finger is not the part of my anatomy that is concerning me at the moment.' He tugged at the zip on his jeans, his eyes on her mouth. 'Something else is.'

Farah's insides clenched hungrily as that something else sprang thick and long from the opening in his jeans. She licked her lips and did what she had wanted to do ever since she'd felt him against her: she reached out and touched him, circling him with her fist.

He groaned and gripped the bench either side of her hips, tension drawing the skin on his face tight. Forgetting all about how awkward and confused he made her feel, she moved her hand experimentally along his smooth, solid length, loving the loss of composure she saw in his expression.

'Firmer,' he rasped, his head bowed back, the muscles in his neck straining.

'Like this?' She stroked him again. Harder.

His nostrils flared as he brought heavy-lidded eyes back to hers. 'Oh yeah, just like that.'

Not giving herself time to think, Farah bobbed her head and took the tip of him into her mouth. The sound he made was deep and guttural, and his hands came up to cup the back of her head. The taste of him was hot and male on her tongue and a rush of liquid heat pooled between her thighs.

'Enough.' Zach urged her head up and yanked his T-shirt over her head, pushing her back on the bench and following her down to clamp his mouth over hers. He pushed her legs wide, his finger sliding inside her, and he groaned again. 'So wet, so ready, *habiba*.' And then he was there, sliding her forward off the bench and onto him.

Five minutes later, Farah was a sweaty mess on the bed with a heavy male panting on top of her.

'Farah, hell…' He raked a hand through his hair and levered himself off her. 'I was at least planning to feed you first.' Her stomach grumbled and he rolled her over so that she was on top of him. 'Sorry, sweetheart.'

'It's okay. It was…'

'Good?'

'Yes.'

'Shockingly good?'

'Yes.' She sighed, trying not to think too hard about anything. 'Is sex always like this?'

'It's called making love and, no, it's not.'

Making love? 'Ah, Zachim?' She wrinkled her nose as she smelt something burning.

He stroked his hand down the curve of her spine. 'Mmm?'

'Did you turn the stove off?'

'Holy—' Unconcerned about his nakedness, he vaulted from the bed and ran to the other room.

Grabbing his T-shirt again, she quickly donned it and followed, to find him rinsing a steaming pan under a tap, the inside charred to black.

He looked over his shoulder at her. 'I hope you like your bacon well-done.'

She laughed.

Later, they finally ate, and not a minute too soon, because Zach was sure his stomach had been about to feed on itself while he fed on her.

He looked across at her curled in the window seat, nursing a fresh cup of coffee and a faraway look as she gazed out over the tranquil blue waters of Talamanca Bay. The remains of their breakfast—eggs *sans* bacon—were pushed away on the breakfast table between them.

The air was balmy with late morning, the waters calm, and his thoughts somehow just as peaceful. The restless emptiness he'd been experiencing a few weeks ago strangely settled. *By this woman?*

The question threw him a little because he had no idea how she felt about him.

It was a surprisingly angst-ridden thought for a man who was used to women who would watch paint dry if he told them he found it fascinating. Not that Farah would. She'd no doubt roll her eyes and tell him a camel had more brains than he did. The thought made him smile and he was determined to remove the pensive look on her face.

Feeling strangely bereft of the skills that had led him arrogantly to claim that he was good with women and horses, he cleared his throat. 'You look troubled, *habiba*. Want to share?'

She glanced at him, her eyes guarded. Slowly she set her mug down on the table. 'It's nothing.'

He cocked an eyebrow and waited, resisting the need to haul her into his lap to comfort her and pet her. '*Nothing* seems to get us into trouble. How about we try some other word?'

A faint smile tugged at her lips. 'Okay, I was... I was thinking that we don't really know each other very well.'

'Well, we do,' he corrected lazily. 'But that's not what you meant.'

Her smile turned wry. 'No.'

'Okay, well, I know that you take your coffee white with one and you know I have mine black. What else would you like to know?'

'I don't know.' She made a face. 'What is your favourite breakfast?'

'Bacon,' he delivered, deadpan. 'Yours?'

She laughed and he took it as a small victory. 'Eggs with sumac, hummus on flatbread, yoghurt and dates.'

'What about toast with Vegemite?'

She frowned. 'What is that?'

'It's something I discovered on a tour of Australia. You will love it.'

She rolled her eyes. 'Naturally.'

He smiled. 'Favourite colour?'

'Too many to choose. You?'

He looked at her hair. 'Chestnut brown.'

She blushed beautifully. 'Favourite pastime?'

'Tinkering with engines. Yours?'

'Reading.'

Zach smiled as he felt some of the tension ease out of her. 'See? Already the marriage is working.'

'What about love?'

He stilled, his heart hammering. Was she about to tell him that love was important to her? That she didn't love him? 'What about it?' he asked gruffly.

'Your mother said you always wanted to marry for love.'

'My mother talks too much. Tell me how you came to use a sword so well.'

It was an obvious change of subject but Farah let it go because for some reason talking about love bothered her as much as it seemed to bother him. 'How *is* your arm?' she asked. 'I noticed this morning it still had a mark. I'm sorry I sliced you.'

'It was more of a nick, but I'm sorry I underestimated you. You're very good.'

She pulled a face. 'Hardly.'

He leaned over and tapped the edge of her nose. 'It was a compliment. So, what made you learn?'

That slight, vulnerable look he'd seen before briefly crossed her face and he was almost sorry he'd asked. Then she shrugged as if it didn't matter and he knew that it did. A lot.

'When my mother and unborn brother died my father was devastated and nothing I did seemed to help. One day while I was weaving a basket to sell at the markets, I saw how much fun the boys were having and how strong they looked, sparring with each other. It made me hate being a weak girl, so I asked to join them.'

'I'm surprised your father let you.'

'He didn't know.' She gave a rueful grimace. 'For a long time he was sort of absent. But I knew how badly he had wanted a son and I wanted to impress him. So I trained hard and entered the tournament that we hold at the village once a year—and I nearly won.'

He smiled. 'I have no doubt. And was he impressed?'

Farah looked across at Zach and realised just how much she'd told him and how easy he was to talk to—something else she hadn't expected. Deciding that she might as well continue, she hugged her knees into her chest. '*Shocked* is probably more the word I would use.' She pulled a rueful face, trying not to recall her father's harsh disapproval and her utter sense of hopelessness at the time. 'Sometimes it felt like nothing I did was—' She stopped, feeling more exposed than when she was lying before him naked.

'Good enough?' He filled in. 'Don't look so surprised, *habiba*. Your father isn't the only man to doll out conditional love.' His expression grew grim. 'My father was of the same ilk.'

Conditional love? Farah had never thought of it like that. Was that what her father gave? It seemed so obvious now, but always, in the past, she had thought there was something lacking in her.

A feeling of lightness came over her and she laughed. 'Why did I never think of that?'

Zach shrugged. 'Our fathers had a way of making us feel otherwise.'

Realising that Zach's father must not have approved of him, either, she leant forward. 'Are you saying you didn't see eye to eye with your father, either?'

Zach gave a short bark of laughter. 'That's putting it mildly. Nadir was always his favourite and he had little time for me as his *spare*.'

Farah heard the layer of pain behind that one word and her heart went out to him, not for one minute having thought that they would have something like this in common. 'And you never resented your brother for that?' Because at times she still felt guilty about her old feelings of resentment towards her unborn brother, certain that her own death would not have wrought half the pain in her father that his had.

'It wasn't Nadir's fault. My father was raised hard and he raised us hard.'

'Still, I admire that you didn't feel second-best.'

'Oh, I felt it. Often. Second-best. Third-best. I did everything to get his attention: being good, being bad, being funny, being smart, being strong... Then I realised that beating my head against a brick wall was only denting my head, not his, so I stopped. I joined the Foreign Legion, did a degree in engineering and started my own company. When I first got back to Bakaan—as you know—there was a lot to do to settle down the unrest. Then I saw how badly things had become and I did what I could behind the scenes.'

Did what he could? Farah blinked. 'It's you,' she said abruptly, instinctively knowing that he was the one who had organised the contraband goods their village—and probably others—received on a regular basis.

He smiled. 'I hope so.'

'No.' She shook her head, still dazed to think it might be true. 'You're the one who organised the medical supplies and educational material that is sent out to the villages in our area.'

He shrugged. 'I know it wasn't much, but it was all I could do while my father was alive. That will change though.'

'Thank you. That was…' She swallowed, struggling for words. For years she'd carried around a grudge against the Darkhans because she had blamed them for the loss of her mother and the happy life she had known before. She hadn't questioned the who, what or why of what had happened but had accepted her father's view and taken it on as her own. How could she have been so narrow-minded? How could she have let the past colour her view of the world so completely? 'I'm sorry. I think it was me who underestimated you this time.'

'Come here. I want to hold you.'

She unfolded shaky legs out from under her and went to him. She let him pull her down onto his lap and opened for him when he kissed her.

'You know, ever since you told me you were responsible for that publication five years ago I've been thinking about something.'

'What?'

'I want to suggest to Nadir that you become the ambassador for change in the outer regions.'

'What?' she parroted, unable to take in what he'd just offered.

'You have a sharp mind, *habiba*. It would be remiss of me not to utilise that. And changing years of cultural norms is not going to be easy. People will resist. They need to feel there is someone they can trust, especially since I am certain Nadir and I will be viewed sceptically at first.'

Farah chewed on the inside of her lip, her heart thumping hard at the thought. What he said made sense, and she would love it, but... 'You would let your wife work?'

'As long as it doesn't interfere with her home duties, of course.'

She felt her tentative bubble of hope burst. *Here it comes*, she thought, *the proviso*. She raised her chin. 'Such as?'

'Such as keeping our apartment spic and span, making sure my clothing is cleaned and ironed, servicing me whenever and wherever I— Oof!'

Farah punched him lightly on the shoulder, realising he was teasing her, and completely thrown by the unexpected playfulness. 'You're joking.'

He laughed deeply. 'For a non-violent person, you pack quite a punch.'

'I am usually non-violent,' she cried. 'I don't know what gets into me around you.'

The look he gave her could have heated the polar ice caps. 'I can tell you what gets into you.' His hands grew possessive, demanding. 'Me. And I have to tell you that every time you get feisty it makes me hot.'

Farah swallowed, instant arousal turning her limbs to jelly. 'Every time?'

As if knowing just how ready she was for him, he drew

in a sharp breath and rose, with her still in his arms as if she were no heavier than one of the cushions they'd been seated on.

'Every time.' He strode inside and dumped her on the sofa, his hands raising her T-shirt and sliding along the sensitive skin of her belly. 'But I was serious about one of those duties.' He fingered his belt buckle. 'Want me to demonstrate?'

Feeling herself melting, and unable to contain it, she reached up and pulled him down over her. 'Maybe a little more instruction might be worthwhile.'

CHAPTER TWELVE

IT WAS SOME sort of loud banging that roused Zach from a sweet dream and a deep sleep. Thinking it was an alarm, he rolled over and thumped the digital clock on the bedside table. Farah stirred beside him and he automatically tightened his arm around her shoulders.

She settled deeper into the crook of his arm and he closed his eyes.

Before arriving in Ibiza, while Farah had slept on the plane, Zach had made some plans about what they would do after they had settled in. First they would explore the beaches around Talamanca Bay, then they'd fly to a little out-of-the-way Spanish restaurant he knew in Dalt Vila, maybe sail around the beautiful island of Es Vedra and watch the sunset from the popular spot nearby.

What they ended up doing was never leaving the apartment—three days in and out of bed eating takeout that was brought by his security detail and introducing Farah to trashy TV—to which his new wife was now addicted. His mouth quirked at her penchant for Doris Day movies and he made a mental note to check the guide before channel-surfing with her again. He'd tried to explain that real men didn't watch romantic movies but she'd nestled more comfortably against him and he'd shut up. And enjoyed himself.

He'd also enjoyed breakfast. Since learning what she

preferred, he'd had the food stockpiled and he liked to watch her potter around, fixing share plates for them both while he brewed the coffee. Then he'd pop the toast in the toaster and over their meal he'd try to convince her to give Vegemite a go. So far she'd steadfastly refused but he'd seen the look of horror cross her face when she'd dipped her little finger in the jar to test it. He'd nearly laughed out loud but instead had kissed her into a stupor before bending her over the table and lifting her—his—T-shirt.

Damn, but he loved her in his T-shirts, with all that dark hair rippling down her back, her feet bare. All in all he'd say she fascinated him and in a surprisingly short space of time, his feelings for his wife had deepened to the point that he now struggled to label them. In fact if he didn't know better he'd think— The loud thumping started up again, breaking his train of thought.

'Darkhan, you lazy bastard,' a voice hollered from downstairs. 'We know you're in there. Your security team told us.'

Farah stiffened in his arms. 'Who is that?'

'Shh,' he murmured as he disentangled himself from her limbs. 'I'll take care of it.'

He grabbed his jeans on the way out and shoved them on. Then he headed downstairs and opened the front door of the villa. Sunlight spilled over the terracotta-tiled portico. Damian and Luke stood there, grinning like tomcats.

'You idiots ever heard of calling first?' Zach complained.

'We did. We've been calling and texting since yesterday.' Damian pushed past him into the foyer. 'You didn't respond.' He slapped him on the back. 'It's great to see you.'

'I forgot to check my phone.' In fact he hadn't checked his phone since...well, he couldn't remember.

Luke ambled past at a slower pace. 'Sweet digs. We

thought you might be side-tracked by a beautiful...' His friend's voice trailed off and Zach followed his gaze to the top of the stairs where Farah stood in nothing but his T-shirt, holding a large chef's knife in her hand. Zach grimaced. He really needed to show her where the suitcases were. And as for the knife... She squeaked out a noise as she noticed the three of them taking in her long legs and darted out of sight.

'Woman,' Damian filled in as Luke still stared wide-eyed. 'And you are!'

'Was that a knife?' Luke asked, confused.

'Ah, a fake one,' Zach parried. 'And she's not just any woman. She's my wife.'

He heard the note of pride in his voice and wondered if his friends did, too, the feeling he was struggling to name swelling inside his chest.

'*Wife?* Well...hell,' Damian sputtered. 'I thought I heard hearts breaking when I woke up this morning. Where was the invite?'

'We kept it small.'

'So, okay...' Luke shook his head as if he couldn't quite believe it. 'So, when you coming to the dock?'

'I don't know. I'll have to check with Farah.'

His two friends exchanged glances.

'You're coming to my party tonight, though, right?' Damian questioned. 'I mean, that is why you're here, isn't it?'

'If the missus says yes,' Luke said with mock seriousness.

'Well, of course,' Damian agreed. 'If the missus says—'

'All right, all right,' Zach growled, half wondering if Damian's party was really a good idea. 'You two morons have had your fun, now shove off or you can forget a present.'

'As long as she's long-legged and big—'

Zach slammed the door on their laughing faces. His

friends were confirmed bachelors and Zach was just glad
not to be one of them any more.

He took the stairs two at a time and found Farah sitting cross-legged on the bed. He glanced around. 'Where's
the knife?'

'In the kitchen.'

He made a mock-salute to the ceiling and saw her mouth
twitch. 'Feel like a walk to the harbour?'

Her face brightened. 'Yes. I'd love it. But I haven't a
thing to wear.'

Zach strolled to the walk-in closet, opened the suitcase
and pulled out a pair of tiny shorts. He'd told her maid to
pack the Western clothing Imogen had organised for him,
but he'd yet to show Farah. He grabbed a white T-shirt he
knew would show off her olive skin and dark hair to perfection, lace panties and a bra he couldn't wait to remove.

She frowned when he dropped them on the bed. 'Where
did these come from?'

'The built-in 'robe.'

'The…' she frowned. 'I thought they were your suitcases in there. Why didn't you tell me?'

'You didn't ask.' He smiled. 'And it wasn't as if you
needed clothing.'

'Oh.' Clearly embarrassed, she picked up the shorts.
'What are these?'

'Shorts.'

She eyed them sceptically. 'And what do I wear them
with?'

'A T-shirt. Flip-flops.'

'Flip-flops?'

'Footwear.'

She held the shorts against her hips and glanced back
at him. 'What else do I wear on my legs?'

'Ah, nothing.'

She frowned. 'On the street?'

'Sure.'

She shook her head. 'No.' She jumped up off the bed and inspected the closet. A century later she came out holding a pair of jeans. 'Where are my usual clothes?'

'I thought you'd be more comfortable in Western clothing.'

Her mouth pinched together and, just as he readied himself for an argument, she surprised him and huffed out a breath. 'I'll try them.'

Thinking the day couldn't get any better, he nearly choked when she came out after her shower dressed in the T-shirt and jeans. She pulled at the denim but they just sprung back into place, hugging her toned thighs as if they were sprayed on. 'These don't fit.'

Zach nodded. 'Turn around.'

She did a quick twirl and he frowned. 'You've just given me another idea,' he said.

'What?'

'I'm going to tell Nadir to make the wearing of jeans mandatory for all women in Bakaan, stat.'

She rolled her eyes and put her hands on her hips and a shaft of sweet pleasure shot straight to Zach's heart. 'Be serious,' she chided.

'I am.' He strolled towards her and curled his fingers into the waistband of her jeans, wondering if he'd ever felt happier than he did right now. 'Very serious about making love to my wife one more time.'

Farah couldn't stop smiling as they stepped out of the villa and into the bright sunshine. She hadn't expected to feel this…this light-hearted about being married; this light-hearted about the man she was married to. She snuck a quick glance at him and tried not to ogle him in his fitted T-shirt, denims and tapered sunglasses.

When he took her hand her heart seemed to skip a beat

and she focused on her surroundings to tamp down the emotions she instinctively knew she had to keep in check.

The harbour town was totally beautiful with its aqua-blue bay, sandy beaches and rows of pastel-coloured high-rise apartments and villas set into the hillside.

But it was the people who held most of her attention, old and young and dressed in every combination of clothing she had ever seen in her magazines. One woman even had a small dog in her handbag with a diamond-studded collar and a bow in its hair. And then there was the trio of eye-catching women promenading towards them. They were slender to the point of being skinny, tanned golden-brown and wearing… She frowned, unable to recall what the word was for what looked like underwear. And they were looking at Zach as if they wanted to eat him alive.

'Careful, *habiba*, you're about to cut off my circulation.'

'I'm sorry.' Farah instantly eased her grip on his hand. 'I just… Those women aren't wearing any clothes.'

Zach chuckled. 'They're wearing bikinis. Swimwear,' he elaborated when she looked at him blankly.

'They're positively indecent,' she whispered.

'Sexy,' he corrected.

'You think they're sexy?'

His eyes skated over her body. 'Sure. On the right woman.'

Before she could ask who the right woman was, he re-directed her. 'Down here.'

Farah continued to be bug-eyed as Zach led her along a beautiful pier lined with yachts the size of tall buildings. At the end was a row of streamlined boats, much smaller and shaped like brightly coloured race cars without wheels. Men were scurrying around them and, combined with the sound of the engines revving and the smell of petrol, the air was alive with a sense of expectation and fun. More girls in bikinis lined the pier, leaning over the weathered railing like decorations.

Sticking close to Zach, Farah feigned a nonchalance she was far from feeling while he introduced her to his two friends from earlier and a group of other men and women who were clearly enamoured by the prince.

When one of the men suggested Zach take the boat for a test run, she saw his face light up. 'And I thought I was going to have to pull the owner card to get the gig.'

Owner? He owned the boats?

Turning to her, he checked if she was okay and she nodded. No way was she going to let him know that she was feeling completely out of her depth and wishing they were back in the apartment. Back in bed.

It was only when the shiny speedboat revved away from the pier and took off in a powerful arc of white water that she felt riveted to the spot.

'Watch how fast he is.' Luke came up beside her. 'There's no one better behind the wheel.'

Farah watched and her heart flew into her mouth when the bullet-shaped boat became airborne before crashing back down, spraying water into the air. 'Is it supposed to do that?'

'Oh yeah.' His friend didn't bother to hide his admiration. 'I wouldn't be surprised if he wants to race again sometime.'

'Race?'

'Yeah, he was unbeatable once, and when he left he said his stint was over and he'd never get back in one of those babies again. But then he said he'd never marry a Bakaani girl, either.' He winked at her. 'Never say never, eh?'

Never marry a Bakaani girl?

Before she could fully process that piece of information, Zach had pulled the boat up to the pier and men were yelling and readying themselves to hold it steady.

The look on his face was one of exhilaration and joy

and she felt a momentary pang that he would never look at her like that.

Brushing off her suddenly morbid thought, she nodded as Luke told her he'd see her at the party before jumping down to join Zach.

'Luke said you might race again,' she mentioned to Zach as they wandered back along the harbour a short time later.

'No.' Zach held her hand again. 'When I finished up, I meant it.' He stopped in front of an enormous navy-and-white yacht with music and lively conversation coming from the upper decks. 'Ready?'

No, she wasn't ready. She wanted to ask him about what Luke had told her but something warned her to hold off. What did it matter anyway? She knew he hadn't wanted to marry her. He'd made that plain.

She glanced up to find Zach looking at her curiously and wondered if he guessed how unsettled she felt. 'Sure,' she hedged, pride refusing to let her lean against him, as if she was the kind of woman who could not take care of herself.

Still, she couldn't seem to stem her unease once they boarded the yacht, and the curious glances she received as more and more people realised she was with the prince didn't help at all. The women especially gave her a weird vibe and didn't seem to know what to make of her once they'd asked where she was from and how she had met the prince. Farah kept her answers deliberately vague— 'My father introduced us'—which earned her a smile from Zach. After that most people either ignored her or saw someone in the distance they simply had to speak with and walked away.

Whatever.

Farah didn't care. For the most part Zach kept her by his side, proudly introducing her as his wife, and she was more pleased than she would have expected to be by that.

Especially given that this marriage had been forced on both of them. Somehow in the past three days that hadn't seemed relevant in the isolated nest of the apartment where she'd come to learn that, far from being an arrogant despot, her new husband was actually a kind and decent human being. But he still hadn't chosen to marry her out of free will, and probably never would have if his friend's unintentionally hurtful words were true.

'Having a good time?'

About to tell Zach she'd prefer to muck out the camel enclosure in her village, she turned her head to find him watching her with an expression on his face that melted her from the inside out. And suddenly she was determined that, yes, she would have a good time in this life he seemed to enjoy so much. 'Yes!' she said, turning her face up to his.

'I'm glad.' He leaned over and kissed her softly before drawing back with his arm slung around her waist. His possessive touch was comforting but, try as she might, she couldn't set aside the feeling of vulnerability that gripped her, surrounded as she was by so many glamorous people, especially those whispering behind their hands as they looked at her. Were they wondering what Zach was doing with her? Or did they all know that he had been forced to marry her? That given a choice he would have preferred any one of the beautiful women parading around on the yacht in their *sexy* triangles of material. Would Zach ever expect her to wear one of those, in public? If so, he was going to be incredibly disappointed, because that just wasn't her.

'Zach.'

Someone—a woman—said his name in a low, throaty murmur and Farah turned to find a slender, elegant blonde looking up at him. She was tiny and delicate and so flawlessly beautiful she was hard to look away from.

Used to having women come up to him by now, Farah

at first didn't pay her any special attention, but then she realised that Zach had grown tense.

'I heard you got married,' the woman said, casting Farah a brief glance.

'Yes.' Something in his tone made the hairs on the nape of Farah's neck stand on end. 'Amy, I'd like you to meet my wife, Farah.' His fingers flexed on her hip. 'Farah, this is Amy Anderson.'

Farah had wondered more than once who the woman was that Zach had nearly married and suddenly she knew she was standing right in front of her. It was obvious in every casually awkward line of the woman's body and the answering tension in her husband's.

The woman had a peaches-and-cream complexion Farah would never achieve even if she stayed out of the sun for a decade, and the way she was looking at Zach made it very clear that, if she could, she would trade places with Farah in a heartbeat. Feeling about as attractive as a desert shrub in a French garden, Farah smiled. 'I'm pleased to meet you.'

'And you,' Amy said with a warmth Farah wasn't sure reached her eyes.

'How long ago did you break up?' she asked a little dully as the beautiful Amy finally wandered off into the crowd.

Zach grimaced faintly. 'Was it that obvious?'

Farah felt old beyond her years. 'A woman knows these things.' Not that she ever would have thought she would.

'Five years ago.'

Five years ago? Farah frowned. Was that because he'd had to return to Bakaan? Had she inadvertently broken up his relationship when she had tried to implement change with her little magazine? It seemed impossible.

She wanted to ask if he had been in love with her but she knew that he must have been if he'd nearly married her. Did he still? The sick feeling she had experienced on her wedding day thinking about the exact same thing balled in her stomach, but there was no way she would ask him because she really didn't want to know the answer. In fact, she didn't want to *think* about the answer.

As if reading her every thought, he took her chin gently between his fingers to bring her eyes to his. 'If you're worried that I'll cheat on you, Farah, I won't. I'm not like that. Amy is in my past.'

Deep down she knew that he was telling the truth but it didn't change the fact that he had once wanted to marry Amy and he had never wanted to marry her—and why was she so fixated on that all of a sudden?

'I'm not worried, I—'

'Prince Zachim.' A large man in a cream suit that stretched across his ample belly and a matching Stetson stopped beside them, an overconfident smile on his face. 'Not interruptin', am I?'

'I've never known you *not* to interrupt, Hopkins,' Zach said mildly, making the man laugh.

'Always did enjoy your sense of humour, Your Highness. This is Cherry, my wife. And you must be Zach's new wife.'

'Farah,' Zach supplied grudgingly.

'Good to meet you, ma'am.' The man took her hand in that deferential manner men did when they were putting women in their place before dismissing her in favour of Zach. 'I was hoping to talk to you about building hotels over in that country of yours, Your Highness, and there's no time like the present.'

'Actually, there is. And now isn't it.'

'Oh, come now, we fly back to Dallas tomorrow. Cherry will take care of your little lady for a spell, won't you, sugar?'

'Of course!' the vivacious redhead exclaimed. 'I'd be glad to.'

'Some other time, Hopkins. Farah and I were just leaving.'

'It's okay, Zach.' Farah put her hand on his arm, knowing from an earlier conversation they'd had how important new investments were to Bakaan and not wanting to be the reason he missed an opportunity, even if the man was a bit of windbag. 'I'll be fine.'

'See? She'll be fine.' The man gave her an oily smile. 'You got to let 'em either sink or swim, don't you, sugar?'

The look on Zach's face told her he wanted to make this man sink or swim and it gave her the urge to giggle. Instead she moved away from him and murmured a greeting to the man's nubile wife who was spilling out of a red polka-dot bikini top above white jeans that looked tighter than her own.

Within minutes Farah found herself amidst a small knot of Cherry's chic friends, including the beautiful Amy, who all wanted the gossip on how she had landed the prince— gossip Farah had no intention of giving them because it would only show them how little she really meant to her husband!

'At least tell us if he's as hot in the sack as they say he is,' one of the women whispered.

'Tia! You can't ask that,' another woman admonished.

'Oh, don't pretend you're not dying to know, Pansy, you tried to get him yourself once without any success. I heard he was into threesomes, as well. Is that true?'

Threesomes? No way was Farah naively going to ask what that was.

'Tia, you're so naughty!' Pansy giggled and took Farah's arm. 'Please ignore our friend. She's had too much champagne and she's had some seriously bad dates.' She glanced down at Farah's empty hands. 'Oh, Lordy, you don't have a drink. Waiter, champagne, *por favor*!'

'I'm fine,' Farah quickly assured her. 'I was sick the last time I had champagne.'

'So?' Tia asked.

'Oh, you're adorable,' Pansy interjected as if Farah was a puppy she'd just won in a competition. 'Isn't she adorable?'

Amy cast her a cool smile and sipped her own champagne as if she had no trouble with the drink at all. 'How long have you and Zach known each other?'

Farah felt the woman's interest like the pointed end of a sword to her solar plexus. 'Not that long.'

'Was it a whirlwind courtship?' Cherry asked, sipping a red drink with a paper umbrella sticking out of the top.

Farah thought about her father ordering Zach to marry her. 'I guess you could call it that.'

'You must have something special going on under the hood,' Tia drawled knowingly. 'To keep the attention of man like that.'

'Have you seen the way he looks at her? H. O. T. Hot,' Pansy said. 'Oh, look, there's the girl I saw earlier with the goody bags. Yoo-hoo, over here.'

Feeling a small glow at Pansy's observation that Zach looked at her in some special way, Farah watched as a much younger woman in a tiny bikini sauntered over with a basket of small delicately fringed purses inside.

'What's in them?' Tia eyed the bags with bored interest. 'If it's not diamonds, I'm not interested.'

'Chocolates,' the woman said.

'Oh, definitely not, then.' She shuddered as if the woman had said snakes.

'I'll take one,' Cherry said, reaching into the bag. 'What about you, Panse? Amy?'

'Which is which?' Pansy eyed the three different-coloured purses.

'There's dark, white and a combination of the two.'

Pansy selected the combination. 'Farah?'

'Oh…' Farah scanned the small purses, suddenly re-

membering the other night when Zach had ordered straw-
berries and chocolate sauce and proceeded to eat most of
them. Off her. She couldn't prevent a small smile from
sneaking across her lips and her heartbeat quickened.
'Dark, please.'

'Really?' Amy stepped forward to eye the selection.
'I'd choose the white if I were you.' She rifled through the
purses as if hunting for the perfect specimen. 'Zach is more
a vanilla kind of guy.' She glanced up at Farah through a
veil of thick lashes. 'If you know what I mean.'

Farah blinked, wondering if she'd heard her right. When
she saw Pansy's wide-eyed stare and Tia's amused smirk,
she knew she hadn't misinterpreted the other woman's
subtle put-down. Heat rushed into her face, making her
insecurities spike. She bent over the basket, pride insisting
she choose the purse holding the dark treats. This woman
might be right about Zach's preferences, but he wasn't hers
any more, and Farah took some comfort from Zach's earlier reassurance that Amy was in his past.

'Maybe he's changed,' she said casually, attempting to
calm her galloping heartbeat. 'Five years is a long time.'

Amy's small smile could have frozen the sun. 'Five
years?' She cocked her head, as if confused. 'I meant last
week.'

Last week? Farah felt herself reel and couldn't stop the
barrage of questions from flooding her brain. *Had Zach
lied when he'd said Amy was in his past?* And what of
the tender consideration he'd given her over the past few
days? *Had that just been his way of making the best of a
bad situation?*

'Oh, look, there's Morgan O'Keefe,' Amy said. 'If you'll
excuse me?'

There was a short, loaded silence as they watched Amy
saunter across the crowded deck and then Pansy patted her

arm. 'Don't mind her,' she said. 'She was obviously looking to start a row.'

'She's jealous,' Tia said offhandedly. 'She was sure she
was the next Princess of Bakaan but it didn't come off.
Move on, I say.'

'Oh, right, like you've moved on from Gary?' Pansy
chortled.

'Do not mention that man around me,' Tia hissed, making the other two girls burst into peals of laughter.

Farah watched them, feeling as if she was listening
to them from afar, a sort of numbness working its way
through her system.

'Ready to go?'

Zach appeared at her side and Farah pinned a bright
smile on her face. 'Of course.'

CHAPTER THIRTEEN

'OKAY, OUT WITH IT,' Zach said, shutting the front door to the apartment and turning to face Farah.

She paused on the first step of the stairs. 'Out with what?'

He came towards her and shoved his hands in his pockets so that he didn't put them on her. Once they were there, her clothing was coming off, but he could tell there was something weighing on her mind that needed to be dealt with first. 'Whatever's bothering you.'

'There's nothing bothering me.'

She continued up the stairs and he followed, trying to keep his eyes off the sway of her bottom in those jeans. 'Pull the other one, it's got bells on it.'

'Sorry?'

Seeing her pained look, he sighed. 'It's just an expression.' He stopped her at the top of the stairs, his eyes searching hers. 'Talk to me,' he said softly. She smiled brightly as she had on the yacht and he wondered if she truly expected him to fall for it. 'Please,' he added.

'Okay…' Her throat worked as she swallowed. 'What's a threesome?'

'A what?' Zach nearly choked at the question. Now, *that* he hadn't been expecting. 'How— Who—' He shook his head. 'Why are you asking about threesomes?'

'One of the women said that you like them.'

'Ah, I see you've been listening to gossip.' His eyes searched hers but she kept her gaze averted, so he guessed that wasn't the real question on her mind, but damn...

He ran a hand through his hair before moving into the kitchen to pull a bottle of water from the fridge, pouring them both a glass. Really he should have just ditched the party when he'd first thought to. Ironic when the whole purpose of coming to Ibiza had been to see his friends and immerse himself in his old lifestyle, to get his spark back. Now all he wanted was to immerse himself in Farah. In fact it was all he could think about. Even when flying over the water in Damian's jet boat, at speeds that usually wiped all thought from his mind, he'd compared it to the joy of waking with her in his arms.

Not wanting to dwell on what that meant, he focused on explaining a threesome to her. 'Okay, well, first a threesome is sex with three people.' When she stared at him blankly, he continued. 'At the same time.'

'Oh.' She blinked. 'I figured it was something sexual but I thought perhaps it was three different positions or something.' She leaned her elbows on the counter top and absently ran a hand up and down the glass of water. 'Is it two men and a woman or two women and a man?'

Zach coughed into his hand. 'It can be either. Why? Are you interested?'

She raised limpid brown eyes to his and her nose wrinkled. 'I've never thought about it before, but...not particularly.'

He blew out a breath. 'Good because I don't share. Which should answer your question as to whether I'm into them or not. But, as interesting as that little diversion was, it wasn't the reason behind your quiet state.'

Surprise flickered in her eyes before she lowered them. 'How do you know that?'

'I have good instincts.'

'You mean you're cocky.'

'That, too.' He smiled to try and lighten the mood. 'Tell me I'm wrong.'

'You're wrong.'

'Farah!'

'Okay, fine. Did you see that woman Amy last week?'

Zach blinked. Hell he hadn't been expecting that one, either. 'No. I haven't seen Amy for five years. Why do you ask?'

'No reason.'

She moved into the living area and he followed. 'Farah, don't fob me off. Why did you ask?'

'She implied that you had…' She shrugged. 'But it was probably my mistake.'

Possibly. Or possibly Amy had wanted to cause trouble between them because she was upset that he hadn't shown any interest in catching up with her. She had definitely been put out to find him married and maybe that was his fault. 'Amy emailed me last week asking to catch up tonight,' he admitted.

Something he'd completely forgotten about until just now. In fact it had been a shock to see her at the party and even more of a shock to realise that he felt nothing for her. Maybe she'd picked up on that and also that he was completely enamoured with his new wife.

Was that how he felt about Farah? *Enamoured?*

Looking at her now, her bedroom eyes large in her face, her hair tumbling around her stiff shoulders, her curvy figure outlined to perfection… A sense of destiny whispered across the surface of his mind. The fact was he couldn't remember ever making outrageously arrogant statements to Amy or any other woman just to make her laugh because it lit something up inside him, nor had he wanted to watch her do the simple act of rubbing the sleep from her eyes in the morning, and he certainly hadn't wasted time on a TV program other than sports just because he'd wanted to hold her in his arms for a little longer.

'So you had arranged to see her?'

It took Zach a full minute to shift his focus from what his mind was trying to tell him to what Farah had asked. When he did, he grimaced. 'Yes, but that was before we married and as I said before, I have no intention of being unfaithful to you. You said you believed me.'

She moved over to the wall of windows and stared outside. 'I do.'

Zach sucked in a slow breath. He'd expected her to be happy at his declaration so he was beyond perturbed when she ignored him in favour of staring out at the darkness. Did that mean she didn't believe him?

'I can see the look of doubt on your face but I'm telling you the truth.' Amy really was in his past because, regardless of what happened between him and Farah, it had been obvious to Zach tonight that his brother had called it right about Amy years ago.

Wanting to eradicate the far away look on Farah's face, he slipped his hand down to hold hers, coming into contact with the silk purse he'd vaguely noticed on the drive to the apartment. 'What's this?'

She stared at it as if she didn't realise she was still holding it. 'Chocolates. They were giving them out at the party. Do you want one?'

No, he didn't want one. 'I want to know whether you believe that I will be faithful to you first.'

'I do.'

'Farah—'

'They're dark, though,' she said, holding up the chocolates as if that somehow made a difference. Personally Zach couldn't care if they were gold-coated and he frowned at the bag.

'You do like dark chocolate, don't you?'

He heard the tremor in her voice and sighed. 'I love dark chocolate.'

That made her lip tremble even more and yet again he found himself at a loss as to how to communicate with this woman. So he said nothing, just stared out at the dark bay beyond the window and waited.

'Dark, isn't it?'

Zach's eyebrows drew down. They were going to talk about the weather now? 'That it is.'

He tried to keep the impatience from his voice when he answered but he wasn't sure he'd succeeded when she stiffened.

'I could have chosen white chocolate instead.'

What the— 'Farah?' He turned her to face him and saw a glittering wetness in her eyes. If this was Amy's doing he'd throttle her. '*Habiba*, sweetheart... What's...?'

'Am I too dark for you?'

He shook his head. 'Too dark?'

'My skin, my hair, my eyes. I realised tonight that I've only ever seen you photographed with fair-haired women and Luke said you had never intended to marry a Bakaani woman. Is that why...? Is that...?'

Zach swore roughly. Perhaps he'd bury Luke and Amy together. 'Listen to me,' he ordered. 'I did say that once but I was young and stupid and rebelling against my father's expectations of me. I'm married to you now so none of that matters. It's in the past.'

Was it?

Farah desperately wanted to believe him, she really did, but it wasn't easy. How could he want her when she so obviously didn't fit his criteria of the ideal woman? And, oh, how she hated the feeling of insecurity that rose up inside her. The feeling that no matter how hard she tried she would never be good enough.

Placing her hands flat against the window, she spread her fingers out like starfish against the cool glass. The move gave her a sense of vertigo and she suddenly knew what was at the root of her current mood. She suddenly knew why it was so important that Zach hadn't chosen her and why Amy and Luke's comments had hurt so much. She suddenly understood that, even though she had guarded her heart so closely and for so long, she had done the foolish thing of falling in love with her husband.

She, who had imagined that such a thing would never happen to her. She, who had always believed that love and marriage limited a woman's chance at happiness—and still did. Bile collected at the base of her throat. How had she been so stupid?

'Farah.' Zach stepped in behind her and splayed his fingers over the top of hers, somehow anchoring her when what she wanted was to spin out into the ether and never come back. Holding her hips roughly, he pressed his groin against her bottom, his erection hard and unyielding through the denim of his jeans.

Sweet sensation swept through her and she couldn't prevent a small gasp from escaping her lips as instant heat and moisture collected at the juncture of her thighs.

'Does that feel like I think you're too dark?' he growled.

Confused and confounded by the depth of her feelings for this man, Farah didn't know what to say without revealing how she felt.

'Does it?' he repeated gruffly.

She shook her head. 'No. But you could be...you could be thinking of someone else.'

The growl turned rough and came from deep in his chest. One of his hands fisted in her hair and brought her eyes to his in the glass. Then he slid his other hand over her belly until it met the snap on her jeans. One flick and the button was released, followed by the zip, and then his hand was on her and in her, and Farah's head fell back against his shoulder as she surged between the firmness of his fingers in front of her and the ridge of his erection behind her.

'Yes,' he growled, the fingers of his other hand going beneath her T-shirt to rub across both her nipples at once. 'You're mine, Farah. All mine.'

Her climax built almost instantly and, just when she was reaching for it, he removed his fingers and worked her jeans down her hips.

'Not without me.' Within seconds he had his own jeans open and then he was there, bending her forward, her hands splayed once more on the glass, as he pushed into her in one powerful thrust. 'Look at me,' he demanded, surging hard. 'Look at me when I take you.' His eyes never left hers as he established a driving rhythm that left her in no doubt as to who was in control. 'Watch my face while I'm inside you. See for yourself that it's you who does this to me, it's you who makes me so damned out of control it sometimes scares me.'

He groaned as Farah pushed back and shattered in a shower of sensation, her body pulsing around his flesh and sucking him in deep. 'Hell, Farah.'

He spilled his release inside her and Farah collapsed limply against the glass, her only support the man breathing heavily at her back who had one arm wrapped around her middle and the other planted against the window.

He leaned forward and nuzzled the sweaty hair that stuck to the nape of neck. 'I didn't mean for that to happen. I'm sorry.'

'It's okay.'

'I've just wanted you all damned day and to hear you say what you did—' He stopped abruptly and adjusted his jeans before picking her up in his arms and carrying her across the room to their darkened bedroom.

He placed her on the bed and stripped off her clothing before switching on the bedside lamp, bathing them both in a golden glow. Then he stripped off his own and came over the top of her, all dominant and elementally male. Farah felt her heart kick behind her rib cage; she'd never seen him so wildly masculine before, so completely out of control.

Holding himself off her with the strength in his arms, he stared down at her. 'I want you to trust me, Farah.'

Trust him...

'I want you to rely on me.'

She didn't doubt she could on some level, but one day he would see that she wasn't enough for him and what then? 'Relying on others isn't easy for me. It's—'

'I'm not asking you to rely on *others*,' he said fiercely. 'I'm asking you to rely on *me*. I won't hurt you, Farah.' He rolled to the side and took her with him. 'In fact you need to know that, if you ever want to leave, you only have to say so.'

'Leave?' She was in such a confused state she wasn't sure that he wasn't asking her to leave.

He smoothed the hair back from her forehead. 'I mean, I won't chase you or force you to stay like my father would have done. Like he tried to do with Nadir's mother.' Farah had heard the story about Nadir's mother, who had been trying to leave the sheikh with her daughter and had died in a tragic car accident when he'd had them followed. 'If we can't make this marriage work, you are free to go.'

Farah's mouth suddenly felt dry. 'You really mean that?'

'Yes.'

'But how? Under Bakaani law a woman is not free to leave her husband.'

'Not yet she isn't. But that is another ancient law that is in the process of being changed.'

She stared up at him. 'And my father?'

'Your father goes free from this moment on.'

His words were a pledge that Farah knew he would keep and once again she felt overwhelmed by the depth of her emotions for this man. She buried her head against his shoulder knowing that there was nothing she could give him that equalled all that he could give her. All that he *had* given her.

She felt the brush of his lips against the top of her head and felt like weeping—she, who never cried.

'It's okay, my little Zenobia.' He sighed and gathered her closer. 'We'll return to Bakaan tomorrow and start our marriage properly. Everything will be good. You'll see.'

CHAPTER FOURTEEN

BUT TWO WEEKS later things weren't good, they were frustratingly bad, and Zach had no idea how to rectify the situation. Ever since their return from Ibiza, Farah had seemed to withdraw from him both physically and mentally and not even bringing her beloved stallion to the palace had made her happy.

He stared down at the list of law reforms he'd been sitting on for a week now. One of them was the new legislation giving women the right to apply to the courts for a divorce, the law he had promised Farah he would implement so that she could walk away from him if she wanted to.

Right now he had a feeling she'd do just that and he knew he didn't want that to happen. It was being so blasted busy that was getting in the way. Since they'd been back, they'd had to attend one state dinner after another as important world leaders came to Bakaan to discuss global issues and future strategies. Having pledged to help Nadir ride out the changes in Bakaan, Zach had done what was required of him and he had also kept his promise to include Farah. Which was both a boon and not, because she had taken to her role as regional ambassador so wholeheartedly that at this rate she could run the country singlehandedly by the end of next week. In fact, she worked so hard she'd often go to bed exhausted. So exhausted that lately he hadn't wanted to disturb her when he'd come to bed and let her sleep. Maybe that accounted for his sullen frame of mind—a build-up of sexual repression.

But he knew that wasn't it. He knew it was because he'd realised some time over the past couple of weeks he'd actually fallen in love with his wife and that she did not love him back. And, even worse, he couldn't help but wonder if her withdrawn state was because she had got what she wanted from him when he'd promised that he would not prosecute her father if they should divorce. Perhaps all she was waiting for was for the divorce laws to be changed and then she'd make her move.

Frustrated and agitated, Zach pushed back from his desk and strode to the window. His office overlooked the stables and his eyes immediately zeroed in on Farah, standing in the sunshine brushing down her stallion's sweaty coat.

The damned horse got more of her attention than he did and he now regretted bringing it to the palace. He'd done it a week ago to surprise her. He'd wanted to lift her spirits and show her how he felt, how much he appreciated her, and—he could admit now—he'd wanted her to tell him that she loved him, or at least cared for him—but she hadn't.

She'd wrapped her arms around the blasted horse's neck and told him she loved him instead. And the damned thing had looked like it would lie down and die for her.

Rubbing at the persistent tension at the back of his neck, Zach wondered what to do about his marriage. Logically he knew that he should just let her go—if that was indeed what she wanted—but he knew he hadn't offered her that so far because he wasn't sure that he could. Even now some deep-seated part of himself that must surely date back to his barbarian ancestors warned him that he couldn't.

It was almost laughable to think that he had once prided himself on how emotionally grounded he was when the truth was that right now he felt about as emotionally grounded as a log. He, who had fought in war zones, who had raced boats at over two-hundred miles per hour, and who had started up his own company without any financial backing was afraid to tell his wife how he felt.

Pathetic.

He watched her lead Moonbeam into the stable, her curvy bottom outlined to perfection in her jodhpurs. A grim smile came to his lips.

It was time he stopped pussyfooting around the edges of this marriage and confronted her head-on. If she happened to throw herself at him, and make love to him in the stables as a result, all the better. If she wanted out, well… hell, he'd give her that, too.

As Farah housed Moonbeam for the night she couldn't help but remember the day Zach had brought her beloved horse to her.

'Is the blindfold really necessary?' she'd asked nervously.

'Yes.'

She sniffed the air. 'We're in the stables.'

'Correct.'

Then he'd removed the blindfold and she'd stared at her white stallion, completely mute. When she'd found her voice, it was to whisper, 'What? How?'

'I had him brought here for you.'

'Oh, I love you,' she'd blurted out, throwing her arms around Moonbeam's neck, when she'd noticed the frown on Zach's face. She'd repeated the words over and over as if she'd been talking to the horse all along, but of course she hadn't, and it had nearly been one of the most singularly embarrassing moments of her life.

Even so, she'd ached to have Zach take her in his arms,

but he'd become even more remote and told her he'd leave her and Moonbeam to get reacquainted.

It had been like that a lot lately—Zach leaving her alone to do her work while he took meetings. Zach leaving her alone to have breakfast while he pounded out a circuit on his treadmill. Zach coming to bed late and then hardly touching her...

Farah felt a lump form in her throat. She knew he was busy and she had no wish to change that but what she'd love to change was the way he seemed to hold part of himself back from her. It was as if he was already regretting their marriage, and she couldn't help but wonder if their trip to Ibiza hadn't triggered a realisation in him that he had been seriously short-changed in being forced to marry her.

Oh, he had tried to reassure her that that wasn't the case, but what else could he have said? That, yes, he did regret it and would now risk inciting a war for his own selfish ends?

Once she would have believed him capable of such a thing. She knew that was no longer true. She knew that honour and integrity was the most important thing to him. As it was to her.

But at the expense of his happiness? Of her own?

With her head aching, she positioned Moonbeam's chaff bucket and leant her forehead against his shoulder as he ate. Lost as she was in thought, she didn't immediately hear anyone come up behind her.

'Farah?'

Whirling around at the sound of her name, she stared dumbfounded as Amir stood in the doorway to Moonbeam's stall with one of her private security detail as escort.

'Amir!'

'I hope this is not an intrusion, Your Highness,' her guard said. 'The palace staff said you were here and Mr Dawad was very insistent.'

'It's fine. Thank you.'

Bowing low, the guard left, and Farah stared at Amir, only then realising how much she really missed being around the familiar faces of her village.

'Is it my father? Has something happened?'

Amir walked towards her. 'No, he's good, although he is concerned about you. I think he regrets pushing you into this marriage.'

'Oh.' He and her both, she thought tiredly.

'He would like to know if you are happy. As we all would.'

'Amir...'

'Before you say anything, I would also like to apologise for my behaviour prior to all this blowing up. I was pushing you because I'm in love with you but that was wrong.'

Farah let out a slow breath. 'Oh, Amir, I... I didn't realise.' She had assumed he had only been trying to cement his place as the future leader of Al-Hajjar.

He gave her a faint smile. 'I know. So are you happy, Farah? Because if you're not I could take you away from all this.'

Farah closed her eyes against his words. She longed to be able to tell him outright that she was not only happy but positively joyous, that she had never been happier, but she wasn't and she had never been able to lie. And his declaration of love made her feel truly awful. It struck deep in her heart because she knew how unrequited love felt and it was debilitating. Every bit as debilitating as she had known love would be and there was no satisfaction in being proved correct.

'I'm not unhappy,' she hedged. Not a lie exactly. It wasn't unhappiness she felt, just a bone-deep sadness that Zach would never return her feelings.

'That's not good enough, Farah. That's a cop-out.'

He reached for her hands but before he could touch her a furious voice made them both jump.

'Who the hell let you inside the palace?'

Jumping almost sky high, Farah turned to face her husband.

'Greetings, Your Highness.'

She threw Amir a dark look to let him know that she did not appreciate his silky tone. 'Zach, Amir was—'

Zach shook his head at her. 'I'm asking him, not you.'

Brought up short by the reprimand, Farah blinked.

'I asked what you're doing here?'

Amir squared his shoulders, although the faint tremor that ran through him slightly mitigated any authority he tried to establish with the move. 'I've come to visit with Farah. Or is that not allowed?'

'No, it is not allowed.' Fury emanated from every tense muscle in Zach's body.

'Zachim—'

'It's fine, Farah.' Amir did not take his eyes off the prince. 'I can go.'

'Yes, you can,' Zach snarled, his eyes alight with murderous intent as Amir paused beside him and whispered something under his breath.

Farah couldn't hear what it was but it only made her husband's eyes turn colder. He raised his hand and security was there in an instant to do his bidding.

Mortified at the way he had just treated Amir who had only been trying to make amends Farah stared at him. 'Why did you treat my friend like that?'

'Why did he come into my home unannounced?'

'*Your* home?'

'Don't play semantic games with me, Farah. What did he want with you?'

'He wanted to make amends.'

Zach made a scathing noise in the back of his throat. 'He is not welcome here.'

Affronted by his easy dismissal of her wishes Farah bristled. 'He *is* welcome here.'

Blowing out a breath he stopped in front of her. 'I did not come here to argue with you.'

'Then stop being such an egomaniac,' she bit out, trying to keep the hurt from her voice. 'If I want to entertain a friend, then I will.'

Feet planted wide apart, he glowered at her. 'Not if I forbid it.'

'Not if you…?' All the confusing, unsettling emotions she'd been feeling ever since they'd returned to Bakaan coalesced into anger. Anger at herself, at him, anger at their whole, damned miserable arrangement. 'Don't you dare try and dictate what I can and can't do. I'm not your possession.'

She didn't have time to say anything else because Zach was on her, his mouth crashing down over hers in a demanding, controlling kiss that left her in no doubt just what he could and couldn't do. 'Yes, you are. You're mine, Farah. Don't ever forget it.'

His! Of all the… Forgetting her non-violence policy Farah lashed out at him, welcoming the spurt of adrenaline that came with a good fight.

Within seconds, however, he'd subdued her. 'Temper, temper, my little wild cat.'

'Oh.' Farah tossed her hair out of her face. 'You great, big, patronising—'

She didn't get any further because Zach's mouth covered hers again, his tongue duelling with her own and, oh, it felt so good to be held by him like this, so good to be kissing him with all the pent-up passion she'd been unable to express.

Moaning, she arched into him, melting against him as

he hitched her thigh up over his hip, angling his body into hers so that she was in no doubt as to how aroused he was. 'You are mine,' he breathed against her mouth. 'And if I don't want you to see someone because I deem it unsafe, then you won't.'

Incensed by his words, by her own traitorous body, Farah shoved against him, only coming up against the horse stall for her efforts. 'I can protect myself if that's what you're worried about,' she panted.

'Like now?'

He forced her hard up against the brick wall, his thigh wedged between her own in a move reminiscent of when he had trapped her in the alleyway.

Moonbeam shifted restlessly behind him, disturbed by all the pent-up emotion circulating in the room. A feeling of utter helplessness came over Farah and the weight of despair descended on her shoulders. Any hopes she had been harbouring that Zach cared for her, that he might one day want her with him because he respected her as his equal, dissolved into nothing. 'I hate you,' she said, unsure if it was him she hated or just herself for loving someone who did not love her in return.

'I don't give a damn.' He released her and swiped his hand across his mouth as if to wipe her taste away.

He didn't give a damn how she felt? 'Nice to know,' she said, before turning with as much dignity as she could muster and walking away from him.

Zach watched as she slowly walked away from him and nearly put his fist through the wall.

Where had all that anger come from? He hardly recognised himself. He, the king of communication, had just acted like Cro-Magnon man with an obsession.

Just thinking about it brought him out in a cold sweat. Usually he was great with women—even-tempered, patient, *considerate*. Just then he'd been…he'd been… Well, he hadn't handled himself at all well. He could admit that.

It had been the confident expression on Amir's face and his snide, 'I knew you wouldn't be able to make her happy,' as he'd walked past him that had done it.

Zach hated to admit it, but he'd got the better of him, because it had struck too close to the bone. And the whole time afterwards he'd been wondering what Farah had told him. What she had revealed to make the soldier so sure of himself.

I hate you.

'Great going, Darkhan. Maybe you can develop an app that will show men how to get their wives on side.'

Not.

He stopped pacing when he reached the back of the stable and clasped his hands over his head, trying to re-assemble his thoughts. One of the junior staff members caught sight of him and quickly scurried for cover.

First, he listed mentally, *you might hate the guy but you can't dictate who she does and doesn't see. You know that.*

Second, you need to pull back. Get some perspective on how this marriage is going to work.

And third… Third, he just needed to apologise to her for being such an idiot.

Feeling that his emotions were on simmer instead of a rapid boil, he took a deep breath and went in search of her.

When he found her in their living room reading a work file, it pulled him up short. Nice to know their argument hadn't interrupted *her* focus.

Glancing up as he approached, her eyes turned wary. He stopped and took a deep breath. 'I was wrong to yell at you. I'm sorry.'

'It doesn't matter,' she dismissed politely.

'Of course it matters,' he said just as politely.

'Look, Zach…' She hesitated. 'Things haven't really

been the same since we returned from Ibiza and if we're honest—' she took a breath '—which I like to think that we always have been with each other, then I can't see things getting any better between us.' She looked up at him then. 'Can you?'

Zach nodded as if he agreed but really he was thinking that he'd been right to assume that she wanted out of the marriage. She did but she was hardly being honest about it.

'The truth is,' she continued, 'we're both victims in this situation.'

Victims? 'You're only a victim if you think you're a victim,' he bit out tautly. 'And I am no victim.'

'Well, that's easy for you to say. You're a man and a prince.'

'I don't care what I am.'

'Fine.' She sighed heavily. 'I was only trying to make this easier.'

Zach paced across the room to put some distance between them. 'You were trying to say that now that I won't prosecute your father there's no reason for us to stay married. How's that for honesty?'

She flashed him a pained look. 'That's not the only reason but with the past laid to rest it certainly means that there's nothing holding us together any more.'

Nothing. There was that word again.

Zach looked at her and saw her eyes shiny with tears. Or was it defiance? Because she had done nothing but defy him all along and he...he'd been arrogant enough to assume that she would eventually fall for him as almost every other woman had. That he could make this marriage work from sheer will alone.

The truth was he hadn't wanted to disappoint his mother, who had suffered so many disappointments in her life, and he hadn't wanted to disappoint himself. But when you broke it down, he'd enjoyed the sex—a little too much

in retrospect—and he'd done what a lot of women he'd
been with had done with him: he'd mistaken lust for love.

'Zach?'

Talk about feeling like a chump.

He turned back to her. 'That's fine,' he heard himself
saying as if he were an actor on set. 'I can see you've
thought this through and, really, I've been so busy I haven't.
But you're right. We have nothing holding us together.'

Shaken by Zach's ready acceptance of everything she'd
said, Farah got up and restlessly moved around the room.
She noticed that the orchid bloom, the gift from his mother,
had fallen from its stem and laid on the table. Carefully
she picked it up and cradled it in her palm, gently stroking the dying petals. She couldn't help but think it was an
omen, as if fate was directing her.

And she knew all about fate from the way her mother
had died so senselessly. They were all at the mercy of it.
Fate gave and fate took away, but in the meantime everyone was in control of their own destiny, and somewhere
along the line she had forgotten that.

Forgotten her desire for independence and self-reliance.
She'd let herself imagine—or rather hope—that Zach was
the man for her when really their whole relationship was
built on an unfortunate set of circumstances instigated
by her father.

Placing the broken petals of the orchid gently back on
the table she turned to him.

'Then when the laws change we can—divorce?'

'We can do it now.' He strode through to his office and
came back, slapping a document on the table beside her,
squashing what remained of the flower of love. 'This is
the legislation that gives you the freedom to apply for a
divorce.' Picking up a pen, he signed it with a flourish before handing it to her.

Blindly she did so and handed it back. 'Congratulations,' he said, 'you can be the first woman in Bakaan to obtain a divorce. I'm sure you'll enjoy that.'

What she would enjoy would be if she had the freedom to go up to him, throw herself into his arms and kiss him. What she would enjoy would be for him to crush her to his hard length as he had done so many times before and tell her that he loved her...that he couldn't live without her.

She thought about her mother and the brother she had never known. She thought about her father who had desperately pined for them both and had held on to anger and bitterness when they had been ripped from him so unfairly. And then she thought about Zach who had wanted to marry for love and got her instead and she knew she was doing the honourable thing, the *only* thing, in walking away. 'So I think... I think I'd like to go home. If you don't mind.' *Did she have to sound like such a wimp?* 'To Al-Hajjar.'

She heard a loud crack in the quiet room and saw particles of the pen she had just held fall to the ground. 'I'm well aware that you have never considered the palace home, Farah,' Zach rasped. 'But unlike a mythical genie I can't rub a magic lamp and make it happen instantaneously.'

'I know that, Zach,' she said, struggling to keep the tremors out of her voice. 'I didn't mean...' Her explanation tapered off when she realised how close he was to her, how fiercely he was looking at her.

Kiss me, she urged silently. *Please.*

'I'll have Staph organise your transportation,' he said.

Farah pulled herself together. She smiled at him one last time and then, before her pride deserted her altogether, she left.

CHAPTER FIFTEEN

WHY DIDN'T ANYTHING work out the way you hoped it would? Zach growled under his breath as he wrestled with the cufflink he was currently trying to force back through his shirt sleeve.

'Would you stop fiddling?' Nadir berated out of the side of his mouth. 'You look like a schoolboy.'

Zach wanted to tell him in no uncertain terms where to go but they were at a formal gathering, waiting for the king of a neighbouring country to take his seat before they all could.

'And where's Farah? You said she'd be here. We don't want to insult this crusty old demon before he's signed the new business treaty.'

'I told you she's gone home,' Zach said.

Nadir frowned at him. 'That was a week ago. How long will she be gone?'

'How the hell do I know?' Finally the gold pin made it through the other side and, just when he went to twist the back into position, the damned thing fell out again. Zach swore just as the room held its breath for the old king to sit down.

All eyes turned his way. Nadir smiled. 'If you'll excuse us.' He nodded at Imogen and gave her a pointed look. Zach rolled his eye and went to take his seat when his brother cupped his elbow. 'You, outside.'

Zach nearly laughed as Nadir propelled him out of the room. 'Hell, I haven't been treated like a recalcitrant schoolboy since...well, since I was one.'

Nadir dismissed the nearby guards and walked ahead of him into an antechamber. 'What do you mean you don't know when Farah is due back? Didn't you ask her?'

No, he hadn't. He hadn't needed to ask to know that the answer was never. Instead he'd tried to forget about her and get on with his life.

Yeah, and wasn't that working out well?

He let his head drop back and started counting the small fretwork panels that decorated the ornate ceiling. He hadn't done that since he'd been a recalcitrant schoolboy either. 'She's on sabbatical.'

'Zach,' his brother said in *that* tone.

Zach blew out a breath. 'Do we really need to have this conversation now?' Because he was starving and a seven-course dinner was about to be served in the banquet hall.

His brother eyed him uncomfortably. 'I don't know. Do we?'

'Not in my mind.'

'Fine. But first tell me why you look worse than you did when you returned from your kidnapping in the desert.'

'I don't know. Perhaps I'm not getting my beauty sleep,' he quipped, deadpan.

Unfortunately Nadir didn't laugh. 'She left you, didn't she?'

'Who?'

'Damn it, Zach, I'm about—'

'Yes, she left me,' Zach grated. 'Happy?'

He stalked away from his brother and vaguely considered hurling an eighteenth-century Persian vase against the wall. It would probably shatter in a very satisfying manner.

'Want a drink?'

He hadn't heard Nadir go to the drinks cabinet and

he stared down at the two tumblers in his hand. 'No.' He didn't want a drink. He didn't want much of anything. The feeling of hollowness he'd experienced just after their father had died had returned tenfold.

'Fine. I'll have them both.'

Zach nearly laughed. His brother was trying to stage an intervention, and he loved him for it, but he was absolutely hopeless at the task.

Throwing himself into an armchair that was about as comfortable as a wooden plank, he regarded Nadir moodily. 'You probably should have told Imogen to come and talk to me instead.'

'Don't be an ass.' His brother took the other plank. 'So, what are you going to do about it?'

Zach looked at him bleakly. 'Nothing.'

'Well, that's healthy.'

'Listen, brother, I appreciate this, don't get me wrong—especially since you've ditched the King of Ormond for me—but my situation isn't like yours and Imogen's.'

'I don't know about that but what I do know is that you've finally found a woman you love and you're just going to let her go.'

Did he love her? This last week he'd convinced himself he didn't but that wasn't working out that well for him, either. 'I promised her I would.'

'Promised her what?'

'If you love something, you let it go. If it comes back, it was meant to be. If it doesn't, it never was.'

Nadir looked like he wanted to crack him over the head with one of the tumblers in his hand. 'If you love something you let it go...? That kind of drivel belongs in fairy tales and greeting cards, not in real life.'

'It was her decision. I'm not going to be like our father and chase her.'

Nadir sat forward and tilted a glass in his direction.

'I tell you, if you don't go to her and tell her how miserable you are without her, I will, because there's no way I'm losing one of the best regional ambassadors I'll probably ever have because you're too screwed up to tell her how you feel.'

'I'm not screwed up.'

But wasn't he?

A long buried memory rose up to taunt him as if it had happened yesterday. It was the day Nadir had argued with his father and left Bakaan for good. Being an eager-to-please thirteen-year-old on the cusp of manhood, Zach had wanted to make things right and had gone to his father and offered himself up as a replacement for Nadir. His father had stared at him for what had seemed like an eternity and then he'd started laughing. And he hadn't stopped until tears had rolled down his hollow cheeks and onto his white robe. Zach couldn't remember much of anything after that. The only thing he could remember was the hot ball of shame in his stomach as he'd stood before his father rooted to the spot.

Hell. He rubbed his hands over his face. He was so madly in love with Farah it had been easier to let her go than to open himself up to that kind of ridicule again. He looked back at his brother. 'Do you need the helicopter?'

'No.' Nadir shook his head. 'But take backup this time, will you? If her father doesn't shoot you out of the sky, your wife might, and with all the changes we're making we can't afford to replace it.'

Farah was tossing and turning in bed when she heard the distant sound of thunder.

Great. A storm was coming. At least she was home in her bed this time, her small, narrow bed that didn't seem to fit her any more. But then what would after the opulence of the Shomas Palace? Not that she missed the palace, exactly, but right now, when she could feel the coldness seeping in from outside, she missed the prince inside the palace. The prince she wasn't thinking about any more.

Slowly she became aware of voices outside her hut and the thunder that seemed to grow exponentially louder with every passing second. Thunder that was so loud it didn't sound like thunder at all.

Quickly climbing out of bed, she felt around on her chest of drawers for her trousers and tunic and slapped her boots against the floor before shoving her feet into them. Hopefully she wouldn't need socks because she didn't have time to look for any.

As soon as she stepped outside she had to put her hand up to shield her face from the circles of light surrounding their village—or what she realised were helicopters dropping from the sky like huge, black alien spaceships.

There was a sense of chaos amongst those who had been woken by the noise and Farah could see her father's men rallying to ward off any attack.

'Wait!' She rushed forward and shoved her way to the front of the gathering group. Her father was nowhere in sight but Amir looked set to kill.

She put her hand on his arm to stay him. They'd had a talk when she'd returned to the village a week ago and had fallen into an uneasy friendship, which basically meant that he avoided her at all costs. Something she completely understood.

What she didn't understand was why Zach was striding toward her, backlit by the now silent helicopters, his security team lined up behind him.

'Hello, Farah.'

Hello?

He invaded her village with an army and said hello? 'Zach? What are you doing here? Are you *trying* to start a war?'

'Not quite.' He stepped forward directly in front of her. 'I've come to talk to you.'

'At this time of the night?' Her heart was racing at the sight of him and she gave up trying to steady it. 'What could be so important it couldn't wait till morning?'

'Us. The future.'

The divorce. He was here about the divorce. Feeling completely stupid she took a moment to compose herself. 'Look,' she began haltingly, 'I haven't put the divorce petition into the court yet, but I will, I'm just—'

Zach took hold of her hands and she was embarrassed to feel them shaking. 'I'm not here about the divorce, *habiba.*' He squeezed her icy fingers. 'But what I have come to discuss I'd prefer to do so without an audience—or a line of guns trained on me. Is there somewhere private we can go?'

Wishing he had just sent a letter—or an emissary— to do his bidding she pulled out of his reach and glanced behind him. 'If you wanted private you shouldn't have brought a thousand men.'

'Only fifty.' He smiled ruefully. 'Nadir insisted on it.'

'What the blazes is this about, Darkhan?' Her father's sleep-roughened voice bellowed from behind them. Farah sighed as he pushed through the growing pack of villagers. So much for hoping her father might sleep through her final humiliation. He stopped in front of the prince. 'You have some nerve turning up like this.'

'Yes, sir. I've come for your daughter.'

Farah blinked, wondering if she had heard right.

'A man should know how to make his wife happy,' her father said. 'I made a promise to her mother many years ago that I would make sure she married well.'

Farah turned to him. 'You did?'

'Your mother said it would take a strong man to handle you. She was right. I never could.' He looked at Zach. 'That night in your shiny palace I saw something in your face when you looked at my daughter. Was I wrong?'

'No, sir. I love her.'

A murmur rippled through the crowd huddling together against the cold. Farah couldn't feel it. Heat was racing through her on a wave of embarrassment. 'By Allah.' She turned to her father. 'He doesn't love me. He's just saying that because—' She frowned, turning back to Zach. 'Why are you saying that?'

He smiled. 'Because it's true.'

'You love me?'

'With all my heart.'

'But…you were forced to marry me. My father—'

'Thinks you need to take this inside,' he said gruffly, directing them both towards the hut. 'And perhaps you should come and see me afterwards, Your Highness,' her father hesitated, 'about that other business.'

Did he mean the kidnapping?

'No, need sir. And the name's Zach.'

Her father nodded once. 'Mohamed.'

Shaking with the rush of emotions surging through her, Farah let Zach lead her inside her home, part of her desperate to play it safe and send him away and part of her aching to believe him.

'Our marriage was forced on the both of us, Farah, but there is nothing forced about the way I feel about you or how miserable I've been since you left.' He cupped her face in his hands and bent to kiss her with such tenderness it made her heart catch. 'I love you, *habiba*. I was just too much of a coward to tell you. And I have to believe that after the way you gave yourself to me, after everything that we shared together, that you have feelings for me, too. That you'll come back to me and give our marriage another chance.'

'Oh, Zach.' A lump formed in her throat as she looked

up at him. She had tried to avoid the pain of love her whole life, yet that was all she had felt since she had walked away from him. Deep down she knew that if she didn't take this leap of faith, that if she didn't fight the insecurities that had made her feel less than her whole life she would never know the joy of truly living. 'I love you, too. I love you so much I can't believe it. I can't—' She stopped talking and kissed him until they were both breathless and dizzy.

'I love you, Farah. I didn't know it was possible to love someone this much.'

'But you let me go.'

'You asked me to and I had given you my word that if you ever wanted to leave then I would not come after you.'

Farah groaned. 'That would be one of the only times you've ever done what I asked.'

'Not true. In Ibiza I did everything you asked. I watched cheesy movies for you.'

'But why were you so distant these past few weeks? I thought it was because you wanted a way out of our marriage. That you were starting to resent it. To resent me.'

He gathered her close and kissed her again, kissed her until she couldn't think. 'I didn't resent you but I could tell you were holding something back and I didn't know how to reach out to you.' He sighed and stroked his thumbs across her cheekbones. 'The truth is, I wanted you so badly I started to doubt myself.'

'You?'

'Yes, me.' He gave her a wry smile. 'Love, I have learned, is not the comfortable, easy emotion I had once envisioned. It's hot and powerful and it brought me to my knees. You brought me to my knees.'

Farah stroked her hand over his stubble, revelling in the fact that she could touch him freely. 'You know, when we first met you annoyed me so much I wanted to do exactly that.'

He smiled. 'Is that a fact? You should be careful what you wish for, *habiba*…'

'Because you just might get it.' She laughed. 'I'm so happy, Zach. I never thought I would feel like this with a man.'

He pulled her in tighter against him. 'You don't feel like this with *a man*. You feel like this with *me*.'

A secret smile formed on her lips. 'So that self-doubt you were talking about…?'

'A blip on the radar. A blip that you have eradicated.'

'I'm glad,' she said, suddenly serious. 'And I'm glad you changed your mind about coming after me. Because without you…without you…'

Tears formed on the ends of her lashes and he used his thumbs to wipe them away. 'You are my destiny, Farah.' He leaned back to look down at her. 'You're the reason I returned to Bakaan five years ago and you're the reason I no longer want to leave. You light up my life, *habiba*, in a way I've been looking for my whole life and never thought I'd find.'

'Oh, Zach, take me home,' she whispered.

'To the palace?'

'To wherever you are.' She curled her hands around his neck. 'I never want to be parted from you again.'

'Good. Because I never plan to let you go again.'

He sealed his promise with a soul deep kiss that was filled with joy and the promise of a wonderful future, and Farah knew that her mighty prince was truly a man she could rely on for the rest of her life.

* * * * *

5_ST19

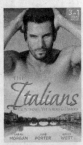